Panama Fever

For Michael,
W. B. Garvey

PANAMA FEVER

Digging Down Gold Mountain

W. B. GARVEY

Jonkro Books
NEW YORK, NEW YORK

First printing 2009

ISBN (hardcover): 978-0-9822294-0-8
ISBN (softcover): 978-0-9822294-1-5
LCCN 2008943057

For all the unsung Jamaican heroes
who gave their lives for
Panama's Great Cause.

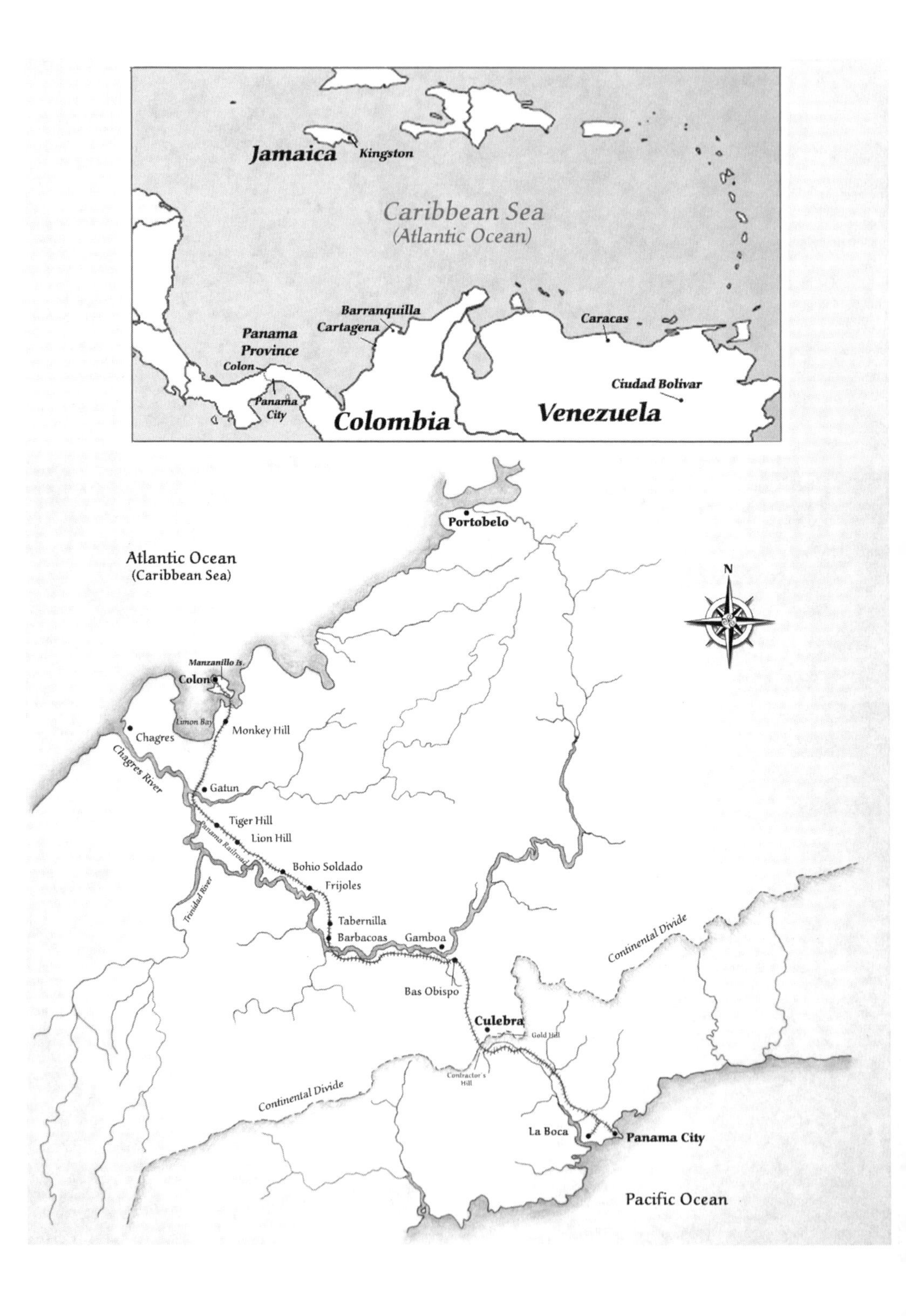

Jamaica
Kingston
Caribbean Sea
(Atlantic Ocean)
Barranquilla
Cartagena
Panama
Province
Colon
Panama
City
Caracas
Ciudad Bolivar
Colombia
Venezuela
Portobelo
Atlantic Ocean
(Caribbean Sea)
N
Manzanillo Is.
Colon
Limon Bay
Chagres
Monkey Hill
Chagres River
Gatun
Tiger Hill
Lion Hill
Panama Railroad
Bohio Soldado
Frijoles
Trinidad River
Tabernilla
Barbacoas
Gamboa
Continental Divide
Bas Obispo
Culebra
Gold Hill
Contractor's
Hill
Continental Divide
La Boca
Panama City
Pacific Ocean

Prelude

BEFORE IT WAS DETERMINED that the earth could be tamed by iron and steam, men steered clear of the square mile of land squatting like a scorpion in the mouth of the isthmus. Even fierce Columbus, probing for the mythic channel that would sail him west to the East, never set foot on that forested swamp teeming with reptiles and insects. Scorned save for itinerant buzzards, the isle had sat unmolested until three decades ago when it was cleared to shelter railwaymen come to speed the chase for gold. Some say the act was a curse and that the settlement still bears its sting.

Isaac Park gone a Colón,
Colón boat a go kill them boy.
Colón *bolow*[1] gone a Colón,
Colón boat a go kill them boy.

Jamaican Folk Song

---

[1] *Bolow*, comrade

CHAPTER 1

Outside Colón, Manzanillo Island, September 7, 1882

THE HEAVENS WERE WHITE and blooming miles above the marsh-strands stretching like fingers inside the lips of Limon Bay. The *Royal Mail* began to labor as a sudden crosswind toyed with its swallow-tailed burgee. Out on deck, the light-brown wag in a Norfolk jacket gave a mordant grin at seeing the empire's scarlet cross and golden crown in a flapping blur. The flag's distress went unnoticed by his comrades. For the island rubes gathered around him, the puffed clouds bursting massively on high were God's own breath infusing them with the heart of Cudjoe and the faith of Accompong. Several dropped to their knees and gave thanks. Some were relieved to have made it this far while others wept, overwhelmed to be getting a chance to show their mettle. Meanwhile, the bumpkins who'd spent two days spilling their guts into the placid Caribbean were busy impressing upon their chums who'd listen that it must have been the food that made them feel qualmish. Buoyed by the clement weather, their comrades smirked and let slide the wobbly alibis while they smoothed their scavenged new suits hoping that after crossing six hundred leagues of sea their true worth would not be cheapened by appearances.

The laggards cut short their excuses and ran to join the men suddenly jostling for a spot near the bow, impatient for that first thrilling glimpse of foreign soil. When what appeared floating above the bay, as if by magic, was a city with roofs of spun gold, a tremor of vindication raced down each tense Jamaican spine. The recruits were still clapping each others' backs and crowing that the naysayers had all been wrong, when the ship lurched west and the near skies blackened. With sucked-in breaths the men felt their scalps begin to prickle as beyond the shoreline's gnarling mangroves loomed a green denseness, vast and impenetrable.

Lightning ripped the lowering heavens and the stunned men were stuck there on deck, facing gloom. The waves grew rough and the steamship shuddered at the thunder's clap, yet not a single volunteer let his comrades see him flinch as the gilded settlement vanished behind a curtain of rain. They had come to link the great oceans. Just like Cudjoe's gritty Maroons who snatched back their freedom by besting the British, they would beat the odds and make history.

The heavy cloudburst had roiled the harbor and the *Royal Mail* prudently dropped anchor away from shore. As the company launches proved slow to respond, three teams of enterprising natives rowed quickly for the mooring. Arriving alongside, they yelled up to the third-class fares to say that for tuppence each they could avoid being shuttled in last and escape another drenching. The recruits gazed wanly down at the little dugouts bobbing on the rough like playthings then shook their heads, still a bit green around the gills. The boatmen continued to bait them until a heavy-set passenger wearing a big beige Stetson and sporting a set of long pointed ears leaned out from the first-class deck and brayed that he would pay a gold Yankee dollar to be taken ashore *pronto!*

After some sharp debate the scullers decided which team had the strongest pair for the job with the pledge that the other two would each get a dime from their windfall. The stretching grins on the winners' faces promptly vanished as they glanced back and saw the man's bulky oak chest being lowered from the hold. Cursing their damned good luck, the rowers squeezed in their buttocks and braced their bare wet toes to the slats of the bouncing *cayuca*. Nerves shooting sweat through each brown pore, their trembling knees bending in tandem, they embraced the hefty challenge, but just as they had set the chest in with care, the fat man came clambering down the ladder and, ignoring a shipload of frantic calls, swung his seventeen-stone into the dugout and tipped them over.

More than an hour had passed before the *Royal Mail's* tenders finally ferried the last of its third-class passengers to land. As the final group made it to shore, dozens of their comrades were still lounging on the pier recounting the image of that fat man thrashing around spluttering profanities as the poor boatmen struggled to fish him out of the water.

"I thought the big man was gonna drown tryin' to save that pretty Stetson!" cried one fresh-faced youth, tears of hilarity streaming on his cheeks.

"Yup! He was fighting like a real heavyweight!"

"Just goes to show—just because him got some big-ole donkey ears don't mean a mule-headed man gonna listen!"

Several of the last arrivals happily joined in the gabbing, unperturbed by the passage of time as they rolled back down the cuffs of their trousers and hunted up scraps of paper to line their wet shoes. It was as if the squall had been their christening and now they were free from all slavish strictures. While the jokesters laughed and grinned their more serious-minded comrades left to inspect the hoard of mammoth machinery that was causing the wharf to sag alarmingly.

There were long metal gadgets that looked like chains with enormous spoons and a giant ladder with rungs resembling huge metal pails. When a row blew up as men argued over the specific purpose for each alien device, the tall young wag grew impatient. Slipping off the damp Norfolk jacket, he tossed it across his shoulder, then picked up his bag and headed for the gates at the end of the pier. As he strolled off on his own, Thomas Judah suddenly realized the stilt-legged hovels perched along the shore like half-drowned terns were the shacks they had mistaken for a fairy-tale city. The roofs his comrades saw as pure spun gold were only straw—in fact, the whole place reeked of a rancid melancholy.

Few even noticed the dreary ghetto as the men settled their differences and sauntered out from the pier. In the daze of their first great adventure, they did not seem to care that parts of the boardwalk were gone or almost rotted, nor that the section's only sign of life was a herd of bony black cats scrounging through drifts of wet garbage. If any pioneer hearts were beating swiftly by the time they neared the hub of town and saw the roads filling with traffic, all qualms were pushed aside and firmly forgotten. Their more pressing concern was how to make it across the brown lake of reeking slop standing between them and the opposite sidewalk.

The squeamish balked and drew back, fearing the ruin of their new rope-soled shoes. They might have wavered there for hours had their comrades who had dashed to the other side with minor mishaps not threatened to go on without them. At last, the four hold-outs tiptoed to the boardwalk's edge, then with acrobatic skips and twists sidestepped a farmer's ambling donkey and leapt to safety inches ahead of two heedless pushcarts. Their nimble dance came to a calamitous end when a passel of naked boys raced up splashing mud while waving fistfuls of cigars and chanting, '*autentico cubano*—two bits *solo*!'

It took only that instant as the splattered men paused for the fruit-sellers to surround them. Unlike the careless boys who'd sprayed them with filth and blighted Spanish, the leather-skinned *buhoneros* greeted the young Jamaicans with a consoling lingual stew that affirmed them as sisters and brothers. The juicy offerings of sliced red melon and yellow star apple quickly rallied the recruits' falling spirits. They had gotten through scouring their jackets for extra change when a ringing command in French brought their transactions to a startled halt. The lucky ones quickly jammed the sweet purchases in their mouths as the French official raced up and scattered the *buhoneros* with his stick, leaving the slowpokes to sulk and re-pocket their pennies.

Crowned by a white sun helmet, a sodden havelock fused to the nape of his neck, the Frenchman, having shooed the disgruntled vendors, went about flashing his black baton to corral the lagging recruits. After he had penned in the last of the stragglers, he paced before them in his drenched white flannels, prickling with soggy discomfort. He erased Judah's grin with a blistering eye and with a sharp pivot shook his stick at the plaza's defunct clock-tower bellowing, *Vite! Vite*! before vanishing around the corner.

Astonished, the Jamaicans were left gaping in wonder at the frozen hands of time until the Frenchman came clipping back seconds later. While young Judah and his comrades struggled not to burst out with laughter, the red-faced official's pinched-in features showed the strain of damping a native urge to take his stick to a few black rumps. Instead, he tucked the baton back under his arm and with a long, disdainful gesture invited the wayward men to please come along. Quietly choking on their grins, they trailed him behind a line of miniature palm-trees and down a short garden path where the rest of their contingent had been put to wait by a hideous red-brick monument. With their sanguine expressions, the men resembled a large corps of small, dark elves standing there beneath three giant effigies of the railroad's Anglo-American founders.

The entire two hundred were pressed in line then marched to the nearby station and packed aboard a waiting train. The hot, stuffy ride was brief, ending with the rails at a forlorn spot where a hand-scrawled sign read, *Camp Gatun*. It was here that France's oldest living legend had stood three years ago and envisioned a sparkling modern Thebes. And just as Ferdinand de Lesseps had inspired thousands to finance his desire for a Suez Canal, he had roused his countrymen to another *Grand Cause*. Over one hundred thousand—writers, doctors, lawyers and widows—had bought over a million shares in the *Compagnie Universelle du Canal Interocéanique,* happy to place all their savings and faith in the man whose genius had joined East to West across Egypt's vast Bitter Lake. No true patriot doubted that with the Great Man directing France's unrivaled expertise this dark forsaken place would someday see a bright new Lesseps City bustling at the entrance to the world's Eighth Wonder. But for now, all that greeted the canal's eager recruits was a clearing in the middle of a tropic wilderness.

For its workers' comfort the company had mounted crude barracks on top of squat concrete pillars linked by a long unfinished verandah. The added elevation was meant to foil both the flood-waters from the nearby Gatun River and the marsh's voracious rodents. The bleak prospect had been brightened with generous swabs of white lime and spacious windows from which to sit and view the jungle. Upon arrival, the diggers were immediately ordered back in line in front of the camp's office cottage. Thomas Judah saw no need to stand another hour in his wet sticky clothes just to sign the official payroll, so while his comrades grumbled and patiently reassembled, he slipped off to appraise his new home, failing to see that he was being shadowed.

"So, Boss—yuh like yuh new Great House?"

"Oh, it's you!" Thomas jerked with irritation when he glimpsed young Byron hovering. "Why are you tracing me? Didn't I tell you I don't like being traced?"

The pint-sized recruit looked taken aback. "Sor-ry—" he muttered, his soft patois lilting in distress, "I thought yuh saw me—"

"Forget it—" said Judah, waving his hand as if to cross out his annoyance as he bent his way inside the barracks. "Better hope you can sleep like country fowl..."

"It don't gots space fi rooster pull on 'im drawers..." echoed Byron, blowing out his breath as he cast a jaundiced eye at the fifty double bunks the company had somehow squeezed inside. "Wonder which one worser—" he muttered, scowling at the tiny span between the berths as his companion plopped down on the nearest cot, minding not to knock his head on the upper bunk, "bumpin' yuh coconut gettin' up from down di bottom—ar fallin' 'pon yuh buddy from up di top?"

"Afraid of heights are we, Sir Eggshell?" Thomas laughed, as he dragged off his boots and pulled out a dry poplin shirt from his leather valise.

"Naw—is you mi thinkin' 'bout—" Byron insisted unconvincingly, then following the other's lead, dropped his own little burlap gunnysack beside the bunk. He was about to slip the limp straw boater from his head when he pointed at the floor with a frightened gasp. "Lawd God!—Thomas! Look!—Is what-it?"

The large shadowy creature had darted from under the bed and hunkered by the farthest bunk, its scaled skin lightening to blend with the barrack's interior. Thomas took a bold step towards the reptile then stopped when it fixed him with its wall-eyed gaze. The two locked stares, waiting to see whose nerve would be first to give out.

Byron tossed off his hat then ducked to peer at the beast from behind his lanky comrade, who made a bolt intending to drive it into the corner. The lizard scurried back across the floor and at a pace that defied its shape slithered up the wall and sailed through the open window with a long green leap.

"Whoa—what a jump!" Thomas cried, rushing up in time to see it escape into the bushes.

"What in h-e-two-sticks was dat? A baby dragon?"

"That, my unlearned friend, was an iguana. We'd still have them back home in Jamaica if the Spanish hadn't eaten them all up—I guess those critters must be tasty!"

"Ugh!" said Byron, making a face. "Yuh mean people would eat such a ugly beast? Tell yuh what—" he stopped and gazed warily towards the open window, "yuh can tek the bottom bed—me can sleep up top—"

Thomas grinned at the country-boy's attempt to sound casual even as beads of sweat showed on his forehead. He was less worried about the iguana than the queer calm to the jungle air still hanging hot and heavy despite the violent downpour. There was something baleful about this land—as if it resented being wakened from its slumber. And while this odd trepidation gave him an exhilarating rush, it was hard to dismiss the fact that they were out in the heart of nowhere.

His unease grew more intense after the next few hours. From the start of dusk the camp had been plagued by the jungle's feral yammer which continued to increase with a mind-numbing crescendo. By dark, between the squawking hysterics and their savage hunger, Thomas and his comrades were beginning to think they'd been brought here just to see how long it took to go crazy. When their own deranged grumbles started to drown out even the shrieking monkeys, a hundred famished Jamaicans marched to the office and demanded to be fed. Finally, one man bawled at the top of his voice that the French were a bunch of frauds just like the English.

The charge brought the chief official rushing from the cottage. He apologized for the delay, explaining that there had been a mix-up in Colón and they were waiting for more supplies. When this failed to quell the loudest of the complainers, the Frenchman added magnanimously that their wake-up call tomorrow would be at six instead of half-past five.

It was ten at night before the train arrived with the missing provisions. Minutes after eleven the harried French cooks finally called the starving men into the camp's enormous canvas tent and in their jabbering tizzy went about doling them double portions. One deep sniff of the rich beef stew and biscuits had Byron and Thomas each testing his stomach for its threshold of pain. When their bellies stuck out in submission they gulped down some tasteless coffee and stumbled far into the bushes willing to expose themselves to the jungle's pesky night crawlers to ease their bloated bodies. Itching but uplifted, the friends groped their way past the long line to the outhouse and back to the barracks, freshly armed for the morrow's epic challenge with company issue of a canal-digger's essentials: a small tin plate, a fork and a candle.

Thomas fell right into bed, glad to lie on anything other than a hard deck floor even if it meant having to sleep with his knees drawn up to his abdomen. Outside, an orange moon gazed down like a stern cyclopean eye and seemed to still the forest which now exuded not even the sound of a chirping cricket. A deep hush settled across the camp like a downy cover and within minutes Thomas had plunged dreaming into the waters of Lethe.

An eye-twitch later he was back at sea, his body aslant, swaying with the steamer's pitch and roll. Only this time they were caught in a storm. They began to tip. He lurched for a hold to keep from sliding off the deck. A giant wave crashed the steamer's hull and he awoke in time to see Byron flailing through the air on his way to the floor.

Men were wailing like howler monkeys, pushing and shoving for the barracks door. Thomas rushed to help up his friend and there was a loud harsh crack as the top bunk tore from the wall. It slammed the back of his head and landed flush on Byron. As red stars flashed before his eyes, Thomas flung the iron frame off his friend and screamed for him to hurry.

Byron lay back clutching his crooked left arm as the veranda gave a creak and started to slip from its footings. Thomas quickly picked up his whimpering friend to jump ahead of the splinters suddenly flying in every direction and went tumbling straight down inside the earth.

Byron's good arm was locked tight around Thomas' waist as the yawning ground swallowed them whole. As they slammed to the bottom, the entire barracks collapsed, crashing into a heap inches above their heads. Sightless in their tomb, the new friends hugged each other tight, quailing at the sounds of bedlam raging overhead. When the furor had largely subsided, Thomas suggested they take turns calling for help, but a few brave tries quickly magnified the piercing pain in his side. He finally confessed that he could not manage it.

Telling Thomas not to worry, Byron yelled until he was hoarse. He was close to giving up when a voice came down through the tomb's deep cover of shattered timber.

"Somebody underneath dere?"

"Yes, yes!" The friends shouted back as one.

"Hold on—help is comin'!" the thick voice replied.

A knifing fissure gashed the earth from where the barracks once stood clear to the center of camp. The catering tent's huge tarpaulin lay flattened—a giant bug mashed by the heel of some prehistoric monster. Incredibly, not a single recruit had been killed. Five, counting Byron, had broken limbs, the rest showed only minor cuts and bruises. All could be patched up except for poor Thomas, who screamed like a child when his deliverers started to haul him out of the earth. Only then did he realize that he must have done serious damage to his side when he grazed one of the concrete pillars during his fall.

Additional hands were summoned and Thomas was lifted gently from his tomb and set to lie on the grass with Byron. The keen-eared digger who'd heard their cries brought out a blanket and rolled it to prop Thomas' head. As their bull-necked savior left to search for any spared belongings, Thomas told Byron he should go along and look after his broken arm, but his friend refused. "Don't min' my little inj'ry," he insisted, "you an' me come here as a team. They can look after the two of we together." But despite his stoic pledge, the night had not far progressed before Byron was getting spooked.

"Lawd, Mas' Tom, mek it stop!" he cried, tightening his spine at every jarring aftershock.

His comrades' ghost-like silhouettes as they rummaged in the yellow moonlight brought back to Byron all the graveyard tales made vivid by half-digested superstitions. The seventeen-year-old began to fret that the French were new age Pharaohs—that they'd all been tricked back into bondage and the devil would have their souls. When Thomas reasoned that it was silly to think the company would harm its own workers Byron grumbled that if this calamity wasn't the work of the devil, then old Busha must have had some evil obi cast a spell to punish them for having ambition and deserting their nation. "I feel worser for you, boss...you never need do this." To which his friend could only smile and shake his head.

Thomas was amused and secretly flattered by the guileless way Byron had attached himself to his side. It gave him added satisfaction to know that even though Byron was eight days his senior and had suffered more of life's hard knocks the little recruit still looked up to him. That Byron wanted so desperately to be his friend when he had every reason to resent him only bolstered his newly-conceived ambition to be the small man's champion.

"Boss...yuh think the world might just end tonight?" Byron asked in a soft frail voice.

"Don't be a ninny! And stop calling me boss!" Thomas snapped, and felt remorse when the sharp ache stabbed in his side. "Sorry old boy—it's just this damn pain is god-awful..."

Although Byron claimed he had taken no offence Thomas could see that the aftershocks were steadily crumbling his facade. At the slightest vibration as the earth resettled Byron would give a tense cry and gripe that they were doomed in hell. He drew no comfort from Thomas' calm explanations for why solid ground was suddenly bucking like a mule stung by a swarm of angry bees. In Byron's view, if it were true there were cracks in the earth far down beneath the surface it was only more proof that the whole damned world was about to break and fall apart.

Happily for Thomas, the blush of dawn brought Byron relief, revealing that despite the night of long cries the world had survived. Upon being told that given time and proper setting his arm would mend completely, Byron revised his intentions. Suddenly, he was no longer in a hurry to catch the next boat home and see the last of this godforsaken jungle.

"The Lawd was only testin' to see if me was up to the challenge!" Byron proclaimed as he rejoined Thomas smiling, his broken arm secured in a sling. "That's why Him made me break me left hand instead o' me right!"

The change was so mercurial Thomas was unable to squelch a laugh which he promptly paid for with more side-splitting agony. Byron's sudden burst of unalloyed happiness reminded him of that moment aboard ship when they discovered that they both loved playing cricket.

"So what you is—bowler ar batsman?" Byron had asked excitedly, curious to know more about this supposed young digger who'd shown up on a third-class deck with soft smooth hands and two-toned Italian boots.

"I have a fair stroke," Thomas replied with false modesty before sporting his waggish grin. "I should have been an opener on my school's first eleven—"

"Man! You went to high school—?" Byron asked incredulously. "Which one?"

Thomas shifted a hard violet gaze to the blue unending sea. "Wolmers," he coldly replied.

Byron whistled through his teeth. "Whew, boss, that's top drawer! How you manage it?"

"It's a long story—"

"Me's a pretty fair bowler miself!" said Byron, his face suddenly gleaming, his chest pressing out with pride. "Yuh know 'bout Millwood's club?"

Thomas stared at him, amazed. Millwood was one of the few established clubs that welcomed players not from the island's pale upper crust but it was still not a team he expected a poor country-boy to be on terms with.

"Mi never usually get to play wid dem," Byron explained, seeing Thomas gape in surprise, "but some of the Millwood boys did a'ready know me. We all used to play down in the gully as children—only me never had a daddy work in post office or land a stush job with some rich man," he said bitterly. "Mi couldn't join dem club but dem come ask me to play because them best bowler took sick just as Millwood was to play a big match at Riddley Park."

"You're joking! Riddley Park—? You mean the pitch for the club with most of the top English players—the ones that get to go abroad and play for Jamaica?"

"That's right—and you never seen such a pretty place. Them have rooms inside with glass where you can change your clothes—and the park have nice green grass all around."

Thomas shook his head. "I can't believe it..."

"It's true—we won the match and I took seven wickets!"

"Right," Thomas said sarcastically. "So how come you only played for Millwood that once?"

The light on Byron's face dimmed. "Millwood had to forfeit—the league's English official said they should have known better than to try and sneak in a little black monkey to play against gentlemen at Riddley Park."

"That's outrageous—pink hypocrites! But keep your chin up, man!" Thomas punched the lad's slumped shoulder. "You showed those snobs who's really the better man! See here—" he went back to bragging, "did I tell you my first bat at Wolmers I could have had a century? First ball I saw—bam!—four runs! I was trouncing them so bad they called the match!"

Byron had been fascinated by Thomas' easy bravado. Even now, seeing his friend leaning crookedly against the rolled-up blanket, favoring his side, it shamed him to feel so afraid in the face of such unpitying humor. Braced by Thomas' wit and the sun's rosy blush which revealed a world much like he remembered it, he was beginning to trust his own feigned confidence when the camp was jolted by a second massive tremor. More powerful even than the first, telegraph poles lay toppled like giant matchsticks among the clumps of fallen trees. Iron rails were curled into twisted ribbons, resembling enormous metal bows. And with the trains out of commission, the injured were stranded beyond easy reach of medical help.

The second quake shattered Byron's new aplomb but he disguised his fear. When he realized that Thomas had grown unusually quiet, his face set in a grimace from the effort it was taking him to breathe, Byron went to convince someone in charge that his friend was more badly hurt than he'd let on. The camp's busy officials tried to dismiss him but Byron was adamant. He hounded the busy canal men until Thomas was lifted inside the re-erected tarpaulin and left to lie on one of the long tables. Half an hour later, the camp bursar and two of the French engineers came inside and after sending Byron to wait outside, took turns poking Thomas' ribs with their needle fingers. When the Frenchmen were satisfied that he had burned their ears with enough Jamaican curse-words they retreated to a huddle and quietly agreed that Thomas' injury was indeed severe and required extended bed-rest and daily care.

"Don't look so glum, *bolow*," Thomas murmured when Byron came in looking downcast. "They're not doctors—what do they know? Give it a week and I'll be back up hitting sixes."

"We don't even start dig and our team done break up already."

"Just for an inning, old boy, just for an inning. We'll be out there digging together before that wing of yours is out its sling."

Byron looked away to hide the sudden trembling in his lip. "Maybe me should ask if them can send me to the hospital with you..."

"You joking?" Thomas rasped back harshly. "Have the Frenchies believing I need a nursemaid? You just hold up your end and don't go throwing up the job before I get back."

"Sure boss—but I already told you me not gonna quit."

The exchange collapsed into silence and Byron stood hanging his head.

With a valiant effort Thomas raised himself partway up on an elbow. "Look—don't take it the wrong way—they warned us this would be a dangerous job—we can't have them thinking that because we're young we don't have the stomach for it."

Though he quietly nodded assent, Byron looked unsure and dejected. He barely smiled in reply when Thomas flashed a grin as they lifted him out to lie in the foul-smelling straw of a pig-farmer's burro-pulled dray and gave his friend two thumbs up.

As Thomas went off on his excruciatingly slow bumpy ride back to Colón and Byron watched his first friend vanish, it was hard to tell which one was fighting harder to draw a breath.

Chapter 2

Six cursed weeks, Thomas grumbled. It was an unbearable length of time for someone young and sound in mind to have to endure the indignities of an invalid. It maddened him that his ribs still made the most routine movement a grimacing ordeal, that his bodily needs were hostage to the kindness of his nurse, and that he was plum out of ways to kill time. He had come to do heroic labor. Instead he was stuck on his back watching an army of tireless red ants crisscross the ward's gray wall in contrary files. Their constant processions brought home the sameness of his long and empty days. He had studied their regimen with scornful interest, waiting to see if a malcontent would be tempted to go off exploring. Up to now, not a single insect had deserted the ranks much less incited a mutiny. Having never observed ants, this surprised him since, as far as he could tell, their back and forth across the foodless expanse sprang more from habit than any useful purpose.

Of late, he had not needed the distraction. He put little stock in psychic hunches, but it was becoming impossible to block the sense that he had made a perilous mistake by rushing to Panama on impulse. It was bad enough that he'd gotten himself injured the very first day. Now some of the very men he'd sailed with were showing up in the hospital, bug-eyed and soaked in sweat. Most were scarcely able to keep their teeth from clicking long enough to plead for some more cold water. Even the big country bucks who'd looked sturdy as club-lump hammers came in griping about thumping headaches and aching limbs. The company doctors were just as baffled, wondering how their hardy young diggers were suddenly as feeble as a bunch of withered old men.

There to assist, however they could, were *Les Soeurs de la Charité.* The religious band of unwed women divulged their strivings to ascend by means of two conspicuous white wings atop their habit's wimple. When the first ones came flapping inside his ward, Thomas' distrustful mind had run to the bodings of an ancient mariner's albatross. 'These gulls will doom us all with raw heads and bloody bones...' he remembered muttering before his suspicions were shamed and replaced by reverence. The nuns showed his humble compatriots the most selfless compassion and none more than the mother superior. A burly French matron blessed with a constitution that yielded neither to men nor diseases and a pair of cobalt-blue eyes that Thomas was sure could bore right to his soul, Mother Agnes appeared in the ward every morning carrying a large clay pitcher. She then proceeded to greet each man by name while she stooped to replenish the saucers of water she had placed beneath the legs of his bed to spare him the extra torment from the spreading incursion of ants.

But the strange contagion mocked her fine intentions and ravaged the ward with increasing fury. Otherwise healthy men who had suffered a broken ankle or a head-wound were now shivering and complaining of thirst. The doctors blamed the infections on vulgar habits and the tropics' toxic soil. When their prodigious theories produced grave nods but no real cure, the women took it upon themselves to provide their patients as much comfort as they could. As the room grew cramped with added beds the sisters fluttered through the aisles with their balled knuckles white from their constant prayers. Sunset was dreaded as nightfall saw fevers shooting to precarious heights, the insidious disease driving its victims to the shelter of insanity. Finally, the women would hunker out in the hall, helpless and despairing, and cover their ears as the dark ward echoed the screams of the distant jungle.

One of the sufferers was an older recruit named Lindell Walker. Thomas remembered thanking Walker for having nipped a budding rumor aboard ship that this young Judah fellow was a company spy. His diction plummy with the Queen's choice English, Walker had haughtily reminded them that for men with a melanistic tint, a fine education was considered as good for digging ditches as it was for hauling wood or drawing water. Thomas had grieved when Walker showed up with his long legs quavering like a Friday night drunk. Since then, the plum-voiced college graduate had gotten progressively worse to the point where his tics and thrashing groans were part of the ward's regular background.

So it came as a shock when Walker's loud stutters suddenly died out and he lay tranquil in his tangled sheets, a mummy resting in state. The digger remained that way for hours before his legs again started to jitter, only now much more rapidly, and his entire body began to convulse in a bone-shaking tremor that had the saucers under his bed rattling like frenzied castanets.

The racket quickly grew intolerable but just as Thomas thought it would drive him out of his mind, it stopped. Walker was bolt upright, glaring right at him. Thomas tried but could not look away. The piercing stare stayed fixed for an endless moment then drifted up, as if drawn to a celestial vision. Walker's face eased with a smile filled with calm and for a moment he seemed to be communing with forms unseen. All at once, he let out a hair-raising yell then doubled over and retched black vomit. For a long while the ward was eerily quiet. So quiet, in fact, that Thomas thought Walker had drifted peacefully to sleep until the two sisters who had hurried in when the digger started to vomit returned to his placid bed and started to weep.

The ward's first death seemed to take a toll on the softhearted sisters. They continued to do their best but their steps were heavy and their flapped wings slowed to scarcely a flutter. Little did they know that those saucers Mother Agnes refreshed so diligently had the *Aedes aegypti* flitting with gratitude. The tiny carriers, far more deadly than the pesky red ants, were delighted to find an easy supply of fresh water to lay their eggs and soon had the doctors scratching more than their heads as they too were gradually infected.

Thomas was touched to see the nuns' tight-shouldered grief and began to stretch his basic French until another anguished nurse was able to strain a smile, grateful that he could translate her patient's unanswered request. Given his long stay and bilingual ability, he became the staff pet and favorite to nineteen-year-old Genevieve, the order's aspiring novitiate. Genevieve's sensitive nature did not rest easy seeing men barely over being boys burning with fever, wilting at death's door. Were it not for Thomas' irreverent sense of humor the young nurse would have lapsed into chronic despondency. Instead, his instinct to laugh when others grew morbid inspired her to do something positive and so she contrived to test her own cures in secret. When one of the doctors caught her administering a pungent tea brewed from white cinnamon and cayenne peppers she was warned to never again interfere with his medical procedures. Incensed, she stomped off to see Mother Agnes to complain that their grand scientific procedures were doing as much good for these dying men as teats on a boar hog.

Although inwardly she admired her novice's passion, Mother Agnes upheld the doctor's injunction and forbade her attempting anymore homemade remedies. "You will learn, my child—over zealousness can cause more harm than good. Modesty, prayer and obedience—those are the watchwords we expect you to honor faithfully..."

The sharp rebuke added a scar to Genevieve's fragile makeup. Her parents and only brother had died when she was ten, just months after they had left Guadeloupe to resettle in Colombia. She'd spent her next eight years living in a convent school in Cartagena plagued by guilt that hounds a sole survivor. After she blossomed, almost overnight, from being a withdrawn pale child to a tall tan beauty everyone expected that her troubles would be solved by a prosperous husband, but Genevieve's rebirth had come through years of prayer. She had searched her soul and finally decided that once she felt worthy she would marry Christ.

She had never been happy that part of her nature tended towards disobedience. Yet she knew she could not long stand by, listening to those poor men plead for water and continue to deny them even a sip on doctors' orders. She thought it a sadistic experiment, its sole purpose to distract from the fact that the doctors had no answer. And if defiance was her second nature, her first impulse was to bring comfort. So when Mother Agnes asked if she could manage the late night shift on her own and relieve her ailing sisters Genevieve took it as no less than divine intervention.

Given a free hand to run the ward she applied her precocious early intimacy with the properties of calming herbs. Within days the midnight flare-ups had been subdued to the point that half of her patients were beginning to sleep straight through until the morning. With the sedatives coaxing snores in place of fidgets and shrieks, Genevieve could spend those restful moments sitting with Thomas, her only favorite. She was thankful to know that if her spirits began to sag and the flask her sisters kept tucked in the cupboard behind the lotions and syringes had been drained of its last nip of brandy, she could count on Thomas being there to amuse her.

"I see you had quite a session last night with one of the inmates..." Thomas accosted her in his usual droll manner when she finally stopped by his bed not long before dawn. "You were on your knees by his bed for almost an hour. What the devil were you up to—have you taken to speaking in tongues and anointing heads with oil?"

"You saw me?" Genevieve demanded, looking surprised. "I thought you were asleep."

"Who could sleep with you and that bugger singing and moaning?" Thomas grinned. "Actually, I woke up in this God-awful sweat and heard you chanting. It sounded very mysterious—like some primal incantation..."

"So you were spying?" she snapped, stepping back.

"I'd hardly call it spying—half the ward must have heard you. Look, I'm not accusing you of anything, I'm just curious what it was..."

"It's nothing mysterious. Just a prayer that helped to calm me as a child..."

"But why would you know such things? Those words weren't in French, nor in Spanish, for that matter. It wasn't Latin, I'm certain of that..."

"Hush! I'll explain it to you later," Genevieve hissed, shooting him a look that warned against more questions. "Now sit up and let's have a look at those ribs."

Genevieve finished removing the heavy binding around his torso but as she began to palpate Thomas' side she suddenly flinched. She darted a brisk hand to his forehead and could only shake her head when he tried to apologize, thinking his trembles were in response to his innocent new lust. She was too busy praying that her darkest fear had not come true.

With her pet's life in danger, Genevieve threw caution to the wind. She smuggled him sips of quinine and water, both of which remained firmly proscribed for patients suffering from fever. Once the lamps were dimmed and the last exhausted nun had retired to the cloister she would shield his bed with the ward's silk screen and hold him in her arms to try and soothe his terrible headache. If he started to moan she would whisper encouraging words in his ear, then force a smile when he grew brave and mumbled back drivel. For five nerve-wracking days, Thomas continued to sweat and shiver until she arrived early one evening and saw the roguish grin again beaming on his handsome face. When he greeted her with a typical cutting quip she raced in like a schoolgirl and kissed his cheek.

She thanked the Lord for answering her prayers but for the next three days and nights she seldom strayed long from Thomas' bed. She passed her free time reading him stories in French and having him tell them back to her in English. And with each traded chuckle her faith grew stronger and her fears diminished; her pet was getting better. Then one night at the start of her rounds she realized Thomas' tawny-brown skin was turning yellow. She tried to get him to drink more quinine but he refused, insisting that he felt fine and was tired of her fussing.

"Look," Thomas said quickly, seeing Genevieve's hurt look, "it's not that I don't relish the company—it's just tiresome to be treated like a cripple."

"Well then, I shall leave you be..."

After that the nurse proudly kept her distance and came to see him only at night during her shift. She felt pleased, seeing the pained look on his face, to know that he missed her but on reflection thought it all for the best. She needed to learn how to keep her chin up after he was gone. For three hard nights she forced herself to treat Thomas like any other patient. It wasn't until she saw his six-foot frame looking more like a whittled stick that she realized that while she'd been ignoring him he had not eaten a morsel.

Even had Thomas not been too weakened to resist, Genevieve would have brooked no more of his protests. Seating herself firmly on his bed, she gripped him by his shoulders and raising his head to rest against her breast pressed the milk from a spoon through his resistant mouth. She repeated the struggle three more times that night only to return the very next evening to find his cracked lips had bled and were starting to scab.

Her lamented efforts only served to double her renewed devotion. The ninth day arrived since she first recognized his telltale trembles and she had an obscure yet growing sense that her faith was facing its stiffest challenge. One lasting conviction sustained her; the spirits had guarded her life through so many tragedies they must have spared her for some great purpose, perhaps precisely this. So every night, while her pet slipped in and out of consciousness, she would sit by his side and thumb through her prayer-book unconscious of the human element actually driving her. She did not presume to prevail upon God's will but when Thomas could no longer speak and his bones looked to shrink inside his skin she could not wait on the doctors to have their breakthrough or abide another of Mother Agnes' commands to spend more time in chapel and trust in prayer. There were more active intercessions left to apply and if they could save her pet she did not care who might condemn her. Slipping a bribe to *Señora* Hidalgo, the hospital's genial Panamanian cook, she had her boil the castor bean plant she'd bought at the market and after drawing the pearly extract into a syringe, refixed the screen to guard against prying eyes and used it to give Thomas a warm enema.

She arrived early the next day to find him on his back, dead still with eyes shut, his face a quiescent mask. She raced to feel for a pulse and a sob of panic clutched her throat. Thomas' skin was fiery. She clamped a hand up to her mouth so her silent screams would not escape and overwhelm her then ran to find the two orderlies. Rushing the men inside, she ordered them to carry Thomas across to the other wing with the hospital's only bathtub.

When they saw the yellow skeleton lying rigid as a plank of wood the orderlies edged back in terror. "That bath is for French patients, we cannot—" one of them protested.

The wings on her wimple savagely fluttering, Genevieve swooped down into his face like a menacing bird. "Little man—I have no time for your petty concerns!"

Seeing the threat of murder gleaming from her eyes the men exchanged sidelong glances and silently complied. They hustled the catatonic body through the other segregated wing, ignoring the string of raised eyebrows as they shuffled on into the bathroom and set Thomas in the deep wooden tub. While they went to fetch the tall clay pots of water for the bath Genevieve dashed off to the kitchen. When she came hurrying back dragging a huge block of ice by a set of large tongs the orderlies stared at her dumbly then shook their heads, clearly amazed that this crazy young nurse had just ruined a visiting dignitary's champagne reception.

The men left muttering, grumbling about not taking the blame, but Genevieve had already drawn out the hammer she'd concealed inside her robes and started to smash the ice then place the chunks around Thomas' scorch-hot body. When she had nestled in the last cold chip she knelt and crossed herself twice on the wet tiled floor then, pulling out a small silver and ebony crucifix and five strands of multicolored beads from her damp habit, softly began to chant her nana's secret mystical prayers.

———

Kingston, Jamaica, early November

As the eighth week began without a word from her son, Josephine felt trapped between preserving a trust and acting on a mother's intuition. She had agreed not to warn his father of his plans but only after extracting Thomas' solemn promise that he would wire her the moment he set foot in Panama. She had scarcely slept since then and the toll had her nerves at a fine raw edge. She despised betraying her word, but consoled herself that she had no choice.

She could tell that Samuel was already fuming as she beckoned him to sit beside her on the drawing-room's George III settee. The flash of irritation as he extinguished his cigarette reminded her that he had never stopping seeing Thomas as the cause of all their troubles. To be fair, Samuel had made an effort to show some fatherly affection if for no other reason than to possess her.

"What more can I possibly do, Josey?" Samuel Judah turned his injured gaze up at the room's high ceiling with its muted depiction of Jacob being daintily fed grapes by his two young concubines. "The boy is thoughtless and irresponsible. Had I known Thomas would dash away the chance at a first-rate education I could have saved myself the trouble—not to mention the expense. Your son doesn't want me looking after him. He has made that much patently clear."

It was moments such as this that made Josephine wonder if her precious scruples were worth the price being foisted upon Thomas. Even though Samuel could still not fully embrace the boy as his own, once his father had died and could no longer threaten his inheritance he had offered to divorce his childless English wife so that he and Josephine could finally be married. But while she would welcome being more than his well-kept mistress, the thought of being the cause of another woman's unhappiness was a stain she refused to bear. And yet, she loved Samuel Judah as much as ever. So much that even after he had wronged her and disowned his own son she had borne him fair twin daughters.

"Darling," entreated Josephine, inching close on the seat's satin cushion to clasp his hand, "I know you're not going to let him just vanish—we need to make sure that he's all right..."

Samuel snatched back his arm and went back to gazing petulantly at the reposing Jacob. "When Thomas agreed to the apprenticeship I'd arranged I thought he was finally showing some sense—then that confounded sister of yours had to go and turn him back against me—"

"I don't think it's fair to blame her for telling the truth. Tongues were bound to wag. I can only imagine the taunts he must have suffered at a school like Wolmers. I'm sure he already suspected—especially once he saw how the twins were welcomed by your family."

"Don't try and lay it all at my feet! You were the one who suggested it might be better to pretend I was not his father. I think our decision was quite sensible. There's no great shame in being adopted. Surely the boy is old enough to understand..."

"He cannot understand if he believes that you rejected him."

"And why shouldn't I?" Samuel retorted. "No matter what I do he thumbs it back in my eye. I procure him a respectable profession and he runs off to the devil knows where! Just how much is that chip on Thomas' shoulder supposed to cost me?"

Josephine squeezed her hands tight to keep her voice from disclosing her panic. "What are you saying?" she whispered, gulping in her terror. "We're to forget he exists and let him rot in some foreign jungle?"

"Of course not," Samuel replied, resting back in the cushioned settee. "I've tried making inquiries but the wire from Colón has not been restored since the earthquake. I did learn that he landed safely. Yes—" he said, seeing Josephine's mouth fall open in surprise, "I knew where he'd gone. After he didn't show up for his internship I figured he'd gone to stay with your sister's family. Of course, Mary wouldn't allow herself to be civil, but after my visit her husband stopped in my office and told me all about the tom-fool plan. Thank goodness that Roberson fellow has his feet on the ground. It still baffles me that such a sensible chap could have fallen head over heels for a pedantic sixteen-year-old."

"I'm just happy my sister's marriage turned out well," Josephine said wistfully. "She only eloped at that tender age because she could not bear living in this house with your mistress—" She stopped mid-thought and her drained beige face turned sorrowful. "I suppose to Mary I'll always be a fallen woman."

Josephine's fair constricted beauty caused Samuel's rough words to smooth and grow tender. "I can understand her despising me—but she shouldn't blame you."

"Never mind, I know in her heart my sister loves me. The question is...what do we do now?" asked Josephine, her hand falling pleadingly onto his knee. "I'm frightened, Samuel. I sense something bad has happened."

Samuel studied the perfect oval face he adored and exhaled with a much-used shrug. "I suppose, my sweet apple, I shall be going to Panama."

Chapter 3

Henri Duvay drew his pistol and coolly took aim. Backed by the eloquence of a loaded gun he was prepared to risk one final stab at trying to reason with the big Dutch bear. "On my honor as a Frenchman, I did not cheat you. Put down your blade and let us play one last hand—winner take all."

The Dutchman leaned his puckered lips across the table and hurled a large gob of spit. "Rot in hell, you stinking yellow thief!"

Duvay wiped the spittle from his eye and sprang to his feet still holding his aim. "Go home to bed, *mon ami*. A night's sleep will lighten your losses."

The drunken bear swept up his paw and flipped the table, spilling the piles of cards and coins across the barroom floor. "Murderer!" he bawled, swaying as he staggered around the mess with his cutlass aloft. He took a wobbly swipe at the little Frenchman who calmly stepped to the right, steadied his gun and fired.

The Dutchman howled and dropped the machete to clutch his knee. "Damn you, Duvay—you shot me!"

The *cantina's* patrons had been ignoring the row, but at the gunshot their raucous voices dipped to a hum. As all ears perked up, alert for the second discharge that would demand their concern and distract from their pleasures, Duvay took advantage of the lull to hail the tavern's raven-haired barmaid. "Estelle, *ma cherie*—!" he called, waving to her with a smile, "bring some dressing—my friend DeBerg requires a bit of mending."

"Keep this up, Henri, and I'll have to throw you out in the alley along with the rabble—" the busty *mestiza* threatened as she arrived and saw the overturned table lying in a mess of cards and coins and splattered blood.

"I'm not to blame, *ma cherie*. It appears the kindly bear is not so cuddly in his liquor."

"Did you have to shoot him?" Estelle complained, frowning at the prodigious drunkard slouching back in his chair, muttering Dutch curses.

"I wasn't inclined to wait and see if he would slice me into pieces," Duvay said curtly as the barmaid stooped and began rolling up the bleeding man's pants-leg. "Anyway, it's just a scratch. DeBerg and I coped with far worse in your jungle."

Few but Henri Duvay had the poise and skill to direct a bullet so that it grazed the exact spot on the Dutchman's knee sure to stop the assault without causing serious damage. Although the Frenchman was not one to gamble for the sake of sentiment, knowing that the wounded bear had gone to heroic lengths to save him made for an attachment that was not easily dismissed.

DeBerg had been among Duvay's team of surveyors just back from blazing a trail from Panama City, the state capital on the Pacific, to Colón on the coast of the Atlantic. They were in the bowels of the jungle when a powerful storm blew up as they were crossing the Chagres River. Within minutes the channel had surged into a roaring monster, capsizing their canoes in the hurtling waters. Duvay would surely have drowned had DeBerg not battled the current and hauled him to land in his ursine embrace. Only nine of the twelve men had made it across safely, they had lost both dugouts with their food and supplies, yet Duvay had refused to turn back. Forced to forage while being stalked by reptiles and eaten by parasites, the surveyors had hacked their way through woods so dense and tall they could scarcely tell night from day. In the end only seven men survived their hellish three-week trek but the little Frenchman emerged triumphant. He boasted that like Balboa and Cortez their names would be immortal—for they had confirmed the fifty-mile path for the long-wished-for Panama Canal.

While she wrapped the immense knee with a rag soaked in whiskey the shapely barmaid studied the sad Dutch face, slightly purple with settling blood. "He is suffering from more than this flesh wound, your friend," she noted solemnly.

"Grief and alcohol are not a good mixture, *ma cherie*," murmured Duvay turning his collected gaze onto DeBerg slumped in his chair like a goliath rag-doll. "His brother was bitten by a *lance de fer* outside Frijoles...we couldn't save him."

"You should have left him to enjoy himself, Henri—not taken his money playing cards!" scolded Estelle, nodding to the chintzy sway-backed girls occupying the laps and swelling attentions of her leather-necked clientele. "They're better tonic—and far prettier!" the *mestiza* chuckled, pinching the middle-aged Frenchman affectionately on the cheek.

"Perhaps—" Duvay conceded, glancing with disinterest at the handful of women adorning the scene with their gaudy dresses and colorful hair-ribbons, "but they'd have exhausted the poor chap far quicker."

His indifference seemed to irritate the smiling Estelle who credited her success as a hostess and then as the bar's sole owner to her special insight into the proclivities of men. Though her Yankee railroaders had gone back to drinking beer and whiskey once they wised to the fact that lavish amounts of quinine-laced champagne had no effect on Panama's diseases, she had splurged on a stock of sparkling wines to encourage Henri Duvay's visits. It fit nicely with her plans to have an engineer of his prestige as a loyal customer but she was flummoxed by this strange little Frenchman who claimed to abhor the delusions of respectable company yet had given her no hint of any exploitable fetishes.

Fluent in Spanish as well as English, Duvay almost invariably came alone and asked for a bottle of Möet, although any 'true' French champagne would do. Selecting a corner table not far from the door, he would carefully remove his jacket, set two decks of cards neatly beside a stack of gold piasters then sit and wait for some sharpie to walk in and take his bait. Estelle noticed early on he would often lose a costly hand in dramatic fashion then proceed to bilk the patsies stupid enough to trust either their skill or their staggering luck. After he had cleaned out the last die-hard optimist Duvay would light up a thin black cigar then settle back and puff while he watched the nightly fondling, as enthused as a clinical anthropologist.

The city's vocational swindlers and cheats quickly learned to stay clear of his table. As a result, the little Frenchman would frequently sit alone for hours patiently shuffling his decks between sips of his sparkling wine, yet not once did he invite a fleshy bar-girl to share his bottle so he could stuff a franc inside her bosom and have her nestle on his thighs. Estelle had thought at first that brown buxom women were simply not to his taste, but with 'American ladies' of every size, age and nationality pouring into Colón as rapidly as the abundant crates of French champagne, it was discouragingly clear that her prized engineer had no craving for easy women no matter their shade or shape.

In truth, Henri Duvay was a rare egg even among the exceptional men Ferdinand de Lesseps had wooed for his ground-breaking project. Raised by a widowed mother of modest means, he won admittance to the prestigious *L'École*

Polytechnique at only sixteen where his talents had shined even in that brilliant constellation. To add exotic luster to his humble background Duvay claimed a blood relation to Chevalier de St. Georges, the French composer of African descent who went from being a Royal Musketeer to winning romantic fame fighting to preserve the Revolution. Unfortunately for young Henri, the olive cast to his complexion was not dark enough to prevent his Roman nose and straight black hair from subverting his proud affirmation. His ridiculed claim coupled with his early addiction to the spotlight finally led five jealous schoolmates to kidnap him one day after class, saying it was time he stopped gabbing and proved he was a man. They bustled him to a dated salon where they stripped off his clothes and thrust him into the arms of the wilted courtesan who, seeing poor Henri's revulsion as proof of her faded charms, appeased her bitterness by making fun of the boy's shrinking member. His humiliation complete when his failure was widely broadcast, Henri had withdrawn from his final year's classes and finished his studies in private.

"He can stay here and sleep it off," proposed Duvay, nodding at the Dutchman now passed out cold, his huge head bobbing to his chest as he snored. "DeBerg is tough as a yak—he'll be fine by tomorrow."

Estelle considered this with visible annoyance. She was delighted that Henri had discouraged the two-bit hustlers from overrunning her tavern and siphoning off money better spent on one of her girls or a bottle of bourbon, but if she was seen allowing drunks to sleep things off all night, instead of attracting more well-paid engineers she'd have every bum in town crowding her joint and pretending to pass out until morning. "Be reasonable, Henri. I close in an hour," she implored, glaring back at the snoring Dutchman, his open mouth starting to slobber. "I'm afraid your friend is going to wake up and spew vomit all over my customers..."

Duvay touched a pensive finger to his lips, his long nose crinkling above his pendulous waxed moustache. "What else can we do? Six of us might be able to lift him but then how would I get him down from the cab? Perhaps, if there was a way to get him up those stairs there is a bed where he could rest, *n'est-ce-pas?*" he suggested with a shrewd glance past the heads of the *cantina's* ardent couples, some groping daintily, others shamelessly. "So many healthy girls, *ma cherie*—I'm sure you take into account your clients might need a little private pick-me-up on occasion—"

"You're an adorable rogue, Henri Duvay," Estelle retorted, smiling, "but if he's to stay here the night and cut into my profits it's going to cost you!" She wiggled a warning finger then bored past him to climb atop a chair. Her chubby arm surmounting the weald of patrons, she made a cryptic signal with her thumb and first finger and in seconds a towering dark figure came worming through the crowd. Without waiting for instruction, the giant man elbowed the little Frenchman aside, then, bending his knees with care, dipped a shoulder beneath DeBerg's armpit and in one fluid move hoisted the slumbering bear across his back.

"*Incroyable!*" the engineer gasped, watching the two retreat so smoothly the bar's engrossed patrons remained indifferent to the fact that a giant West Indian was squeezing past them lugging three hundred pounds of insensible Dutch flesh. "Where did you procure that magnificent specimen? I would pay a king's ransom for a thousand like him!"

"You can forget it, Henri, he's mine!" joked Estelle.

"No doubt, *ma cherie*—who would not covet being lifted in those arms! What grace—and yet such power! He reminds us that success is a matter of balance! That balance now requires a good night's sleep. You shall have just compensation—I'm sure that by morning our injured bear will manage to limp with the aid of a shoulder."

"Just this once—for you, *querido*," laughed Estelle, lightly smooching the Frenchman's cheek. "But I want him out of here by noon."

"On my honor, *ma cherie*. I'll see DeBerg early to the hospital, myself."

———

Light was streaming through the ward's drawn curtains and as he awoke and began rubbing his eyes, Thomas felt tense, afraid that he was suffering another jolting hallucination. His anxiety quickly turned to anger as he realized that the familiar form looming by his bed was indeed his father who immediately launched into one of his tiresome reproaches.

"I suppose you view this little escapade as your strike for independence! After all your mother and I have had to grapple with for you, one would think you'd appreciate our sacrifice."

"Who asked you? You're not going to run my life just so you can ease your bloody conscience!"

Samuel Judah glowered at his son but refrained from answering. He started to pace alongside the shielded hospital bed, his yellow clasped hands making twisting motions as if wrestling to shape an intractable ball of clay.

"No doubt you've gained wisdom from your recent infirmities," Samuel abruptly moralized as he stopped himself from pacing. His voice sounded calm, as if their heated exchange had never happened. "Count on God to provide a dose of pain to shake us back to reality. Your mother has been at her wits end so she'll be relieved to see you've recovered. Don't worry—I've smoothed things out with Dr. Graham—the position has been left open."

"Go home. You're wasting your breath," Thomas retorted, making no attempt to hide his disgust at the quiet certainty on his father's face, the face he assiduously kept out of the sun lest it bronze to too swarthy a glaze. "I'm not going back."

Samuel pressed a hand across his wavy brown hair in frustration. He had come expecting some resistance but had hoped that Thomas would be satisfied to know he could leave Panama without losing face after breaking several ribs and almost dying of swamp fever. Instead, the lad's impudence only reminded him of the constant antagonism that had finally doused the paternal embers he had tried his best to keep aglow. Considering the shades that importunity had placed between himself and his son, he found it hard to accept that they shared the same vital matter. When the boy was born he had been so sure no child that brown could be his own that he had slandered poor Josephine with every vile name he could think of, and in his anger had jumped into a loveless marriage. He wished he could forget the hurt he had caused the woman he loved. He still smarted at the shame he had faced once it became clear that not only did Josie's toddler possess distinct Judah traits, he even had Samuel's dear dead mother's impossibly violet eyes.

"So, is that your plan?" the elder Judah crisply challenged his son. "To stay in this pesthole while your mother goes out of her mind worrying that you've died?"

"She knows why I left. Now you can toddle off and tell her you saw me and I'll be fine."

"I did not come this far to listen to more of your impertinence! You've been incorrigible since the day you quit school. Where does this new arrogance towards me come from? I suppose I can thank your dear Aunt Mary..."

"Yes, Aunt Mary told me why you never married my mother—it was because of me. Apparently, I turned up a shade too dark for a proper Judah. Or was that just a handy excuse so you could weasel out once you'd knocked her up?"

Samuel had his hand raised, ready to strike the boy across his mouth, then thought twice and dropped it coldly at his side. "Damn you, Thomas! Have I not gone out of my way to give you every advantage?"

"I thought you'd thank me for leaving. Now you don't have to worry about trying to explain me to your high-flown circles. Go on home and pretend I don't exist."

A relieved look flashed on the elder Judah's face, as if he'd just been released from a role he could not master. "Don't try taking that line with me—I'm not your mother. You've gotten chance after chance, everything money can procure. You're bright enough to know that more than that is beyond my power. Accept it. I grant you it's harsh and unfair, but such are the realities and they aren't about to change because we might wish it. That doesn't mean your life must be an error!"

"I'm not an error! I'll best you yet, father—just wait, you'll see! I'll start at it right here in Panama, without your self-righteous philanthropy!"

"Doing what? Manual labor? I doubt you have it in you—it would mean doing an honest day's work."

"Then you and I have something in common after all...father—" Thomas sneered.

"How dare you mock me!" Samuel boomed out, stalking in aggressively. "I won't have it—not after I put my family in jeopardy and let you carry my name—the Judah name!"

Genevieve came dashing around the screen with her head-wings flapping. "*S'il vous plait, monsieur!* You must be quiet—there are other patients!"

Samuel ignored the young nurse and went right on upbraiding his son. Genevieve was insisting that he compose himself or go out to the hall when a sharp new voice sliced in.

"Beg pardon, *messieurs!*" A short man, dressed head to toe in fine white linen, appeared at the edge of the screen. He gazed at Thomas in a moment's startled wonder then bowed deeply to the elder Judah. "I could not help overhearing, so please forgive my indiscretion..." The interloper's head barely reached the nurse's shoulder but the gold-rimmed monocle and expansive black moustache lent weight to his imperious manner. He glanced up at Genevieve. "Nurse, you may go. I'm certain *les messieurs* do appreciate your concerns."

Genevieve glared at him before she left and the intruder rattled right on. "Henri Duvay, at your service. " The Frenchman clicked his heels with a vain crisp nod as if the mere stating of his name was enough to explain his temerity. "I am chief engineer for *Couvreux, Hersent*. Our firm has been charged with the noble task of guiding this great canal project. I realize this may appear to be presumptuous, however, I believe I have the solution to the gentlemen's disagreement."

"This is no concern of yours...sir," Samuel responded with asperity.

The Frenchman pressed the white fedora in his hand against his chest and addressed the elder Judah with solemn deference. "Fate has seen fit to introduce us and we should never shun its fortuities! As it happens I was just recently acquainted with your family's accomplishments. I was told that when it comes to doing business there is no name more respected in the British West Indies. I consider it an honor to meet a gentleman of such means and high standing."

"I thank you for the compliments," Samuel replied stiffly. "However, I must insist you respect that this is a private matter."

Duvay neatly transferred the monocle to his pocket and turned to Thomas who had pried himself higher in bed, enraptured by the little Frenchman's performance. "I agree with your father—menial labor is out of the question. It would be a waste of all that inherited talent." Duvay bent in nearer to Thomas who spotted the conspiratorial twinkle in the beady green eyes. "For a resourceful young man out to test his strength against outrageous obstacles this project offers unparalleled opportunities. I assure you its scope is something the world has never seen, Master Judah—I understand perfectly why you'd want be part of it!"

Only the hard lesson learnt that a circumspect tongue was the wiser choice on most occasions kept Samuel Judah from replying with something rude. "We thank you for your interest, sir, but as you can see, the boy has not yet recovered. Panama is simply not the place for him—he has suffered severely broken ribs already..."

"*Oui, oui! Je comprends!*" Duvay concurred, nodding vigorously. "But suppose I could arrange something more suitable—say...as my personal assistant? It would be largely a clerical position. No cracking of the ribs, *mais oui?*"

Thomas opened his mouth to object but the Frenchman covertly silenced him.

"You'll find the compensation quite satisfactory under the circumstances—and the experience is certain to reform him..." Duvay abruptly left Thomas' side to speak quietly by Samuel's ear. "And there is one other small matter I intend to propose which I'm confident will prove worth your while."

Samuel's inclination was to reject this pushy overture, but as he weighed the Frenchman's credentials against his other options his back slackened to its more natural indulgent pose. "Why not?" he agreed with a shrug. "I can make time for a worthy proposition."

"That is all an honest supplicant can ask, *n'est-ce pas?*" Smiling, Duvay quickly turned back to Thomas. "Isn't that so...young master—?"

"His name is Thomas," Samuel said quickly, "my most exceptional offspring."

"Well, it has been an exceptional pleasure to make both your acquaintances!" Duvay winked back at Thomas as if the two of them had just pulled off a bloodless coup. "I must tell you, sir," he said, extending an arm for the elder Judah to join him in the hall, "I sense the three of us shall each gain immeasurably from this happy encounter."

Seeing Thomas' sly little grin as he bade the Frenchman good-bye, Samuel felt suddenly encouraged. If it could indeed be arranged that the hotspur's welfare was placed in such prominent hands, he could return to his darling Josephine with a most attractive compromise.

CHAPTER 4

"GOLD-OH! GOLD-OH! Gold dey at mi yard-oh!"

The pique in that constant refrain cut deep into Byron's psyche. The more its sarcasm weighed with repetition the more his hatred for it grew. He had spent his whole first month in Panama fetching water for a pittance as he waited for the crack in his arm to heal. Now the thought of earning twenty cents for every little dump-car he filled with rubble left him sure his pockets would soon be jingling merrily. But ever since he'd been sent to level the spine of the Continental Divide with a pick and shovel his gang's cynical chants had been getting louder and much more common.

"Monkey rub de fiddle-oh!—Gold dey at mi yard-oh!"

Byron slammed the ax-head against the crest's hard slab with a mighty tooth-rattling ping! then glared at Jackson Free working a lazy shovel a half-dozen yards to his right. As much as he rejected its bitter irony, he had to admit the lament fit their task to a tee: crush the rock then scoop up the rubble, crush the rock, scoop up the rubble and repeat—ten hours a day, six days a week until the sands of time poured right over All Saints and Christmas.

He brushed aside the thought and struck the granite six times in succession hoping the sharp reverberations would keep the hated lyrics from weighing on his brain. But each time the sound of his pick started ringing across the ridge Free pressed his baritone to a more piercing register until Byron began to feel his forearms burn from gripping the ax in anger. He finally tossed down the pick in disgust and Free promptly stopped singing.

Byron stood to glare through the hot gusting dust and saw Free start to wipe the white salt grit from his black-baked neck then ease his lanky body up to scan the dented sierra. Free surveyed the mountainous chain with a long leaden gaze then bawled out, "oh, what de raas!" and bent back to his shoveling, droning a sorrier tune all to himself, "jes' so mi bawn, jes' so, mi bawn...yuh can wear long boot, but is jes' so mi bawn..."

Byron was determined to beat back the discontent he could sense taking hold of his entire camp. Unlike some of his fanciful comrades he had not come to Panama praying to dig up a trove of lost treasure. The pot of gold he was after was the respect he would command once this challenging venture succeeded. He merely had to glimpse those massive machines scoring the mountain's low flanks like smoke-snorting bulls to remember that he was part of something momentous. So when the work seemed to drag, instead of agreeing that they had been sold a bushel of French blarney, he reminded his unhappy comrades that the eyes of the world were on them—and besides—the pay was enough to fill a fat man's belly.

His cheering efforts only drew more resentment. No one liked to be proved wrong and after digging for almost a year Byron's comrades were compelled to admit that they stood less chance of finding a cache of Spanish gold than a mongoose becoming governor of Jamaica. Even the young hayseeds escaped from off-the-map places like Wait-a-Bit and Buck-Up without two pennies to rub together felt shamed, knowing they'd been abused by their own ignorance. Where Byron understood that while he was starting at the very bottom there were more than two rungs on the social ladder, for them the bridge between privation and wealth was no more solid than a dream, and that span could only be crossed in a single sanctioned leap—like Joseph being plucked from slavery and made the Pharaoh's high counselor.

"Gold-oh! Gold-oh! Gold amber gold-oh!"

Byron swore, hearing the tiresome refrain start up again and decided to counter it with a light-hearted ditty of his own, "there's a blind boy in the ring—tra-la-la-la-la-la." As his voice grew stronger he dug more heartily, egged on by the livelier rhythm. He was nearly done scooping in another barrowful of rubble when he noticed Jackson Free drop his shovel and rush a hand to his dripping forehead. Byron yelled out to the stumbling digger who made a woozy pirouette and crumpled to the ground.

Byron hurried to where Free had fallen, shouting for someone to bring water. The men closest by saw him waving frantically from his knees and raced in quickly. They crowded around the two prostrate figures and saw that Free was out cold. A heavyset digger at Byron's side suggested they rouse Free with some snuff made of dusted pepper but an older man argued against it, saying a sudden big sneeze might hurt him. The water-boy arrived with his pail and Byron pleaded for the men to step back and give Free some air then doused his own handkerchief to swab the unconscious digger's face. Free's eyes fluttered open, but seeing Byron he squeezed them shut with a hateful scowl.

The men carried Free to rest in the spot of shade by the giant excavators leaving Byron to battle his emotions. He was hurt by Free's open scorn and troubled by the fact that it was not the first time he'd seen a comrade suddenly faint and topple over. Even though he told himself that he was still young and fit as a corn-fed rooster, he wondered who would come to his rescue if he passed out working in the blazing sun. It was at times like these that he dearly missed Thomas. He wished he had gone to see his friend in the hospital, despite his objections. Instead, he'd been too timid and now the months had gone by and they remained out of touch.

He had taught himself to read at a basic level but he had a hard time writing more than the letters in his name. So when some of his upland gang prepared to leave for vacation he had enlisted a comrade's help and cobbled together a note to Thomas in care of the hospital to wish him a nice Christmas and let him know he'd been transferred to the camp at Bas Obispo. When he got no reply his comrade suggested his friend had probably gotten cold feet and run home to daddy. But Byron refused to believe it.

There was no denying the job was proving tougher than he had bargained for, yet Byron held to his belief that every penny it let him save was worth the strain—at least until the month of May signaled the dry season's end and he found his earnings stifled by the oppressive humidity. Not only was the steamy heat the sworn enemy of speed, the daily torrential squalls had him constantly ditching his work to scramble for cover. Still he was reluctant to complain, as even on his worst days his limber back and increasing proficiency were netting him close to two gold dollars a day, more than triple what he had earned back on the plantation.

"By gum, boy! You done full-up one mo'?" The beefy new overseer had nothing but compliments for his smallest digger. He beamed, seeing the slender Jamaican already hauling up his eighth load of rubble that day.

"Yah, boss," Byron grinned. He liked the slow-talking Cajun who claimed to be from everywhere in the great U-S-of-A except Boston or 'Frisco and said his men were free to call him anything except for 'Mr. Charlie' or 'hey—Yank!' "But mi goin' up back to fill two more—so don' tally me up yet."

"Well, butter my biscuit!—if I cudden use a barrel o' darkies like you! I reckon we'd be halfway outta this pepper patch by now."

A swell of satisfaction rose in Byron's chest as he watched the big Southerner lick the tip of his pencil then scratch another mark beside his name. "My back say yuh got dat right, boss, but we got more rock still to crumble an' mi pocket not complainin'."

"Ain't no lying 'bout that," the foreman grunted. He slipped the tally sheet into his sleeve and started to hitch the full Decauville to the miniature train of dump cars. "Only thing is—at this rate—" he stammered, puffing from the exertion in the torrid heat, "these high-on-the-hog Frenchies are gonna end up swallowin' all their money before this crackpot job gits done...hell—I could buy haffa Alabama for what these peeshwanks splurge in a week just on champagne."

While the Cajun struggled to fasten the last car-load of rubble behind the rail's toy-sized locomotive Byron slouched back up the ridge confused and freshly deflated. He had taken it for granted that if there was a set of people with the skill and the money to carry off something this big it was the French. Everyone he knew agreed they were cleverer than the English. It seemed impossible that after all the talk about their 'glorious enterprise' being splashed in every paper, that Mr. de Lesseps would let them fail. But he was not quick to slough off the Cajun's opinion. The man clearly knew a thing or two. For instance, once he realized his Jamaican crew had no experience with blasting powder or dynamite the big Southerner had taken the time to show them how to handle high explosives without blowing themselves to bits. And he'd been right about the French needing more diggers—although Byron wondered, when new recruits began showing up in droves, how that squared with them running short on money. Either way, the job was falling short on gratification. And that was before Byron was unnerved by all the disappearances.

Of late, after the little Belgian train had chased the ruby-red sun down the back of the mountain to dump its last load, Byron would trudge into camp and sense that more comrades were missing. Sometimes, while waiting to wash up at the cistern he would ask the man beside him in line if he had seen 'so and so' around in the last few days and receive either a shrug or a pinch-eyed stare as if Byron had broken a taboo and tempted evil. When Jackson Free was nowhere to be found, despite having been back at work the day after his fainting spell,

Byron decided he'd best broach the matter with the bossman, but the big Cajun did not seem bothered.

"Don't go gettin' yer britches in a twist—most nigras ain't wu'th your salt. That lazy griper was barely clearing four bits anyways...Free and those boys prob'ly just bin dippin' into too much moonshine and they're lyin' off someplace three sheets to the wind."

The speculation seemed reasonable enough until Byron remembered that Jackson Free never touched hard liquor—called it the white man's curse. So he asked the overseer why he thought men would want to take off in the middle of the week and not wait for pay day.

The big Southerner had to stop for a minute and scratch his chin. Maybe, he said, they were out to fool the Frenchies into thinking they'd taken sick. That way they could weasel out of their contracts and still wangle that free trip home.

Although the inkling in Byron's gut did not jibe with the Cajun's theory it was hard to quibble with his contention. He knew more than a few of his comrades could be tempted to nip off for a short unscheduled vacation after swigging a tad too much rum. Having reasoned out his suspicions, Byron set about squeezing every dollar from his digging until one muggy breeze-starved evening he walked into his barracks and found the Fiddler quivering like a rabbit.

Johnny Fingers was Byron's one close buddy in camp. The eighteen-year-old digger's last name was not really Fingers but everyone called him that, or simply the Fiddler, because Johnny was a genius on the violin. Byron had noticed that every day, once the sun went down and the air felt cool, Johnny would wander off in the dark and be gone for an hour. He decided to trail him one night after supper and discovered that his friend was simply after someplace quiet to play his fiddle and stay nimble after a hard day's digging. Since Byron didn't care to waste his money on moonshine or risk it gambling, most evenings found him crouching somewhere politely out of sight listening to Johnny Fingers' inspiring talent.

With little in camp to entertain them, the highlight of the diggers' week came on Sundays when Johnny would oblige to step out in the yard with his bow and fiddle and promptly launch into a breathless quick-step. It took only a handful of those flashy notes to trill the air before men were breaking up their card-games and slapping down their dominoes to stamp and clap to the Fiddler's homespun virtuosity.

When he had everyone worked up to a rip-roaring frenzy Johnny would slyly ease up the tempo and shift to a stately quadrille. Upon hearing the dignified dance meter, the men would bow to their pending partners and form in two-set pairs. The smaller man in each couple would then gaily tuck in his stomach and swell a milkless bosom, giggling in his role as the bashful female when a hand or a thigh 'accidentally' brushed his bottom. Once this playful grazing of flesh had both dancers aroused the Fiddler would impishly slide into a slow serenade. Carried away by the throbbing melody, the men were soon cheek to cheek, their eyes pressed tight to guard their inner rhapsodies against the confusing delight of muscular arms and scratchy whiskers. When the couples began to look lost in their bodies' ardent heat, Johnny would snap them from their dreaming caresses with a lightning-fingered reel. Finally, a few bold souls not left wearily huffing and puffing would run and fetch a beat up old guitar or a rusty concertina for the chance to boast that they had once played with the great Johnny Fingers.

Just as Byron had been stunned to come across a fellow like Thomas Judah on a steerage deck, he had been curious to know how the Fiddler ended up in Panama plying a shovel.

"My daddy was a great banjo player," Johnny explained after he and Byron got more friendly. "He used to travel all over the island playing for dances. He gave me my very first fiddle for my sixth birthday. It really wasn't much more than a toy, but he made it himself—sawed it from a piece of pine and an old cigar box. He even made the little horsehair bow. When he wasn't off playing his banjo, he'd come and make sure I was balancin' the little fiddle the right way under my chin then he'd teach me a scale or a short little tune. Then one day he left and never came back. I think he got tired of Mummy always accusin' him of carryin' on with other women and decided he might as well go ahead and prove her right—folks say my daddy drew women like honeybees to cane syrup," the Fiddler boasted with a grin.

"...'bout seven years back he turns up out of the blue. I'd been sawing on that cigar-box fiddle that whole time—my ear could pick up anything dat grab me. When he heard me play *'Fan me soldier man, fan me!'* some long tears came in his eyes. He said I'd been blessed with a load of talent and by hook or crook he would get me a real violin. That's it right here—" Johnny nodded vaguely towards the slot between the barracks wall and his bed where he kept the violin hidden inside its black cedar case. "My daddy came back and gave me it in time for my thirteenth birthday." He stopped then looked up at Byron defensively. "Nobody knows if this is the god's honest truth...people were always jealous that my daddy had a bit more money than the average...Anyhow, rumor was that after he finished playin' for a dance at some big man's plantation the busha's prize mare went missin'. The bad talk mussi did reach Mum's ears 'cause I remember her asking where he got the money for such a sweet-soundin' fiddle. I never know my daddy to get angry like he did that day—he told Mummy she had no business cross-questionin' him when he was out crossin' this island on foot to keep that roof over her head. He told her if he was a rich man he could ride a fine horse clear and free but since he was born poor he had to pay tax to our white monkey government just to ride his blinkin' jackass."

Johnny paused again with a bitter look but kept both eyes drilled on Byron's face.

"Yuh think your daddy stole the white man's horse to buy yuh dat fiddle. Yuh ever have chance to ask him?"

"Nope," Johnny replied, shaking his head. "He left again right after he and mummy had that fight. I have a bad feeling he might be in prison but my mum would never answer when I asked if it was true what people were saying. She told me if I wanted to help my daddy I should find that big man and offer him my violin." Johnny screwed up his face and stared at the fiddle's secret spot. When he looked back up there were tears in his eyes. "I couldn't do it, *bolow*—I couldn't give it up! I asked her if they never found the horse how did they know for sure who stole it but she wouldn't listen. Daddy had stopped coming back to bring us money and with all the labba-labba people in our parish, mum was afraid the boss might take back her new job cleaning at the bakery. She said if I didn't do like she say she was gonna tell the police and have them come and take it. So to put her off I said 'all right, Mummy,' packed up the fiddle and caught the next boat to Colón."

"Yuh did right, Johnny. Who's to say where your daddy got that money..." Byron said with a cagey wink, "maybe it's the tax money he saved from selling his donkey..."

"Byron..." the Fiddler grinned, "you're what I call a true friend."

Johnny's confession, shared as a precious confidence, prompted Byron to assign himself as the Fiddler's impresario. He coaxed his friend to take Saturdays off from shoveling to play in Colón or better still, Panama City. He seemed about to prevail when the monsoons came and Johnny began to mope like the soggy weather. Byron would pester him to play '*La Paloma*' or '*Three Acres of Coffee*' but as the steady rains began to coat everything metal in an ugly orange rust, Johnny griped that the dankness had opened a seam on his fiddle and ruined its tone. When Byron still persisted Johnny grumbled that his fingers ached and besides, he had lost his feel from so much digging. So even as Byron trumpeted the young digger's talents and helped spread the Fiddler's fame far beyond camp, those delightful rollicking Sundays stretched back to their dissolute slow routine with the magic violin left silent in its case.

———

"Yuh should go in hospital, Johnny." Byron was worried. He had just returned from a fourth trip to fetch him water and the Fiddler was still wrapped inside his bedclothes, shivering.

"I can't afford it, *bolow*. Every day they want to keep me in that infirmary is gonna cost me two days shoveling."

"But how yuh gwine work in your condition? Maybe they can give yuh some medicine."

Johnny Fingers eyes grew wide with fear. "Look how many men done gone in that hospital and I have yet to see one come back out!"

"If you don't want to go in hospital then you better stay here and rest."

"No—I gots to try and hold up! If that big Cajun finds out I took sick he'll make me leave camp. What'll I do then? I can't risk going home yet—not until I can pay that rich man for his horse and clear my daddy's name..."

Byron felt his throat clamp shut as if it had been choked with some of the mountain's rubble. He understood only too well. His friend was caught between a hard rock and the devil. For men like him and Johnny life always seemed to boil down to this: if a sickness didn't kill you off quick then starvation would finish you slow—but only after it stole your spirit.

Touching a hand to Johnny's shoulder, Byron wrapped his friend more snugly and promised to stay by his side. He told himself that so long as he faithfully kept watch the Fiddler would find the strength to survive.

That night, the minute he sensed his eyelids start to dip he forced them back wide and busied his mind imagining the short eulogy he could expect were he to take ill here and die. At least if Johnny was alive his death would be marked with some music. But who would be there to hear it if no one came to mourn? Would his end be just another ordinary day—like the one those long years ago back in St. Catherine—the day that began like any other but which, by its end, saw the heart of his brief existence wrenched away?

She had left him early that morning. He had been made to stay with the estate's toothless barrel-maker a few times before and feared the old buzzard. The seventy-year-old cooper with his crooked long-nailed fingers and scab-gummed grin seemed to like nothing better than to frighten a five-year-old child. When he had cried and clung to her side, pleading with her not to leave him, she had brushed away his tears and asked him to be her brave boy. She said she would be gone for only a little while until her blown-up belly could push out its new life. But by afternoon the new word he had learned was death.

There are no more special days when you're five and straining to grasp the meaning of 'bounder' and 'indentured ward'—and why you hated the way the big round cook mutters 'whorish' and why she always cuts you in half with her eyes. Then the awful truth dawns and you realize, standing by the open pit, that the center of your life is not going to jump up from that ugly crate laughing and say it was all just a game to tease you as she picks you up and smothers you with kisses. For that child, there will never be words some drab gray preacher can intone to tell you why some folks grow old and lose their teeth while others still full of life and bright white smiles suddenly close their eyes and die; why at ten you were willing to risk another bloody nose if just once you could jam 'hey, coolie-boy, where yuh long-foot tata deh?' back down the throat of your tormentor even if he was three years older and a good foot taller because you didn't know who your daddy was and damned if you cared.

So he began to search for anything, a slip of paper, a generous word, that would confirm the reason for his existence. He finally found it in a Bible lesson during his Sunday school class. The district's drab preacher had quoted from the book of Samuel and the passage had left him believing the Lord could at anytime work his magic, even on him:

> The Lord maketh poor, and he maketh rich,
> He bringeth low and lifteth up,
> He raiseth up the poor out of the dust, and
> lifteth up the beggar from the dunghill
> to set them among princes...

Thinking back on those wondrous verses, Byron realized they had carried him through all those discouraging years. They gave him the courage to believe he would rise from that dusty dunghill and attain a self-respecting manhood. He could never go back to do slave-wage service. Yet, as someone who'd spent his life as the lowest among the low, seeing Johnny chilled with fever he shared the goose-bump flesh of a homeless man's terror. The Fiddler was his one close friend after Thomas—he could not fall asleep and not be there to hold his hand and say good-bye.

Byron woke with a startling sneeze and the three men bunched at a small shared mirror stopped shaving to glance at him curiously. Seeing the filtered sunbeams sketching the barrack's wall, Byron chided himself for dozing off. From the reach of the patterned light it appeared he had slept right through breakfast. As he stood to shake the cramp from his legs after the night-long vigil, his comrades came and patted him on his shoulder before hurrying out to start work.

"Byron?" Johnny whispered as they left. "Cover for me, today? Please—me beggin' you!"

As he leaned back down and got a whiff of the Fiddler's bedclothes Byron realized his friend was too weak to even get up to pee. "Is awright, Johnny—yuh jus' stay and pick up your strength. But once you're up yuh got to promise me you're gonna pick up that fiddle. I'm dying to hear you play *La Paloma...*"

"Thanks, good buddy," Johnny said weakly, with a rheumy-eyed smile. "Don't you worry—come Sunday the Fiddler's gonna play everybody's request..."

That day Byron strained his back for the shovel, pretending half his loads were actually Johnny's. When he told the foreman to jot another mark for his friend, the Cajun peered at him suspiciously.

"Where is that mangy fiddle-player diggin'? I ain't caught sight o' him all day yet he's scoopin' up dirt quicker than a yaller dog scrapin' for a ham-bone. Y'all pulling a fast one on me, boy?"

"Nah, boss." Byron pointed up his nose to the jagged ridge fairly glistening with black bodies. "The Frenchies got so many of us nigras out here shovelin' how yuh supposed to keep track of all of we?"

The southerner weighed him with a long hard glare. "I'll tell yah one thing that'll make a nigger stand out in my mind and that's bein' a smart one."

"Whatever you say, boss," Byron answered meekly, feeling the knot unwind in his stomach when the big Cajun shrugged and scratched another mark for Johnny.

"You're a real good worker, boy..." said the foreman turning solemn, "so I'm gonna give you some free advice—don't go lettin' some huckster con you. A real smart fella looks out for hisself—keep that nugget in yer noggin..."

"Sure, boss," nodded Byron, swallowing back his grin.

By the final whistle Byron was so sapped from his feverish pace it took him twice as long to stagger back to camp. When, at last, he hauled his aching bones into the barracks he was shocked to see the Fiddler's bed lying empty. He told himself not to panic—maybe Johnny had taken his advice and gone into the hospital. He dragged off the blanket on the empty bunk and stalled with fear. There in place at the foot of the bed, safely away from friendly scorpions, were Johnny's boots. He checked the covered slot between the mattress and the wall—sure enough there was the hidden black cedar case. Knowing his friend would not have gone far without that fiddle, he rushed to look inside. The violin was there still neatly swathed in its green silk cloth. Drawing a breath to try and stay calm, he checked the little compartment where Johnny kept the tiny cake of resin for his bow. Inside was a stash of coins and a thick roll of Yankee dollars.

His strained muscles burning as if they'd been through a roasting fire, Byron stumbled down to the catchment where about a hundred diggers stood in groups, chatting lightheartedly. He approached a set waiting to wash the rimed grit from their faces and necks and asked if anyone knew what had happened to Johnny Fingers. Several reacted to the question irritably, asking how the devil could they know that. Others simply grew quiet and shrugged their shoulders. Later, in the big tent, when most of the camp was there having supper, he stopped to inquire at every table but no one could recall when last they'd seen the Fiddler.

Byron skipped work the next day to head for the nearest canal office. He was told there was no record of his friend being admitted to either of the company hospitals or terminating his contract. He decided to tramp up and down the web of rails moving dirt and men across the center of the canal line thinking someone must have come across Johnny. He waylaid Yankee roughnecks and annoyed the Chinese peddlers. He even held up the local farmhands busy helping their wives prepare to sell that morning's produce. He was sure that someone had to have recognized the celebrated Fiddler until it came to him that without his violin Johnny Fingers was just another dark digger among thousands.

Drained and downhearted, he returned to camp in time for the last call to supper, but vowed to hunt for Johnny one more day. The next morning after girding himself with a roll and a strip of bacon he headed to work with his crew just like usual then snuck back down the ridge and followed one of the side-trails threading through the bush bordering the line. After wandering for an hour without any luck he found himself at one of the makeshift settlements strung up by his more independent-minded comrades who were happy to dig to earn their bread but had grown allergic to French food and binding contracts. Seeing no one around, he called outside one of the flimsy shacks tacked up with bamboo and scraps of lumber and was greeted by a freakish-looking man with a severed arm.

"The Fiddler gone?" lamented the man, also missing an eye and half of his right cheek. "I had a chance to hear him play one Sunday—did my heart good—the one time I ever enjoy myself since I came to this damn country."

Byron added the missing arm and damaged cheek to the collapsed eye-socket. "Dynamite?"

The man glanced at his half-empty sleeve and shook his head. "Black powder. I was settin' it in just how they show me then—blam!—fire blind my eye and I'm flying dead to Jesus. When me good eye open I'm thinkin'—rawtid!—is so-so white people up here in heaven!—til' I realize it's the Frenchies' hospital me into. They said I was lucky to be alive—" the man paused and shook his head, "lucky to be half-blind and a goddamn cripple..."

Byron made no effort to respond. The last thing a lamed man wanted to hear was an able-bodied man's pity. The fellow had no clue where Johnny Fingers had gone but said he admired a man who looked out for his buddy and invited Byron inside to share some boiled yam and pumpkin from his garden. Byron thanked him kindly and declined. He had to keep looking, even if deep in his heart he knew that, somehow, the Fiddler had vanished...just like the rest.

That evening, back at camp, the big Cajun came by the barracks to warn Byron that if he missed another day's digging the company would charge him for food and rent and could decide to void his contract. Byron felt an urge to snap, 'who the hell cares?' It peeved him that no one else gave a fig about the Fiddler, but he held his tongue. His being out of a job wasn't going to help him find Johnny. So with a heavy heart he gave up the hunt and took back up his shovel. He tried not to dwell on his misery but he fretted for his friend day and night. The mental strain took its toll on his body and with his pace already slowed by the constant showers his first three days back digging saw him struggle to clear a dollar. And then it started to rain in earnest.

To run their trains and work the towering dredges with scooping buckets strung on mechanized ladders, the French had carved three-staged terraces around the flanks of the cordilleras. Two straight days of battering rains had churned up the slopes and left them spongy. The third day the weather finally relented but chunks of the terraced roads were either missing or in ruins. The tracks not sagging loose down the side of the mountain lay covered in debris and Byron's unit was assigned to dig out the buried rails and repair the damage. With track work scaled at fifteen cents an hour the others were content to be making roughly their usual pay at a more leisurely pace, but feeling energized by the first blue patch of sky seen in days, Byron was anxious to get back to his more lucrative digging.

He tried urging his dawdling comrades faster up the slope and was laughed down with scorn. They called him a fool for wanting to wear out his body for an extra half-dollar and Byron finally lost his temper and went storming on ahead. Before he knew it he had jogged to the top of the mountain but as he headed down its far-side to the damaged terrace he suddenly slipped and went skating down the embankment. The shovel flew from his grasp and went spinning through the air. He twisted around his body to jab his feet into the sliding topsoil and promptly lost a shoe as the dirt gave way. Suddenly he was flat on his face, skidding on his belly. As his momentum picked up speed, his heart was ticking a rapid staccato against his chest. He shut his eyes and flailed out blindly and by some miracle, just as he pictured his body plummeting down through the sky, his hand caught a stump and with the reflexes of a man watching his life flash by, he held on tight. Afraid he might pass out, he forced his eyes open, unable to breathe as the adrenaline left him trembling when the anchor held and braked his fall.

His healed arm began to ache as he held to the stump with all his might. He could hear his comrades yelling his name as they circled up the hill from the opposite side but with his heart still pumping in his throat he lacked the strength to shout in reply. When his throbbing pulse begin to slow he gathered his nerve to search for a way to escape. Slanting himself to the side, he spied a shelf of jutting rock not far to his right. It was just over an arms-length from where he lay but he dared not loose the death grip he had latched to the saving stump. With gingerly care, he swivelled up his legs and stretched up his right arm until the tendons in his shoulder felt ready to snap. He finally touched the ledge's lip and squeezing his eyes against the pain, he clawed the rock with five desperate fingers. His heartstrings thrumming, he snaked up slowly through the mud, then grasping the ledge with both his hands, hung there while his body drained its tension.

While he waited to stop trembling he scanned the slope to plot a safe route across to the undamaged roadbed. He was girding himself to crawl those last twenty yards when morbid curiosity pushed him to peek back down the mountain to where seconds ago he was about to fall to his final rest. As he peered to the hundred-foot drop a rush of bile surged to his throat.

In the water-cut gorge lay his vanished comrades, some adrift, others strewn in clumps. Byron had to look away to keep from being sick. He realized some fiend must have chucked them down the back of the mountain knowing the dump-trains would soon come and cover them up with spoil. Had the pounding rains not exhumed their bodies no one would have ever been the wiser. But there they lay, rotting in the sun, forgotten, save for the vultures greedily pecking their naked flesh. When one of the bodies appeared to be Jackson Free, Byron crept closer. He squinted to see if he could recognize any among the dead who still had faces. His hand flew to his mouth a fraction late and the vomit came gushing through his fingers. On its back, both eyes plucked out, was Johnny's shoeless corpse.

When he was over being sick, Byron climbed slowly back up the slope on quivering legs, except now his shaking was from rage. He finally found his gang at work on the lower tier. Apparently they had been called back to shore up the road before clearing the tracks. Some of his comrades, relieved to see he was safe, ran to greet Byron cheerfully, then stood in disbelief as he shared his terrible discovery.

Several of the men left to see for themselves while a few cut Byron with sharp, silent glances before returning to pound more gravel. The heinous deed confirmed, the men in his gang all loudly agreed it was a barbarous wicked act. Yet not one man deigned to venture a guess as to who might be the culprit. Disgusted, Byron stalked off to confront the big Cajun.

"Look, I'm a fair Christian fellah. It don't sit right with me neither," he said sympathetically after he'd listened patiently to the young digger's rant. "What am I s'posed to do? Tell the Frenchies, sorry, I gotta halt this dig 'cause some dead darky needs to be hopped down to Monkey Hill so ya'll can bawl at his burial? Hell, I'd have to stop work every other day! You're a smart enough nigra...you tell me—would that make any sense?"

Byron came close to hollering, "why not—you'd a-done it for a rich man!" then he remembered the first rule of the plantation: 'a poor man never gets vexed'—not when a job and a place to live were so hard to come by. "Yuh right, boss," he muttered, his rage suddenly submerged beneath deep sadness, "it sure don't make no sense."

That night at supper everyone was real upset. One after another, men got up to toast the Fiddler and mourn his talent. Many shed crocodile tears. Others promised the Lord would wrest retribution from the heathen who issued the godless order. But more than one hand had to have pushed those men over the cliff to be buried under rubble. Everyone confessed the whole thing was a scandal and sin. Not one ever confessed their part in its careless evil.

Chapter 5

Estelle Morales let her vision glide from the threadbare velvet sofa to the Kashmiri rugs tinged with mildew. She used to take pride in her cozy sitting room's eccentric style. Today it appeared less quaint than simply shabby, its mellowed flair flirting dangerously with a scent of mold. If she intended to last, much less thrive, her *casa-de-cita* demanded major updating.

The new canal-works were bringing a bonanza Colón had not seen since California gold had sent every dreamer and misfit in the world rushing to cross the isthmus. To squeeze real cash from this promising cow she needed to skim more of the social cream which meant paying for girls with prettier faces than the best of the cheap she'd lured from the stalls of her fly-by-night competitors. This was still a nasty town in an untamed country but when the scummiest little pimp was starting to ask for caviar with his French champagne it was time she upped the ante.

Buying that old Bottle Alley tavern had been a gamble. Luckily, now that the canal-men had started to arrive, it was fetching such stunning returns she could have her stylish new saloon ready to open by early next year. The thought made her sink deeper in the overstuffed chair and smile—she would fit the Last Frontier with a secret entrance leading straight upstairs. That way, while her brothel was being redone, she could still cater to her important customers anxious to guard their reputations. The one question that vexed her as she bent to massage her ankles was how long she could go on standing all night in those thin French heels.

"*¡Tia, tia!* There's a man out in the garden—he told me to get you, *pronto!*"

The honey-brown pixie came skipping in looking breathless. A tangle of tight black curls bounced down the back of her smudged yellow dress.

"Isabella!" cried Estelle, shaking a scolding finger. "You promised to stop scrambling up my almond tree. Look how filthy you've gotten! And where are the shoes I bought you to wear?"

The squirming feet stilled and their little owner stared down at them as if they'd been disobedient all on their own.

"It's time you learned to mind your appearance. My—look at that untidy hair!"

"But *Tia Estella*, I was only trying to catch Pompey—suppose he flies away and doesn't come back?"

"Don't you fret, *mi vida*, Pompey knows better than to stray. Who else would care for such a naughty little cockatoo? Now, no more scaling trees—you could hurt yourself!"

"But you clapped and laughed when you saw me climbing mama's coconut tree...and I was two years littler then!"

Estelle controlled a grin at the child's alert comeback. "All right, Isabella," she smiled, reminding herself that her niece was only six, "who is it that wants to see me? And why did you leave him standing out in the yard?"

"He wouldn't come unless I called you first. He seemed very nice but..." Isabella's eyes grew wide with intrigue and her voice fell to a whisper, "his eyes looked very red! Is he sad like the crying man last night?"

Alarm-bells set to ringing inside the madam's head. She reached and pulled the child in by her tiny wrists. "What crying man? Did you sneak out of bed when you should be sleeping?"

"No, *Tia Estella*! I only woke when I heard him crying. It was scary—my room was so, so dark...and it was really, really loud!" The child stopped again in curious thought and her big hazel eyes grew even larger. "Was he being bad—? Was he hurt?"

Estelle quietly held her breath, stunned that for all her precautions—she had gone so far as to cover her niece's bedroom wall with doubled rugs made from knotted seagrass—those sharp little ears had still picked out the voice of the newlywed vice-consul whose peculiar needs even she found disturbing. However, in a town where one's fortunes could change overnight she was lucky to have outstanding clients like the young British diplomat who was grateful for her discreet accommodation and just as eager to trade information. "No, *muñeca*, he wasn't bad and no one got hurt. Everyone leaves your auntie's house feeling happy. Now you run along upstairs and ask one of the girls, once she's awake, to wash you up and comb that hair."

As she watched the child go bounding up the stairs, sure-footed as a little capuchin monkey, Estelle could not decide if the stab inside her chest was anger at her sister for letting Isabella grow up half-wild or the pain of knowing that only Constancia's ill-health had allowed her niece to come for a visit. If she could have her wish, when the time came to take Isabella back to Portobelo she would stay on in the country until the two of them could truly bond. But as much as she longed to invest in her own blood and undercut the specter of growing old alone, if she was to survive Panama's chicaneries, she needed to be on the spot with her ear to the ground.

Muttering at the fickle needs of men, Estelle stood and slipped the torturing shoes back on, then paused at her gilt-framed mirror to pin a few truant strands of her lustrous black hair with her jeweled barrette. She despised it when clients dropped by in the middle of the day. They either had to be cajoled into making a later appointment or they were bearing bad news. A rotten hunch told her it was the latter.

Estelle's dark eyelashes fluttered as she stepped into the sunshine and crossed to the porch rail left bald by the paint-stripping rains. She peeked down the side of the house to the garden but saw no one there. She started to wonder if her niece was playing a prank then dismissed the notion. Little Isabella was already sharp enough to know it was not the sort of game *Tia Estella* would find amusing. She moved to her lowest front step where the sight of the full-grown nut tree reminded her pleasantly of how far she'd come. She no longer feared the advent of middle-age. She even relished her figure's new plumpness because it projected her more solid sense of place. She felt rooted, ready for her branches to spread like those perfect boughs on the almond tree she had meticulously nipped and pruned as a sapling and which now stood crowned by a leafy laurel of large green teardrops. She thought about strolling to the garden for an admiring look when there came the deep thuds of beating wings and a huge snow-white cockatoo swooped in to the balustrade.

"Come back for your supper, eh, my naughty Pompey?" Smiling, the madam stuck out two fingers to the imperial-looking bird but instead of lighting on her hand it squawked, *"¡cuidado, cuidado!"* and flapped away just as Estelle sensed another presence. She twisted around and nearly crashed into the black-clad figure. Her relief as she recognized the man's features lasted only an instant. "*Señor* Prestàn! What do you mean stealing up on me like a cat stalking its pigeon?" Estelle was well-endowed in ways men liked, excepting her height. Even so, in her two-inch French heels, she found herself looking down at her bantam caller who greeted her wry smile humorlessly.

"Your niece is a beautiful child—I hope she does not suffer seeing her aunt degrade herself entertaining degenerate foreigners."

She was tempted to scoff at this stuffy little capon with his rod-straight pose and English bowler. 'And what are you in that gloomy three-piece suit?' she wanted to jeer at his insult, 'the noble solitaire marching to the graveyard at the head of a *bombero?*' but she didn't dare. "It's safe to come in, *Señor* Prestàn," she said curtly, seeing his shifty backward glance to the gate at the brothel's hedged fence. "I do not make appointments at this hour." She moved to lead him inside then stopped when he hesitated yet again to gaze at her second floor windows. "Don't worry, my girls neither see nor hear. Besides, they're probably still sleeping."

Prestàn took a quick contemptuous scan of the cozy room as they stepped inside and stood by the red divan covered with harem-style silk pillows. After tilting his head to listen for any voices coming down from upstairs, he marched to the shutters and started snapping each one shut. The day was still bathed in bright sunshine and the loss of light left the little parlor in partial gloom. "Don't be alarmed—" he said reassuringly, "it is for your own protection."

Estelle was furious at having her salon rudely commandeered, however, she felt it wiser not to object until she learned why Pedro Prestàn believed she needed protecting, and why a deputy in Colón's assembly wished to speak with her in secret.

Prestàn snapped in the last wooden shutter then twirled back abruptly. "Have you heard? That traitor, Nuñez, has refused to step down. It seems our *presidente* believes that losing an Election is a promotion to dictator!"

Estelle pulled out the handkerchief she kept in her bosom and dabbed her nose to conceal her reaction. Since declaring itself a federation of self-governing states, Colombia's politics had turned from a hopeful comedy to a tragic farce. Young Harcourt, the British vice-consul, had told her there was trouble down on the mainland, but Panama was so isolated from the rest of the country she had hoped that by the time the turmoil reached this far the worst would already be over. "Come now, *señor*—you know that women have no place in politics," she retorted, smiling as she eased herself onto the velvet sofa and gracefully stretched an arm for him to sit.

"This is no time to play games, Estella—we both know what's at stake." Prestàn perched like a bird on the edge of the overstuffed armchair and set the black bowler primly on his knees. "If we do not accept his fiat, Nuñez is threatening to dissolve Panama's assemblies! I am sick of these turncoats! You help them gain power then the minute they get to Bogotá they sell the country's cream and leave our children sour milk!"

Now that her eyes had adjusted to the murky light, Estelle could see the angry neck veins like ropes rising at the sides of Prestàn's collar. She wondered if she would ever fathom the vain urges that drove such scrupulous men. Here was a man who, despite his mother's dark Jamaican blood, had become a respected lawyer. With his brilliance, by this age he should have had riches, then money could have done his talking. Instead, he'd spent his energy trying to remain upright as if one honest man could put to sword a country of thieves.

"I'll grant you Nuñez has turned out to be a cruel disappointment, but our people are used to being their pawns. Why come to me? How can I help you resist the federal government?"

"We've known each other many years, Estellita—" Prestán said, almost pleadingly, "long enough for you to know that as much as it pains me to see the path you've taken I would never wish to see you harmed. The people are angry. They supported Nuñez because we told them he would defend Panama's right to its own revenue. Even if the assembly is intimidated and votes to surrender, the people will not sit still and let the traitors bleed us dry." He said this with a resigned heavy look that hardened as he once again surveyed the intimate bordello. "I know you are cozy with the British vice-consul. I need to know the *gringos'* view. Will they go on supporting this corrupt government when it is a dictatorship or are they ready to respect the people?"

"I'm not sure it's my place to address such matters..."

"I warned you not to try your games with me, *señora*—you are no innocent. Everyone knows you are planning a new establishment. That means you know enough to have bribed the right people. I'm sure Mr. Harcourt would not find it strange that you would be concerned about Panama's future."

Noting the vein still bulging on Prestàn's neck, Estelle tried to appease him. "Yes, we do occasionally talk about such things, but I cannot say with confidence that the vice-consul would be candid about his government's intentions," she answered, truthfully. "My sense is the English would prefer to wait and see the outcome. The French are much more worried. They will support Nuñez as long as he can promise them stability. A French patron of mine is concerned that certain elements are trying to stir up his workers—" as she heard the words come out of her own mouth Estelle suddenly guessed Prestàn's ulterior plan.

"Oh, *señor*—those men are poor British subjects—you should not involve them in our politics!"

"*Tonteria*—British subjects! They have been involved in Panama's problems from the very beginning. Jamaican blood ran in rivers to build this town. Are they to be scorned while their sons are back here working like dogs?"

"Of course not—but let's not kick the bucket over just as it's filling! We've waited centuries for this canal—this is a time to be patient!"

"Why? So while we are dying with patience the rich can bribe our rulers? The poor gained nothing from building their railroad. Now the French come bragging about bringing us progress and what do they do? They spend millions for a pretty suburb right next door then sneak here at night to despoil our women and leave us their garbage. Every day Colón gets more vile! No, Estella, the people have been bled of their patience. If Nuñez traduces our Constitution we will raise an army to defend it. Tell the *gringos* that if they want these men to go on digging they would be advised to stand with us."

A sickly suspense came over Estelle. She had lived through such spasms before. In Colón, where the power was firmly in the hands of the Anglos these tantrums changed nothing. But until the bullets decided which side would get to wield its rubber stamp, the parties would go around bribing the poor to follow and extorting the rich to buy them guns. Then one day the foment would erupt, more fools would die, a new government would be seated and the *gringos* would go right on running their railroad and most of Panama's business.

Estelle jumped up from the couch rubbing her palms as she stalled for time to devise her response. In the past, buying protection had cost no more than a hundred dollars and some free liquor but with her reserves already committed any new violence would cost a great deal more than her plans could afford. "Where are my manners! May I offer you coffee, *señor*, or would you prefer a glass of sherry…?"

"Nothing—thank you!" said Prestàn, stopping her mid-dash on the way to the kitchen. "But when the time comes I trust I can still depend on your largess."

His words were vague but his tone held an acid threat. As she stood with her back half-turned Estelle could feel his eyes patrolling her body, alert for the tiniest twitch that would betray her.

"You seem unsure, Estellita—" Prestàn said sweetly, sounding hurt. "Do you no longer trust me? Or has all the money you've been making hardened your heart against the poor?"

Estelle drew a breath to ease her shoulders before crossing lightly back to the sofa. She had backed Prestàn's foray into politics because as a young lawyer he had saved her mother's farm from being seized by a land-grabbing *caudillo*. She had done so quietly because even though his Liberal party's leader, ex-general Aizpuru, was a former president, Prestàn was branded a 'Radical' by the curl in his hair and the bronze in his skin. She hoped that in time such biases would end, but business was business, and her best clients were all staunch Conservatives.

"It's not a matter of trust, *Señor* Prestàn. Your party does not control the army, and a few hungry diggers cannot match real soldiers." Estelle's answers gushed out in spurts as her mind raced just ahead of her words. "I'm told your lovely wife has just given you your first child. In her place I would be trembling—why gamble their futures?"

"Yes, we have a beautiful daughter. I named her América—would you care to know why?" Prestàn asked with contempt. "Because the new world I will die for shall be a place where she is not forced to choose between living on her knees and spreading them."

The remark unsheathed the barb in her tongue Estelle had been restraining. "So in this fine new world of yours we women are to be granted a choice—how marvelous!" she sneered. "Will you hold a referendum so you men can decide if we deserve a vote? Can we join the party if we promise to lock our knees?"

"You twist my words to make it sound as if I'm the one who stole your decency."

After being deserted by her father and then deceived by her first lover, Estelle was not about to allow any man to judge her, not even one as well-meaning as Prestàn. "No man can speak to a woman about decency! Not unless you can pass a law that every woman who vows to stay upright will be cared for when she has no more husband and she's left to raise his children. We cannot live on your fine principles."

Prestàn waved a dispirited hand. "Never mind. I am not a priest. I did not come here to condemn your sins."

"You want to know sin?" Estelle replied, her anger still rising. "Asking men to die for an impossibility—that is a sin! What are your saintly wives going to eat when you fail? Your leftover bullets and machetes? No, *señor*, it is not *my* sin that makes the rot in this world!"

Prestàn stayed with both arms rigid on his knees then slowly got to his feet, shaking his head with a downcast look, as if picturing a field full of shattered dreams and broken heartedness. "We do what we must, Estella," he said, lingering on her name's Spanish ending as he slipped back on his bowler. "You have been forewarned. I trust you will choose the proper course."

When he had left and she was sure he had passed her gate, Estelle dashed to open her shutters. As she watched Prestán vanish with his crisp short stride she wondered why men's hankerings always began and ended with war while in the respite they could be tamed in a woman's warm bed.

The sunny day was in full retreat and as her nose picked up the scent of dampening mud Estelle could hear the plinks of quickening raindrops. There was no telling when the storm would break or if her plans could still be saved. One thing she was glumly sure of—not even the noblest of men lived up to his promises.

Never, from the day she'd been saved, had Genevieve doubted her calling. Now, despite her prayers, she feared the place in her heart she had desperately reserved for her Lord and Savior was being usurped. It had been a shock to feel the burn of envy when her pet was given over to the care of that arrogant little Frenchman. She realized only then that the sharp wit, the chiseled cheeks, and those guarded, impossibly violet eyes had all conspired to snare her soul.

The end of each shift found her more drained and depressed. Men were dying in her care but instead of falling into bed and rising refreshed she would toss and turn worrying about Thomas. When her mind was not eased by prayer nor her spirit healed of its own loathing she asked the Blessed Virgin's forgiveness and indulged in a tiny deceit. A letter had arrived for Thomas days before Christmas and with the credulity of the sexually obtuse, Mother Agnes had asked Genevieve if she would forward it by hand. It was past eleven the night after Christmas when Thomas showed up late in back of the deserted post office expecting to find his old buddy, Byron, and found Genevieve standing there instead.

"I've been waiting here since ten!" she whispered anxiously when Thomas rushed up to greet her and the sound of a horse-drawn carriage went clacking through the dark nearby. "I shouldn't have come!" She had come with no intention other than to spare her nervous dread, but seeing him healed, looking so divinely straight and tall, her spine turned to jelly.

"Why on earth not?" said Thomas, as each glimpsed the joy on the other's face and felt surprised by their unacknowledged longing. "Is it not the season for goodwill towards all men?"

"Don't joke like that—it's blasphemous!"

"Blasphemous? Is this the same Nurse Genevieve who giggled about Mother Agnes boosting her chastity with a little cognac in her coffee?" Thomas asked wickedly. "How is the old blue-eyed spinster? Still soft as nails and warring with ants?"

Genevieve could not help smiling at his familiar dry humor. "She misses you. The ward has felt like a morgue since you left. Mother Agnes and I must be the only ones who haven't been struck by a touch of the fever." She turned her head, suddenly embarrassed. "That's why I came—I needed to be sure—sure that you were still all right..."

"Seeing you now, I've never felt better! What a bully surprise! I thought angels never flew far from their cloister!" Thomas drew closer so that his hot breath warmed her cheek.

As she stood in the lamplight with her wings replaced by a masking cowl and her flushed face tingling Genevieve felt as if she had been taken over by a wanton spirit. A strange thrill raced straight through her as he caught her hand and moved to kiss her.

"Stop, Tom—please!" she begged, feeling her own frightening surge of desire.

"You're a changed girl, Genie—why not just admit it? Perhaps you're not cut out to be a virgin saint."

"Don't say that! It's been a gift, finally getting to see you—but I've got to get back. Oh, my—!" she whispered fearfully as two drunks came stumbling up the road from Colón, bellowing the *Marseillaise*, "who's that coming?"

"For goodness sake, calm yourself, Genie. It's just two frogs hopping home with a bit too much holiday spirit."

"I should never have come," she repeated, nervously squeezing her hands. "What if they see us? I'm sorry—I need to get back!"

"You can't show up and then run off on me just like that!" Thomas pleaded, seeing her stoop to pick up the small lantern at her feet. "No one's going to see our faces in this light...and I doubt anyone would recognize you without your angel wings."

"God knows I don't deserve to wear them..."

Thomas again moved in to caress her. "Maybe you're not quite the angel you thought."

"Thomas Judah! Behave! You almost made me forget—I came to give you this—"

Before she could reach inside her cloak for the letter, Thomas had pressed up against her, straining to nuzzle her cheek like an ardent puppy.

"Please, not out here—"

Picking up the lamp, she led them across a dark open span then behind a row of low palms. But instead of continuing on towards the hospital she veered from the shore and into a fenced-in orchard, potent with the smells of fermenting fruits. When they were safely concealed behind a plum tree, Thomas rushed to cozy up close and in her daze she started to chatter, voicing each chance thought that came into her head. She pretended not to enjoy the needy hand she felt stroking her neck while she described how the fenced plot had come to be leased to her sisters' order. To ground the startling lightness in her being, she attempted to portray Mother Agnes' horror when the dredging in the bay corrupted the garden's well with salt water.

She went on babbling until Thomas was out of patience. He clutched her by the waist and searched a hand to rub the excited breast pressing inside of her robe. Before her brain had time to refocus they were sucking lips and brushing noses.

"No. I can't. I must go," she whispered, pulling herself away. She gathered up her hem to flee but Thomas held her by the arm and begged to see her again. Afraid that if she stayed a second longer the night would end with her fall from grace, she told him that if he released her now she would meet him here on New Year's night. In response, he flashed her a faultless look full of love and right then she knew that if she dared a next time he would break her resistance.

She was nearly to the cloister before she remembered that she had not given him the letter. Whether she had forgotten consciously or not, as she began her shift that night she was far from distressed, knowing that it meant she had to see him again.

Chapter 6

March 30, 1883

Thomas stretched up from the unyielding hardwood chair and yawned out the kinks in his spine. He had been craning at his desk for hours trying to decipher the scrawls some buffoon incapable of keeping a ledger had jotted on myriad scraps of paper and now his bleary eyes were seeing double. The job's sheer tedium was urging him to rethink his disgust for the odor of sulfur blended with bay rum and becoming a druggist. His agreeing to work as a secretary had been a tactical concession—it was sure to appease his mother and keep his father off his tracks—but he'd be damned if his whole youth would be used up inside an office.

To be honest, it had been hard to turn down the offer once he realized the salary of a hundred and fifty gold *piasters* worked out to over thirty Yankee dollars each week. Not only did it make up for the months he'd wasted in hospital, but since he was living in the Frenchman's posh villa cost-free he was able to tuck aside most of his income. He reasoned that even at its dullest, working for an important canal engineer had to be better than being stuck inside a Kingston drugstore assailed by disinfectants and toxic gossip. And unlike at home where his dubious pedigree left him forever betwixt and between—not nearly good enough for some, yet superior to most—no one in Panama, apart from his sponsor, seemed to care one whit that his last name was Judah. He admitted being surprised by how much he was enjoying the social entree being thrown open for Henri Duvay's exotic new assistant. He especially liked it that his boss seemed glad to play along when he would fabricate some romantic biography just to bait one of their snooty fellow guests. And yet as much as he relished his chameleon liberties, he might have said goodbye to the isthmus already had his heart not been lost to Genevieve.

The new year had not long started before the canal was fighting for its life. The company was still discarding its dead from swamp fever when a lashing hurricane wiped out months of digging and a rash of cholera followed murderously in its wake. The actual death toll had been kept from the public to stave off shareholder panic, but hundreds of personnel, from doctors and cooks to stenographers and accountants, needed to be replaced and the project's day-to-day expenditures were spiraling out of control. Then, just when fresh recruits had been enticed to Panama, *Couvreux, Hersent* announced it was pulling out and returning to France.

The surprise announcement sent Henri Duvay into a week-long tantrum. Thomas regularly fetched damp towels to cool the Frenchman's head and was careful not to antagonize him lest he erupt and rupture his spleen. Still in a fury, Duvay published an excoriating letter, charging that the directors of his firm were abandoning France like rats when the mother-ship was imperiled and vowing that either his final breath or a Panama Canal would come first.

The canal company was delighted when Henri Duvay quickly agreed to stay and advise the American firms that would replace *Couvreux, Hersent*. With this new appointment Thomas' facility in English and French was even more valuable. But unlike before, when he was able to join Duvay on his frequent field trips, his more clerical duties found him bound to the boredom of his office.

Each rain-free day left him envying his pal Diego. They had met on a surveying trip led by Diego's uncle Victor Sosa, Panama's well-known explorer who was often employed by Duvay on his long expeditions. Born and raised in the hills outside El Coco, Diego seemed to enjoy the kind of life Thomas had always wanted. When the young rodman was quick to brag that he had tracked and killed a white-tailed deer by the time he was ten, Thomas had known right then he had found a kindred spirit.

Not only was the young surveyor also seventeen, like Thomas, he had never experienced the special pride that comes with a father's praise as his had died when Diego was only three. With such similar temperaments it had been no great surprise to discover they both tried to emulate lore's rugged breeds—lowborn men with enough guile and swagger to build their own kingdom, and if need be kill, with no more regret than a cut-throat pirate. In the jungle, Thomas was wise enough to defer to his far more experienced friend, but wanting to impress, he sometimes took risks that raced beyond folly, like the time they were surprised by an infant boar and Thomas rashly charged and landed a flying kick on its snout. Luckily, the boar had strayed far from his mother and quickly ran off, but Diego had to sternly caution him to always stop and engage his senses. "*Amigo*, out here the hunter lives to prove his valor by using his *cabeza*."

Given the slightest opening, the friends would sneak off to explore on their own. Thomas was always amazed when Diego could name each weird plant they came to; he envied the ease with which his friend could always find the way back to camp without having flagged a single branch. He remembered his elation on their last side excursion when Diego taught him how to set ripe fruit to lure a coati and the way one checks the trunks of trees for tiny scratches to pick up a puma's trail that had seemingly vanished.

That had been way back in January and now Easter had come and gone. When he began to pine for those lost adventures Thomas set his thoughts on the weekend when he would meet Genevieve. She seemed no less eager to see him but she had so far resisted surrendering him her all. As his sap rose unspent, so did his youthful frustration. He would be in the midst of tabulating the amount of dirt the big excavators had dug out last month and find himself dreaming about the perfect little scoop at the base of Genevieve's throat. As a result, he often ended up glossing over his figures which meant having to redo each boring sheet down to the most infinitesimal irrelevant digit. Duvay had clearly lost patience with his sloppy work, yet for some reason that mystified him, the pedantic engineer gave no hint of wanting to fire him. No matter how harshly Duvay criticized him at the office, by the time they were back home together the Frenchman's demeanor would turn almost ingratiating.

Thomas noticed that his sponsor's goodwill would last the longest when, out of sheer lassitude, he stayed downstairs past dinner and listened with half an ear while Henri enumerated all the stupid reasons the project was progressing poorly. The engineer's late-night rants grew even more petulant when one of de Lesseps' sons showed up from Paris and the canal company responded as if Panama had been blessed with a visit from royalty.

"I missed that wit of yours tonight, *mon fils*," Duvay muttered, returning from another compulsory champagne banquet to which Thomas had not been invited. "More bloated toasts to '*Le Grand Français*'—God, they've gotten tiresome! There I was—stuck beside some doltish Kansan who insisted on fascinating me with the fortune he'd made peddling hog manure and bibles. I understand the company's need to seduce these rich speculators but unless we adjust to this canal's technical challenges a billion dollars still won't save it!"

Duvay was finally mollified when the company's newest director proved to be an austere manager. However, it clearly rankled him that more and more of the canal-work was being parceled out to the Americans. "I grant you those cowboys build whopping machines," the Frenchman reluctantly conceded when Thomas pointed out that the new excavators were doubling his numbers, "but they lack our expertise and commitment—their only genius is for making a buck."

Thomas had begun to suspect that Henri's new waspishness sprang from feeling ignored and under appreciated. He decided to test his curious hold on the temperamental Frenchman and see if it could be turned to some practical advantage.

"*Monsieur*, you took me on as your personal assistant, and I accept that my work has not been its best of late..." he opened candidly as they sat at home over a fruit dessert, "but my mind keeps pondering the great strain you've been under. I know you're busy working to present Mr. de Lesseps with a modified plan—yet all I've been doing is toting up dirt in cubic meters. I thought if you'd teach me—you know—about design and mechanics—I could help do the drafting. That way I'd feel as if I was doing something to help you—something meaningful..."

For the first time since *Couvreux, Hersent* abandoned the project, Duvay looked bright and cheerful. "Monique!" he called abruptly towards the kitchen, "my brandy snifters from the cupboard—if you please! I have something wonderful to celebrate!"

A slender ebony girl in a black maid's uniform came in with two bulbous glasses.

"Thank you, Monique, that was a very fine meal. Go and enjoy the rest of the evening, you can clear up what's left in the morning!" Duvay declared, his tone light and expansive, as he launched up from the table and headed for the small liquor cabinet.

Monique gave Thomas a wide-eyed look as she set down the glasses and he slouched back in his chair and shot her a cocky wink. The maid hurried off, her pretty face delighted with surprise, as Duvay returned carrying the cognac and his special case of Havana cigars.

"I must tell you, Thomas," he said effusively, "tonight you have heartened me no end. I only hope our lessons will inspire you to work with diligent care. If we lose our way in Panama the loss—even for innocents like humble Monique—

will be incalculable! But enough dour speeches!" Duvay cut himself off and held out the blue-silk-lined humidor to his young assistant. "Not ready to start smoking?" he said, closing the cigar-box when Thomas shook his head. "I understand—it's an acquired taste."

As he opened the bottle and began to pour, Duvay's hand was quivering. "The most satisfying things in life often take time to appreciate. A good cognac is no exception." He paused and demonstrated how Thomas should gently twirl his glass then stick in his nose to breathe the bouquet. "It takes years to nurture the best grapes and our vineyards are just recovering from being ravaged by American aphids. But you'll taste and see—we French survive to rise again!" He raised his snifter for a toast. "Here's to our new collaboration and a victorious canal!" Duvay waited for Thomas to take his first sip. "So—what do you think of the world's finest cognac?"

Thomas eyed the peppery amber liquid thinking he would happily trade it for five warm minutes with Genevieve. "I confess, *monsieur*," he replied with a devilish smile, "there is yet another experience in life I fully intend to become more intimate with."

———

Genevieve awoke feeling flushed and realized that the vivid dream had left her body wet and restless. It appalled her how far she had regressed. She kept expecting to recover but there was a ravishing force inside her she could neither confess to nor control. She had wanted to be at peace when she swore her vows, not anxious that she was affirming a lie. Ever since her mother had died her life spirit had been tucked behind barricades—first as a miserable frightened child locked safely in her nana's bedroom and then as a schoolgirl sealed inside the convent. She had hoped her work in Panama would free her from confusion. Instead, the power of her devotion as she nursed Thomas Judah had seen her cross the divide between charity and love.

Torn with guilt, she slipped out of bed and padded to the hospice chapel hoping no one saw her as she slowed to savor the feel of the cold stone floor against her hot bare feet. At the Virgin's shrine she added to the amber expanse of burning candles then knelt before the blue-robed image cradling her infant Jesus. She mumbled a short prayer and asked for the clarity that would restore her to grace.

She tried unburdening her pain to the gilt-framed image but struggled to express what first drove her to disobey. Why in Thomas' case had she been so quick to cross the line she had been unwilling to transgress for her other patients? Was it simply cowardice—fear that her unorthodox measures would be discovered and her acceptance to the cloister denied? Or had she inherited a special kind of madness—a cross she had to carry all her life? But although she confessed she was not proud of her defiance nothing could shake her conviction that Thomas would have died had she not used the gifts her *nana* had imparted.

Drained, yet still conflicted, she lifted her gaze to the virgin's portrait and, all of sudden, there appeared, glowing goldenly before her eyes, a passage from the gospel of John. It was her Savior's words after He'd been denounced for healing a man on the Sabbath: 'I have come into this world—to give sight to the sightless and make blind those who see.'

Genevieve tiptoed from the chapel and crawled back into bed, greatly comforted. While in the dark recesses of her conscience she knew she would have bargained with the devil if it meant healing Thomas, Jesus' words had assured her—no law could deny the virtue of saving a life. "Now, dear Lord," she whispered, feeling her eyelids growing pleasantly heavy, "if you'll just let me sleep until noon I'll try and find the strength to end my madness and save my soul."

Chapter 7

The Jamaican canal-men were seething. A sense of persecution was now added to a year spent digging through sickness and surrounded by death. The company had replaced its old Decauvilles with new dump cars and though they held exactly the same amount of spoil the foremen exploited the opportunity to announce that it would now take two full loads to earn what a single one had paid before. Byron had groused along with the rest, knowing they were being cheated, but when the big Cajun stoutly denied it, there was nothing to be done, short of quitting.

To make things worse, three men had just been killed and five more dismembered after the dynamite they were trying to tamp into solid granite exploded. Tempers flared and there was talk of staging a protest when a rumor that two Jamaicans down in the Cut had dug up a chest of gold doubloons swept through camp like coal-dust through a work-train. Byron tended to agree with the cooler heads who contended that even if the unlikely story was true there was no point rushing down to Culebra since they stood as much chance digging up such a fortune as a dive-fisherman spotting a pearl on the ocean floor. But when half his gang left anyway, seeing he'd barely cleared ten dollars since the day he climbed down into the ravine to bury Johnny, Byron decided he might as well follow. A change would ease bad memories and maybe even improve his luck.

He tried not to obsess about unearthing a fortune, but shoveling knee-deep in sludge the hope was never far from his mind. Many rainy months later he had dug up just a lot more mud. Day after day he wriggled into the same cold damp clothes that never got dry. When a sudden avalanche buried twenty men alive, Byron began to suspect all that talk about buried treasure had been started by those wily French to trick fools like him to come and dig their treacherous Cut in monsoon weather. Yes, there was a reason *culebra* meant snake in Spanish.

The pummeling rains had battered the ground into paste, and work in the canyon had slumped to a crawl. What had been an active scene featuring hustling trains and six hundred arms working shovels now seemed a pantomime of toil in slow-motion. As Byron labored, hoping he wouldn't go deaf from the roaring excavators or suffocate from their belched black smoke, his morale began to lag along with the pace of his profits. Not only did it take twice the time to meet his quota, the earth was like glue and had to be perpetually scraped off his shovel with a stick. And as if that was not bad enough, the bosses were getting testy.

Their objective was to cut through the saddle of the two steep hills, but the daily storms left the earth so soggy that the deeper they dug the more gummy soil slid in to take its place. They tried tempering the angle of the slopes. But that meant flattening the channel bottom and having to scoop out even more dirt. Worse, once the ground became saturated, the weakened crests began to slip. The slide would start slowly—like heavy batter drooling over the edge of a giant whipping bowl—only to suddenly accelerate and become a colossal rolling blob as it gobbled up locomotives, railroad tracks, men, and anything else in its devouring way. As a result, every day some irate engineer was bawling for Byron to stop his work to go and help reset rails buried half a mile away or rescue his sunken steam-shovel.

The entire Cut was a quagmire of blue-green mud. The French, seeing their caterpillar dredges floundering in the slop like dinosaurs trapped in quicksand, abandoned their massive contraptions and swelled the ranks of their diggers to over nine thousand men. The mosquitoes, having found the pocked earth's rain-filled pools ideal for hatching their eggs, boosted their own numbers twenty times over and sent them to feast on all the fresh blood.

By the time the holidays arrived a third of Culebra's new men had been stricken. It was Byron's second Christmas in Panama but with nothing to celebrate it came and went without a happy murmur. His only gift had been a nasty head-cold. When a tightness grabbed his chest as he thought about his comrades who had died or left for home he reminded himself that if he gave up now he would always be a failure. Besides, he had no loving arms to return to. The one hard cold fact he could not get over was that, despite having lived like a miser all year, he had not saved anywhere near enough for a good piece of farming land back in Jamaica.

An unexpected present arrived shortly after the New Year. A chap from his old gang had been transferred to Culebra and came bearing a letter from Thomas Judah dated the 1st of October. Thomas apologized for not responding to him sooner. He blamed the lapse on his job which he claimed was both important and dangerous as it involved spending days inside the deep jungle. Thomas signed off by wishing 'Millwood's best fast bowler' well adding vaguely that they should get together in the coming year. Byron read the letter through four straight times until he captured the gist of the unfamiliar words then folded it neatly back into its envelope and hid it with the money he kept in Johnny's fiddle case.

Summer brought a respite from the rain. Byron's nagging cold was finally gone but more diggers were falling ill and new protests were springing up across the canal line. Their grievance was simple: if a digger was up against yellow jack, dysentery, beriberi and typhoid fever—any of which could kill you—he deserved to get paid while he was down. The problem for Byron and his comrades was that their contracts clearly stated that while they were entitled to be housed and fed, as indentured labor they were only paid for the amount that they worked.

Byron's new boss, faced with an increasingly hostile crew, had promised the men that if they worked hard all summer and made him look good he would make sure they got a raise in pay and some extra vacation. When the end of September arrived and the Yank was only offering up more promises, Byron figured that since he had fulfilled his two-year contract, it was as good a time as any to take a break from digging.

Once he quit he would have to give up living in the barracks but he was wary of Panama's cities. He'd seen too many comrades come stumbling in on a Saturday night crying that they'd been robbed by a pair of armed hoodlums. Of course, half the time, once they got around to telling the whole story, it turned out they'd gambled on a nice plump girl or a teasing hand and had their pockets picked clean. But before he went scouting a fifty-mile-long canal-line looking for a job he needed a place to sleep and someone to trust. So after collecting his final pay, he packed his small cloth bag, grabbed Johnny's violin and hopped the train to Colón to find his good friend Thomas.

He nearly turned back when he saw the city's streets all layered in filth and moldering garbage. Only a dung fly would care to breathe the air, so overwhelming was the stench from the open sewers. As he left the Front Street depot, huge crates stood blocking his way, the exposed wood blue with mildew. It seemed as if the entire shipment had been casually abandoned, either to rot, or for some ambitious thief with the means and desire to take it. One container had so disintegrated Byron was able to stop and glimpse the curious device inside.

Seeing its rusted metal arms fitted with two long trowels he pictured it moving up and down like an enormous orange seesaw. He walked on trying to imagine its purpose and came within an inch of a shimmering black heap. He grabbed his nose to dodge the smell and had to wave away a rush of startled flies. As he shied back in disgust he realized that someone had piled over a dozen dead cats onto a horse's carcass and now the whole atrocious heap was crawling with maggots.

He quick-stepped for the nearest alley, keeping Johnny's fiddle tightly under his arm as he clutched his nose. When he felt it was safe to breathe he paused to let his starved lungs recover and saw that he was standing before a monument nearly two stories high made entirely of empty champagne bottles.

He was still marveling at the decadent tribute to human ingenuity when a sallow-faced man showing day-old whiskers straggled out from the alley struggling to button his trousers. Byron had his eye on the man's weaving movements when a rat the size of a small dog came scooting for his feet. He snatched up his bag with a yelp and pasted his body to the alley wall. The rat bared its long spiny teeth and looked ready to plunge them into Byron's ankle when it veered at the very last second and scuttled off. When he saw that his legs were trembling Byron decided that finding Thomas could wait a bit longer. If there was ever a moment to forgo his scruples and test the calming effect of a good strong drink, this was it.

It appeared that the stumblebum was a leftover from the night as all of the bars he came to stood quietly closed. There was something sinister about the sleepy alley with its line of sleazy-looking stalls. He was about to change his mind about that drink when he glimpsed a nicely-dressed couple ducking out of a brightly-painted *cantina* a few entrances ahead. He hurried through its swinging doors then clambered onto a stool at the counter, sticking Johnny's fiddle between his knees. Seeing the buxom *mestiza* casually saunter up, he tipped his hat and said, '*buenos dios, señora,*' then copying his comrades, asked for a white rum with bitters and some coconut water.

The barmaid drilled him with a dark-eyed stare then slapped a glass down from the shelf letting her arm nearly brush his nose. She held her gaze while she uncapped the bottle, making no attempt to disguise the fact that she was sizing him up. A smile seemed to sneak across her lips seeing the youngster struggle to keep his eyes off her cleavage.

She still had not said a word, and as she slowly poured his drink Byron could feel his temperature rising. He had not been close to a woman in years and her presence was both seductive and daunting. When she continued to closely assess him he was glad he had thought to wear his suit, even if it was a decade out of style and the clammy weather had given it a rather fusty, wet dog smell.

"There's no one here to chop open any coconuts," she finally answered him, shaking in the red dash of bitters, "—if you want I can give you a side of water." She paused from wiping a spill off her counter. "I see you've been working down at Snake Mountain—"

Byron blinked at the barmaid with her raven hair coiled in twists, wondering if she was a witch or a first-rate fortuneteller.

"I saw the green mud on your shoes when you came in. Looks like you could use a new pair."

Byron glanced irritably down at his shiny cracked boots. He'd spent half of last night rubbing them with lye and linseed oil trying to get rid of that blasted mud.

The barmaid filled a second glass from a small brown jug while she watched him through her long black eyelashes. "Lucky for you I've started opening at eleven—most joints around here won't serve you a bottle of pop before two. Be careful who you ask for water—it can kill you in this town. Don't worry, I get mine fresh from the country—or I boil it first," she reassured him, seeing Byron stop and cringe mid-sip. "So—what brings you up here to Colón?"

He was about to answer then promptly choked on his first gulp of rum. "Yuh know how it goes—" he said, coughing while trying to hide his embarrassment, "the work it keep gettin' harder but the money it keep gettin' smaller—plus mi back needed a rest from all that shovelin'."

The barmaid gazed at him questioningly. "But you're a musician..."

Byron gawked at her in confusion then remembered that he was safeguarding Johnny's fiddle. She went on before he could explain.

"So you figured you'd take a break and see if you can make a little extra playing in the city—maybe pay for those new boots. Am I right?"

The barmaid stood confidently awaiting his confirmation and a quick bright smile lit up the stunning features starting to fade inside the plumpness of her no longer youthful face. Byron glanced at the fiddle with a plumped-up grin and saw no reason to contradict her.

"I knew it!" she exclaimed, puffing up her luscious bosom. "I adore the sound of a violin—would you honor me with a little tune?" She leaned towards him across the bar and made him inhale her strong perfume.

"I'd like nutting better—" Byron answered weakly, realizing too late he'd been trapped by his own pretense and now he was too overpowered to try and escape, "unfortunately, after all that diggin' my fingers them not fit to serenade you right as yet—"

"Pity—" she replied, drawing back, "I was thinking I might hire you on. I've been looking for something different—something that could give my place a little extra class..."

Byron ran through his mental image of the smallish tavern with its raw planked floor and cheap pine tables, its only customers two grease-fingered leathernecks looking like they'd slumped here straight from their night shift in the railyard. He was impressed that a woman owned the best bar on the alley but her air seemed awfully puffed up for her surroundings.

"Give me little time to do some practice an' maybe I'll answer you diff'rent," he told her. He hated to lie but he was much too flattered by the respect he saw shining in her eyes.

"I look forward to it! There's not much to tickle a woman's fancy in this town—all the menfolk want to do is drink and gamble—not that I'm complaining, mind you," she added with a chuckle. "So what shall I call you, *muchacho*?"

"Byron—"

The barmaid held out her hand slightly bent at its wrist and for a moment Byron had the sense she'd have liked it if he bowed and kissed it. "Welcome, Byron," she said, smiling as she took firm hold on his bashful hand. "I'm Estelle Morales. I tell all the Jamaican boys if you want to have a good time and stay clear of trouble stick with Estelle—she doesn't water her rum and she keeps a clean place. That's rare in this town."

"I'll mek sure an' remember," Byron responded, feeling unusually warm as he sipped his drink and pictured himself entrancing her with Johnny's magic fiddle. "Say—" he said, setting aside the pleasing fantasy, "yuh know how to get to a place named Christopher's Column?"

Estelle stuck a hand on her hip with a hefty laugh. "Christopher's Column! That's a good one! I guess you don't speak French or much Spanish for that matter. You must mean our new little suburb—it's Christophe-Colomb," she explained with a more cynical chuckle. "You'll see that we in Colón are one lucky tamale—our treasured town has French plantain leaf on one side and Yankee corn husk on the other. Go back across the tracks and after you cross that open grassy patch you'll be there. But around here we call it Cristóbal-Colón. You know—for the great big fellow standing in the harbor."

Byron wanted to fall through the floor, mortified that he had not put two and two together. He remembered seeing the bronze statue when his boat sailed in and even a fool without real schooling should know enough to recognize Christopher Colombus.

"Don't feel bad," Estelle encouraged him, "it takes awhile to get the hang of a new language—and besides you're a musician. You do your talking through your music. It pains me to think of those trained hands working a shovel—but I suppose making music is too pure a calling to earn you a decent living."

"That's so true, miss," Byron replied, nodding sadly as he thought about talented Johnny. "Poor men can't afford that much pure enjoyment."

Estelle grinned, taken by his answer. "You're a pretty special fellow, Byron. Not too many boys come up from Culebra wearing a tie and collar, asking about the French Quarter. Someone working there a friend of yours?"

"Yep—the two of us came here together."

"And you say he lives there in Cristobal?"

"Why—something wrong?" Byron asked anxiously.

"Nothing's wrong, it's just unusual. I take it your buddy is not here working as a digger."

"I wudden think so. Thomas wrote say his boss is some big man named Henry Duvee—or Du-something or the other—"

"Henri Duvay?!"

Byron shrugged. "I guess...that sound right. You know 'im?"

"Henri used to come here almost every Saturday night. You know—I bet that was your friend I saw come in with him a couple of times...didn't really drink or want to cuddle—just sat and watched Henri play poker." Estelle wagged her head in distaste. "Too bad—all the girls were ready to eat him. Good-looking boy—had these striking eyes...like pretty violets."

"That's him—that's Thomas!" Byron cried. "Yuh know which house he lives?"

"Sorry—I don't know his address but Henri's a very important engineer. Once you're there I'm sure somebody can direct you."

Byron stood to down his rum, suddenly in a rush to get going.

As he paid her for the drink Estelle peered at him gravely. "Wait till you cross that grassy patch to stop and ask—Colón is not a place you want to be wandering around with a violin. We have some bad men in this town."

"Thanks—I'll remembah," Byron replied already on his way through the swinging half-doors.

"Don't forget my offer!" she called after him. "And don't be caught out there too late—there's a 10 o'clock curfew!"

"Ah, *jovencito*," Estelle muttered when she realized he had not heard her, "you touched my heart seeing myself looking out of those innocent eyes. Just don't end up like the stupid girl who came to town and lost pride and treasure for a promise."

———

Byron was as delighted as he stepped to Christophe-Colomb as he had been disgusted by Colón. Its pristine streets lay straight and exact and were stylishly bordered with slender young coconut trees. Its sidewalks sparkled, free of filth and rotting cats, and its only odor was that of crisp sea-air, the only sound the gently lapping surf of Limon bay. At the water's edge, neat rows of identical white cottages sat shaded by pale green jalousies, each dwelling with its own seaward porch sporting a bright-colored hammock in which to lie and enjoy the breezes at sunset. Walking through the hamlet after the muck and mud of Culebra, Byron experienced the moment when a nightmare blessedly recedes as one wakes to light.

The cottages appeared mostly empty and rather than spend time knocking door to door, he decided to ask a passer-by if they knew the Frenchman and failing that, where he could find the town's canal office. He came upon an elderly Chinese man using a sickle to trim the weeds from a lawn abutting the sidewalk. The gardener at first looked irritable as if not wishing to be bothered but when Byron thanked him politely and tipped his straw boater he seemed to relent. He pointed a finger west then held up two more fingers, waggling them to indicate he needed to go two more blocks and then veer north. "You find post office..." the old man explained as he stooped back to his work.

Following his instructions Byron came to square one-story building. The letters in a curve above its arching entrance read: *Bureau de Poste*. He joined the short line in front of a brass-barred window and quickly became anxious when he heard everyone else speaking in French. When his turn arrived he asked where he might find Mr. Henri Duvay, praying the damp-haired clerk spoke English. The Frenchman proved to be fluent and willing to offer him detailed directions. Byron was still pinching himself inside for the day's amazing string of good luck when the clerk abruptly added that he understood *Monsieur* Duvay and his young valet may have recently left for the jungle.

Byron thanked him, feeling subdued but not discouraged, and in minutes he had made it to the address which offered a lovely view of the nestled cove with its pink-white sand and emerald water. Compared to its neighbors, the two-story dwelling looked positively regal behind its guarding crotons flaming in reddish maroon and golden yellow. Byron gave a chuckle as he recalled Thomas' indignant claim back aboard ship, that he was coming to be 'just another plain digger'. But as he followed the walk's polished inlaid stones to the villa's oak door, he gave himself a mental kick for waiting so long to change his own fortunes. On his fourth gentle tap a stunning black girl in a white cap and apron came to the door and smiled at him quizzically.

"*Si? A qui voulez-vous parler?*"

As he stood twisting the wilted boater, Byron could not decide if it was the rum's lingering effect or simply the sight of such a pretty girl that was cramping his tongue. "Is this...um...is this the home of a Mister—ah—Duvay?"

"*Monsieur* Duvay, *oui!—De quoi s'agit-il?*" When Byron mumble something, inaudibly, the pleasing face sharpened with annoyance. "*Oui, oui?*"

"I'm a friend of Thomas—Thomas Judah...?"

"*Ah, oui—jeune Tom!*"

Byron relaxed seeing the smile light her face divinely. He asked if Thomas had left for the jungle and, if not, did she know if he was expected later today. As he finished with his questions he saw that she was staring at him, clearly bewildered, and now began chattering back in French, leaving them both in a soup of confusion. Unable to catch a word, Byron started creeping back from the door, bowing every few steps, his face fastened in an inane-looking grin while he stabbed a finger over his shoulder to say he would wait out here by the road.

When the sun had burned to the bottom of the sky the pretty maid came out to see him, her ebony face crimped with concern. After a frustrating minute with her babbling while waving her arms and jabbing her fingers, Byron finally recognized the word *gendarme* and grasped that with the day spent to its shadows he could not loiter in Christophe-Colomb. He mimed a gesture for her to let him leave his name. Then, with a wistful '*merci*', he bid the lovely Monique farewell and sadly crossed his way back to despicable Colón.

CHAPTER 8

"SO, THOMAS—HAVE THOSE figures the Americans sent all been reviewed and entered?"

Duvay had appeared unexpectedly inside the office bungalow and caught his supposedly reformed assistant with one leg slung over his chair, absently tossing pennies at a corner.

Thomas straightened up in a flash and jammed the coppers in his hand back in his pocket. "Nearly through—" he answered, rushing to neaten the mess of rumpled slips littering his desk. "They should be done by tomorrow midday."

"Tsk, tsk, that's a pity—" said the Frenchman, shaking his head. "Victor Sosa is willing to lead a survey of the Chagres River early tomorrow. I was hoping to have you come along, but you'll need to stay and finish up those figures."

Thomas' face crumpled in dejection. Henri had been hinting about some mysterious mission for weeks but when nothing came of it he had reckoned it was simply a dangled carrot to inspire his efforts.

"But, *monsieur!*" Thomas complained, "you didn't tell me you needed them right away!" Nothing did more to restore his self-image than a chance to test his nerve in the jungle. He grasped for the straw that might win him a last ditch reprieve. "What if I stay and work all night—" he suggested, before his voice trailed off and his chin sank to his chest. There was no point in going on with the charade. They both knew those numbers could not be checked and copied in one night.

Duvay toyed with the end of his immense moustache then unveiled a lurking grin. "All right, do as much as you can—but carefully! You may not get much sleep—we leave at dawn."

Thomas raced to hug his mentor who beamed at him smugly. "Don't worry, *monsieur*, I'll stay chained to this desk!" he promised, quickly sitting down to transcribe with intense devotion more recorded volumes of dredged-up dirt.

The early morning bloomed in a mournful gray, its cold steady drizzle dampening even Thomas' exuberance already dulled from lack of sleep. As he and Duvay met up with the explorer's outfit, Thomas waved joyfully at Diego who shrugged and stood looking grim. Arriving at the three long canoes Sosa's men had rowed from the shore to where the Gatun River joined the Chagres, Duvay insisted that his instruments, already wrapped in oilskin, be tightly sheathed inside of canvas in case a sudden storm blew up and they capsized. "At the moment, that apparatus is much more valuable than men."

The equipment and provisions secured, the eight-man team cast off through the swampy murk. The river was silent save for the splashes of their smooth dipped oars, the gloom revealing little beyond the outlines of gnarling mangroves and evil-looking vapors that wafted up from the channel's inky surface. Every so often, when the lofty trees still standing to the south obscured the pale threads of light, a rower would cautiously stick out his paddle to check for the bank. Thomas' loaded boat was gliding a mere fraction out of the water and while Diego rowed he kept a half coconut's hollow shell, ready to bail.

Like all of Sosa's men, Diego plied his oars with the fluid ease of a ripe old fisherman yet at each slight bump as the canoe struck rock, Thomas grew tense. He knew that caimans rarely troubled themselves with attacking humans but with every new splash or loud gurgle he pictured one of the slimy reptiles slithering down the bank to dog their trail until the time came to strike.

The three canoes made it to the second tributary in well under two hours. When the men were through hauling the boats up on land, noting that the drizzle had thinned to a spraying mist, Duvay ordered half of the dynamite unloaded from its covered crate. Thomas had already peeled off his confining slicker, his hopes for a day of adventure rekindled even though the sky remained drab and cheerless. After the rest of their gear had been carried to land two of the men grabbed their machetes and went about clearing sight-lines while Duvay scouted for a level spot to mount his scope. Sosa left to supervise the two men preparing the dynamite needed to blast the nearby rock formation so that the debris could be collected for later analysis.

Thomas and Diego had been sent to plot the distance back to the road then plumb a quadrant one point three miles square to mark off a potential site for new workshops. It was a tedious chore that involved one of them constantly overlapping the other as they alternated flinging the bunched-up wire ahead as far as one could and grabbing it up to straighten the metal links and make the next measurement. As the day warmed and grew muggy Diego wanted to stop and rest, but Thomas persuaded him to plunge on so they could finish sooner. By midday they had covered almost the entire stretch back to the rail-line.

"That's it for me, *amigo*—" Diego announced wearily after Thomas had tossed him the bundled chain in a perfect arc and it uncoiled like a snake near his feet, "you have me sweating like a *pendejo!*"

"What's the matter, slowpoke—no stamina?"

"Screw you, *awebao*—pass me some water!"

Thomas took the time to pull on the linked chain's brass handle and mark its sixty-six feet before slipping the hide bag of water from the side of his knapsack and handing it to his buddy who glowered at him fiercely. "If you don't dawdle like an old woman we can be done with this dull nuisance. I left a honeycomb in that last canebrake while you were busy measuring. I want to try and catch that big tayra we saw dart back inside there. I have my new throw-net—"

"*¡Mierda!*" Diego grumbled, swiping a hand across his lips after guzzling the water. "That tayra isn't sitting there waiting for us to come back—he's up in a tree laughing at those two idiots slaving like *negros!*"

"All right, all right," grumbled Thomas, grinning as he conceded the clever point. "We can take a break—but I hope when the lazy spickadee is feeling better he'll show me how he goes about tracking white-tailed deer...or was that just talk?"

Diego crouched casually, wagging his head of black curly hair. He smirked at his friend so full of bluster. "Hear that racket, you tenderfoot *chango?*" he mocked, his deeply-tanned brown head trained in the direction from which the beating sounds of air drills and hammering could just be heard in the distance. "No deer is coming this close while they're busy dynamiting this part of the line. And besides," he said, curling his thinly haired lip, "unless you packed a pistol inside that knapsack I'm not about to shoot one with my invisible blow gun."

"What the hell is the matter with you today?" Thomas griped. He sat up and picked up a stone from the grass and hurled it at a far-off tree in exasperation. "You don't want us setting any traps and you say it's a waste of time looking for any deer—so what do you propose doing?"

"Just that we go a little slower, *amigo...* Uncle Victor said your boss is on a very strict schedule. He made me promise not to stray off with you, today..."

"So!—the brave *explorador* is now a lick-finger *chico!*"

"Better than a *gringo's* little *puta!*"

"*Puta*—? What do you mean—calling me a little *puta?*" Thomas looked bewildered, astonished to sense that his friend was no longer joking. "You trying to say I'm somebody's whore? What the devil are you getting at?"

Diego glanced down to hide his smirk. "If you really don't know, then forget it..."

"Forget it—? I'd forget it if I thought you were joking, but you weren't!" Thomas yelled, hopping up angrily. "The only *putas* I know about are the fat strumpets up in Colón curling their fingers at you from an alley."

"I bet your *patrona* never stops to look at any of them—not when he's got his own *mariposa moreno*," Diego hit back, grinning lewdly.

"Henri's no poof!" cried Thomas, recoiling at the obscene notion. He knew in a vague abstract way that there were men who preferred boys to women, but the reality seemed as distant as ancient Greece. "He's no invert with me—that's for certain!"

"Maybe he's impotent and just likes looking..."

Thomas gave the bundled surveyor's chain a vicious kick. "Damn you, Diego—I thought we were friends! Why would you want to spread such a disgusting lie?"

"I'm not the one spreading anything—I overheard my uncle's men joking about what some saloon girls said about you and *Monsieur* Henri—they call you his *guapo negrito...*"

Thomas paled. "They're making molly jokes...about me...?"

"It's just silly bar-talk, *amigo*—I doubt they really believe it," Diego added quickly. "But you're right...I shouldn't have said it. I was just angry at you for calling me a lick-finger *chico*. I hate being called *chico...*"

Thomas stopped listening and went storming off to lick his wounds. It never occurred to him that his relationship with Duvay would be seen as something deviant. He racked his brain trying to think if his mentor had ever shown any perverted tendencies and the only behavior he remembered striking him as at all peculiar were those times when they'd visit that Bottle Alley *cantina* and he'd catch Henri stroking his black moustache, staring at some tipsy couple snuggling with the timid wonder of a child.

"Don't be furious with me, *amigo*—" Diego said breathlessly, as he caught up to Thomas inside a vale that seemed ablaze from its overhanging vines laden with crimson passionflowers. "*Mujers* gossip and *hombres* repeat it—I didn't mean anything by it. Perhaps it's better you know what some people are saying. At least now you can show they are wrong."

Thomas turned sulkily towards his friend. "Yes, but what about you? Do you think it's wrong—my living with Henri?"

Diego shook his head. "I think you're lucky to have a man like Duvay look out for you like a father. So long as you trust him—what a few stupid barmaids think does not matter."

For the next few hours Thomas barely said two words and Diego wisely left him to his brooding. Working at their less hectic pace it was nearly three by the time they'd finished mapping the quadrant and made it back to the river. There, to Thomas' dismay, they found half of the men already packing up their equipment.

"Don't they look hard-pressed—" he sneered loudly to Diego. "So much for our rushing back here. What a waste..."

"I'm sorry my work strikes you as trifling!" snapped Duvay as he tramped back from the shallows.

Thomas stood looking chagrined. He did not want Henri to think he was complaining. "I did not mean to suggest the work is not important, *monsieur*, I was just surprised that you'd gotten finished this quickly..."

"Oh, but we're not through—not by a long shot. Now that my suspicions have been confirmed the real work begins. Unfortunately, Victor Sosa could only spare me his service for today—he has a previous commitment he must prepare for. Don't worry—" he said quickly when Thomas looked even more downcast, "he's leaving us his best guide and young Diego. You should be ecstatic with what we've accomplished here! We may have just saved this magnificent project from a most ignoble end!"

Duvay began pacing in circles, his arms waving with jubilant gestures like a schoolboy stunned to learn he'd aced a tough exam. "You look mystified, *mon fils, ne t'inquiétes pas*—I've not gone mad," he said exuberantly, seeing Thomas standing agape. "No madder than my teacher, the great Godin de Lépinay de Brusly. Oh, how the pygmies maligned him! But he alone was correct! We must tame this mighty river and make it our ally, not our enemy!"

Thomas continued to look puzzled. After having lived with Duvay for two years, he thought he already knew the name of every top engineer even slightly connected with the canal—names like Gaston Blanchet and Gustav Eiffel. "*Monsieur*...who is Godin de Lépinay?"

"Perhaps the finest scientist in France—if not the world," Duvay exuded with rare self-abnegation. "I have just tested his prophetic assessment and confirmed his genius! We have been courting disaster by dismissing his wisdom. Our great de Lesseps is not a scientist—he won fame in Egypt because that canal was dug through sand. To take the same approach disregarding Panama's weather and terrain is an outrage to both Science and Nature! This new director is another simpering toad but now I have the proof and a plan to convince him! A sea level passage is impossible. We must lift our ships and sail them above the mountains!"

Energized by his vision, Duvay pointed a victorious finger skyward at the very moment the sun burst through the filtering clouds and spread its brilliance. Judging it yet another felicitous omen, the engineer launched into a cockeyed high-stepping jig.

"Your patron is *muy loco*, eh?" Diego whispered, inching up beside his friend as Duvay started stamping about in circles, babbling in French. "So, this is your chance, *amigo*—let's go now—quickly!"

But Thomas stood engrossed. He'd been able to catch snippets of the engineer's joyous rambling and was fascinated to realize that the giant iron locks Duvay had been explaining in his lessons were to be built at the mouth of the river and that a massive earthen dam would one day cover the very ground on which they stood.

"Do you want to go and check your trap or not?" Diego hissed near Thomas' ear. "The jungle is waking—see?"

All at once the forest appeared throbbing with life as if animated by the sun's return. From the treetops a macaw began providing shrieking commentary on a contest between two tribes of red-haired monkeys quarreling to decide whose howls were the loudest. Flocks of birds were flying in reckless loops and when a rare quetzal went speeding across the sky like a flaming arrow Sosa's men roared a spontaneous cheer.

With Duvay still prancing about, lost to his muttered thoughts, the men finished stowing their gear then wandered off, shrugging their bemusement. Sprawled in the nearby grasses, they rushed to pull off their boots and pick out the fleas and chigoes burrowed in their ankles and between their toes, happy for a chance to soak in the sunshine.

"If you don't get a move on there won't be time, you contrary Jamaican!" Diego snapped, spying his uncle on his way back up from the river after repacking the unused dynamite. He was ready to jerk his friend by the arm to get him moving when Thomas pointed out the low blue cloud floating up from the green savannah.

"Blue morphos!" one of the men gasped reverently when the rising cloud turned out to be a swarm of radiant butterflies.

"Uh-uh—something's coming!" Diego cried, his keen black eyes shifting excitedly as two southern screamers shrilled an alert then flapped to a higher perch inside the forest.

"Shh!—listen!" Victor Sosa whispered, as he crept up from behind, a warning finger at his lips. "The monkeys are silent."

A shimmer of gold glinted in the grass twenty yards from where the men lay loafing. Seeing them start to wriggle back like crabs, Diego gave Thomas a shove in the small of his back and the two friends lay with their chins on the ground, their eyes latched on the rippling in the green savannah. The waterbirds' screams grew frantic and the men stopped their sideways crawl and crouched on all fours. The high grass shivered less than five yards ahead as the yellow stripe blazed and flashed in closer.

Thomas froze at the sound of a sudden loud pop and the movements ceased. He snapped around his neck and saw Henri Duvay poised like a statue clad in high rubber boots, his outstretched hand gripping the smoking pistol. As Thomas sat there gaping, two of the stouter-hearted men inched to the static spot and cautiously parted the flat green blades. On the ground was a spotted young jaguar, dead, a small dark circle in the center of its skull.

Thomas finally jumped up for a closer look and the rest of the surveyors converged behind him. He stared at the thin black trickle oozing on the fur between the cat's opalescent staring eyes then back to Duvay. For a long moment no one spoke. They were too consumed with reverence, awed by the beauty of the sleek golden creature and the skill required for such a kill. Thomas was first to break the spell.

"*Monsieur!*" he blurted in admiration, "where did you learn to shoot like that? You will teach me how to do that...yes?"

"We'll see—so long as you're sure about what you're aiming at," Duvay replied, tucking away his pistol. "For now, our energies must focus exclusively on the great task at hand."

Thomas felt let down by the cryptic answer then instantly relieved. As Sosa's men continued to argue over who should get to sell the cat's valuable hide and divide the profits, he advanced on Diego, leering in triumph. "This should put an end to their slander," he crowed to his dumbstruck friend. "Tell me—what poof could make a kill like that!"

Chapter 9

The approach of twilight was muting Colón's wretchedness in wistful blues. Now that he was no longer fixed by its stench, Byron noticed that every store on Front Street shared the same wood frame and a second-floor gallery set on posts planted flush to the curb. He was surprised to see that the signs were all in English, including a confounding one that said: *Welcome to Aspinwall.* No doubt, had he ever ventured as far as New Jersey, the boardwalk's seedy hotels and Chinese curio-shops would have convinced him that he had wandered to a chintzy stretch of Atlantic City.

The red sun was dying before his eyes and the day's warming serendipity had already ebbed and gone cold. As he left the immaculate Christophe-Colomb he pictured the naked children somewhere off in the shadows hungrily sucking the rind from tainted refuse. It seemed unreal that such a contrast could exist separated by a short patch of grass and no one noticed.

A whining steam-whistle was advertising a street-vendor's fresh roasted peanuts and Byron suddenly realized he had not eaten since early that morning. Feeling his mouth begin to water, he was about to go buy himself a pack when the air filled with shouts and an angry mob was seen converging at the next intersection. Half in bare feet and showing mud-caked shins, some waving shovels or sharpened sticks, the men were attempting to form a column behind their leaders loudly chanting '*¡Libertad!*' and '*¡Justicia!*'

The fast-striding men quickly overtook the slow-moving traffic. The four in front, dressed in mismatched uniforms and hoisting large cudgels, barked for the marchers to halt but not before two of the little carmietta carriages had been jolted into the gutter. The first coachman got down to try and coax his frightened horse back out of the ditch while the second ran at the demonstrators swinging his fists. Their stranded passengers, fearing they were about to be caught in a riot, hurried to escape and knocked back down the poor old wagoner the mob had left sprawling in the street, wailing beside his upturned load of guanabana and custard apples.

The brief flare-up subsided and a few courteous souls broke ranks and came to the aid of the weeping farmer who cursed them as they helped him to his feet, vowing vengeance as he gazed at his produce lying splattered to a pulp. Byron was engrossed listening to the old man haggle bitterly with the men about his just restitution when someone knocked hard against his side in a rush to push past him. Encumbered by his bag and Johnny's fiddle, he lost his balance and was about to trip into the sewer when a kind hand reached out and steadied him.

"*Détendez, mon ami!*" the man declared, when Byron shied back in fear, seeing the huge sword hanging at his side. "Don't be—eh, *craintif*—we *noires sommes tous les frères!*"

The Good Samaritan, a short, stout moon-faced fellow with deep obsidian skin was sporting a navy-blue regimental tunic with gold-stringed epaulets fringing his shoulders. Byron noticed that, unlike some of his indigent-looking comrades, the fellow could have passed for an officer of currency and weight decked in those cream-colored breeches and snappy red boots, except for the fact, that like the stained tricolor sash across his chest, his costume was clearly a relic from victories lost and forgotten.

"What's all the carryin' on about?" Byron wondered, after nodding the man his gratitude.

The soldier made a few faltering stabs at replying in English then finally surrendered the attempt and pointing to his decorated chest with a gleaming smile. "I am Reynal—*nous avec le coeur devons combattre pour La Liberté!*"

Byron gathered enough to understand that he was being urged to join a pressing cause. When he questioned its purpose, the militant clicked the heels on his shiny red boots and saluted majestically, his free hand grasped stiffly to the hilt of his scabbarded sword.

"*À la justice et à l'égalité! Allons, allons—ecoutez le chef!*" Reynal exclaimed, scuttling off to catch up to the departing protestors.

Intrigued, Byron shambled along behind and trailed the reordered march a short distance until those furthest in front stopped before a tin-roofed warehouse. As the last of the marchers funneled to a standstill the rest of the street stood largely deserted. A pale sprinkling of well-dressed ladies and gentlemen had drifted out to observe from some of the second floor balconies. His Good

Samaritan had disappeared inside the mob and Byron quickly drew off to the side and took stock of the roughly three dozen men, all of whom were now raising an ax or a shovel and chiming for justice. He was impressed to see that while the majority was made up of his countrymen, the other long aggrieved faces diverged between several distinct nationalities.

A voice up ahead hollered, '*¡silencio!*' and rising onto his tiptoes Byron was just able to make out a tiny yellow-skinned man being lifted onto a shipping crate rising about four feet above the ground. As he perched there in a dour black suit, scowling down with his short arms out rigidly from his sides, he bore the countenance of an implacable raven. On the street, right below him, four fierce-looking men stood hoisting what Byron had taken for cudgels but were now revealed to be long torches. The amber flames lent a baleful cast to the evening's blue gloaming and the raven-man stayed grimly silent until the chants had petered out and everyone stilled with solemn expectancy.

He started out with a barrage of stirring slogans, drawing cheers from the noisier half of the crowd before he launched into the theme of his speech. Byron was only able to pick out strands as the speaker fluctuated his sentences between Spanish and English. Byron glanced around to see if anyone else was having trouble and noticed that his moon-faced rescuer was quietly interpreting for some fellow Haitians. The firebrand must have sensed he was losing command of his audience as he sharply increased his intensity and continued only in English.

"The time is near, my hardworking brothers, when you may be called to man the barricades against the encroachments of tyranny!" The speaker paused to let the import of his words take effect before continuing. "The *gringo* may claim it is not your fight—that your rights must be submerged for his canal. If he does so, tell him, fine!—that's your right—here's my shovel—start digging!" The firebrand mimed a pompous man clutching his chest in horror, sending the diggers rocking with laughter. "Tell him your fathers and grandfathers did not rid this land of vermin so that their sons could be preyed on by reptiles!" he resumed more aggressively. "The very ties beneath our roads are soaked in their blood—were their lives not worth more than a slice of watermelon?" A murmur rumbled through the crowd as the native Panamanians placed the reference to a deadly riot spurred when a rich Yank refused to pay a poor *buhonero* for his melon. "Our treasonous leaders betrayed you then, just as they are betraying our country now. But a cry is rising from every grotto and vale in Colombia! It says: we, the people, will not be cowed!—we will defend our land!—we will preserve our Constitution!"

The firebrand's voice rose to a smoldering pitch and the crowd ignited with cheers. As he listened, Byron's blood was racing. He had never been near such passion. He was amazed by this little yellow-skinned man who showed such audacity with white men in earshot. He was clearly important enough not to fear them. Byron had never imagined that he might possess a right unless it was the right to be paid for his labor—and even then he knew of no law that would enforce it—and yet this tiny straight-backed man spoke as if he was proclaiming great truths. Still, the thrust of the speech disturbed him. He was here to find Thomas and, with help and some luck, land better employment. How slim would his chances be if there was a crisis—would he need to choose sides? "One cocoa at a time fills the basket, Byron," he counseled his restless mind, remembering an old Jamaican proverb about keeping cool and having patience. "Purpose is a fine thing—" he mused as he edged off from the crowd, "but all the proud feelings in the world ain't about to make a poor man king."

The cramp of hunger was again gnawing at his gut and he put off returning to the barmaid's tavern to scout out a place to eat that looked clean and cheap. He headed back to the boardwalk when he noticed an exceedingly tall man in a floppy slope hat hard on his trail. He needed no more warnings to feel anxious about being out alone in Colón at night. He held Johnny's violin closer to his side and doubled his pace but had not gone six steps before the man's long strides had them almost even. He wheeled to confront his stalker, his mouth open to call for help, when he saw the snug tapered pants and flashy silk shirt and recognized the favored attire of his compatriots who made good money working on the docks or for the railroad.

"Sorry to bother—" Byron appealed innocently, to cover up his fear, "but can yuh tell me what that was all about?" He nudged out his chin to where the protest was ending.

The man peered down at him coldly. A long chewstick wiggled between his teeth. "Monkey trouble is what that is..."

"*Attente! Attente!—mon frere!*"

The voice rang excitedly, and Byron felt a surge of relief seeing his Haitian Samaritan come dashing up from out of a group on its way from the rally.

"*Ah, mon frere—je t'ai vu là—tres bien!* You join...yes? *¡Viva la causa! ¿si—si?*"

Byron made a show of welcoming the militant's warm greeting. The sharply-dressed Jamaican spat out his reed in disgust, then stalked off muttering 'hard-ears boy burn in sun-hot.'

The back-home warning gave Byron an anxious twinge as he watched his countryman vanish. He was still wondering why the man had wanted to trace him when he felt Reynal grab him by the elbow and start to prod him back to the alley where a light-skinned man in a check-patterned suit stood jotting down the names of two men Byron recognized from the crowd. A second man then slipped them each a five dollar bill with whispered instructions.

When his turn came to sign Byron tensed and held back. He wished he knew enough to weigh the risk. He could certainly use those five dollars. While he stood there wavering, Reynal left to speak with a watchful group loitering quietly on the street by the lamppost. The men all looked famished, their expressions churlish as they stared at their muddy bare toes.

Byron finally decided that while the cause might be just it was simply not worth his getting involved. He turned to slip away with the men already heading for a nearby billiard hall but Reynal rushed to detain him, one hand steadying the long sheathed sword while the other waved a pamphlet along with a small wad of bills.

"*Cinq dollars, mon frere—pour vous!*" he announced, looking pleased with himself as he held out the cash Byron was apparently free to accept without signing. "*Allons!* We talk—*oui?*" Reynal lifted the hand from his sword and pointed back to the hungry-eyed men now being enticed by the man in the light checked suit. "We go eat—*bien?*"

Held by the Haitian's engaging smile, Byron was again trapped in two minds. He was about to relent and tag along when the tall Jamaican suddenly reappeared along the sidewalk. "Hey, you! Young fiddler! My lady would like a word with you! Come on, country-boy—" he barked when Byron looked skittish, "don't keep her waiting!"

Eager to escape, Byron told the Haitian to keep his fiver then snatched the leaflet from his startled hand promising to read it. He could hear Reynal calling after him as he ran to catch up to his departing countryman. He was starting to sweat from trying to match the man's quick pace when they pushed through the hinged half-doors of a raucous saloon and his heart stopped mid-beat. Disoriented by the sudden rush of noise and sweet smoke, he stood with muscles clenched for a full thirty seconds before he realized the huge leopard with its spike-toothed jaws poised to tear him limb from limb was made of bronze and paper mache. He walked past the immobile cat feeling foolish but more than a little bit queasy when its glowing agate eyes continued to follow him as he searched for his escort, now lost among the tavern's glittering patrons.

The men at the linen-topped tables were all too pale, their chins to weak to be his imposing giant. As he scrutinized the faces happily ignoring him he was struck that, unlike the downcast looks he'd left outside, inside the countenances were mostly carefree. It was easy to understand once he had counted up the number of pretty women in soft satin gowns with bright looming feathers in their hair catching eyes like princesses, yet there was an edge to the boisterous voices which seemed pitched too high to be completely at ease. His eyes grew wide admiring the saloon's gleaming walnut bar and wide gilded mirror until he saw the bumpkin staring back in his musty old suit and felt instantly small and out of place. "Byron," he muttered to himself, "you got a long way to go to be a real somebody..."

He was lurching back out through the knot of tables cluttered with carafes and black-stockinged thighs on his way to the street when the tall man again materialized. The giant put a mighty hand on Byron's neck and ushered him back through the noisy tavern to a darkened room.

"I warned you to watch your step in this town..."

The hard female voice came out from a choking cloud of incense and rich perfume. In his state, Byron did not notice that his escort, his touch as light as a ghost, had relieved him of his bag until the man tugged at Johnny's violin. He clasped the fiddle in tight, praying he had not stupidly blundered into the hands of high-class criminals.

"It's all right, Longers," said the woman, her tone melting sweetly, "a good musician doesn't allow his instrument out of his sight."

Her tall stooge grunted, shoving him forward and for an instant Byron thought his hunger had his mind playing tricks. Estelle smiled at him through the dimness.

"So, my handsome young fiddler—not here a day and already plotting Revolution?" she asked, looking like a queen at her lonely table.

"Naw, naw—nothing like dat! I was just curious..." Byron shifted nervously, hearing the giant's snicker.

"Hungry cats can be too curious—you'll see they have very short lives in this town."

"Sit there!" the man called Longers ordered. He pulled out a chair at the singly-set candle-lit table, then vanished yet again.

The violin safely between his feet, Byron tried to nod at the appropriate moments while Estelle lectured him about the danger of mixing with radicals. As he did his best to look attentive, he struggled to square the woman in the high-necked gown with her face talced white and the one who'd beguiled him with her gypsy eyes and soft brown bosom. Her black hair, no longer in braids, was pinned with sparkling gems in an elegant pouf and her two voices seemed astoundingly different—where the first had been sultry and inviting, this one was guarded and businesslike. He was deciding whether to try and demand his bag or simply flee when the tall ghost returned with a plate of seasoned rice and two cold tamales.

Estelle poured out some champagne into a thin tapered glass and she and the colossus shared a chuckle when, after a dainty sip, Byron promptly sneezed as the bubbles tickled his nose. He laughed along and was hungrily smacking his lips, wolfing down the spicy wraps of corn and chicken, when it dawned on him that his inscrutable hosts had been communing the whole time in some silent code. As he polished off the last morsel, mumbling a child's honest thanks, Estelle reached out with her thumb and brushed a stuck rice grain from the edge of his mouth.

"I take it you didn't see your young friend."

Byron stared forlornly at the empty white plate and shook his head.

Estelle glanced knowingly up at the giant who stood impassively just behind her right shoulder. "You should have come to see me instead of getting roped in with those ruffians...if Longers hadn't told me he'd spotted the boy with the straw hat and fiddle you could have gotten yourself in a pot of trouble." The more distant Estelle leaned back in her chair. "So, here we are..." she said, pausing pointedly before peering at him more closely. "Longers said they were bribing you boys with cash..."

"I neva took their money..."

"Good...but if you had I wouldn't hold it against you. Everybody needs money. Did they offer you a place for the night?"

Byron wagged his head no.

"You never considered my proposition? I should have mentioned that you'd be playing here at the Last Frontier—not that little Bottle Alley tavern..."

As he recalled her offer, Byron found everything that had puzzled him begin to make sense. If this woman had the brains and means to run this fancy saloon it made sense that she might want something different to make her business stand out. Now that he had grasped the picture he started to panic. How was he to explain that he couldn't play a tune on Johnny's fiddle to save his life? How could he dare it with that giant staring down on him? Who could tell what the man might do if he confessed right after gobbling his food?

"Like I told you earlier, miss—my fingers them not been feelin' too right—I think I mussi did sprain them down at Culebra..."

"*¡Que lastima!*—what a pity! An artist should not have to hurt his hands on a shovel! I see you're embarrassed. Don't feel bad—we all do what we must to eat. I remember these two young vagabonds used to stop in my Bottle Alley bar almost every night—turned out they were picture-painters—apparently quite well known in Europe, but here they were, digging in our ditch. Being the person I am, I thought, poor artists—they never have money! So I offered them fifty dollars if they'd do my portrait like the ones you see in the bank or the *sala* of a wealthy *padrona*." Estelle's white-talced face glazed with anger. "Do you know one of those *pintors* had the nerve to insult me?—said he'd rather get the clap than ever paint me like that!" Her fury gone as swiftly as it arose, she smiled at Byron warmly. "You, on the other hand, were so gracious when I asked you for a tune—you declined but you didn't insult me. I admire a man who is humble about his talent. How about this—?" she bent across the table towards him as if bursting with sudden inspiration. "The men in this town with a crumb of ambition are all employed, corrupted or dead. Managing two places is turning out to be more than I can manage. I could use another hand at my little *cantina*. I can't pay you any wages right off—but you'd be sure of a square meal like that every day. You needn't worry," she said quickly, seeing Byron's uneasy look. "You'll stay with Longers. I have a little house that I've been renting out that's not far from here. What do you say? This way you wouldn't have to go back to hoisting a shovel before those fingers had a chance to mend. I'm not one to look past a genuine offer...I intend to hold you to your promise that you'll serenade me someday."

Byron nearly laughed out loud, but his head was shaking 'no' even as his heart cried, 'yes'! When he felt her touch his hand and beg him to reconsider, his heart won him over. Had he not wished for a break from shoveling? And who knew how long it might be before he caught up with Thomas? For richer or poorer, it seemed that he was meant to get to know this woman better. So while his conscience commanded him to stop trading on his dead friend's image, it was not an easy order to follow when that magic fiddle was bringing him such amazing luck.

Chapter 10

The snake's headless body thrashed furiously, oblivious to its own belated death. Thomas stood quivering, the branch hanging useless in his hand. He still had not budged when Henri Duvay came racing to the logwood tree, his pistol braced to re-fire.

"Are you bitten?" he shouted anxiously.

It took a moment for the question to seep into Thomas' consciousness. "Not me, *monsieur!*" he cried, "Diego!" He aimed the trembling branch to where his friend had sunk with his back against the fluted tree-trunk. "I was ahead when I heard him yell. I came as fast I could—the snake was on his neck! The bloody thing wouldn't let go...it wouldn't let go!" Thomas slammed the branch at the huge brown snake on the ground, still twitching violently. "Oh, Jesus—Diego!" he cried, seeing his friend start to jerk with convulsions. "What do we do? We need to get him to a doctor!"

"I'm afraid there isn't time..."

"What are you saying? We can't just fold our hands—surely!"

Thomas ran to stoop by his friend as the seizures which had been becoming more rapid and frequent, suddenly ceased. Diego gazed up at him weakly and started to speak but then his lashes sagged heavily and a trickle of blood leaked out from his eyes. "For God's sake, Henri—help him!"

With starch-faced calm, Duvay holstered his gun and knelt by the diamond-backed snake which now lay still after twisting the last thrashes of life from its tail. "Young Valladares was extremely unlucky...that's a lethal bushmaster." Duvay got back to his feet without looking at Diego. "It's too late," he said with ice-cold frankness. "Look—there's no point your staying here to weep," he snapped when Thomas choked back a sob, "—I'll have one of the junior men help you with the measuring. I told you before we left that I only have a few days to complete this survey—we've barely gotten started..."

Thomas was no longer listening as he bent down and hugged his friend. Diego's light blue shirt was slowly turning scarlet as the gruesome flows increased. Blood began to stream out of his ears and nostrils and as Diego sat up to gag, a bright red geyser came gushing from his mouth. When the bleeding youngster finally drooped as if falling asleep, Duvay nudged his protégé gently on the shoulder but Thomas pushed him off roughly. "Move, if you're not going to help!" he cried, grabbing for the knife at his belt. "Diego showed me what to do!—I need to cut a cross at the wound and suck out the poison—" he muttered, his hand shaking as he searched the blood-smeared neck in vain for the marks from the viper's fangs.

"I told you—it's hopeless. The venom has already spread to his nervous system. What blood he has left is turning to water..."

"No, God! No! He can't be dying!"

Duvay grasped Thomas with a fatherly grip and pried the knife from his trembling hand. "There's nothing to be done. He won't have long to suffer..."

"Damn you—he's still breathing! We're not that far out—can't we at least carry him back to Gatun village?"

"To what purpose? I can't waste valuable time. You know the doing it took for me to get this many engineers to help us today."

When Duvay tried to pull him up from Diego, Thomas pushed him back and charged off. He ran on heedlessly, seeing nothing but blood. He crashed through brush and low-hanging branches then suddenly felt sick. He stopped with his scratched hands braced to his knees and saw that his trousers were splashed with blood. He puked a long thread of saliva then collapsed onto the ground. He sprawled there feeling his head set to crack from its furious pounding. From back in the copse he could hear the junior engineers who'd just arrived to replace Sosa's men shouting out for Duvay.

Minutes passed before Thomas was able to force his fluttering legs to hold him up and stagger back. He was almost there when he heard a chorus of ooh-la-la's erupt from the gathered Frenchmen. He arrived in time to see them staring with cautious excitement as Duvay held up the murderous bushmaster and sliced it down the middle to prove his prediction that the snake was heavy with eggs. Behind him, Diego lay slumped against the tree, covered in blood.

The last thin straw snapped inside of Thomas. He prayed that when Duvay displayed the depth of his callousness Diego's soul was already free of that bloodied, bloodless corpse. He charged through the engineers' fawning circle ready to curse his gloating mentor when he saw that two of the shirtless *macheteros* were busy digging a grave in the canebrake nearby.

"Have you no feelings, Henri? How could you have them bury Diego out here?"

Duvay glanced up from measuring the length of the snake stretched out on the ground. "I told you why already. There is little time left before it will be dark and I have far too much to get done to waste a day and turn back. Would it suit you better if we hauled along his stinking corpse?"

"We could at least wrap him up and carry back him to one of the villages."

"Look, it's unfortunate, but Diego is dead. Where he is buried doesn't matter to him now."

"I can't believe you! You claimed Victor Sosa was your friend. How are you going to tell him you left his nephew to rot in a makeshift grave?"

His outburst drew glares from the other Frenchmen who followed Duvay's lead and stepped around Thomas without a word to continue their surveys. Meanwhile, the *macheteros* had rolled Diego's body into the hole and were hurrying to pack in the last shovels of dirt so they could return to hacking off more tree-limbs impeding Duvay's sight-lines back to the river. As they finished the hasty grave and resumed their chopping, the jungle's animal dwellers seemed to join in Thomas' tantrum. Even normally reticent birds began a crazed whooping, beating their indignant wings as they joined in outcry against the destruction of their natural homes.

The tapering off of the displaced monkeys' howls seemed to moderate Thomas' temper. When their babble had diminished to where he could hear himself speak, he ventured one last appeal to Duvay using a far less combative tone. "Forgive me, *monsieur*," he said as he found the engineer on one knee with his monocled eye set keenly upon a sample of soil in his hand. "I should not have allowed my emotions to get away from me. I understand your work is important but couldn't we spare a moment to say a few words about Diego?"

Duvay got to his feet and briskly dusted the dirt from his hands. "*Non, non, non, c'est impossible!*" he said emphatically as he brushed past Thomas and began to mount his alidade onto its tripod to employ his freshly cleared sight-lines. "We have no time. Now please do as I asked and find someone to help you map the shortest route back to the quarry. I will brook no more of these childish interruptions!"

"Suppose it was I who had been bitten, Henri? Would you have covered me with those few specks of dirt and left me to the buzzards?"

The Frenchman let the question hang unanswered while he bent and squinted through the lens. When he was satisfied with the alignment of its focus he rose looking mildly mystified. He answered Thomas in a voice that was faintly tender. "*Oui—mais alors, rien n'importerait*—were our efforts here to fail, neither your death nor my tears would matter."

Duvay quietly returned to his telescope and Thomas stood impaled by the sheer puniness of his existence. It shocked him how easily the glorious script he had sketched for his new life could be rubbed out and he was filled with rage and even deeper despair. Seeing the *macheteros* finish axing down a wild avocado tree plump with fruit he wandered alone back to the patch of freshly shoveled ground. He knelt and touched a hand to the still warm grave, then covering his eyes, released the flood of dammed up tears for his own dead hero.

———

In addition to bussing tables six days a week at her Bottle Alley tavern in return for his food and shelter, Byron had agreed to keep Estelle Morales' little boarding-house neat and clean. He'd been less than overjoyed to learn he had to wear an apron and wash dishes like a plantation woman, but after Culebra the job felt like a vacation and tidying the lodgings was a simple matter since Longers worked all day at the shipyard and her only other boarder had recently been killed in a railway accident.

Byron had twice made return pilgrimages to Christophe-Colomb but neither time, despite knocking at the Frenchman's door over several hours, had the pretty maid been there to answer. So although he worried about not saving up any money, he felt lucky for the chance to stay in town without digging a hole in his pocket while he waited for Thomas. It helped that Estelle's fearsome giant seemed less hostile when they were alone at night in the boarding house. When Byron would express his doubts about hanging around Colón without an income, Longers was quick to offer his gruff encouragement. "Forget dat pick and shovel drudgery—git you a trade!" the giant would growl.

"Take it from a sea-worn sailor—in this here world you gots to grip that keel hard but if you're sinking and somebody throws you a lifeline you better hurry and grab it!"

"So who roped you back to land?" Byron finally dared to ask the solemn giant, grinning, thinking he already knew the answer.

Longers stretched one of his endless legs on the low coffee table, careful not to disturb the ceramic figurines of festive folk-dancers and musicians Estelle kept safe in the little boarding-house. "I stowed to sea the day I turned thirteen and she carried me on her back for twenty-five years but she's a damn hard mistress and after a while you get tired of her always shoving you around. A man can't set roots in the ocean. I guess you could say I found somebody who got me thinking 'bout planting good seed instead of just sowing wild oats..."

It had been an easy guess that Longers was sweet on Estelle. Every evening, after working in the shipyard, he would show up at the Bottle Alley tavern sharp at six cleaned and dressed in his loud silk shirt and matching neckerchief to escort the freshly-powdered and gowned hostess to her upscale establishment. Longers would then spend the rest of the night quietly observing, a stout iron bar at the ready should any of her patrons get stupidly drunk or try to start trouble.

"So you stayed here on account of Miss Estelle," Byron suggested forwardly.

"I'd been in pretty rough ports in my time but when I landed here it seemed like the vermin from every pesthole in this globe was in Colón searchin' fresh blood. Miss Estelle was a rose floating in a cesspool but you could smell her ambition. She saw this boom coming from way back then and, yeah—" Longers drawled proudly after a pause, "I kept the jackals from tearing her down. The only ones I couldn't help her handle were those two-faced officials." For Longers, the worst snakes in Panama were its gamblers and corrupt politicians.

"These ginnals got folks here believin' all they need to do is bet on a big enough goose and they'll have fresh golden eggs every day. Go ahead—laugh—" he chided, hearing Byron start to snicker, "you were swallowing their fairy-story right along when I first saw you. You think that ginnal lawyer, Prestàn, is the first one ever climb up on a soapbox to try and make poor folk think they can have rich man's freedom? I'd quicker trust a hustler with the aces up his sleeve than some bonehead sloganeer strutting around like a little toy soldier."

Byron did not find anything Reynal had said to be stupid or ignoble, but at well over six-foot-four, Longers McCatty was not a man he felt eager to dispute. Byron had not thought about the rally in the two and half weeks since he'd been in the Last Frontier, so it came as a surprise when on his third Friday night

Longers showed up in the Bottle Alley tavern an hour before closing to say Miss Estelle wanted to see him right away.

"Is everything all right?" Byron asked, anxiety frothing in his stomach as he threw off the apron and dashed out after Longers.

"Just come," the sailor said tersely.

At the Last Frontier Byron squeezed past the staring leopard and was impressed to see the tavern walls even more blanketed with vivid lithographs. Despite its brighter decor, the room's tenor held the same false note he had sensed in the edgy laughter, except tonight it was even clearer. As he sidled along the walnut bar behind Longers, a red-cheeked popinjay scrambled on top of one of the white-clothed tables and began holding court in the middle of the saloon. The blond dandy had obviously imbibed too many and as he waved his glass to start his toast the champagne went sloshing past the rim to his elegant laced sleeve.

The popinjay was struggling to rouse some more enthusiasm as Byron followed through the bamboo curtain shielding the softly-lit room in back and Longers nodded for him to wait at the table. The sailor vanished and Byron noticed for the first time that there was a hidden door behind the room's floor-length draperies. He was creeping over to poke in his nose and see where it led when the secret door pushed open and Estelle came striding in on the arm of a tiny Frenchman with a huge black moustache.

"There you are, Byron!" Estelle exclaimed, catching him off guard as he rushed back from the door. "This is your friend's employer, *Monsieur* Duvay. Shall I leave you two alone?" she asked, turning back to address her short companion.

"No, please stay, *ma cherie*. These are simple questions," Duvay crisply replied.

Byron was taken by the fact that as the three of them stood by the table they were roughly equal in height. He was bursting to ask about Thomas, but knew to wait and be spoken to first.

"I understand you've journeyed to my domicile more than once hoping to communicate with young Master Judah—but you have not succeeded?"

"No sah, I came by dere few times but nobody was 'ome—" Byron replied, wishing he could remember to speak more clearly and make his patois less pronounced even when he was nervous. "Mas' Thomas all right?"

"No one can be sure. It seems your friend has gone missing..."

"Missing?" Byron gasped, his sudden happiness leaking away. "The canal office had me to believe he went with yuh to the jungle—"

"So indeed—however he and I both returned days ago. I had to leave the next morning for Panama City. When I got back Thomas was gone and no one seems to know where he might be found. You're quite certain you're telling me the truth? He hasn't written you? Or perhaps arranged for you both to meet in secret?"

"No sar! Is me the one searching for him!"

The Frenchman shot a glance towards Estelle, then considered Byron with deeper interest. "*Señora* Morales tells me you were digging for us down in Culebra. Was seeing young Judah the only reason that brought you up here to Colón?"

Thomas gone missing had Byron groping through a swamp of emotions but his mind was sharp to the fact that here was the chance he might never have again. "Thomas wrote and told me he was working for an important man," he said speaking slowly to enunciate every syllable as a properly as he could. "I did think that, if I got the chance to meet you, I'd ask if you might help me get a different job...I don't—"

Duvay cut him off with an impatient gesture. "If I were you, I'd go back to Culebra and finish the job I was brought here to do."

"Byron plays the violin, Henri," Estelle broke in. "He needed a break to save his hands—I've heard tell he's quite accomplished."

"I see. Well, I suppose that's a bit different..." said Duvay, his severe manner easing slightly. "So, you're a gifted young man with ambition, eh—?"

Byron shunted his face to the side. "I won't tell you different, sar..." he mumbled. Strangely, his discomfort seemed to create a more favorable impression.

"In that case, I shall trust you to be candid—you've no doubt heard there are serious troubles down on the mainland. Are the rebels trying to draw our workers to their cause?"

"I don't know much 'bout that, sar..."

"But they did approach you about joining them, is that not so?"

Byron darted a dismayed look back to Estelle. "I was only lissnin'. Most of the talk was just about askin' for better wages—"

"They didn't offer to pay you to fight?"

"Not really, sar...at least that's not the way I did take it..."

"Did you take the money?"

"No sar!"

"Let's both be clear," Duvay said evenly. "They knew you were a digger—they tried to sign you on but you declined...is that it?"

"Yes, sar! Like I tole yuh—I came 'ere lookin' fer a job, not to spark up any trouble." Byron insisted, too agitated to remember what Estelle told him about slowing down his words when he wanted to speak properly. "Dat's de God's hones' truth—I swear!"

To his relief, the Frenchman seemed satisfied.

"Très bien! You appreciate the seriousness of the matter and what we have at stake. You must tell *Señora* Morales immediately should these rascals contact you again."

Before Byron could ask what he intended to do about Thomas, Duvay had strutted out through the bamboo curtain and back to the main *sala.* The encounter had left Byron's head swimming; despite its glimmer of promise, he felt discouraged and slightly resentful. He wondered why Estelle had wanted to tell the Frenchman about him stopping at the rally. On the other hand he was grateful that when Duvay suggested he go back to digging she had jumped to defend him.

Estelle appeared to read his mind as she clasped him by the shoulder. "Don't get downhearted over what Henri said. We're all on edge about the political situation. We cannot let things get so out of hand that the canal is in jeopardy."

"But why you had to let him think I got mixed up in all this business?" Byron asked sullenly. "Now he'll never help me get a job..."

"I'm not the one who first told him," Estelle claimed somewhat touchily. "There are as many keen eyes in this town as there are loose tongues and with that violin you stood out in the crowd like a big sore thumb. You needn't worry. I think Henri has special feelings for your handsome friend—I'm sure the poor man's beside himself with him gone missing," she added with a lascivious grin.

Byron touched a hand to his muddled head. He had no clue what Estelle was hinting at. "Maybe Mas' Thomas just decided to go back home..."

"I doubt it. Henri said he left behind all his belongings and is still owed his last month's salary. I can see you're disappointed—just don't rush back to hefting a shovel. If this foolish war can get itself settled I'm planning to have a small cabaret in Panama City. When those fingers heal I could use your talent. I couldn't pay much right from the start but it would be a seed for the future."

Byron was about to break down and confess that he was only keeping the Fiddler's violin to take it back home to his mother, when Duvay's voice burst out from the saloon in a bilious tirade. Back inside, the red-faced popinjay had climbed off the table and was standing with his drunken arms outstretched, sputtering apologies for having just vomited all over the engineer's vest and trousers.

While Duvay stood venting his rage, Estelle hurried to take charge. She ordered one of her girls to try and find some clean trousers, then gave a thankful smile when Longers loomed carrying a basin of sudsy water. As she coaxed the Frenchman back to her private room, she hissed through gritted teeth for Byron to help Longers convey the rich dandy outside discreetly and see him onboard a carmietta.

With Byron's hand prodding his back and Longers' inflexible grip on his elbow the popinjay had no time to kick up a fuss before he found himself hustled outside to the sidewalk. When Longers left to track down a cab, the dandy stuck his glabrous face so close to Byron's nose that even in the dim gaslight he could see the faint scars from a childhood illness.

"*Où va-t-on?*" the popinjay demanded, his words slurring drunkenly. "*À la Madam Morales' seraglio—tout-de-suite!*"

Befuddled by the request and the liquor heavy on the dandy's breath, Byron drew back for air before mumbling an equivocal reply.

The large popinjay leaned most of his weight onto Byron's shoulder and started to hiccup. "*Nous sommes tous qui vont vous mourir ici savons—tu ne comprends—?*" he stuttered, tears of grief glistening in his red-rimmed blue eyes. "I burie-ed *ma fiancée et mon beau-père aujourd'hui...*" When Byron responded with more blank confusion the dandy fumbled to recover the words from his poorly-learned English. "Your mistress—she has girls, *non*?" he grumbled, sticking up a thumb to count between hiccups. "She promised me a negress—hic!...a mulatto—hic!...and a quadroon!" he cried, thrusting the three raised fingers in Byron's face. "If I am to die in zis infernal *tombeau* I wish to die a man—hic!...*tu comprends*?"

When Byron still said nothing, the popinjay angrily shoved him aside. Muttering lewd curses in French, he stumbled out to the middle of the street and after a slow and clumsy effort unbuttoned his pants then turned and aimed an arcing yellow stream back to the sidewalk. Byron dodged to avoid getting splashed in urine but before he could think of a way to get even, Longers had arrived with the cab and the dandy quickly rushed by and into the carriage.

Back at the rooming-house later that night, Byron shared his unpleasant new insights with Longers. "Miss Estelle has herself some biggish customers but how she makes her money is not too upright. I thought she had more class—"

The words were no sooner out of his mouth than he realized he should never have taken the liberty of criticizing Longers' adored Miss Estelle. For a moment it looked as if the giant was about to clout him flat, but instead he shook his fist in Byron's face and berated him for his gross ingratitude.

"Not too upright!" Longers scoffed. "You should thank your stars that woman has a soft spot for musicians. You think she takes in every Tomfool-Harry-and-Dick she sees in the street? And who the hell are you to be talking about class?!"

Byron absorbed the insult and tried to diffuse the sailor's temper by sharing his curious exchange with the sad young dandy.

"What puppy know 'bout anything?" Longers groused. "Don't go mixing up class and virtue. Virtue ain't for us to judge and preaching it don't make you kind and generous."

Byron realized that, whether out of love or simple admiration, Longers clearly had his own worth invested in Estelle Morales. It surprised him that for all his worldliness, Longers had despised hearing it mentioned that Estelle ran a popular whorehouse. Byron, however, drew a small consolation from knowing she provided sexual favors for men like the wealthy young popinjay. If nothing else, when he was forced to confess, she was sure to understand that sometimes the devil comes up with a bargain too rich for a humble man to resist.

Chapter 11

Its temper more lamb than lion, the volatile Chagres had been mercifully sleepy, allowing Henri Duvay the time to judge how best to rob the mighty river of its power. His team had traced the dormant channel south to where it cascaded three hundred feet to the buttresses of the railroad's latest bridge at Barbacoas. The hulking six-hundred-foot span, girded in stone and belted with wrought-iron, would be lucky to survive the next great flood when a million gallons of roaring water could rush downstream inside a heartbeat. To spare the canal such predictable destruction, Duvay's solution was to divert the Chagres' feeding tributaries to a manmade lake which ships entering from the Atlantic would then access by a flight of locks.

Thomas had seen the mission to its end, but every day more bitter loathing and a pining for revenge had been sharpening like a stalactite dripping guilty night tears for his dead discarded friend. When he had managed to sleep, he'd been beset by nightmares: a giant stalking cat with eyes of fire pouncing on a wandering child, the boy's frail limbs jerking helplessly as they snapped inside its monstrous crunching jaws; dark bleeding men with snake-like bodies begging for water while they thrashed in the mud which churned red and viscid the more they squirmed. More than once, he had thought of packing it in and sailing for home, then realized that for him to turn tail and leave now would only confirm his repulsive cowardice. If he was to retain a shred of self-respect he had to stay on and face Diego's mother. So when Duvay turned querulous and ordered him about, he had curbed his tongue, content to wait while he devised a way to get even.

Although he could scarcely remember having ever been content, he had never felt lonely. Yet here he was, feeling strangely abandoned inside his mentor's commodious residence. Exhilarated by his findings, Henri had left for Panama City immediately after their return and Monique was still off enjoying her first vacation. As Thomas reclined in the soft wicker bed, the touch of the morning breeze wafting through the French windows added to his melancholy. "Admit it, Mister Crusoe," he muttered, pushing aside the gauzy white netting that had granted his first night free of biting insects in many weeks, "you're a fraud."

That he was lying here in ease while Diego lay dead disgraced him to his core. Telling himself he'd come back to Christophe-Colomb because of Genevieve only inflamed similar feelings. The cold truth was he had already failed his promise to live like other hardworking men. He'd gone soft. Worse yet, he had traded on his father's reputation.

He had been battling deep self-doubt ever since Diego had shared his ugly rumor. The fact that he had frozen when he was called to act bravely had all but killed his swashbuckling image. It still pained him in the extreme that Diego had let stand, even for a laughing moment, the nasty lie that he was Henri's little invert. He kept reflecting upon the times he and Duvay had shared an evening out together and wondered who could have conceived such a scurrilous notion. He racked his memory, searching for some impure or effeminate gesture he'd seen from his mentor. The only spark for the slander he could think of was that Henri was in his forties and still unmarried, yet showed no taste for Colón's 'American' ladies.

Certainly, Thomas mused in his mentor's defense, that doesn't prove anything. A man in Henri's position would not care to frequent some Bottle Alley trollop. In fact, his most remarkable memory of Henri's behavior towards a woman seemed to disprove the rumor. The company had insisted they attend a champagne reception for the railroad's new Yankee superintendent and whether to annoy the director he referred to as de Lesseps' toy poodle, or for his own amusement, Henri had gone about charming the honoree's wife. Duvay had captivated that beautiful young woman so completely that her poor husband had spent the entire afternoon dragging her back from the Frenchman's side. He smiled, recalling how Henri had the superintendent's wife hanging on his every word as he described a night at Paris' *Les Folies Trévise* in lurid detail, knowing full well the American penchant for deriding French morals. Yet Thomas realized now, more than anything, he hated to think he'd ever been foolish enough to trust his mentor's affections.

Exhausted from his grief-filled labors, he could not drum up the will to climb from the bed and get dressed just to spend the day indoors poring over Duvay's insipid numbers. Sulking, he lay back and closed his eyes, deciding that if anyone asked he would say he'd taken ill. He pictured being back with Genevieve hoping to slip into a comforting dream. He imagined her on his lap softly nuzzling his neck until her lips became fangs and in her place the squirming bushmaster had latched to his throat. A voice bawled *'¡mijo!—¡mijo!'* and he saw a dark-haired woman clutch her chest and collapse into sobs. He pressed it from his mind but the vision returned each time he started drifting to sleep. He began to wonder if he'd gone mad. Finally he threw off the covers and raced downstairs for some water. As he leaned on the kitchen table and downed a second glass he was hot and shivering. He panicked, thinking it was a relapse of fever. But as the cool water soothed his throat his pulse quickly slowed and he no longer felt flushed.

The rest of the day passed by in a fog as he lay in a listless state, trapped between slumber and wakefulness. When the next morning found him dragging about aimlessly, he knew he would never have another decent night's sleep or stomach a full meal while Diego persisted in that unworthy grave. In the past, overconfidence would have led him to believe that retrieving a six-foot corpse on his own was no real challenge. Being humbled had left him wiser. He made up his mind to stop in Gatun Village and hire on help. After downing an egg with a cup of warm tea he left for the station, deciding he would stop in Colón to buy a light shovel and some canvas to wrap the body.

As he left the store with his purchases strapped to his back, Thomas noticed there were federal troops milling at every corner. The handful of people he passed on the street wore strained expressions, their gaze aimed blankly ahead as if determined to block out the ominous armed presence. Relieved to hear the bell begin to clank to alert the departure of his ten o'clock train he shoved the added anxiety from his mind and hurried on board.

They had barely stopped picking up speed when the tension cropped back up as the brakeman locked his wheels, bringing the train to a sharp screeching halt. Thomas sprang from his seat and joined the other passengers who had jumped up nervously to stare through the car's smoked-glass windows. The racket from grinding metal and gushing steam died out and inside the compartment singing voices were heard advancing behind a dirge of flute and drum. Thomas quickly lowered his window and sticking out his neck saw an ancient locomotive trudging slowly across their path dragging a short dark train fluttering with brightly colored streamers. Rolling by last was an open flat-car, its honored bier decked with garlands, shielded from the sun by a blazing white canopy.

Next came the thirty-odd mourners marching solemnly behind, their melodious voices uniquely attuned between grief and celebration. As they passed close by, Thomas saw the depth of his ancestors' burdens carved in the black perspiring faces. Although he was willing to concede that these moving processions provided a feast for the ear and eye, they had become so commonplace he found their affect on him greatly diminished. There was something pathetic about these men all scrubbed and polished in their Sunday suits and borrowed shoes, the women in hats and bright mended gloves not quite matching their calico dresses. It was as though living had become a glum submission, a mere preamble to the liberty of dying.

The pageantry passed on by and as the flamboyant funeral train started its slow chug for Monkey Hill cemetery, the motorman blew his whistle with a long respectful toot and the brakeman released his pins and shunted them onwards. With the engine throttle full out to make up for lost time, the train covered the eight miles left to Gatun in under twenty minutes. Descending to the platform with his bundle, Thomas glanced across the tracks and was discouraged to see the sprawling settlement beyond the river showing scarce activity.

He went to speak with the wrinkled old woman he'd glimpsed on a bench outside the station fanning at some fat stubborn flies. As he came closer he saw that she was guarding a stand with loaves of the local micha bread and a pot of dark brown honey. His lost appetite beckoning, he paid for a slice with honey and while she readied her long serrated knife explained that he was in the village in search of a guide.

There are no burros, the old woman replied pertly in Spanish, flashing away an eager fly as she pried the wax lid from the jar of honey. "Two soldiers came by early this morning and bought the last ones anyone could spare." She handed Thomas a hunk of the sweetened bread spread thick with honey then glanced towards the heavens. "Thanks to the Lord," she said, her wrinkled hands clasped prayerfully, "the good young people were already on their way to town to sell the new oranges. Our lazy rascals prefer to stay and sleep so the soldiers came and took them—"

"Against their will?"

The old woman shrugged. "Not once the soldiers promised them money. *¡Estúpidos!*—they think they're gonna be better off if there's war."

"So there isn't anyone left who can help me?" asked Thomas, greedily chewing the gooey sweet bread.

"*Pide Horace. El es el hermano de mi marido muerto.*" The old woman pointed across the river to the squatter settlement saying he could speak to her brother-in-law who was home making sure his son stayed inside and was not tempted to join the other ignoramuses. "I told him he needn't worry about that meager boy of his being killed. If it turns to any real fighting, he'll be the first to turn tail and run. You just go and ask for Horace—he knows this jungle better than a white-faced monkey."

Thanking her, Thomas gobbled the last of his bread, surprised it had taken this long for him to realize he was ravenous, then hurried to the footbridge spanning the river to the village. He called to a naked little boy spinning bottle-caps on a hard dirt path and asked if he could tell him where to find *Señor* Horace. Giving Thomas an old man's serious look, the boy aimed a finger towards a plank board shack set back from the dwellings along the village's central lane. As he left the boy and approached the hut, Thomas glimpsed what he'd come to recognize as one of Panama's Jamaican old-timers. The man was standing at his door, waving a corn-cob pipe to press a point to a feather-thin chap slouching just inside. Thomas hailed to Horace cordially and greeted the reedy fellow as his son even though the "young rascal" was clearly on the long side of thirty. Neither man appeared all that fit, but after listening to his story old Horace insisted that renting a *cayuco* was a waste of Thomas' money. Quickly pocketing his pipe and dragging on a hat to cover his head of white wool hair, the old man claimed that for a 'so-so extra hour' he knew a way they could carry the body back on foot and bypass the river and those nasty crocodiles altogether.

What the shrewd old goat had failed to mention when Thomas agreed to add two more dollars to their fee, was that the first half hour they'd be in mud up to their knees plodding through swamp on the lookout for snakes. Thomas breathed in happily to see them back on solid ground as the forest welcomed them with an embroidered veil made of white and yellow orchids shaped like stars and rows of wild hibiscus the shade of blood-red oranges. Every so often the path would flame with crimson-tipped heliconias as the thickets grew dense and the onerous heat and filtered sunshine both withdrew. In the shaded grove sprang airy epiphytes and bearded lichen above the lush green ferns sprayed at the feet of the mighty *cedro espinos*.

A brisk wave of redemption washed over Thomas as he found his way back to the canebrake. As the three of them stepped from the shelter of the hundred-foot tall trees, Thomas screened his eyes from the sudden sunlight and then stumbled to a sinking halt. He barely felt the featherweight's light tug on his shoulder as his blood ran to ice. Dark languorous wings glided patiently around the sky.

"Coyotes," the old timer murmured, spotting the plundered grave specked with dried blood and tissue.

Thomas stood rooted, barely breathing as his guides picked out a grisly trail leading to a cotton-silk tree where Horace knelt and retrieved half of a finger and a severed ear.

"It's a wonder they left any of his parts them at-all!" the son blurted out thoughtlessly, earning a quick wallop across the mouth from his father as Thomas staggered over.

"Something's not right 'bout this," Horace muttered, rubbing the thin white stubble on his chin after scouting the nearby thicket and finding part of a hand. "Something—or somebody drove off whatever animal was feasting on your friend because they dropped his parts piece-piece all over..." The old timer raised his soft duck hat and scratched his head. "So what happ'n to the rest of the body—and the clothes him was wearin'? I doubt you did bury him naked..."

An hour's search yielded nothing but part of a fibula gnawed to bone and one of Diego's rubber boots. Only after they returned did Thomas notice that a severed vine with magenta and white orchids sat a few feet off from the pilfered grave. The way the flowers lay arranged gave the hint of human touch. He pointed the men to the affecting display. "Diego told me the jungle isn't what we perceive—that there can be tribes living right nearby—only they stay hidden so we can't see them."

"You don't want to go mess with them forest people," the featherweight piped up, his black eyes drawing wide. "Could be those savages decide to dig him up and eat him!"

"Shut your foolishness about savages!" Horace snapped angrily, threatening his son with another hard smack. "I don't know who put that there ignorance in his head—not me!" he apologized to Thomas. "Your buddy was right but the forest people don't always mind showing themself to folks like us. Back in the day when the railroad money finish, a lot of us was out here foraging to keep from starving. The Wuonaan people would bring food and give us. It was the Spanish they didn't want to mix with."

"You think you could find your way to their village?" Thomas asked him hopefully. "I don't want to have to face Diego's mother with just his ear and part of a leg bone."

The old timer shook his head. "I wouldn't bother. Them not gonna give yuh back his body once they done pure it. And I can't see to blame them—I wouldn't want your friend to come haunt me neither..." Horace stopped and put a shriveled hand on Thomas' shoulder. "You were probably right about those flowers beyond his grave. If the Wuonaan laid your buddy down there to pray over him, he's at peace. Let it be—just trust the rest to God."

Chapter 12

"Psst!—you!—¡*mozo!*—over here!"

Byron pondered whether he should set down the heavy crate and confront whomever was hailing him from a Bottle Alley stall or just keep moving. The sun was out, so most thieves, like the women who sold their used-up bodies here in the masking moonlight, would be somewhere sleeping. But Longers had made a point of telling him that Colón tended to turn good men into desperate gamblers. And desperate men were known to do desperate things—even in daylight.

"Back here, fiddler! Just a word—"

The stranger's startling solicitation heightened Byron's dismay. Apparently Estelle was not the only one in town to mistake him for Johnny Fingers. He wondered if by taking his friend's violin into his safekeeping he had been bonded to the Fiddler's spirit. The thought both pleased and upset him. He would give his eye-teeth to play like Johnny but he could not go on living such an obvious lie. When no one came out of any of the recessed stalls, he shifted his grip on the case of bottled whiskey and decided to keep on going.

"You're late coming to work this morning." The stranger's voice sounded vaguely accusing. "I had to stand here out of sight—"

The brown-skinned man in the check-patterned suit stepped out from the alley stall and blocked Byron's path.

"Let me pass! I don't need any more trouble!" Byron said firmly, recognizing the tall Haitian.

"Keep it down, *mon brave*! The *federales* are like lice these days—they're pestering us everywhere we turn!"

"Nobody not botherin' me—that's why I'm not gettin' mixed up in any bad business," Byron stated bluntly. He had not been happy when Reynal and two others from his party showed up at the Bottle Alley tavern and urged him to attend their next meeting. Although he supported what he knew of their goals, he had come around to Longers' opinion that by pushing things so hard the fruit of their struggles would be forced-ripe and less lasting. "Maybe if it wasn't for reckless people like you, those soldiers wudden be here pestering people..."

The militant considered Byron with a pitying eye. "Man, they've really got you sold. I bet you came here full of ambition—look at you now—" he said, clucking his tongue, "a good little coolie for a Spanish harlot! And here Reynal thought you had some backbone..."

"Reynal doesn't know me!" Byron said resentfully. "I got backbone when I need it."

"That's more like it!" said the man, reaching out his hand. "I'm Pautrizelle—Anton Pautrizelle, at the people's service!"

"Nice to know—" Byron replied, ignoring the familiar gesture. He made a quick move to try and swerve by but was hampered by the carton of whisky. "Kindly let me pass!" he cried when Pautrizelle shunted him back towards the stall.

"I won't keep you long," the militant promised, coaxing the crate from Byron's tired arms and setting it on the ground crusted with bits of old rubber and splintered glass. "I want you to see what we just got through printing—" Pautrizelle handed Byron a pamphlet charging the Bogotá government with violating Colombia's Constitution and usurping Panama's rights. Below the words, which surprisingly were in English, an artist had sketched a bandit with bandoleers crossing his paunch and a blood-tipped dagger in his teeth. Beneath his heel, a prostrate woman shed tears onto a severed scroll labeled Statehood. "We need these posted across town but most of our members are being watched. Reynal thought you might help with the job. You could hide them in your fiddle-case. We can pay you..."

"Not a chance!" Byron cried, recoiling. "I told yuh a'ready—I want no part of trouble!"

"You don't get it, do you, my good fiddler? You're going to have to choose, *mon brave*. Trouble is about to find you...like it or not."

Byron shuddered inside as Estelle's warning came flooding back: 'you get caught up with that rabble and you'll end up sunk.' I should never have stopped at that stupid rally, he thought bitterly.

"This got nuttin' to do wid me!"

"That's where you're wrong, *mon jeune ami*, this has everything to do with you—*et moi aussi! Les blancs* bleed us, then make us pay for what they corrupted, and call it progress. Well, Mr. Prestàn is not corrupted—he believes in justice."

Pautrizelle's voice was calm and cultured. Byron was impressed that, despite his accent and cracked hands of a laborer, the Haitian's English was much more polished than his own.

"That's well and good but it's not my country."

"The reactionaries won't care where you come from—either you'll be with us or against us. Would you want to take a bullet for your oppressor?"

"They can't force me to fight—I'm a British subject, by law."

Pautrizelle assumed the discouraged look of a doctor unable to convince his new patient that he was sick from taking snake-oil. "They don't believe in the Law, my friend," he muttered, shaking his head when Byron stooped to wrest back up the crate of liquor.

Heavy-booted strides were approaching and Pautrizelle turned to dart a quick peek up the alley. "*Federales*—better let them go by!" he whispered, ducking back inside the stall.

His arms again aching from the weight of a dozen liters of whiskey, Byron ignored him and moved to be on his way.

"I said hold it!" Pautrizelle lifted the edge of his light checked coat and revealed a large revolver.

Byron froze as he saw the gun then relaxed, knowing Pautrizelle was not going to shoot him with troops from the Colombian guard just yards away. "You can stay—me not afraid—" he said with a haughty grin, hitting back for the slight about him lacking backbone.

Backing out into the alley, Byron saw the two soldiers were almost level with the stall. They glared at him then at the case in his arms labeled Sour Mash Tennessee Whiskey. Steadying the long rifles slung on their shoulders, the soldiers stepped briskly towards him, barking in Spanish for him to stand where he was. They wore the restless looks of men who felt they deserved more of life's pleasures and made up for the deficit by aggrandizing the joyful brutishness bestowed by a military uniform. They set about questioning Byron roughly and he soon surmised that they suspected him of stealing the whiskey.

Neither soldier seemed to understand his English and Byron was worried that they were about to haul him off to jail when he noticed Pautrizelle sidling out of the streetwalkers' stall with his felt hat slanted low. He looked quickly for the big revolver and breathed more easily seeing it safely out of sight.

Pautrizelle bowed to the soldiers so deeply he was practically groveling at their feet. He vouched for Byron in Spanish, his proud voice oily in its servile disguise. He straightened up and promptly made an off-color joke about a '*puta rico*' that Byron guessed was at his expense when the soldiers both leered at him and winked. The three men traded a few more racy quips then one of the soldiers pointed for Byron to set down the crate of whiskey and with a wink at the simpering Haitian casually bent and helped himself to two of the bottles.

Byron yelled, "hey!" seeing him pass a bottle to his partner, but the soldier ignored him. Grinning at their loot, they each gave Pautrizelle a tap on his shoulder then strolled off, chuckling.

"You—! You told them they could take that whisky!" Byron stormed when the soldiers were out of earshot. "Who the hell gave you permission?"

The tall Haitian gazed at him coolly. "Would you rather have spent the night in the calaboose and let them have the whole dozen?"

"That would be robbery!"

"Exactly."

"That was Miss Estelle's good whiskey! What mi supposed to tell her?"

"Tell the harlot she was lucky—it would have cost her a lot more to bail you out and pay the magistrate."

"Then I guess I should thank yuh...mi suppose..." Byron mumbled, not sure if he believed him.

"I understand the fix you're in," said Pautrizelle, his proud tone back but stripped of its ridicule, "you're dead broke but tired of shoveling, so the hussy has you over a barrel." He folded one of the large leaflets and stuffed it in Byron's shirt pocket. "Take this and think it over—there's an address on the back when you come to your senses. This is a lawless country—*Señor* Prestàn wants to change that." The militant took a long look at Byron's pained face then gave a snicker. "He doesn't want to see you fellows stay here and die of *melancholía*."

Pautrizelle disappeared down the alley and Byron stood brooding about the lost whiskey and this mysterious disease the Haitian claimed he might die from. Each time he ran into one of these radicals he ended up wondering how much of what they said he should believe. Sure, the soldiers were pretty hostile but who could blame them when over half of the town resented them being here. He decided Pautrizelle could think what he wanted. Since he'd met Miss

Estelle he'd been living better than chaps who had to work five times harder. And though she might not be paying him, she had bought him a new pair of shoes and dungarees so he'd look respectable on the rare nights he was asked to help at the Last Frontier. Were it not for his lack of savings, he would say life had never looked better.

When he was through telling Theresa how he'd managed to lose two bottles of Estelle's best whiskey walking between her two taverns Byron asked her about Pautrizelle's strange parting remark.

"*La melancholía...*" the stately hostess echoed, expelling a dubious breath. "This radical who stopped you—was he Chinese?"

Byron shook his head. "No. He seems to have been here for donkey's years but I believe him come from Haiti—"

Theresa cut him off coldly. "So it's just by chance he brought it up and now you decided to ask me what I know about *melancholía?*"

Theresa had been with Estelle the longest of all her girls, and was a notoriously poor sleeper, so she'd been the natural choice to take over running the Bottle Alley *cantina*. Byron would have been shocked to know that the slender cocoa-dark hostess with the exotically turned-up eyes and an ingenue's pert breasts was years older than her madam. What did not surprise him, once he'd gotten to know her, was that Theresa was as happy managing inventory and tending bar as she was miserable with her old profession. She was quick to boast that she had taught herself to write and reckon and Byron suspected Theresa's erratic flights of temper stemmed from the fact that she had never found the nerve to try and follow in Estelle's entrepreneurial footsteps.

"Sorry, Miss T—it was just a harmless question..." said Byron, glad to forget it and let his crazy day start over peacefully.

"Do you have more harmless questions to go along with your harmless lies?"

Her reproach made Byron's heart drop. Unlike Estelle, who had expressed annoyed surprise at his clumsy fingers, Theresa had quietly replaced the glassware that had ended up broken while he learned to maneuver inside a crowded *cantina*. Depressed after his latest attempt to see Thomas had again been fruitless, he had told Theresa about his secret shame—how he'd never expected in a hundred years she'd become his employer and he was tired of living with the daily dread of being caught out. He had been relieved when Theresa sounded sympathetic, calling it a sweet little dilemma. But she had advised him against telling Estelle the truth until he had been around long enough to convince her of his true character.

"Estelle and I have one thing in common," Theresa went on now in her sudden dry huff, "we don't waste time crying over men who lie to us just for fun!"

"What would make mi want to lie 'bout it? I never even did know a person could get a sickness call *melancholía*. People can sure act strange in this country sometime..." Byron grumbled, turning towards the washroom to change into his work-clothes and apron.

Her shortness spent, Theresa called him back and asked him to hand her up four of the bottles from the case of special holiday whiskey. "Never mind what I just said—it was an old sore talking," she explained as she reached to put the bottles on prominent display on the shelf of liquor in back of the counter. "I knew you had an honest nature the day you brought me that money you'd saved to pay for those broken glasses. I just don't trust anything coming from the mouths of these scheming politicos—" she said, turning back and smiling down at Byron.

The bar had not yet opened for customers and, suddenly in the mood to talk, Theresa had him put off sweeping the floor to come and sit with her in the back. She apologized for her fit of temper but said he had brought back some ugly memories and that was saying a lot for a girl who'd spent her entire life living in a brothel.

"I kept only two things from my childhood—" she told Byron, her eyes softening, "a little straw doll and a red and yellow spinning top. They were gifts from my father—my mother said he made them both himself. I never got to ask him—he died just months after I was born.

"For years all my mother would say was that his name was Huan Yue and he had come here to work on the railroad. She would never talk about what happened. When I got older, I asked a woman in our house who said my father was one of the Chinese opium heads who'd committed suicide. I asked my mother if it was true my father had hung himself because the railroad refused to give him more opium and she went crazy and slapped my face." Theresa stopped and stared at Byron fiercely. "It was the last time I let anyone hit me. After that she cried and said the other girls were all jealous vipers because Huan Yue had been tall and good-looking and was saving up money to marry her. She said he would never have killed himself—that he only took a little opium to keep from getting sick. She claimed if anything it was the railroad that killed my father. I was never sure if I should believe her. The year she died I learned that the railroad had promised to provide those coolies with opium medicine as part of their contracts." Theresa rose proudly to her stately height. "Everybody in this country loves to look down on the Chinese—but no one can convince me that a thousand men decided to kill themselves because they were homesick—because of *la melancholía.*"

She stamped off to prepare and open the *cantina.* As he dusted off the tables, Byron wondered if Pautrizelle really thought that things in this country might get so bad men like him would be tempted to take their own life. A dark thought took shape in his reflections—what if Johnny had been sick but still alive when they dumped him over that mountainside? He shoved back the notion, finding its horror too terrible to contemplate. He was not sure why Pautrizelle wanted him to know about *la melancholía* but if the Chinese he'd seen in Panama were any example, being scorned and belittled did not rule out becoming better off—even respectable.

Chapter 13

THOMAS DID NOT RELISH the prospect of facing Diego's mother. He could not bring her the few measly parts they'd recovered and then try to explain why he had failed his friend. Instead, he went to see his barber who'd grown exceedingly rich midnighting as an undertaker and asked that Diego's remains be sealed in his finest mahogany coffin. From there he went to the hospital and waited for Genevieve to come off duty. He reasoned that if *Señora* Valladares was anything like his own mother, his only hope of dissuading her from wanting to peek inside the casket would be to somehow convince her the seal had already been blessed and made sacrosanct.

He met with Genevieve briefly in the waiting-room lobby where they agreed to reunite a half hour later on the sheltered strand not far from the hospice garden. At the beach, he told her about the murderous snake and the hasty makeshift grave then implored her to go with him to Diego's home in Cocle Province. She immediately said no, she could not possibly travel such a distance and forsake her duties—no—not even for a day. When more fervid pleading failed to change her mind, he got to the reason behind his asking.

"Please Genie—I fear for *Señora* Valladares if she sees what was done to his body," he said, encouraging the new quaver in his voice to underscore his torment. "I was tempted to dig a deeper hole and put him back in the ground where I'd left him—but that seemed too heartless. The poor woman deserves something of her son to cry over. I thought, maybe if she believes you're a nun you'd be able to persuade her the coffin has been prayed over and that the seal should not be broken."

Genevieve glared at him wrathfully. "Have you no scruples? You want me to help you deceive a grieving mother and transgress my oath in the offing? This is too much, Thomas," she said, looking down at the rust-colored sand and shaking her head, "—even for you!"

Thomas had anticipated her resistance but over the course of the year, as their relationship became more and more intimate, he had discovered a way past her defenses: he would throw back her own words.

"I'm not asking you to lie—but did you not once say it's better to be merciful than to blindly obey?"

The reminder drew Genevieve's quick withering glance and she stormed off in silence. He might have felt worse, knowing he was rubbing her sorest spot, had he not overheard Mother Agnes observe that her novice's young spirit seemed too chafed to rest easily inside the cloister. When Genevieve kept walking without looking back, he rushed to catch her up.

"Forgive me, Genie," he said, tugging her by the arm, "I seem to have adopted Henri's callousness. To think I'd been growing fond of him! I swear there's a timepiece in that man's chest in place of a heart—of course, knowing Henri, he would take it as a compliment if you suggested he was utterly devoid of human sentiments..."

Genevieve turned to face him then went to perch on a dying beach-tree's sinuous bared roots. She had still not said a word as he came and sat beside her. Thomas feared that his tack had failed, then saw the thoughtful furrows on her brow and dared to hope that perhaps he had struck the right nerve after all.

"Are there not times when it is more charitable to lie?" he coaxed her, convinced that she was rethinking her answer. "Take a dying man for instance—does he really need to hear the truth? Is it so important to be impeccably honest even if it causes someone more unhappiness? For years my mother lied and pretended Samuel Judah was not my real father—" Thomas stopped and stared angrily into the distance. "Finally my Aunt Mary told me why the snake refused to marry her—it was because of me. I think my father only granted me his name so he could get back in my mother's bed after he'd jilted her. Don't get me wrong—I adore my Aunt Mary—but I wish she'd never told me I had such a dastard for a father."

Genevieve drew his hand and held it gently in hers. "Believe me, I know the emptiness you carry around. There is no greater void than to feel oppressed by one's own blood...but had your aunt not told you the truth, you were bound to wonder and eventually blame your poor mother. I understand why she wanted to shield you, but we must be careful about falling into deceits too glibly. Anyway," she said, her voice dropped low as the two of them joined to stare at the thorny marsh out in the bay, "the truth is what heals us in the end..."

"Can you accept this truth?" Thomas asked, switching his gaze to look at her deeply. "I've changed—and so have you. Genie...I want us to be—"

She put her palm to his lips and stopped him before he could go further. "You Judahs certainly know how to beguile a poor weak girl," she teased him, only half-jokingly. "Is what you're feeling at this moment love or a guilty conscience?"

"I'm ashamed of nothing except, perhaps, my own cowardice..." he said, his voice wilting slightly. Sensing her sympathies had at last been aroused, he decided to share the vision that still haunted him. He described seeing Diego's mother, her face warped from terror as she tears her hair, wailing madly before she falls into a swoon.

"You poor dear—how awful!" Genevieve caressed Thomas' arm as he finished telling her what they'd found near the grave in graphic detail.

"I mean, how does one show up with part of a leg and half an ear?" he asked miserably.

"I see now why you're afraid to face her...and she has no other children?"

Thomas shook his head. "Diego's father died while he was an infant. He was her one and only—"

Genevieve sat quiet for a moment, chewing her lip. "I take it she's Catholic..."

"I'm fairly certain."

"Could we see her and be back the same day?"

"Sure..." he said vaguely, not wanting to press her by sounding too hopeful.

"All right," Genevieve murmured, rising from the twining mangrove. "I'll come. It will be easier on the poor woman if a believer is with you."

Mother Agnes was fully in favor of her young nurse taking a day to go and comfort a grieving mother. "You apply yourself so intensely for these patients, my dear. I often worry you'll drive yourself sick. Yes, a break and a bit of crisp country air might be just the tonic!"

Since she had promised to be gone just for the day Genevieve resented it when Mother Agnes went on to express her hope that she would traveling with a suitable escort. *Les Soeurs de La Charité* were not cloistered but tasked with performing good works, so she never understood why no one thought twice about a priest journeying on his own yet sisters had to roam in pairs. It vexed her to have to pretend with Mother Agnes, knowing the mother superior's knack for spotting a lie, but she felt constrained to mention she was making the trip to

El Coco with Thomas Judah. In the interests of time and prudence, Genevieve insisted that she and Thomas catch the five A.M. express to Panama City and ride in separate compartments. Reuniting outside of the station after crossing the isthmus in just over two hours, they made it to the coach-line terminus and the battered *diligencia* just as the driver was checking the straps on his two bay mules. He took one glance at Genevieve in her novice habit and rushed to re-open the stagecoach door, firmly refusing to accept the money that Thomas presented for the fare to Penonomé.

"*¡Monja bella!—oraciones para Placido*—you light a candle for Placido, *si*?" said the driver, removing his grimy hat and bowing to the nurse's sandaled feet when she tried to force him to take the two piasters. Afraid he might suddenly bend down and kiss her toes, Genevieve colored with embarrassment and quietly thanked him, promising she would do as he asked.

As she and Thomas climbed aboard the hulking *diligencia,* an elegant woman inside crossed herself and murmured Genevieve a solemn greeting while nudging her young daughter to sit back close beside her so that 'the nun and young padre' could have seats together.

"Why are you blushing?" Thomas whispered impishly in English near Genevieve's ear.

"Because I'm not worthy...not yet..."

"Don't be so rigid! It's not as if you're harming anyone."

"*Tu ne comprends pas*—you don't understand! Can we please not talk about this now?" Genevieve hissed, peeking at the five other passengers to see if they were being listened to then quickly looking away when the small swarthy man seated directly across her way lifted the brown fedora on his head with a tiny smirk.

From the pace he pressed his mules their driver did not appear to share Genevieve's mounting concern that the next crater in the road would see his creaking old *diligencia* go crashing to its splintered end. At times it seemed the highway was no more than a husbanded footpath that the recent rains had gifted generously with fair-sized rocks to give its travelers some good shuddering jolts. Two and a half back-wrenching hours later saw their first merciful stop at Chorrera.

"How much farther?" Genevieve asked as they got off to stretch their legs at the open-air station outside the village square.

"It shouldn't be much longer," he assured her, though in fact he had no idea.

"I hope not—I promised I'd be back by evening. The train back to Colón won't be running past the ten o'clock curfew."

"Mother Agnes gave you her permission so she obviously trusts you. Ah, look—" Thomas pointed to the coachman returning from an iron-roofed *pulperia* nearby carrying two large wooden buckets. One was filled with feed, the other slopping with water for his mules. "Maybe they have something for humans. I'll see what I can rustle..." he said, hurrying off.

He was almost at the roadside market when he saw three rough-looking *lanceros* come swaggering out. They were blabbering loudly and kept having to balance the old blunderbusses slung clumsily across their backs as they passed around a large bottle of beer. 'So, Colón is not the only town where the government is calling out the thugs,' he thought dryly, recalling the time he'd been stopped by a couple of uniformed ruffians on his way back from seeing Genevieve. They were drunk and it was after curfew so he'd felt lucky when the four piasters in his pocket had been enough to keep them from bashing his brains in.

Thomas steeled himself, prepared for a hassle as he neared the boisterous conscripts who clearly seemed excited by their new perquisites. There was nothing more profitable than a war for the morally deficient. As he approached the *pulperia,* one of the bearded young mercenaries glanced past his shoulder to where Genevieve stood with the sun gleaming on her white winged habit and hurried to hide the bottle of beer behind his back. He bowed to Thomas who nodded back with solemn piety, restraining a grin when the other *lanceros* stepped quickly out of his way, mumbling *buenas dias, padre.*

"They had *pipa* juice!" Thomas announced triumphantly, as he rejoined Genevieve carrying two bamboo cups filled with water and a jar of filmy white liquid. "And they let me have the two mugs for free! I have to say one gets reverent treatment traveling with a nun."

"You're incorrigible—taking advantage of people's credulousness! And for the last time—I'm not a nun!"

"And my heart leaps with hope to hear you say it!" Thomas retorted happily.

Back on board, the old Indian woman who'd spent the first leg drowsing over her basket of stacked straw hats sat snoring with her thin neck bent at an awkward-looking angle.

"Has she been sitting there like that the whole time we've been stopped?" Genevieve murmured anxiously. "I hope she's not taken ill!—do you think I should wake her?"

"Why? She decided to stay out of the sun and go on with her nap. She is obviously a vendor and, no doubt used to doing a lot of traveling."

"How can you be so sure?"

"Because those items on her lap that are so popular with the *gringos* may be called Panama hats but they are not made here, or anywhere else in these Disunited States of Colombia for that matter. They come from Ecuador and my guess from the gold necklace around her neck and coral bracelets on her arm is that she does too—or travels there frequently. Look, anyone who can calmly nod off on these seats while their bones are being rattled like maracas has probably made the trip a dozen times."

Genevieve seemed less than assured as she continued to stare at the dozing old woman.

"That face!" she whispered in a breathy voice. "It's been haunting me since we came on board. Her skin looks scarcely wrinkled. And see how her jaw draws down to that dainty chin? If she was a shade darker she could be my Nana Binta..."

"Your Nana Binta...? Was that your grandmama?

"No—she was even dearer to me—" she replied inscrutably. "My Nana Binta was small and slight—just like this woman—but she was strong and full of life—" Wetness started to glisten in Genevieve's eyes as she watched the sleeping woman's cheeks dimple with each loud breath puffed from her delicate mouth. "Nana used the last of her strength to make sure I'd be safe—then she passed away..."

"It's not fair, you know—" Thomas chided as Genevieve's voice trailed off. "I've told you about myself and my father's family—yet I'm left to guess what on earth could make you suddenly look gray as a ghost—"

For an instant, Genevieve's semblance revealed the terrors of a victimized child then she closed her eyes for a long deep breath and it was gone. She glanced to see if the small swarthy man who'd eyed them with a smirk was about to reboard but saw that he and the mother and child were outside awaiting other transport. She breathed out to relax then with one eye on the old woman's breathing, attempted to explain her sudden grip of panic.

"Nana Binta was part of my mother's family from before my mother was even born," she said, feeling free to speak when no new passengers appeared inside the *diligencia* for the next leg of their journey. "She'd been kidnapped from her home in Senegal and sold as a slave when she was eleven. Curious—that was the age I was when mother died—" Genevieve's voice again hung mid-thought as if she had come to a block in her memory. "From before I can remember, Nana Binta ran our household. If my brother or I were hurt we went to Nana Binta—if we'd gotten into mischief she was the one who punished us—but never harshly. She would have us help her with her chores or make us sit and read a book. I learned more helping Nana in her kitchen than from any of my tutors."

"I thought you said you grew up in a convent?"

"That was later. I was already ten when Father had us move from Guadeloupe to a ranch outside Cartagena. My mother and my brother both ended up getting scarlet fever—they died six months later. There were no homes near our ranch and we were new to Colombia so we knew very few people. Nana Binta must have weighed no more than ninety pounds and she was long past sixty but she managed to hitch up one of our mules and drive the thirty miles to the city so I'd be safe in the convent."

"But what about your father? Why didn't he look after you after your mother died?"

Genevieve pressed her lips white and she again went pale before glancing away. "My father did not want to go on living if he couldn't be with his beautiful wife..." Her tone turned brittle. "I thank God every night for my Nana—she was all I had left..."

Thomas was about to ask what she meant about her father when the Indian woman opened her eyes and, struck by Genevieve's moist gaze, slowly cheered her with a soft warm smile. "*No te preocupes, hija de Crista. La abuela necesita descansar.*"

"See—I told you not to fret—" said Thomas after they'd all exchanged greetings and Genevieve appeared to recover her practiced calm. "She only needed some rest."

"*¿Quieres un sombrero de Panamá, joven padre?*—would you like a Panama hat, young father?" the old Indian woman asked, lifting a particularly elegant example from her stack, its creased bell crown trimmed with thin black ribbon. "It's a Montecristi...real *toquilla*—see?" She crushed the straw hat in her hand then watched as it popped back perfectly in shape.

"Sorry," Thomas replied solemnly, "it's very handsome, *madre*, just not for today."

The old Indian quietly considered Genevieve's tight face then nodded knowingly. "*Entendido. No es un día alegre—debemos esperar hasta mañana.* I understand—it is not a joyful day—we must wait for the morrow when the sun always rises."

It would be three more stops and several hours later before the *diligencia* arrived in Penonomé having acquired two fresh mules and three new passengers whose worshipful salutations promptly nudged Genevieve back into silence. By the time they had transferred to the hack that would take them the last two miles to Diego's, it was going on four o'clock.

"We'll never make it back in a day," Genevieve complained as they finally arrived at the Valladares' gate. A dog whimpered from somewhere in back as they ventured in and passed through the small villa's vegetable garden. "But you knew it all along, didn't you?" she hissed accusingly, as Thomas rang the tiny rusted bell hanging from a string outside the front door. "To think anyone could mistake such a reprobate for a priest!"

"Chastise me as you like—I am willing to bear the scars. You see, someone once told me doing a kindness is always worth the trouble. But then, perhaps the arduousness of the trip has left you not yourself..." he added slyly, drawing Genevieve's husky laugh.

"That's your cunning art, Thomas Judah!—you know how to charm and exasperate me all at the same time. But you're right," she muttered quickly, hearing Diego's mother arriving to answer her door, "this is one transgression I may be forgiven."

Thomas' other shrewd guess proved equally perceptive. Genevieve's presence in her novitiate's robe appeared to restrain the poor mother's hair-pulling anguish as with stops and starts Thomas finally explained how Diego had died and how it happened that his body had been left in the jungle.

"But he's been retrieved and has a lovely coffin...unfortunately there was a mishap in between...we are missing some remains..."

Señora Valladares had them sitting on her either side on her drawing-room couch after insisting they both have a cold refreshing drink made from the guanabana in her front garden. She was a sturdy handsome woman who seemed to bear her misfortunes with a peasant's grace but hearing this, she stared at Thomas with eyes like saucers.

"Missing—? *¡Dios mio!* You put my son in a casket with parts of him missing? Why—how much is he missing?"

When her lips began to tremble, Thomas shot a pleading glance to Genevieve who nodded back firmly for him to continue. Before she had agreed, Genevieve had made it clear that they were to tell the truth, saying it was better not to try and gloss things over and have her find them out later as liars, "—besides, she is his mother—she deserves to know."

With more agonized halts and stammers Thomas explained that it appeared the interim grave had been discovered by coyotes but there was a good chance most of Diego's body had been rescued by an Indian tribe and buried respectfully.

Señora Valladares had been hanging on his words, catching herself each time she put her hands to head ready to tug at her loosely combed black hair. Finally, she could contain herself no longer. She seized Thomas fiercely by his forearms. How, she cried, a flash of fury breaking through her sorrow, was her son's pure Christian soul to join his Maker when his body had been defiled by dogs and godless heretics?

She began to weep and Thomas could only sit mum, seeing his awful premonition spring to life before his eyes. Then, just as he'd hoped, Genevieve rushed to his rescue.

"Let us not let our suffering cause your son's soul more ill, *señora*," she said, using her authoritative nurse's tone as she pried the mother's vise-like fingers from Thomas' forearms. Like many modest country homes, there was a small shrine to the Virgin Mother mounted in a corner of the *sala*. Softly, Genevieve urged them both from the sofa to kneel beside her at the miniature altar. She embraced Diego's mother around her shoulders and began chanting a prayer for the dead. Out in the yard, the whimpering dog lengthened his cries, as if singing along. With quaking fingers, *Señora* Valladares picked up her rosary from beneath the altar and Genevieve managed to ignore the dog's loud whines clear to the prayer's end and a recitation of the believer's creed.

"Your son is at rest, *señora*—trust in His Mercies. Come—" She coaxed up the weeping mother, still on her knees clutching her rosary. "Sit and hold my hand and let us share a moment in honor of Diego." As the words left her mouth, the dog made a last, long cry and fell silent.

Thomas struggled to find a few apt words in tribute but what little he was able to express was so intensely heartfelt, Diego's mother was moved to suspend her grief and comfort him.

"It's hard, losing a good friend when one is so young," she told him soothingly. "That poor dog—you hear how he howls? He knows. I had to chain up Pobrecito or he would have gone searching for his master. When you lose a friend it's like you lose a piece of your soul. It's uncanny—but you'd swear that dog knew the instant Diego was killed. Now he and I can only sit and sniff at our food. Why eat when there's no taste left in your mouth?"

Señora Valladares again broke into sobs and Genevieve once more alertly interceded. "*Señora*, I understand—your yoke must feel very heavy. If you'll allow me," she said, warming to her ecclesiastical role, "I'd like to share what helped me through the darkest time in my life. A young priest came to teach at our convent—we girls all cried when he left so quickly because he was kind and had the patience of a gentle saint. One day, I asked him why it was a person can do something terrible and be forgiven yet will burn in hell because he's so sorry for what he's done he wants to die. Father Rodrigo said that Jesus came so there would be no more hell full of demons—to assure us that despite our sins, even at death we are still God's children. He told me that it is for us to accept His forgiveness in heaven—"

"We'd like Diego to receive mass in the main cathedral," Thomas broke in, remembering the other purpose behind their visit. "I trust we have your permission to arrange it?"

Señora Valladares' eyes brightened for an instant then the light flickered out. "You have both been so kind—coming all this way. A funeral mass in the cathedral sounds very grand—but as you see," she said, waving a tired hand at her chintz-cloth tapestries and the room's simple bamboo furniture, "since my husband died we've had to live very humbly. My brother may be the acclaimed Victor Sosa but you would be surprised how little an explorer earns to risk his life. I cannot impose on him further—Victor has done enough..."

"You let me worry about the cost, *señora*," Thomas said boldly, realizing what was left to be done once he returned to Christophe-Colomb. "Diego will not be used and callously forgotten. Someone is going to pay for what he has done."

Chapter 14

New Year's Eve, 1884

Inside the Last Frontier the champagne corks are popping like pistols. Cackles of laughter cover the loud groans as the white-gloved croupier declares, *vingt-cinq, rouge* and primly places his marker. The losers shrug off their failings and double their stakes just in time. The wheel spins again and someone else chortles with joy as the ball takes a late fickle skip and lands on *dix-huit, noir.* As she wends through the crowd in her low-cut burgundy gown, Estelle is bubbling. She greets the governor's nephew and stops to kiss a white-tied gambler's chips for good luck. Longers stands aloof at the bamboo curtain, a glowering thundercloud in his black tuxedo.

Smiles come much more easily when your bets have all hit their mark. Pretty escorts fetched a premium during the holidays, but Estelle had never been able to fully exploit that fact before this year. She owed a lot to Byron, who'd happily taken on the seemingly endless tasks that needed to be done in time for Christmas, allowing her the liberty to expand her services. It was no cheap trick, finding enough girls willing to pick money over virtue who could also fit in at a canal company picnic. A girl like tall and slender Theresa, who would be craved for in private, was generally ruled out by shade—although if the shape of her nose seemed as dainty as her manners you might darken the boundary and hope the man she ends up escorting is not so thin-skinned that he's embarrassed by some porcelain wife's crass snicker.

Ironically, the rebellion on the mainland had made it a banner year for recruiting. The desperate young widows she could not house in her *casa-de-cita,* Estelle had appended to the canal company's payroll and (for a cut of twenty per cent) they were now officially receptionists and personal secretaries. Three of them were here adorning her tavern and, from the trailing looks as they moseyed the floor in their crinoline gowns and velvet flocked satin, the costly camouflage of French couture seemed sure to pay off soon after midnight. As she counted the full dress tails bunched around her new roulette wheel, Estelle had to pinch herself—no, it wasn't all a rich dream! Yet, as she wandered to the bamboo curtain appearing not to notice Longers' immovable scowl, the knot in her stomach sharply twisted.

"There you are, *ma cherie*—we wondered if you had forgotten us!"

Henri Duvay stood gallantly at the back room's linen-covered table and then bent to breathe on Estelle's ringed fingers. The vice-consul raised his bottom an inch off his chair smiling pallidly as she sat down between them.

"Are you saying nothing can be done? There is no way your people can head this off?" she asked irritably when Longers left after bringing in an ice-bucket with more champagne.

The young vice consul colored and shot an exasperated look at the Frenchman who sat smoothing the ends of his extensive moustache. "The Yanks' superintendent has already cabled Washington...the Americans are being a bit cagey this time 'round—they're taking the line that this is strictly a Colombian affair..."

Duvay pounded the table with his fist, rattling the silver half-shells of pâté and the three crystal champagne glasses. "*Exécrable!* Panama should not be dragged into this confounded war. Is it not its own state—with its own assembly and state president? We must demand that it be allowed to stay neutral!"

"Our leaders may treat us like an ugly step-sister," Estelle said dryly, "but so long as you promise them a grand canal they'll hold onto Panama. We're their golden goose."

"It may not come to anything. So far it's been relatively quiet and the local garrison seems loyal to the federation," the vice-consul suggested before Estelle cut him off.

"You're mistaken! Aizpuru and the Liberals see this as their chance to get back power. Prestàn has been warning those of us in business that we had better provide him funds to defend the city. I tried to warn you they were gearing up to fight! I thought when martial law was declared you would have Nuñez arrest the upstarts and keep them from starting trouble."

Estelle tried not to sneer seeing the young vice-consul respond with a hang-dog look. She sometimes wondered how the English had managed to plunder half the globe if a man like Harcourt was considered good enough to represent them. Then, remembering it had been only a month since his lovely young bride had died of yellow fever, she decided that she was judging the poor vice-consul too harshly. It can't be pleasant being stuck far from home trying to prevail among people no less hostile than the climate. But then young Harcourt had never been all that happy.

"We're so isolated here in Panama!" she complained, appealing to the long-faced diplomat much more pliantly. "If we wait for the mainland to respond it may be too late. Your ears are longer than mine—what are you hearing of the crisis?"

"To be honest—? Nothing terribly good," Harcourt admitted, his neck hunched inside his white-tied collar as if the saloon's sporadic cork pops were incoming fire. "The rebels have wide popular support. They took Barranquilla with ease and completely routed the *federales* outside of Tunja. That's not to say they are up to taking Bogotá or even Cartagena. But Colombia's federation is, at best, a wobbly creature. If Aizpuru can muster enough fighters who won't scamper at the first good skirmish, I doubt Nuñez has the manpower to hold the provinces and still keep charge of Panama."

"But that could spell disaster!" Duvay exclaimed. He cast an urgent glance at Estelle. "If Aizpuru is viewed as a dangerous radical, the canal could lose its investors!"

"Things work out as they shall, old boy," the vice-consul replied with a shrug, serving himself some more of the pork paté. "Delicious—" he praised Estelle with a watery smile. "All is never lost when Miss Morales can provide such tantalizing peculiarities! After she warned me about this Pedro Prestàn, I did some digging. He may be a fine lawyer but he has no support in the circles that matter. The Brahmins may loathe paying Bogotá a ransom in taxes but they despise him all the same. I was surprised to hear the little patriot referred to with the kind of venom one might have assumed Panama's esteemed *caballeros* reserve for us niggardly *gringos*."

"That's on your part, *Monsieur* Harcourt," Duvay retorted, a supercilious thumb poking up the shiny lapel on his evening jacket. "We French pay them fairly for our franchise. And I doubt it creates much warm feeling that you Anglos insist on naming everything in their city for an American railwayman—the new governor of Colón barely speaks two words of English."

"I see," said the Englishman, sounding droll. "So I take it French modesty has mitigated against naming your proposed canal hub Lesseps City?"

Duvay chuckled at being deftly outwitted. "*Touché, mon ami!* And I concede that on the tongues of our American friends Aspinwall is immensely preferable. Although, considering all the filth in Colón—I would count having one's name attached to it as a dubious honor."

"Careful, Henri," Estelle cautioned him good-naturedly, "if we do free ourselves the Anglos are not the only ones who'll be paying the piper!"

"I assure you, *ma cherie*, we will make your city the envy of the Americas!" Duvay declared, before finishing off the last of his champagne. "You should know, *monsieur* vice-consul," he continued, turning back to the Englishman, "that our company is prepared to pay its share to safeguard our properties—but we will not see our canal held hostage. Am I right in assuming the Americans retain the authority to intervene to protect their interests here?"

"Indeed they do. Both ports and the railroad are to remain in operation by treaty. But there's no point to go poking a stick in the ants nest. My government is keeping close contact with Colón's provincial governor, as Miss Morales so forcefully suggested. I am confident that, should there be a serious hint of trouble, Prestàn and his ilk will be found and detained."

"Mr. Harcourt!" Estelle gasped, a palm pressed to her powdered neck. "I thought you were helping to prepare charges so they could arrest him, now! Prestàn may be a joke in your genteel circle, but he is considered a champion among our poor. If you wait until he's bought them all weapons, you'll never get near him!"

The Englishman made an arrogant show of pulling on the gold watch chain in his vest pocket. After pausing to note the time, he shifted himself upright, his tone suddenly abrupt and bristling. "The little nigger can collect a thousand pounds, for all I care! The last I heard Remington rifles were not one of this benighted country's manufactures. He still has to get those weapons shipped in. And I doubt seriously the yellow ape has a fleet hiding somewhere under a pillow..." Then promptly regretting having betrayed his temper, he cast an imploring look to Estelle. "I thought it the wiser course, *señora*. No need to get the beggars into an uproar. Don't worry, we're keeping a steady eye on Mr. Prestàn."

"You should hope so, John, or I shall thrash you myself!" Estelle admonished him with mock severity as she popped another bottle to pour the smirking Frenchman more champagne. "This canal is too important to be lost to prejudice or spineless politics."

"Hourra! I'll drink to that—success!" Duvay cheered, lifting the refilled glass.

"And to getting what we all so richly deserve." As Harcourt stood to add his toast his long face looked sad and bitter. "Now, I'm afraid you both must excuse me. It's getting late and I need to make my appearance at Lesseps Palace. I'm surprised you managed to duck out if it, Duvay," he said, wrapping on his white neck-scarf. "Wish I had the option. These huge balls can be such a colossal bore. Thankfully, they've planned some smashing fireworks."

"I find that decision in extremely poor taste, what with our director's wife lying in hospital, practically at death's door. I'd take ill myself having to watch enormous sums much better spent burn up in smoke!" Duvay answered churlishly.

Harcourt tapped on his black silk hat and his droopy eyes grew distant. "I understand perfectly, old boy, but this is Panama. War or no—you still have to buy those 'warm feelings'...Never mind. It all amounts to naught in the end. To misquote Marcus Aurelius, 'only death is the release from the vagaries of the mind and the hard service of the flesh...'"

"Poor Harcourt," said Estelle when the Englishman had left. "His wife was everything to him—even though she could never please him."

"A most peculiar fellow," Duvay observed. "I know you trust him, *ma cherie*, but don't you think it strange that these tensions scarcely seem to faze him? The British own half of the city's real business. Were things to dissolve into outright anarchy they'd stand to lose as much as anyone."

"The *Ingleses* are a race of pirates. So long as you French are bearing the cost of this canal our little squabbles do not worry them. There's no need to fret if you have insurance—and when you have the greatest navy in the world you have plenty of insurance."

"Pity they lack the vision to make the most of it!"

Estelle smiled back weakly then held out her arm for Duvay to escort her back out to the floor so they could mingle with the revelers while the minutes ticked uneasily towards the coming year. As they parted to greet their separate acquaintances, she could still feel the link of their shared apprehension. They had both gambled it all and now could sense the harsh wheel turning. Even among the happy celebrants singing themselves hoarse and drinking themselves numb there was a chord of desperation, as if all of life's pleasures needed to be squeezed out now, before the clock struck midnight and every hope and joy in the world died beneath yet another brutal headache.

The New Year found Thomas in better spirits. He had returned from El Coco full of vim and vigor, prepared to defend his absence and harass his mentor until Duvay agreed to pay for Diego to have a high-church funeral. He guessed rightly that when told about the pilfered grave, Henri would be anxious to square things with Victor Sosa. Indeed, not only did the Frenchman not chide him, he praised him for taking the initiative and promised he would speak to the company about providing *Señora* Valladares with a small annuity.

The cathedral ceremony in Panama City had turned out grand. Victor Sosa, back from Nicaragua, served as head pallbearer and Genevieve had induced Mother Agnes to spare her and two of the other sisters for part of the day so they could add their limber voices to the choir. Thomas' true consolation had come at the graveside, when *Señora* Valladares pressed his hand and said she knew that her son was safe with God because he'd been blessed with a noble friend.

Thomas returned to Christophe-Colomb after the long emotional afternoon to find a letter from his mother. She had written to remind him that he had promised he would visit her this Christmas and it pained her to think he had simply forgotten. He had crumpled the letter, knowing she was right, but resenting the reminder. Christmas was not a time he looked forward to spending with his family. His father was sure to be a perpetual presence and he had no desire to watch him being fussed over by Thomas' twin younger sisters who, blessed with their long pretty hair and adorable light color, treated the end of year holidays as merely the indulgent peak in life's endless party. So while he longed to see his mother, he knew that in such a cherished atmosphere he was bound to be disagreeable.

However, as the weeks rolled on and he settled back into his dreary office routine he began to think that a short trip home might allow him the time to better assess his future. He was still furious about Diego and his mentor appeared to sense it. Since the year began, Duvay had been unusually distant. It was partly due to the fact that with de Lesseps' son here on an official visit the Frenchman was spending more time in Panama City. Thomas had taken the chance to see Genevieve more often during the week but if Duvay had noticed his extra long lunches he had not said a word. In fact, they spoke to each other so rarely Thomas was beginning to wonder if the busy engineer had forgotten he had an assistant.

"I was in Colón this afternoon—" Thomas ventured provocatively as he and Duvay sat sharing a rare dinner together at home. "There was not a federal soldier in sight. Word has it they've all been shipped off to save Cartagena from being taken by the rebels."

Duvay set his knife down briskly on the edge of his plate. "That's impossible. The government has assured us the guard is here to defend Panama." He peered at Thomas more closely. "And what were you doing in Colón this afternoon, may I ask?"

"I was looking about booking a passage back home," Thomas lied, although the thought had occurred to him after a frustrating visit with Genevieve. "This place is a powder keg just waiting for the spark that will light the fuse. I thought I'd better see about getting out now—while one still can."

Duvay wiped the grease on his mouth then tossed his bulky serviette onto the table. "Is this what a British education does—wither their subjects' spines? I never took you for a coward who shrinks at every threat!"

"At least I'm not a fool! Don't you read the papers? Your precious canal has become a quagmire. It will either perish in this war or die a natural death!"

"Spare me the judgments of guttersnipes who fancy themselves as journalists! Did they imagine the greatest canal in the world would be built in three years? They said we were doomed in Egypt—your English masters called the notion of a canal at the Suez a bunch of cockle-shells. If we had listened to the half-wits then, men would still be crossing the Arabian desert on foot!"

"I'm merely applying your own words, *monsieur*," Thomas retorted, his tone vindictive. "Or do you deny ever saying this project has turned into a huge boondoggle?"

This seemed to diffuse some of Duvay's anger. He picked up the crumpled napkin and stuck it back inside his collar. "I will not deny it," he conceded, cutting aggressively at his pork loin. "Our progress should be better. I've tried explaining the technical challenge to the younger de Lesseps but the son is as thick as the father and just as bullheaded. But all is not lost. While he's still too cautious, I think this director is willing to try my approach. It won't be easy—that's why I'm so disappointed that you'd want to leave now, when I need you here helping me."

The concession came like a bolt from out of the blue. Thomas had thought his mentor had finally given up trying to make use of him.

"Why, Henri? Why do you suddenly need my help?" he asked suspiciously, always keen to divine the slightest truth to Diego's distasteful rumor. "Any fool who can count up to ten could tot up those figures."

"Hardly. Look—about what happened with young Valladares—it was wrong of me to be in such a hurry. I should have had them bury the poor lad deeper. My plan will work but I don't have many allies. You are someone I can trust. While you can be a bit lazy, you're eminently teachable."

Thomas related Duvay's half-baked apology when he next saw Genevieve. After he shared what the engineer said about his being loyal and teachable, the two of them enjoyed a hearty laugh.

"So now I'm not erratic and sentimental, I'm trustworthy and loyal," Thomas snickered. "Do you suppose the tyrant might actually have a heart?

"You're like an opiate in the effect you have on those who get near you," Genevieve mused abstractedly. "We know we shouldn't need you, but we can't give you up. It's as if you lurk darkly in our hearts ready to devour all our senses."

Thomas rose quickly up onto his elbows wishing he could see more of her face. After their trip to El Coco they had become full-fledged lovers and as a result his swagger was reviving, but of late Genevieve had turned into a puzzle. Now, each time they met she immediately announced this time would be their last. He would smile and say let's wait and see, and sure enough, by week's end she would weaken. Her behavior once they were alone had become more and more reckless. When they met for lunch, instead of grabbing a snack from one of the vendors to eat at the beach or a secluded spot, she would have them make love in some old warehouse or behind the plum tree in back of the hospice garden. Today, as if to test his ardor and her nerve, Genevieve had them climb to the top of a ninety-foot orange tower erected ages ago to keep tabs on the volatile Chagres River. Now they, along with the sun's dying rays, were thoroughly spent, happy to lie on the fluviograph's dusty floor and rub skins, blanketed by the falling darkness.

"Darkly lurking? What am I now—Dante's leopard? I'm more the star-crossed sod in a penny-dreadful whose fallen for the fair conflicted heroine," he said sarcastically.

"No need to get huffy! Obviously I didn't mean it literally. It's just that there can be beastly things one fears about oneself—urges just too painful to face."

"Those beasts have been haunting you far longer than the time you've been with me," Thomas retorted unkindly and felt bad as he sensed her stiffen.

"But you did come along, didn't you!" she said resentfully. "Can't you see? It's what I've been trying to tell you all along. I prayed for years to make the guilt and sorrow go away and they did because I promised myself to Him and Jesus forgave me. His was the only comfort I ever needed until I had to watch those poor men die in my care." Genevieve raised a crooked arm and covered her face. "Why was I made so weak and wicked? If Father Rodrigo is wrong and there is a fiery hell I'm sure to burn in it! My God! If someone was to say before I came here, that I would violate my sacred promise and lie with a man I would have told them they were cruel and deluded. Yet here I am, beside you, naked as a lamb..."

"I don't see how God can hold you to some guilty notion you had as a child. Even the Bible says children are innocent."

"'Suffer the little children...'" she whispered softly. "I'm afraid, Thomas." Her voice was dry and heavy. "I'm afraid some sins are only cleansed by an innocent's sacrifice..."

Thomas felt the weight of her pain upon his chest. He did not feel guilty about his love for her, only about his inadequacy to make things right. A rare day passed when he did not feel alone and diminished for having failed his friend at the fatal moment. Listening to Genevieve's deep hurt, he knew that while he might never get back all his old swagger, every sense he retained of himself would be lost were he to shrink from trying to save his conflicted lover.

Chapter 15

As it began, the rumblings were faint. From a distance came the beats of swift feet. Then a blast, no louder than a hiccup, seemed to trigger the sounds of terror taking over the streets. The wind, which had been strengthening through the night, sent a mighty gust whipping against his window and Byron was up and alertly awake. The break of dawn was adding its reflections to the screams of panic and as he dragged on his dungarees Byron tried not to shake from nervous tension. He scooted down the stairs still pulling on his shirt and saw Longers peeking through a corner of the window shade, already dressed and in his hat. "What's hap'nin'?"

Longers gave a grunt without turning his head. "I was leaving for the yard and I heard guns fire. Look like Miss Estelle was right. Best not to go rushing off to work today."

A surge of irritation made Byron forget his fear. Why did this ruckus have to start up now? Colón had been seething ever since the occupiers disbanded its militia and installed an eight p.m. curfew. To show they were now in charge, or simply to relieve the extra boredom, the *federales* had begun to use the town's poor vagrants and drunks as target practice, adding to the people's malice. So when the army patrols had been suddenly withdrawn, Byron had hoped that today he might finally dare to return to Christophe-Colomb and catch Thomas Judah at home.

"I thought Mr. Prestàn's men were back in charge," he said to Longers petulantly. "Weren't those his men we saw doing their drill parade down Front Street yesterday morning?"

"Monkey soldiers," Longers scoffed. "What they think—they were gonna hold this town with broomsticks and machetes? They could strut around like big rooster these couple days because the guard had to leave to fix the mess down in Panama City." A faint roar blared from the direction of Monkey Hill two miles away. "Hear that? Sound like Gonima's troops are back from taking care of the upstarts. Watch—they'll put an end to Prestàn's mischief."

Byron came and stood by Longers, pressing his nose to the small glass pane to glimpse the street. "Why you and Miss Estelle keep callin' it mischief?" he asked defiantly. "Everybody I talk to was happy to see those cruel troops leave and Mr. Prestàn take over. Miss Theresa said a bunch of high-class ladies the soldiers was pesterin' went and thanked him personally."

"Nobody with sense is thanking that fool," Longers retorted. "If Gonima can't put him in his place, the Yanks have a gunship sitting in the harbor. And you can be sure the Brits have one ready for him as well. These bungo-head rebels might be turning things upside down on the mainland but they won't be running the show in Colón for long—you can put that in the bank."

Byron was befuddled trying to figure what side to take in all of this looniness. Everyone he spoke to apart from Longers and Miss Estelle—and Miss Theresa, depending on the mood she was in when you caught her—despised the government troops and were hoping Prestàn and the Liberals would be their saviors. Then again, these were the same folks who spent their days in the Aspinwall Post Office or the Aspinwall Bank in the Aspinwall Municipal Building next to the Aspinwall Station and then knocked off work to have a few drinks while they cursed the rich *norteamericanos*. Times like that he remembered Longers' words when he shared the mayor's outrage that the army would try and keep Mr. Prestàn in jail on bogus charges. 'Listen, country boy,' the sailor had said, 'I sailed this globe for almost thirty years—I've seen how things operate whether it's Calais or Zamboanga. Justice may go begging, but her daddy is rich.' Byron had to admit his seemed the more sensible view. Better not to bite the hand that's feeding you.

"Watch them nuh—" Longers jeered as a pack of ragged children dashed past their window, their little arms laden with pilfered loaves and sweet-buns. He shook his head as the girls and boys ran giggling. "I guess they just done loot the bakery...hard to blame them when you have grown-up people runnin' around like chickens widdem head chop-off! Boy, you should kiss Miss Estelle's big toe! If it weren't for her you'd a-been mixed up with Prestàn and all his foolishness."

The words were not out of his mouth when the small house rattled at the powerful burst of a close-range cannon.

"Lawd, Longers! It's really war?"

"Git back from that window and lie on your belly!"

Byron ducked down beside Longers on the floor a split second before shards of glass showered across his back as he rushed to cover up his head. The ground seemed to be trembling under his belly and for an instant he saw himself back in that sightless black hole, clutched to Thomas with his left arm smarting from pain. This time the shaking was not from a violent earthquake but the impact of a thousand stampeding feet. The pings of gunshots rang in through the broken window. Feeling his hands start to sting as they speckled with blood he wanted to run but could not budge from his stomach. Besides, he realized with a frightened shiver, where was he to run? There was no safe place to go.

The screams grew louder as the deep sleepers woke, the wailing wind adding menace to their terror. A hysterical voice rang out above the panic: "They're burning the city! They're burning the city! Run! Run for your lives!"

The shrill cry jolted Byron off the floor. He raced back up the stairs, ignoring Longers when he bellowed for him to stop. Trembling, he dragged on his socks and shoes, grabbed Johnny's fiddle then bolted back down, vaulting through the wide open door ahead of a sharp wisp of smoke.

The scene on the street was bedlam. Against a dawn sky lit like a flaming cigar and the flares from distant artillery, Colón's poor were streaming inland. Byron stopped by the curb to search for Longers and was nearly bowled over by two huge puffing women, their knees working like pistons as they juggled two squalling infants and three raffia bags stuffed full with rescued possessions. The heat was intense and with the smoke in burning pursuit Byron was forced to join the mad sprint. He scoured the swift human tide as he ran and felt sick seeing no sign of the giant. He had assumed Longers had gotten out ahead of him. Now he suddenly felt unsure and all the smoke and noise made it hard to think. He was deciding if he dared to turn back when the frantic rush began to stall.

Angry shouts rang out from behind as the crush of refugees was pressed to a standstill. Byron was about to try and fight his way back when he spotted the brigade. It had apparently converged with the fugitive wave at the boulevard crossing. The burnt-out citizens, calmed by the sight of order, saw the rebel patriots striding in lockstep double-file and paused to watch. Some even managed a tepid cheer as the city's volunteer defenders came marching through the haze of gunpowder, smoke and soot, their only insignia a strip of blue ribbon sewn to a collar or tied to the crown of a coarse straw hat.

Byron was rocked by a clash of emotions as he recognized Reynal and the lanky Pautrizelle among the militia's two hundred. He feared that theirs was a losing cause—half of their recruits were barefoot, shouldering sticks in place of shotguns and rifles—but it was impossible not to admire their drilled-in courage. Reynal's moonface was beaming as he passed by the crowd, his chubby black hand cupped proudly to the hilt of his impressive naked sword. Finally came the starch-backed hero himself. He was still in his somber black suit and bowler, except now he sat perched on a magnificent white stallion like a tiny all-conquering Caesar. Prestàn's appearance drew more respectful applause but as Byron scanned the homeless faces there were fewer smiles than jaws clamped tight with anger.

As the insurgents faded inside the screening smoke to take up their defensive positions more flaming embers were being picked up by the wind and starting to light down roof to roof. An orange fireball flashed out from the alley and several in the crowd raced screaming in blind directions. Byron turned to shield his eyes from the red-hot cinders and realized that the sudden stink was the smell of his own hair being singed from his eyebrows. The street now close to deserted, he stumbled back to the little boarding-house and felt his heart fall to his boots seeing it completely consumed in flames.

"Hard ears boy—you lucky you made it out in time!"

In typical fashion Longers had just appeared from heaven knows where.

"Didn't you hear me telling you to get out o' there before the whole house fill with smoke? You nearly let that darn fiddle cost you your life!" berated the giant, catching sight of the violin just as Byron doubled over hacking violently as a slip of ash blew in his mouth and scorched his palate.

After he had kept the burning fleck from sliding down his throat, Byron suddenly remembered the cherished figurines Estelle had left with them for safekeeping. "Shame...shame on us, Longers," he whispered glumly, knowing that somewhere in that fiery pile burning like worthless kindling were Estelle's cherished folk-dancers and the little peasant fiddler he had found so lifelike. "We didn't even think to save Miss Estelle's nice things."

"There wasn't time, boy. Smoke can kill you faster than fire."

"She gonna be broken up over this..." Byron muttered, his memory recalling the drawing-room's stylish pictures and the daguerreotype of Estelle as a dark-haired young beauty that Longers had framed and hung on a wall in his bedroom.

"Once water's done been thrown away you can't pick it back up! We're not helping her any standin' here blubberin'—let's go check and see how the Last Frontier made out."

Byron wiped the smoke-drawn tears from his eyes and shifted his hold on Johnny's fiddle to follow obediently. The streets were no longer jammed but the blaze was spreading, sending more people dashing from their homes in perplexed agitation. At a block that had been mostly spared, men had set themselves to chopping down the old tinderboxes in the crazed belief that they were denying fuel from the swirling flames. As he and Longers made it through the hectic fray Byron's sinking hopes had reached the brink. Half the waterfront was ablaze.

A railroad tanker trying to cross through the flames spilled its oil and caught fire, torching the dock and igniting bales of unloaded cotton along with the crates of abandoned equipment left carelessly to rot. The gusting wind was doing the rest. By Estelle's swank saloon the boardwalk was a raging inferno. Seeing the flames start licking their way, Longers grabbed hold of Byron and hauled him back to the alley behind the tin-roofed warehouse where Prestàn had addressed the rally.

Meanwhile the sounds of rejoined battle were ringing anew. People were yelling in fear and consternation, confused as to whether it was wise to try and dodge the flying bullets and risk being trapped by the leaping fire. The handful of municipal police not fighting on one side or the other had given up trying to keep order and gone to help the railway leathernecks struggling to save the rest of the city. Battling through the plumes of billowing smoke they made it to the seaside terminal with the company's water storage tanks but before they could finish unknotting the first long hose most of Front Street had burned to cinders.

Byron and Longers could only wait helplessly, praying that the tin-roofed warehouse did not catch on fire. When at last the blaze seemed nearly snuffed out, they rose from the alley on shaking knees and ploughed through the carnage to Estelle's new saloon. As they both feared, the Last Frontier had been among the first buildings gutted. Longers stopped to stare with his mouth shut tight. Byron was struck by a sense of unreality seeing the menacing leopard now a puddle of paste and plaster, its gold agate eyes aimed at the smashed chandelier dropped from the caved-in ceiling. The new roulette wheel lay careened on its side, looking bent even as it slowly kept spinning. Longers watched it turn for a long seething moment then gave Byron's shoulder a hard shove, saying they needed to see about Miss Estelle.

"That upstart Prestàn better pray she came outta this all right," Longers muttered. Nearing Bottle Alley, they saw that the towering champagne monument had been reduced to a low mound of bleeding glass. Nothing but a blackened shell remained of Estelle's little *cantina*.

They finally found her sitting alone on the bordello's front step, her uncombed black hair falling wildly to her shoulders. An enormous white cockatoo was cradled in her lap. Seeing Longers, she tried to smile but the effort failed her. She looked years older and smaller than Byron remembered. As he and Longers hunched down beside her, one on either side, she explained in a cracking voice how Pompey had tried to warn her of the fire but when she came downstairs and opened the shutters he had flown at them in a panic to escape the rush of smoke and broke his neck.

Longers got up and walked off without a word. Estelle stayed sitting with a vacant look, stroking the dead bird as if to soothe it back to life. Byron worried that he was being left to break the news about the Last Frontier. An awkward tension filled the silent space and he was beginning to have a hard time breathing when he saw the sailor returning, looking calm yet grim. Longers tugged the smoke-stained cockatoo from Estelle's caress and, leaning down his shoulder to bear her up, led the two of them back to the garden where he had dug a small hole beneath her spreading almond tree. When they had buried the noble Pompey and processed back to the brothel's front steps, Estelle launched into a tirade against her worthless government.

"They had Prestàn in jail. Why? Why did they have to go and release him?" she cried before diverting her ire towards the *gringos*. "They are the cause of all this! Everywhere you turn they remind us this is their town. Look on a *gringo* map! You won't find Colón—no *señor*! This is Mr. Aspinwall's city! The *norteamericanos* have a gunboat sitting right in Manzanilla Harbor—so why didn't they step in like they always do? First we are made to endure occupation—now this?" Her voice broke from tension. "—and I warned them..."

She slumped back on the step and Longers stretched a quick arm to comfort her. Sensing suddenly that his presence was an intrusion, Byron stepped up towards the charred front door hanging askew beneath the singed eaves, half-open. He leaned to peek inside and saw the old world furniture reduced to a smoky mass of junk.

"Miss Theresa and the others, them not still inside there...?" he murmured in a timid voice.

"No. Thanks to Pompey, we all got out in time. Theresa took the girls without family to stay with friends she has in the countryside. Are the trains from Cristobal running? I heard it was left untouched..." Estelle muttered jealously. "I don't suppose my little *cantina* made it through the fire—I hope the Last Frontier didn't fare too badly..."

Byron looked guiltily off into the distance and Longers drew close to the madam and lovingly clasped her hand. Estelle listened without changing expression while he told her all they had seen, absorbing each blow as if she knew it was coming.

When he had finished she squeezed both eyes shut and sat in silence. "That's it, then," she whispered finally, from somewhere far away, "you cannot trust them..."

As he saw the depth of Estelle's resentment, great questions began to form in Byron's head, questions about injustice and what it meant to be loyal. In some small obscure way he felt responsible. Not just for having never thought to save her precious keepsakes, but for having joined with those who had taken advantage of her trust. He hated to think that it would be one more stone upon her heart when she discovered his lie and realized he had never deserved her kindness. To cover his shame and show his loyalty he blurted out that the three of them should forget about this crazy town and sail away together on the very next ship.

Longers dismissed his flash of inspiration with gruff disdain. "How many thousand you think are right now fightin' like crabs to book their passage? Besides, Miss Estelle is not some little country bumpkin. She can't pick up and leave just so. She'll be all right so long as I'm here to back her up."

Byron felt his face start to burn as if it had been scorched by more hot ash. It was not the first time Longers had been quick to slap him down. Since the new year started the sailor had seemed out of sorts and unusually ill-tempered. Yet listening to him tell Estelle the horrible news, Byron sensed he had gotten back his old stolid self-possession. It was almost as if Longers had drawn comfort from the Last Frontier's destruction, knowing that the unmet wishes he had invested in Miss Estelle were no longer threatened by her swift success.

"The boy is just being sensible," Estelle objected, surprising Longers who reared like an injured bull to hear his ruling disputed. "Even if I could afford to repair the damage, there won't be much business here for me right now. I think I'll go and stay with my sister, assuming she doesn't turn me away—" She looked imploringly up at Longers. "That way, at least I'll be able to spend some time with little Isabella. I need to figure out if this town still has a future..." Estelle halted midstream and a tacit line seemed to strain in between them. She turned her head to avoid Longers' wounded look. "The real question is what to do about the two of you," she went on quickly. "I hate to think of you roaming the city with nowhere to stay..."

"Don't go fretting yourself about me," Longers snapped, his nostrils flaring and his eyes glowing red. "I'll manage."

"I know you can manage, but I shall worry all the same," Estelle answered quickly, touching his arm to try and soothe his ruffled hide. "It would ease my mind to know where you were and how to reach you."

The tender admission seemed to draw the heat from Longers' ire but he was not ready to let pass the fact that his original position had been wrongly disparaged.

"That won't be simple if I have to go wandering across the country. And where the devil would I go? Everybody I know lives here in Colón. I might as well go back to living on the sea."

From the gleam in Longers' eyes it was clear he was testing to see how much he was going to be needed. Estelle caught on instantly.

"I should know better than to contradict you. You're right. It would better if you were someplace close by, but it has to be somewhere safe for our young fiddler..."

"You mean the one I never hear practice?" Longers put in snidely.

A trickle of fear began to churn in Byron's gut. He braced, expecting to finally be exposed, but instead Estelle again jumped to defend him.

"And whose fault is that? You decided you needed to work full-time at the shipyard. The poor boy's been busy helping me. He's probably been too exhausted."

"Exhausted?" Longers echoed with dripping sarcasm. "What's he been doing—digging you ditches?"

"Byron's done everything I've asked and more! You know it's true," she said, seeing Longers' quick glower, "because you said so yourself!"

Byron hated to think that, on top of everything else, he was now an issue between them. He decided to remind them he was not a child or a stupid bumpkin. "Don't worry 'bout me either! If Cristobal never catch on fire I can stay with my friend Thomas—"

"No!" Estelle shouted in command. "Cristobal is bound to be heavily guarded. If you're lucky they'll only arrest you and not just shoot you as a looter. No. There must be somewhere safe you two can stay until I can find a place for you..." She paused with one sooty palm pressed to her forehead. "That's it!" she burst out finally. "Longers, you know that English church—the one the railroad company built for their Anglos?"

"The one down by the sea? Yes! I catch your thinking! That little church is solid rock-stone. They couldn't burn it down! But you're sure they'll take us in?"

"Well, it wouldn't be very Christian of them not to!"

Longers sat back to mull the proposition.

"You know you've been my right hand and my left," said Estelle, addressing him more gravely. "I want you to swear you won't let this young fiddler out of your sight. I'm going to need you both and I don't need any more burdens on my conscience. Promise me you'll stay put in that church until you hear from me. It shouldn't be for very long."

Any objections Longers may have been pondering melted on his tongue the moment Estelle grasped his hand and set it fondly on top of her knee.

"You sure you can manage?" he asked, his gruff voice so faint and filled with care it was almost melodious. "I don't like leaving you..."

Estelle rested her small palm on the back of Longers' large black hand. "I know," she whispered gratefully.

Byron moved away, his arms cuddling Johnny's fiddle. He felt uncomfortable seeing the rugged sailor in that woeful pose.

"You need to go," Estelle murmured gently. "Promise me you won't let him wander? Promise me—"

Longers bent his imposing frame and kissed the backs of her plump smudged hands. "I'll look out for the boy. You have my word on my dead mother's grave. Come on, young fiddler!" he barked, standing abruptly. "You and me need to lie low for awhile and not be a burden."

"Now listen," said Estelle walking up and cupping Byron's face in her hands. "I still have big plans for you, so I don't want you getting into any more trouble. You're to stay with Longers until I can send for you, *comprendo*?"

Byron pulled away self-consciously. Apart from his mother, he had never felt a woman's soft touch. Even with her round face marred by ghoulish streaks from tear-borne ashes, with Estelle so warm and close his body responded. Its reaction upset him, as it had the day they met, except now his shame was compounded and much more acute. He groped for something manly to say. "You done enough for me a'ready," he mumbled. He wanted to thank her and say he was not a boy, he could get by on his own, but her closeness stopped him. "I—I'm sorry 'bout what happen...I shoulda did think to save your pretty things..."

Estelle crooked a sooty finger and lifted his chin. "Byron, look at me! Who needs a little stick fiddler when I have one in the flesh?" Her strong gaze held his eyes. "Those things are not what matters. I've known what it is to have nothing. I'll have something again, and so will you. I'm keeping you to your promise—I want to hear that fiddle in your arms sing just for me."

Her projection of his promise into the indeterminate future touched him like a reprieve. Somehow her words had woven him inside a mystical web and he felt himself nod yes, as if in a trance. As she gave them her last instructions, Byron's wild imaginings were possessed by those wishful ambitions which flow from the fount of a second chance. Who was to say, he thought magically, what he might not still achieve with a little practice?

Chapter 16

Bidding Estelle one last farewell, he and Longers began their slow cross-town pilgrimage in pensive silence. There seemed to be no one else around, as if the people had all vanished with the wind. What remained of the familiar grocers, haberdashers and curio shops were mere broken shells, their split beams in piles on scorched-black plots. Colón's night haunts, where wanton escapades had eased the pain of Panama's everyday tragedies, lay smoldering and dashed to pieces. Yet, as he trudged through the tranquil streets lying empty and dusted white where hours ago he had been tripping in mud and moldering garbage, Byron felt a strange exhilaration—the vile city had been cleansed.

As they came to the Last Frontier for the second time, Longers looked ready to erupt. His brooding countenance was that of a broken general, furious that some quirk of fate had managed to surprise him, demolishing every hopeful cause he'd fought for. For a long while he stood transfixed, his eyes burning on the ruined roulette wheel that was no longer turning. Then he abruptly snapped himself erect and walked on with his seething gaze aimed straight.

The two of them quietly pressed on, hiding their faces as the wind came howling back and blew up more eye-stinging cyclones of dust. Longers had still not said a word but his thoughts were resounding in Byron's skull like rolling thunder. When he sensed the anger rumbling beneath the drawn-out silence beginning to fade Byron ventured to ask the sailor how long he reckoned they'd have to stay cooped up in that church.

"You heard Miss Estelle—until she says it's time to join her!"

Byron knew better than to press it any further. He was starting to regret having stuck with the grouchy sailor but there was no one else around save the two lost souls he'd seen combing through the rubble, clearly out of their minds. Of the buildings he could see only the freight house and the brick train station were intact. Here and there he passed a damaged home still partly standing but the only ones that appeared to have been spared were far to the west in the Yankee section down by the lighthouse. He was beginning to fear that Miss Estelle had been mistaken and they would find no sanctuary in town at all. He had almost given up hope when he glimpsed the brown stone belfry and the little red-roofed church sitting off on its own against the background of the gray green sea.

The white-haired vicar came wheezing towards the gate to meet them and his anxious gray eyes seemed greatly soothed as they rested on the fiddle in Byron's embrace. He said they were welcome so long as they agreed to stay inside, out of hostile view. Byron's first instinct was to thank him and leave right then. Seeing that the most of the fires had already burned out and the streets were virtually deserted, he was finding all these fidgety precautions to be ridiculously overblown. If anything, Colón seemed safer than ever. But as he considered it twice, he realized that it would be foolish for him to refuse food and shelter while he made new plans.

Once inside the narthex Longers quickly dragged off his hat and his immovable scowl magically melted away. Father Chickering, whose waxy visage could have belonged to an embalmed apostle, turned to Byron, rubbing his pale hands. He said he trusted most musicians were peaceful souls but would ask that they both surrender any firearms. Byron grinned, ready to assure him they were unarmed, when Longers pulled a flintlock pistol sheepishly from the back of his jacket. He handed the old relic to the vicar who received it as if it were a newborn presented to be blessed and promised to keep it safely under lock and key.

"There's water, tea and biscuits in the apse—I'll leave you to make your own acquaintance with those inside," Pastor Chickering advised before departing with the gun.

"You mean all this while you had that pistol under your jacket?" Byron hissed as he and Longers came in from the vestibule.

"Nope. Don't usually need to...but trials alter cases..."

Longers abruptly stopped his reply and hurried in past the rosewood pews to where a man and four small children sat in a huddle on the floor by the transept.

"Is that Yick Wo?" the sailor exclaimed, as Byron tagged behind curiously.

The man turned to the booming voice and in the church's yellowy light his face looked freakish, like a spooky wax-figure. "Longers?—you the last man I expect to see in here!"

Byron barely recognized the Chinese shopkeeper he would often see standing outside his store trying to solicit new customers. The weird translucence to Yick Wo's face was from a nasty burn that ran from his left temple to the bottom of his jaw, so that half of his face looked melted. Byron shifted his startled eyes to Wo's children whose exotic blended features made him think of Theresa. None seemed a day over ten. They all looked terrified by Longers' huge presence.

"Oh, now I see why you are here!" Yick Wo exclaimed as he noticed Byron, "you are hiding one of your *chango* rebels! Get away—get away and leave us be! You criminals have done enough to us already!"

As Yick Wo looked down and began to sob, Longers stood by looking intensely distressed. Byron could not tell if he was hurt by Wo's accusation or embarrassed to see a grown man bawl in front of his children.

"Calm yourself, Wo. The boy is no rebel," said Longers, reining in his temper. "Miss Estelle had him working at her tavern. She asked me to look out for him till the crisis is over."

The children all started crying, clutching onto Wo and looking more and more frightened as he seemed gripped by hysterical weeping.

"Why you lie?" Wo cried, as sudden anger checked his wails. "I saw him! Yick Wo saw him talk with Prestàn stooges—two time!" he shouted, sticking up two badly burned fingers. "I remember I think uh-oh—he new in town so prob'ly mean trouble! But what Yick Wo can do? Cannot trust either side."

Byron began to defend his innocence but Yick Wo turned his back and waved them away.

"Come—let's go," said Longers, seeing Wo open up his arms to console his bawling children. "We can try again when he's a little calmer."

"What makes him think I joined with Prestàn?" Byron whispered indignantly as they retreated up the aisle. "Because he saw me with that Haitian—? And what the devil is a *chango?*"

"That's what the Spanish-speakers call you and me behind our back," Longers replied with a sour look. "And our follow-fashion Jamaican monkeys couldn't wait to go an' jump inside their business!" He snorted with disgust. "You'd think they'd have the sense to realize that once this war is over they'll still be the wasters scrubbing the deck. Who I feel bad for is poor Mister Wo. He worked thirty years to build that shop—finally found himself a strong young wife—" Longers paused and glanced wistfully back at the weeping family.

"Damn-it-all!" he swore, his voice briefly choked up, "—I'm pretty sure Wo had five children..."

Byron was furious to hear Longers side with Yick Wo and try to blame the fire on his fellow Jamaicans. It reminded him of when the plantation fires being set to ready the cane for harvest ended up sending smoke inside Busha's great-house. It was always the fault of the lowly field hands—as if they had control of the wind. He was so tired of the injustice. A week ago men like Wo were praising Prestàn and his men for restoring order.

"When me was diggin' down at Culebra nobody talked about Panama's politics," Byron rebutted after he and Longers had settled on a pew a considerate distance from the Wos. "Yuh shouldn't be lettin' them put us all in the same damned boat. There were plenty Panama people happy to follow Mr. Prestàn."

"It's not my doings—that's just the way life works when you're in anudder man's country. A few bad apples make the whole crop smell rotten."

"Yeah, we're the bad apples now but I bet you Mr. Wo cheered with the rest when they thought our boys were gonna help defend them against those govament soldiers. Now, all of sudden, I'm to blame for the town burning down? It make no sense!"

"You right it make no sense—but it make a crazy kind of sense once you take time and query it," Longers suggested sagely. "Don't you feel proud saying you're a Jamaican?"

Byron hesitated, troubled by the question and wondering where the sailor was leading. "I suppose, I have to—it's what I am...it's where I born an' live..."

"That's where I'm drivin'! People here feel proud same way—and there's nothing a dog hates more than to go and mess in his own yard. So if some big mess ends up wrecking your town who you would rather blame—yourself—or the dog from next door?"

Byron sensed there was something wrong with Longers' logic but then guessed it was part of his point.

"You know what's been the hardest thing to get used to since I gave up the sea?" the sailor continued, "—people tying me to a place I ain't set foot since I was thin as a fly-pole and my little soldier-man started to itch. I hate it that folks want to judge me for the scrap of ground where my mama happened to be squatting when she pushed me out her womb. They use it to name us even though it ain't never been really ours and it's too small to feed us—if we belong to any land at all it's back in Africa. You can forget all that patriotic rubbish when you're out on the ocean; the ship is your country and all nations are the same. The sea can be a mean old witch but she's every sailing man's yard. If she starts up with her mess, you better just button your lip and stick to your best mate—you don't care a mango that his last name is Huang or that you're following Captain Vardulakis' orders."

"Dat may work out at sea, but me was born here on the earth," Byron shot back. "I think God meant every man to have himself a piece o' land in his own country...and me never come 'cross one man yet who wants to go live in the bush down in Africa."

Longers scowled with a contemptuous look then stepped angrily out of the pew, saying he needed some air to cool his spirits. Byron was about to remind him what the vicar had said about staying out of sight then thought better of it. Seeing Wo had clearly put Longers back in a nasty mood. The fact that Wo's wife and youngest child had apparently died in the fire and Estelle was coping without him seemed to have left him unmoored. Byron wondered if Longers was afraid of what might happen to her without him or simply worried that his dear Estelle was sailing beyond his reach, and would be lost to him, forever.

The image of the hard-boiled giant pining over a woman each night as he climbed into his empty bed gave Byron a chuckle. Then he reflected upon his own life and on the fact that he'd spent all these months in Colón and never found the nerve to learn about women. He picked up Johnny's fiddle and set it down on the pew trying to forget that he was going to be twenty this year and still a virgin. He snapped open the case telling himself to remember why he was in Panama. He was here to make money—so that when he went home he could afford a good woman.

Opening the case's small compartment, he drew out the envelope with Thomas' letter and counted the ninety-three dollars he'd saved from his two-years wages and the five gold piasters Estelle gave him at Christmas. It wasn't bad but it wasn't nearly enough. Although part of him did not want to face it, if he was to afford that land he was going to have to give up Estelle's sweet company and find a real job. His best bet was to contact Thomas. His lucky friend was bound to have some ideas. If not, he would either be going home broke or shuffling back to Culebra to do more shoveling.

Longers came back carrying a goblet of water and two dry oatmeal biscuits.

"Here, you're probably feeling peckish—" he said tersely, handing Byron the obvious peace offering. His new pious look had returned yet he seemed more like his old gruff self.

"Thanks—I guess me was a little hungry..." Byron said appreciatively, taking a greedy crunch out of one of the biscuits.

"Pastor Chickering is making up some soup. You sit here and rest—I'm gonna try talk sense with Mr. Wo."

Longers departed again and Byron sat pensively sipping his water. He was already starting to feel like a prisoner. Two or three days at the most—then I'm gone, he thought to himself as he sat and took stock of Panama's only Protestant church. The nave was small, much like a Jamaican country church. Its stained glass windows were far from grand with their colors dimmed from salty grime, but the altar's setting stood white and gleaming, attended by a host of chubby pink angels. The center of its large white cross appeared studded with rubies, its heart and extremities shining with gold. It was a far cry from the plain wood tabernacles that he was used to and yet as he gazed upon the altar he began to feel strangely at peace. The comforting sensation surprised him knowing that Sunday worship was famously reserved for the Yankees working for the railroad and the British expatriates brought down by their shipping companies. The only exception was during Christmas when the leathernecks' colored brethren were invited to worship together in the back.

It was an aspect of religion that had long confused him. The preacher would talk about how Jesus loved the poor and forgave us our sins, yet it was the whites who had the most money he put to sit up front and better hear God's word. As a child he had decided it must mean that the rich were in greater need of forgiveness until he grew up and realized most poor folks who went to church came praying to be wealthy.

All at once the church was thick with a banging sound. After the long quiet the echoes rang like a fusillade of close artillery. Byron snatched up Johnny's violin and was out of the pew before he realized it was the tolls of a bell loudly pealing. When the long strokes stopped at eight he took it to be the pointless call for the start of curfew. The nave's stillness returned and a moment later the vicar appeared, his red face wet from his ringing exertions. He fled inside the transept still wiping his brow then came back to announce that he would be serving them bread and warm soup out in the apse.

Longers hurried off to help in the tiny church kitchen and Yick Wo's children shot up from the floor to race each other to the apse, the promise of food banishing the tears from their dark gloomy eyes. The smell of the soup made Byron's stomach begin to gurgle and he quickly followed them out to the apse's long table. He waited until the smallest child, a curly-haired almond cherub who looked about three, had her own little bowl of soup but as she greedily carried it off steered by an alert sister's hand, Longers swept in and pulled him back.

"Mr. Wo is starting to come around but for now I think it's better if the two of us keep our distance." Longers cast a worried look back to the disfigured shopkeeper who had gone to stand alone against the wall behind the table. Wo's eyes were two furious black holes trained on Byron. "I don't want any loud argument blowing up in Father Chickering's church."

"So what—? I must wait for them to finish and drink cold soup?" Byron griped.

"I never said so—after I get through serving Mr. Wo I'll bring you your bowl inside—I explained it all to Pastor Chickering and he says it all right for us to eat in the pew."

The soup turned out to be thin, tasting of a hint of soap mixed with year-old beef gravy, but Byron drank every drop. As he and Longers sat cleaning the last from their bowls with some small heels of bread, Longers shared Wo's unhappy story.

"It seems that right after Nuñez declared Panama was under martial law Prestàn went to Mr. Wo asking for a loan. He told him the Americans were on their side and if Wo helped him buy his men more weapons Panama could finally be free of Bogotá's dictatorship. Wo said he didn't trust Prestàn and his radicals but he understood that being a successful businessman he was expected to contribute. Once Colón was under occupation, Wo ended up paying the *federales* so their thugs would not steal from his store. Wo said he was tempted to leave town altogether but felt he was getting too old to start over. When Prestàn came back demanding more money, Wo told him he could not spare it and still feed his family.

"Prestàn big liar!" Longers rasped, mimicking Wo's broken English. "He told Wo not to worry, he would still protect him—Wo says Prestàn lied about the Yankees wanting Panama to be independent. He blames Prestàn for thinking he could beat an army with some barefoot *changos*."

"But why does Wo blame me?"

"Mr. Wo said to me, 'your friend he's not from here so he don't care.' He looked straight in my face and said, 'you *changos* no care!—so you burn down town—kill Wo's wife and baby boy!'"

Byron was incredulous. "I hope yuh told him we had nutting to do wid any of it!"

Longers looked down and shook his head. "He won't listen...one of Colón's two-faced officials owns the store next to his. He put it in Wo's head that Prestàn started the fire so his boys could escape." Longers shrugged. "Who's to say it's not true...?"

"So now every Jamaican he comes across Wo's gonna blame him for the fire?—yuh think that's right?"

"I never said I thought it was right—the poor man's crazy with grief and I can understand it. He just lost his wife. If you love a woman that is life's hardest blow. Give him some time."

Byron stared off irritably. "Fine by me—I'll keep my distance."

Byron spent the night on the floor, finding it more conducive for sleep than a narrow pew. He awoke with aches in every joint from his neck to his ankles. The apse had a welcome meal waiting but the vicar's notion of banana porridge turned out to be as watery and insipid as his soup. Byron had swallowed as much of the breakfast as he could stand when Longers commandeered him back to the kitchen to help with the washing up.

The sailor quickly left him to do the drying, saying he wanted to try again to placate poor Mr. Wo. Byron returned from stacking the dishes and was stunned to see his friend, having apparently failed to thrust himself back into Wo's good graces, kneeling in a front row pew in a pose of deep meditation. The image defied comprehension. Here was the man who claimed to have no need for religion, the heretic, unashamed to admit he had never been baptized, acting all holy. It made Byron want to puke up his porridge but as he walked on by he was grateful that the giant's temper seemed to have eased overnight.

Lunch proved a discouraging rehash of breakfast scarcely improved by some slices of half-ripe banana. A trip to the garden's small privy was a relief for more than his bladder and as Byron lingered to enjoy the sunshine he noticed there was a half-hidden gate inside the back hedge of golden trumpets. Walking over, he saw that it opened directly onto the beach. He unbolted the latch and was taking off his shoes for a short stroll in the wet sand when he felt Longers' shadow looming.

"Better not—who knows who might be out there prowling the beach."

"Me just out for a little walk—I'll make sure nobody sees me—"

"Can't be taking that chance," said Longers, sticking an arm in the youngster's way. "Father Chickering said we must keep inside—I'm sure he has good reason—"

"Tchuh, man!" Byron snapped, slipping back on his shoes then banging the gate shut. "The old vicar is just worried that his congregation might get vexed if they find out what color people he's harborin'—"

"Father Chickering don't strike me as a man who cares a damn what people say. Use your brain!—if he's worried about anything, it's us—he could just as easily turned us away."

Byron was about to ask why no Jamaicans worshiped in his church even though they were also Protestants but knew he'd be wasting his breath. Longers seldom questioned the way things were and seeing he was nearly six and a half feet tall few men ever questioned him. Having started out as nothing but a stowaway, the sailor figured all a man needed for a rewarding life was the sense to know where to anchor his ambition. It explained why he hated to see working men gamble—he saw it as a doomed attempt to bypass the world's natural order.

It poured with rain the entire next day and stuck indoors Byron found the pale solemnity of an Episcopal church ideal for deepening a gray depression. Here he was trapped for God knows how long, and Longers was behaving like a monk who'd vowed an oath of silence, the Wos continued to keep to themselves, and the vicar spent most of the time shut in his chamber, emerging only to ring his bells or bring them more weak tea and stale biscuits. He was itching to leave and search out Thomas but no sooner did the rain seem to end than it would start pouring again, even heavier. As he sat alone listening to raindrops fall quietly at dusk he thought, this is how a man goes slowly mad. He tried to think of something happier and suddenly remembered Johnny's violin. He lifted out the magic fiddle and began to pluck one of the catgut strings gently with his thumb.

He had been strumming absent-mindedly with his eyes lightly closed, weighing if he should wait to hear from Estelle or escape this unbearable isolation, when he heard something move close by his feet. He peeked beneath the bench and saw Mr. Wo's little honey-skinned cherub and the other youngest girl crawling out from under the pew where they'd been hiding. The children had apparently wriggled clear across the stone floor, drawn by his plucking. He beckoned them over with a friendly grin but their little eyes grew wide and they dashed back to stand with their siblings watching him keenly from a safe distance.

Byron wished more than ever he could do more than strum six or seven sorry notes. It was clear they'd all been waiting for him to finally get around to playing a tune. When the four of them still looked hopeful, seeing Mr. Wo nowhere in sight, he approached them gently with the fiddle outstretched. The tallest girl, her skin's sheen and color reminding him of a lightly fried breadfruit, glanced around the church with anxious eyes, obviously on the lookout for her father.

"It's all right—I won't hurt yuh," Byron said softly, holding up the fiddle when she rushed to gather in her siblings. "I'd play yuh a song but me just start learn miself—if yuh careful yuh can have a turn to pluck it..."

He paused where he stood so as not to scare them and the little brown cherub tugged out from her sister's grasp then ran up to shyly stretch her tiny finger and touch a string.

"No man—" Byron teased her gently, "yuh gotta pluck it harder than that if yuh want to make music."

Emboldened, the little girl took her thumb and gave the G string a long hard snap, giggling with joy when the buzzing note echoed in the nave's arched ceiling.

"Are you a musician? Longers never say—"

Mr. Wo came up holding a towel to his badly burned skin after a drenching trip to the outhouse. His surprise sounded cordial but guarded.

"I can't rightly call myself a musician—but I'm—"

Before he could go on Yick Wo stepped in and stood protectively between Byron and his daughters. "Go, and leave us in peace—Wo tired of so much double talk!"

Byron again tried to explain but Wo tossed the towel rudely across his shoulder and turned to shepherd the crestfallen girls back to their separate corner.

That night's dinner turned out to be a treat as the vicar had discovered some forgotten cans of stewed pork and beans beneath a stack of old boxes in the back of the church pantry. "What you expect?" said Longers as he and Byron sat down to eat alone in their pew. "This town is full of crooks and here you're hauling around that fancy fiddle and like I did suspect you can't even play it. Mr. Wo probably thought you were out to try and hustle him."

Byron cringed, knowing he'd just been tagged as a liar—or worse—maybe even a thief. What hurt the most had been the looks he'd gotten from Wo's children. It didn't matter that the image of him they saw was nowhere near the truth, it was burned in their wide-eyed little heads, and would stay there, probably forever.

The sun rose brightly again the following morning and Byron decided he would wait until Longers had finished his post-breakfast meditations then confront him about leaving. He wanted the chance to tell Estelle the truth himself and he was afraid that if he left Longers would say he was not grateful for all her help. He was not eager to sever that tie but he could not stay cooped up much longer without losing his mind or, at least, his temper. He decided that while Longers was enjoying his quiet introspection he would take a stroll on the beach and try and come up with a good argument for leaving. He had just finished yanking off his shoes when he saw four men come running up from across the sand. He grabbed for his shoes to dash back inside the gate when he heard one of them calling out his name.

"Byron! Well—God sure answers prayer—it's my good friend, Byron!" A rail-thin black man hopped up, gasping. It was Jake, one of the diggers from Byron's stint in the uplands.

Their short run up the beach had the four men all bending with their hands on their knees, struggling for breath. As they gasped for air, Byron saw that their thin limbs looked oddly slack and their torn clothes were filthy and dappled with wet sand.

Jake moved to grab him in a bear-hug and Byron deftly avoided the embrace. Jake was unfazed and hurried to explain that they were hoping the church might let them have some water. The men looked half-starved and although he doubted the vicar would be pleased, Byron knew Father Chickering would not turn the four of them away. He waved them in through the gate then thought to have them stop and brush the sand from their clothes out in the garden. He was leading them all inside when they ran into Longers lurking outside by the belfry tower. The sailor stared at the four shabby strays then back at Byron as if to say, 'have you lost your mind?'

"Don't worry—I can vouch for them—Jake and me used to dig together on Lion Hill."

"Hard-ears boy never get too far—" Longers grumbled, stalking back inside the church ahead of them.

Pastor Chickering's serene expression never changed as he followed the scowling sailor out of the rectory and saw the four disheveled vagrants skulking in the aisle next to Byron. He said they were welcome to stay and regain their strength but unfortunately his resources were not unlimited and so, except for the children, they would have to be satisfied with one meal a day.

With murmuring thanks to God and the vicar, Jake and his friends made short work of some offered strips of dried meat and four cups of hot mint tea. When they had taken the edge off their hunger the men sat down with Byron, eager to share their recent adventures. They had left camp to spend their two free days in Colón and gotten arrested on their very first night when they were caught out on the street not realizing there was an eight o'clock curfew. The next day an army officer had shown up at the calaboose saying he needed more volunteers and the four of them would be released without charge if they joined his battalion. "I told him we were in Panama to dig not to shed people's blood," Jake started to explain and one of his buddies promptly chimed in. "We tried to tell him we had a contract to work for the French and they were expecting us back in Gatun—"

"He just gave us a dirty look—" the third digger butted in. "Him look down him nose and say—'then I guess you cowards are gonna be spending this whole war in jail.'"

"They had us in there five whole days when this black-skin soldier showed up in the calaboose with these two barefoot Jamaicans. He said something about the invaders being in retreat and that General Prestàn had ordered all prisoners who hadn't been sentenced by the magistrate released," Jake recalled, taking charge of the story. "I'll never forget that proud black man with his shiny red boots and his big-ole sword."

"Reynal!" Byron gasped.

"You know 'im?" Jake asked with sharp surprise.

"Sort of...not really...go on—" Byron said quickly, praying Mr. Wo was not within earshot.

The digger from Belize, who the three Jamaicans jovially referred to as Runnylip, picked up the story. "It took us awhile to draw some sense outta what Red Boots was sayin'—then we realize him was lookin' for us to fall in line behind his general. Since only a dummy would let a ghost fool him the same way twice, Jake and miself figure is better we all go along with Red Boots and get outta this jail—then first chance we get we can scamper."

So the four had joined up with the rebels but instead of handing them rifles and teaching them to shoot, they had them sweeping up Colón's foul mess. They were in the middle of shoveling raw filth when Red Boots ordered Jake and Runnylip to go and bury a man the government troops had shot dead in the street and left for some giant buzzards to eat. Then, once they were done cleaning the street, the four of them had to haul in these big heavy carts loaded with barrels and help barricade the whole town.

Jake paused and looked at Byron miserably. "That's when we knew we'd gotten mixed up in sumpun serious—but we was so dog tired from all that haulin' and diggin' we didn't have strength to scamper. When the madness start we were all lying in the police-house sleeping..."

"Not all-o-we was sleeping! Don't listen to Jake—if it wasn't for me them three fools would probably burn up!" boasted Runnylip, who claimed to know who started the fire.

"Red Boots had told those of us without any weapons to make sure keep inside but when I heard the gunshots start coming closer I decide I better check the street and see what was happ'nin' in case we need to hightail it outta there. Day did just barely light as I was climbing up the barracks' back wall—and when I peer down to the street I see this man sneaking around in back of the armory. It look like him was going around pouring kerosene oil from this big-ole tin, then I see him glance back over him shoulder then him quick duck back down the alley. I ran to wake these fools and couple minutes later we all heard this big explosion—Jake thought it was cannon but soon after that is when we heard men shouting, 'fire! fire!'"

In the turmoil the four friends had managed to escape. They ended up running clear to the docks and straight into the arms of six of Prestàn's men guarding the wharf and holding two Yankee officials in custody. Jake and his companions were ordered to sit right on the dock with their hands behind them. They had seen the barracks where they'd just been sleeping send red flames into the dark morning sky. As the fire spread, people had swarmed to the docks, hoping to board one of the standing vessels. In the confusion, the two white men had escaped and when their guards turned to search, the four friends managed to sneak off once again. They had been on the lam, struggling to survive, ever since.

"Praise God, it rained. We could cope widout any food but by the third day we were ready to drink the sea-water," Jake confessed, knitting his brow as he recalled their growing desperation. "I defy any man to convince me that dying from violence or even starvation is as bad as dying for just a sip of fresh water..."

Longers, who had come up quietly and had been following the whole grim story, called out to Byron. "Just think—if Miss Estelle hadn't made me promise to keep you in this church you could have been out there with them, going crazy, drinking sea-water."

Before Byron could express his annoyance at being teased in front of his comrades he heard Mr. Wo start to speak. "You say fire start in police barracks—where militia sleeping?" Wo came wandering up and stared at the newcomers gravely, one by one.

"That's where it started all right," said Runnylip, nodding bluntly. "I was the first one smell the smoke—"

"I hate to say it but the big talker is right—who the hell knew we were sleeping next to dynamite? That big nose of his gave us the time to get the hell outta there!"

The blood drained from Wo's burned face and he stood silent and perfectly still, like a man suddenly cored of his essence. Finally he turned towards Byron and bowed deeply. "Please accept Yick Wo's apology...sorrow make Wo judge too quickly."

Byron smiled inside but did not reply.

The advent of the four young exiles transformed the atmosphere in the church almost instantly. The children seemed to have forgotten their grief and by the next day were happily playing countless games of hide and seek with Jake and Runnylip. With his compatriots there for company Byron was no longer in a rush to set off on his own, especially after hearing their story. Even the vicar came out of his shell and began to invite Wo's three eldest children up to the belfry to help him ring his bells. And each day, after their single midday meal, he and Longers would disappear into the rectory and converse there, sometimes for hours.

As their first Sunday in exile loomed, Byron found himself sharing the refugees' collective yet unspoken urge to restore the church's sober decorum. His own nose was acutely aware that it had been days since any of them had washed or changed clothes and he feared how their presence would be received by the white congregation. He made them all pledge to sit out of sight up in the choir loft but when Father Chickering learned of their plan, the vicar insisted they share the pews right in front and those who had been baptized accept communion.

Byron spent the early morning trying to shake the rankness and smoke from his shirt and trousers while counting the minutes until the nine A.M. service. The awaited hour arrived with the eleven exiles sitting primly in the second and third rows, straining to repress their anxiety. They sat there silent and on edge for fifteen minutes until finally a single worshiper, an English spinster in her mid-to-late forties, appeared in the aisle and quickly sat in the pew next to Byron.

She seemed not the slightest bit put off by the grubby exiles and while they waited for Father Chickering to read his opening sentences she whispered her apologies for her missing fellow congregants. "They've all been evacuated to Panama City except for the nervous willies who are afraid to even set foot from their homes. I tried to tell my North American friends that Panama's little squabbles aren't all that dangerous—they're what these hot-blooded country-puts use for a bit of entertainment."

Throughout the service Longers' expression was that of a new convert lost in rapture. His face seemed positively beatific when Pastor Chickering, looking even smaller and more frail than usual inside his bulky chasuble, assured them Christ's kingdom was a harbor for the downcast and the outcast alike. Stressing that forgiveness was despair's divine comfort the vicar shifted his benevolent gaze from Byron to pensive Mr. Wo. When near the end of the short sermon he asked if there was someone who needed a special benediction, Longers rose to ask if the good one did could make up for the bad. Father Chickering regarded Longers with an incandescent smile and answered yes, there was a place in God's heart for all, even the most misguided.

"Then I'm asking Him please to protect Miss Estelle Morales and guide her to her honest salvation," Longers declared with great passion and a special confidence appeared to pass between him and the beaming vicar.

"When we leave this church you'll be walking with a new-made Christian," Longers whispered proudly in Byron's ear.

Except for Longers and the quiet Wos, everyone went to kneel at the altar rail and accept communion. After the twelve raised their disharmonious voices for a ragged Gloria in Excelsis, Pastor Chickering delayed the final blessing and asked that everyone join him out in the narthex for a special sacrament. When they had formed themselves into a circle he had Longers kneel by the large stone fountain. Dabbing the sailor's brow with the holy water he made the sign of the cross three times while chanting the anointing benediction. He asked the eleven witnesses to bow their heads for one last prayer then loftily said, "rise, Joseph

Douglas McCatty and be of good cheer—you are now part of Christ's episcopal family."

The novelty of Sunday's communion service and baptism was followed by the vicar surprising them with a treat from his private stock of chocolates. The rich sweets along with his two tiny glasses of some aged port wine made Byron's Monday pass with intolerable slowness. By evening, having imbibed his fill of soapy soup and Runnylip's drawn-out anecdotes, he was openly begging God for deliverance. He awoke Tuesday morning to find his prayers magically answered. The railroad superintendent appeared before the listless refugees like the Angel Gabriel disguised in Yankee flesh. He announced that his company had set up camps on an eastside beach and that all were welcome. Even poor Mr. Wo jumped up with a smile and hugged his children who began to dance and clap with joy. Byron had Johnny's violin back inside its case, and was halfway down the aisle when Longers strode up and blocked his path.

"Miss Estelle told us to wait until she could send for us and that's what we're doin'."

"Yuh stay if yuh like, I'm going!"

"You made her a promise—what's the hurry?"

Byron stared up at Longers with eyes glazed. "What's the hurry?...yuh never hear the saying—'nuh bettah to walk than jus' siddown?' I'm going crazy!"

"Hey, *bolow*—yuh not coming? The Yankee man says he's leaving!" Jake called out impatiently, peeking in from the narthex.

"Just give me a minute—" Byron yelled before returning to plead with the fearsome giant. "Look—the poor reverend is runnin' out of food. Can't yuh just thank Miss Estelle for me and tell her where me gone?"

"I'm not gonna let her waste time searching you out—or have her blame me if anything should happen—"

"Nutting's gonna happen!"

"You don't know that!"

Exasperated, Byron tried ducking out under his arm but Longers was too quick and shoved him back. Seeing that pleading was doing him no good, he tried using ridicule. "What a thing! A big-ole strapping sailor hiding in here like a church-mouse while a little white lady think nutting to climb in her buggy and drive herself to church. I bet is she that went and tole them to come help us—if she can do all that I can't see what yuh so afraid of."

"That's fine for her—she can poke her English head in the lion's mouth. She's the one who trained it."

Byron looked off with a sigh, hearing the vicar telling Wo's little girls goodbye and spied Jake signaling him from the door to say he was leaving to catch up with the others. Although he was boiling mad, he still did not have the courage to challenge Longers. He slumped back to his pew, bitterly resigned. But time was on his side. Sooner or later Longers would turn his back. He just had to wait and be ready to fly.

Chapter 17

WITH THE *FEDERALES* HELD down in Colón by Pedro Prestàn and his motley band of heroes, ex-president Aizpuru seized the capital and appointed himself the People's High Commander. Our new potentate somehow imagined the Americans would be so pleased to be free of Bogotá's greedy lot they would overlook his dark skin and liberal politics and wreathe him in garlands. It was a sad calculation. I am sorry to report that Panama's brave strike for independence has not been greeted with flowers or shiny brass bands. The U.S. Marines are about to land and will no doubt support the new dictatorship. So, I expect the spot our enterprising Mr. Aizpuru shall soon be commanding will be one from the gallows. As for the clever Mr. Prestàn, it seems he has escap—

Thomas swore under his breath as the bent nib leaked ink, smearing more of his words before he could use his blotter. He grabbed fresh paper and started over, removing mention of the gallows, but after reading the altered paragraph, he cursed again, this time out loud. Get to the point, he muttered, crumpling the fifth aborted sheet—details just serve to confuse and make matters more complicated.

However, the thorny problem still remained. By now his mother was certain to have read the sensationalized newspaper reports and be in a fearful state. For his plan to succeed, he needed to convince her that he understood the dangers, his health was good and while the entire southern hemisphere was not facing Armageddon, he would be safer someplace else. The trick was deciding just how much of the country's current intrigue to get into without provoking any maternal hysterics.

His strategy finally balanced, he sat up at his desk and started the crucial letter from the beginning one last time.

Christophe-Colomb
April 22, 1885

Dear Mother,

I am living up to my promise and letting you know the latest on conditions here. Henri and I are beginning to have our disagreements. He has been remarkably kind these past two years, however, you can imagine the intense strain he is under with all this uncertainty. I do think it may be time to let the air clear between us.

It was a great relief that Christophe-Colomb was untouched by the fire. Even so, the canal work seems ready to unravel. Our latest director gave it his best but he has returned to France in despondency having lost his entire family to the last scourge of swamp fever. I suspect the gods or dark angels (or whatever one calls them) take ironic pleasure in smiting man's arrogance. Not a day went by when the poor fellow was not pontificating about clean-living being the great bulwark against harmful diseases. Let me say now, mother, that if such notions hold any merit then I deserve your absolute faith as I suffer with nary a cough nor a hint of my earlier ailment.

I must confess the atmosphere in Panama is very ugly. Prestàn completely humiliated Colombia's new government. The newspapers are blaming him for Colón burning to the ground—personally, I think the little rascal should get a medal. If nothing else, he has cleansed that vermin-ridden city. The French are convinced the Americans deliberately delayed taking charge in order to undermine the project. Henri does not believe it was a wholesale conspiracy but is convinced that some foreign cabal has been manipulating de Lesseps and is looting the company. At any rate, the Yanks have become extremely unpopular. Suddenly, almost everyone here seems to detest them.

So you can see, mother, that while I have survived unharmed so far, it behooves me to seek greener pastures. I have stinted on all indulgences so I should be able to scrape up enough to make passage to Venezuela. Now don't go worrying, I am told by estimable sources that for a capable man with a tidy bit of cash there are excellent profits to be made there.

Before he signed off with greetings to friends and family, Thomas perused his handiwork with satisfaction. If his reckoning proved right, not only would his mother be grateful for his prudence but she would wish to ensure his well-being (and her continued influence) by making her next draft especially generous. For though neither his pride nor cunning would allow him to ask for funds directly, one thing he had learned watching Duvay clean up at poker was that having a pot of loot at the start greatly improved one's chances at the end.

———

The tardy Yankee invasion and occupation coincided with the start of the dreaded yearly rains. Soon, just as Thomas had predicted, the French project was teetering near collapse. Another director had come and gone, stricken by herpes and pneumonia, and like the rest of the American firms that no longer felt welcome, the outfit that wrote Thomas' paycheck announced it was leaving. The decision had not been unexpected but Thomas had hoped the job would last, at least until he heard from his mother. If she turned him down, he would need every available nickel, dime and dollar to finance his plans in Venezuela. He was trying to divine some way to stay on and still make decent money when Henri proudly disclosed over dinner that he had arranged for them both to stay on as part of the canal company.

"No need to thank me," Duvay declared with a sniff when Thomas looked delighted and surprised. "This new director understands my insights are indispensable. Our project is about to undergo drastic changes. You won't be bored very much longer—that I can assure you!"

Thomas' euphoria was at an end even before his new position became official. He and Henri had not yet been assigned an office so the two of them were stuck working together at home, the engineer huddled downstairs in his study while Thomas made do in his upstairs bedroom. In constant mental agitation, Duvay seemed determined to exact his return for Thomas' past delinquency with compound interest. Contrary to his promise, there were more dreary statistics to be tabulated and transcribed—in triplicate—*tout de suite*! Worse, the Frenchman kept popping up at his side, his arms laden with new charts and designs he wanted copied. It was exhausting Thomas just listening to him bounce up and down the stairs and when he found himself working twelve hours a day, six days a week and half of Sunday, only the thought of his adventurous plans kept him from quitting.

Adding to his miseries, Genevieve seemed to have finally made good her threat and was avoiding him. When the chaos after the fire seemed to have slackened, he had rushed to the hospital and found his old ward standing half in ruin. He asked for Genevieve and was told she was gone. She had apparently induced the four Yankee leathernecks who had heroically arrived in time to save the building to help carry her invalid patients down to the brick Freight Station, but she never returned. All that Mother Agnes could tell him was that she'd heard from one of her priests that her young nurse was off caring for the sick among the homeless thousands.

It ran counter to his nature to exist in a self-pitying state, but the longer Genie was gone the more he regretted how abruptly they had parted. That night in the fluviograph tower, he had pressed her to share her dark secret. At first she would only whisper that before her Nana Binta passed away she had told her that she was good.

As someone who'd been betrayed by his own, Thomas could understand how Genie might have trusted—or even loved—an old Senegalese maid more than her own family. What he found much harder to swallow was that after being raised in a convent school and granted some passing knowledge of medical science his lover continued to put stock in primitive rituals involving such absurdities as animal sacrifice and the blessing of stones. He had not planned on starting a row but he had finally lost patience. He told her that imagining her pain could be cured by chanting away invisible goblins was even more nonsensical than believing one could sprout angel wings or walk on water. He regretted having hurt her, but how else was he supposed to react after she kept on insisting that some hoodoo African potion had saved his life.

When they both had calmed down he told her he was sorry and again begged her to tell him the whole story. Holding her close, he said he knew her pain was tied to her mother's death and it was time she eased her mind and told him why her father had died.

"A ten-year-old cannot be trusted to know what is evil about her nightmares..." she had replied as a teardrop wet his arm. "Do you really think I'm good?" she whispered after a long silence, her shy voice that of a child.

"Of course. You're my angel..."

When she failed to meet him as usual the following week, at first he had shrugged it off as her needing time for reflection. But now that Panama was again growing tense, knowing the person he loved most in the world was out on her own, at the mercy of anarchists and desperadoes, he found it impossible to carry on as if nothing had happened.

"An honest heart need not be troubled," Mother Agnes said obliquely when he came to ask a second time where Genevieve had gone. When Thomas gazed pleadingly at her face, the nun's ice-blue gaze bore the shards of censure. "The Lord giveth and He taketh away...trust His mercies. Grace and Genie's faith will preserve her."

He realized then that Mother Agnes knew more than she was telling him. He left her half in shock, appalled that no one else seemed troubled by Genevieve's recklessness. He saw now why the mother superior may have questioned Genie's readiness for an ascetic's life. Her biggest demon was her passion. Genie wanted it locked in a cloister and put safely out of mind. In the glow of his new burning devotion, Thomas concluded it meant they belonged together, eventually as man and wife.

Genie had clearly suffered something so onerous for the mind of a child that only her God, being permanent and omnipresent, could repair. He feared, seeing the reproach in Mother Agnes' eyes, that Genie had finally confessed and her going off alone was an act of penance. If that was the case, there was no point his chasing her shadow—better to wait and hope that given time she would forgive herself for falling in love with him. The more he pondered it the righter it seemed. He had to be patient. If he was going to compete with God, he had to prove he could provide what he decided she wanted most—a home where it was safe to feel loved. He had come to that conclusion having watched his mother slowly trade her pride for the shelter of his father's fortune. It had been hard for him to forgive her that submission, but he had come to accept that there were real advantages to having money. The challenge for him now was how to go about getting it!

His solution to his troubles did not make his day-to-day existence any more hopeful. He rarely smiled and his more serious demeanor had only encouraged Duvay to increase his workload. A large new drafting board was procured for his upstairs bedroom so that he could better copy the flood of new designs issuing from the engineer's feverish pencil. Thomas gave it his best, hoping to earn a healthy bonus, but frothing, the method Duvay now demanded, proved extremely fickle. It required wetting a sheet of copy paper then delicately rubbing a coin across his tracing cloth. When his mentor came and rested a guiding hand on his to gently demonstrate the correct amount of pressure, Thomas quickly jerked himself away. "No need to squire me like a woman, *monsieur*! I'll get the hang of it—"

"As you say—but I expect no more clumsy imperfections!" Duvay snapped back as he stormed out looking wounded.

It had been a purely paternal embrace but Thomas had never enjoyed a father's touch and he was still haunted by perverted rumors. Several spoiled tries later he decided it was easier to throw away the coin and use his thumbnail to transfer the markings. Even then, the merest slip rewarded him with an unsightly ridge or gouge which proved, after much swearing and painstaking effort, completely irreversible. It did not help to steady his hand that he was still sleeping poorly or that thanks to his boorish reaction Duvay was back to being his old abrasive nitpicking self.

Life seemed to hang in suspense as he waited for his mother to reply. He worried more each day that she had shown his letter to his father and he had bullied her into turning him down. Without the extra money Thomas feared he would be forced to put off his plans or perhaps abandon them altogether. He had given up hope of earning that bonus, until it occurred to him that he was working many more hours without a penny of added pay. A commensurate raise seemed only fair. His mentor, however, saw things quite differently.

"You complained that you were bored just totting up figures—so I entrust you with work of immense importance and instead of concentrating upon the task at hand, all that's on your mind is your pound of flesh. Money, money, money! Is that all you were bred to think of?"

Thomas resented the coarse insinuation but with his future in mortal limbo he was not about to indulge his temper now. Besides, knowing Henri, he was inclined to overlook the bigoted remark and chalk it up to the effects of sustained mental stress. It had taken a good deal of lobbying to convince Gustav Eiffel and those other top engineers in Paris to back his revisions and present them to de Lesseps, and having succeeded, poor Henri was locked in a hopeless race against failure. Still, being denied even a token raise did not help settle Thomas' nerves. It seemed his tracings grew sloppier the harder he tried. After bravely laboring on while being flayed by his mentor's caustic criticisms, he was primed to strike when Duvay came racing in to address him.

To his surprise, instead of damning his latest efforts, the Frenchman announced that he had been summoned to meet with the canal board tomorrow to discuss his new plan. "We're nearly there, my boy—we're nearly there!"

The next morning, after joining Duvay for breakfast and wishing him luck in Panama City, Thomas sat down to tackle his work and was suddenly grasped by an irresistible whim. The rainy season's normally torrid air felt endearingly light and the glimpse of sunshine coming through his window hinted at a rare blue sky. Telling Monique vaguely he'd be back in a while, he strolled to the station and boarded the next train, thinking he'd enjoy a refreshing trip across part of the isthmus.

Just to be back outdoors brought a sense of liberation. After settling upon a seat in the mahogany car, Thomas drew down his window and stuck out his head like a schoolboy. In his sleep-starved state the effect of the warm wind whipping his face while the jungle flashed densely by was hypnotic. He hung there for several minutes with his mouth stretched wide then slipped back into his seat feeling weightless, as if floating at the delightful edge of sleep. He barely heard the train bell's clang or felt the coaches rattle and roll to a jerky stop. He sat up rubbing his eyes and was startled to see the stalks of green bamboo he'd first imagined as sentries guarding the rails climbing up and into his car. It took a moment for his eyes to convince him that it was actually two soldiers in plain green uniforms lugging their big outdated rifles. They wore the world-weary look of jaded peasants but he could not tell if they were part of the militia that had sided with the *federales* or fresh conscripts brought in from the countryside.

Their broad Indian faces darkened as they caught Thomas staring their way. When they made no attempt to hide their hatred as they slouched down directly across the aisle, Thomas wondered at its cause. Was it that they could see he was a foreigner and they were tired of all the foreigners? Were they farmers bitter to know that whether or not Panama got its grand canal, the land was no longer theirs to cherish? Or was their contempt saved for men like him who, having lost claim to land of their own, appeared like mooching nomads, groping for what fools like Pedro Prestàn called freedom. If that is what stirs their wrath, Thomas sneered to himself inside, then the joke's on them. Any man taking orders is a slave—even if his pride tells him to scorn the *gringo's* shovel and carry a gun.

The soldiers glared at him one last time then faced away, the brims of their high-peaked straw hats touching as they sank into quiet conversation. Although they both seemed happy to ignore him, Thomas kept them under watch from the corner of his eye. It was widely known, from even before the fiery insurrection, that Panama's poorly-paid soldiers were not above extorting cash from some hapless Jamaican, so he was relieved when they stood up to get off at Bohio Soldado.

The old locomotive chugged on, straining stoutly to make the steep grade. As they parted from the canal line, leaving behind the mechanical sounds of air drills and steam-run shovels, Thomas picked out the roar of the Chagres moments before it came majestically into his view. In his wariness to pass by the armed soldiers he had stayed on board much longer than he'd planned, but as they crested the slope to Tabernilla and he saw the long white plunge of cascading water, he was seized by a second rebellious whim.

———

"How long you say you been in Panama?"

The belabored question was plainly designed to rankle. The stick-limbed Jamaican had already ruined Thomas' smugness at having guessed from the man's starched khaki shirt and the hitch in his step that he was a straw-boss for one of the crews digging down in the canyon, but he still insisted on being a pisser.

"Look, we've been over this three times—" Thomas griped in frustration. "I tell you I've been with the company going on three years. We both know the Cut needs diggers, so what are we standing out in the hot sun quibbling over? Point me to a shovel and I'll get started!"

The straw-boss looked incredulous. "Dressed like that?"

Thomas suddenly remembered he was wearing his red satin vest and pin-striped trousers. "I know a bunch of these men," he lied smoothly. "I'm sure one of them won't mind lending me his extra dungarees."

The foreman's face, scored with pits from a bout of smallpox, scrunched with a look that said he was struggling to decide if Thomas was a pampered scamp or some poor loon put off his head by sickness. He took one more craving glance up to the little camp store where he'd been heading, then dug inside his back pocket and pulled out a small slip of paper. Stopping to lick the tip of his thumb, he unfolded it carefully and pointed to the bottom. "Write your full name here," he commanded. "If the French boss says it's a go you can start tomorrow. Just make sure you're back here by six o'clock, sharp."

"Um...I was hoping I might spend the night in camp..." Thomas cajoled, stepping in again to block the foreman's path.

The middle-aged Jamaican looked towards the heavens to silently ask why he was being punished with this crazy impediment intent on keeping him from that pack of snuff. He turned back to Thomas with a caustic snarl. "You need a signed contract before I can let you sleep in camp."

"No need to act so touchy!...I'll sign one now."

The foreman drooped and again gazed skyward before peering at his pest with a smirk. "You say you been working here almost three years—then you should know that before you can get a contract you need to have a physical exam. Then if you pass—you gotta swear you'll stay here and dig for no less than two years."

"Look, I'm offering you an extra back for a week or maybe two—I'm not out for a whole career!"

Thomas watched in dismay as the straw-boss swore under his breath and folded up the paper. The problems with his unconsidered impulse were popping up faster than he could bat them down, but the challenge kept egging him on. His only chance now was to try and bluff.

"All right," he admitted. "I see I'll just have to be square with you—I work for the Eastern Division's top engineer. He's been complaining about progress down at the Cut being awful slow..." Thomas stopped and fixed a bold look on the baffled Jamaican. "I'd like to be able to report that my hardworking compatriots are doing a smashing job under trying circumstances."

The foreman studied him coldly. His eyes looked small and mean. "I don't know what game this is you're playing but if they catch you out don't bodda pretend you got my say so—'cause I'll deny it—" He shoved the crumpled paysheet against Thomas' chest and handed him a pencil from inside his sleeve.

As he stooped to scribble his name, Thomas could feel the foreman's unblinking glare warming him from his head to his toes.

The straw-boss grabbed back his paper and barked over his shoulder as he headed up the ridge to the little camp store with his haughty high-stepped gait. "Make sure when you show up tomorrow you have on proper poor man's clothes."

Thomas felt exhilarated, though somewhat astonished that his ploy had succeeded. Just as he had approached that canal-recruiter in Kingston on a caprice and ended up in Panama, he had produced this abrupt new adventure on a lark. It never occurred to him that the foreman was simply anxious to be rid of him.

Thomas thought about slipping into one of the barracks while the diggers were still at work then decided it was safer to wait and mingle with the men returning to camp. He would have liked to follow along to the hillside store and buy himself something to eat but he dared not risk a second encounter with the foreman until he was dressed in dungarees and holding a shovel. It was not quite three so he wandered back up the ascent towards the station not far from where Culebra's French engineers resided in their quaint little clapboard row-houses. A short walk down the settlement's new dirt road brought him to a tiny open shop snuggled in the shade from a half-grown amarillo tree. He paid the Chinese proprietor for a small spiced bun and a bottle of 'wash'—a mix of sugar and iced water flavored with a tiny squeeze of lime.

He hid from the sun beneath the amarillo's flowering branches and was promptly discovered by three stray dogs who sneaked up, coyly sniffing the air, at his first bite of bun. When he decided to simply ignore them, the dogs sat back patiently and watched him eat, their sad eyes drooling at the bun like expert beggars. It was clear why they had adopted the little French village as, apart from some patches of sparse fur, their coats looked remarkably sleek for Panama strays. "Sorry, chaps, I need this more than you," Thomas muttered as he polished off the bun and washed it down with one last gulp.

He left the disappointed dogs to sniff for crumbs and headed for one of the long looping trails leading to the flanks above the canyon. His only glimpse of the notorious Cut had been from a passing train and he reckoned now was the ideal chance for a closer look. The day had mercifully started to cool but the stretch along the ridge with the choicest view was like a furnace. There, the water that had seeped deep inside the earth was gradually heated to steam and came spurting back up through the rock at separate spots hundreds of feet across the surface. Thomas was weighing whether to try some other direction or retreat to lower ground when he spied a hollow safely away from the spouting geysers where part of the mountain shale had apparently been knocked free.

So this is the famous Culebra Cut the world has been flocking to see, he thought, as he gaped at the hillside bleeding blended shades of green, blue and red from three years of implacable digging. The mountain's weal of vivid striations was so staggering to the eye he wondered why the cash-strapped company had not thought to charge their visiting sightseers admission. At the trench's bottom, he saw what appeared to be close to a thousand diggers. From where he sat they resembled an army of black ants sprinkled in clusters around one of the

Cut's huge excavators. The machine was rumbling like a famished beast as it belched black smoke from two enormous pipes that threatened to blind him with their refracted sunlight. The diggers seemed to work with scarcely a pause. The only time some would stand and pause their shovels was when the next miniature train arrived to haul away more rubble.

Between them Thomas could see the pale-skinned French engineers busy running a mechanical chain with buckets connected to a pair of thirty-foot ladders. As the contraption scooped up mud with its slow systolic movements, he imagined a giant caterpillar lazily pushing its feed through its long fat body. Suddenly one of the dark clusters began rushing for the side of the mountain. One of the dump trains had made it partway up and stopped and men were dashing to help its frantic crew shore up the rails where the road-bed was beginning to crumble.

Against Culebra's sheer size, the thrashings of man and machine seemed valiant but puny. Even if he was wrong and their task was not hopeless, at the rate this dig was going, it would be at least thirty more years before any ship would be sailing between oceans across this mountain.

Miraculously, the men had managed to secure the shifting rails before they tumbled. Returning to follow the earth-eater's ponderous motions, Thomas felt his eyes growing heavy and he finally dozed off. He'd been drowsing for over an hour when he was stirred by the drift of human chatter. He ducked out from his hollow and raced headlong down the slope, overjoyed when he recognized the burly recruit who had heard their cries when he and Byron lay trapped in their tomb after the earthquake. The digger was lumbering up, bare-chested like his weary comrades, a soaked blue shirt tied loosely at his waist. The men all stopped as one seeing Thomas charging towards them, waving like a lunatic.

"Long time no see, partner! Glad you haven't let this rough job wear you down!" Thomas held up short when the sturdy young digger stood looking befuddled. "You don't remember me—? I'm the chap with the mashed ribs you saved from an early grave."

The bull-necked digger still looked puzzled then slowly unmasked a dazzling grin. "Oh yes—kiss mi granny! Sure—now I remember! You're de rich boy dat got himself hurt savin' his little buddy!" He gave Thomas such a lusty slap on the back he had to struggle to keep from wincing. "We all thought you were long gone from Panama!"

Thomas shared a husky laugh and gave the Jamaican a friendly hug. The sudden gesture made some of the passing men stop and stare, trying to make sense of the improbable couple: one half-naked, his dark molasses skin caked in salted sweat and mud, the other a cool light brown in a red satin vest and striped wool trousers.

The white-toothed digger put a hand to his jaw as he stood back to admire Thomas' expensive clothes. "Looks like yuh landed back on your feet pretty sweet..."

"Let's just say I've had my ups as well as my downs."

"So, what yuh doin' down in this pest-hole rubbin' shoulders with us meager quashie?"

"You look pretty fit for a man you call meager," Thomas replied, admiring the digger's thick muscular body. "I've been behind a desk so long my body's almost turning to water. I figured I could use a little hard work out in the sunshine so I came to give you fellows a hand."

"Yuh playin'!"

"No sah—yuh can tell ole granny me dead serious," Thomas mimicked with a chuckle. "By the way—the name is Judah—Thomas Judah—"

He stuck out his hand and the digger held back but then, as if deciding it wasn't a trick, swiped his palm across his muddy trousers and accepted the greeting. "Me christen name Godfrey—Godfrey Patterson—but everyone prefer call me 'Cuffie'.

"Good to get reacquainted, Cuffie...I still owe you—" said Thomas before drawing the Jamaican aside and slinging another brotherly arm around his broad shoulders. "I do have one more favor to ask you..."

By the time the sun had fully dipped, Cuffie had hunted up a pair of cast-off dungarees and for a nominal price talked the comrade using the single bed beside him to yield it to Thomas. When the cooks refused to serve Thomas without a tag, Cuffie prevailed on three of his friends to put aside some of their portions and sneak them back to the barracks. Presented with the torn-off crusts of their mold-topped bread and some gray-looking mutton, Thomas gave a sickly look and said, thanks, but he was not all that hungry.

"Yuh better eat if you expect to work for old Deggy," Cuffie warned as they sat on the ground outside. "Yuh gonna need every bit of your strength come tomorrow."

Thomas chewed as much of the leathery meat as his jaws could manage, then happily tossed the rest into the bushes when Cuffie was distracted by some arriving comrades. To show his thanks and join the fold as the friends gathered to sit and shoot the breeze, Thomas regaled them with fantastical accounts of his jungle adventures. When he sensed them getting restless and start to surreptitiously swap rolling eyeballs, he would bow his head with a sigh and admit there was no point his going on with his story: "You're right—it just sounds too crazy—even I wouldn't believe me..." and each time he managed to tease back their willingness to be deceived. "—when that big-ole alligator tipped our canoe into the water all I could think was the brute is gonna bite one of my legs-them clean off! Meantime the rain is pouring in buckets and the river is swellin' and startin' to roar like an angry lion! I just had to hold that crocodile's long mouth tight and pray its big ugly tail didn't cut me in two!"

When the men had swallowed all the tall-tales they could stomach, they straggled off to bed, agreeing that even if they had to carry this big talker, he was sure to provide some good entertainment. Cuffie, who'd been silently beaming, hanging on Thomas' every word, was thrilled to be able to call such a smart engaging fellow his friend. Back in the barracks he showed Thomas where he kept his private stash of phosphorus matches. "I had to hide them because chaps were always beggin' one to light up a smoke," Cuffie explained. He pointed to a shelf above their heads a few feet to his left. "I put it up after the Frenchies finally took out those darn top bunks so I'd have someplace for my personal things. Just so you know—I keep a box of extra candles up there—the ones they give us are hard to light and the minute you breathe on them they're ready to go out. Just help yourself, anytime—" He quietly slipped Thomas one of the candles along with a copy of yesterday's paper. "I lifted it from one of the fellows," he whispered with a grin. "I know an educated chap such as yourself looks forward to his nightly read."

Thomas was too wound up as he lay back in his bunk to focus on yesterday's news. His mounting disappointments were still heavy on his mind. Had this blasted canal lived up to its promise, he could have left here a hero. Instead, he was left to pray that his mother would save him from hearing his father brand him a failure. No, he muttered to himself inside, tomorrow could not come soon enough. A few days hard labor would clear his head. Instead of fretting about his future and getting frustrated with Genevieve, he would take it all out on the glorious Cut.

The mountain paid him back in short order. In his fury he had started out at a reckless pace. His palms were raw before he was halfway through his first day digging. The second day he learned to handle his pick with more prudence but still ended up shredding his skin, leaving his hands two scarlet claws he could no longer fully open. By the third day, the claws were two slabs of tender pulped meat wrapped in gauze to staunch the bleeding which, despite his willful pride, had him laboring at a loafer's pace. His pains seemed to tickle Old Deggy, who kept stopping by just to needle him.

"Remember, Mister Big Man's assistant, the deal was—if you quit before finishing out the week you gotta pay for that bed and all this food I been letting the Frenchies feed you."

"Don't mind Old Deggy—" said Cuffie when Thomas muttered that he was tempted to show the pock-faced pimp he could still use his fists, "after all—he must've done some pretty smooth talking to get them to hire you."

"Maybe so—" Thomas grumbled, not bothering to mention his bluff and biting his lip against the pain as Cuffie started to unwrap his red-stained bandages, "but it takes a hard man to grin at seeing another man bleed."

Thomas' fourth day in the Cut was a near calamity. Mid-morning the sky had abruptly gone black, and lost in his own world, dreaming of Genevieve, Thomas failed to notice when the rest of his team all grabbed up their shovels and made a dash for higher ground. By the time he heard them shouting the heavens had opened. Within seconds the churned-up ground was a river of sliding mud. Thick raindrops were falling like bullets but after wrenching his back the previous day he was clumsy and slow-footed. By the time he managed to shamble across to the slope and start the awkward climb, the terrace sixteen feet above was beginning to slip. Before he had climbed three steps he was sinking deeper in mud. He tried to dig his way up with the shovel but the toppling earth kept pushing him back, pressing his knees like a large fondling animal. He shut his eyes against the pelting rain and went stumbling backwards. He was about to fall when he felt a sudden tug that, for a moment, left him half-floating on top of the sludge. By some miracle, a stout rope was now cinched around his shoulders and he was face down, sliding upwards, struggling to keep the mud from his nose and mouth.

He dragged himself onto his feet, no longer aware of the pain in his back as he grasped the thick line with desperate fingers. The rain was a dense gray sheet but he felt sure the hefty back he saw up ahead belonged to Cuffie. His bull-necked friend must have hiked back down with the rope around his waist, tossed the lasso around Thomas' shoulders, then signaled the men up above to haul the two of them up to stable ground.

As they both crawled panting onto the crest, the diggers greeted them with hugs and hurrahs. Thomas learned that anytime an avalanche did not cost a man his life, there was reason to celebrate.

It was an hour before the deluge tapered to an end. The ladder dredge lay ruined under four feet of mud, as did Thomas' three days of agonizing labor. The reality that he could have easily lost his life for a worthless job made him wonder how anyone could get up each day to face such a callous joke. He grew even more depressed when he tried to thank his friend for his courage and Cuffie, in his simple straightforward way, told him to save his praise for Old Deggy. "He's the one run to fetch dat rope and made the lasso."

It took a nasty gulp of humble pie but Thomas steeled himself and went to thank Old Deggy for saving his life.

"I hope it was worth it. Now, don't go mashing up your mouth—" the foreman said when Thomas started to grimace, "you and I both know damn well you weren't raised to do hard labor. By gum—I never thought the fellow who came here spouting all that rubbish could swallow that much crow! I guess you got a lot firmer stomach than I did credit you for."

"Thanks—I guess..."

"You're all right, Judah," the foreman grinned, clamping a bony grip on Thomas' slouched shoulder. "Stay on if you like—but here's my advice: you got a head start up life's mountain—stop trying to show how tough you are with your back—show us with your head."

Chapter 18

It had only taken an hour once the other refugees had left for Byron to feel oppressed by the absolute quiet. He missed hearing the stone church suddenly echo with a child's quick laughter, or feeling Jake's elbow nudge into his side when Runnylip got tripped up during one of his long winding fables. Now, even those sensory recollections had lapsed into the void. His hope of escape seemed to have vanished as Longers had apparently guessed his intentions and attached himself to Byron's side. He could no longer even go out to pick some fresh mint for the vicar's four o'clock tea without the sailor showing up on his tail like a ball and chain. He had planned to slip away while Longers and Father Chickering were having one of their long private sessions, but the vicar had decided, now that they were the last two exiles, to hold their afternoon talks out in the nave so that Byron would feel welcome to join the discussion.

Byron bided his time the entire week waiting for the moment when a break in the rain found Longers safely at a distance and out of view. Finally, one sunny Friday morning, his chance arrived. He snatched up Johnny's fiddle and made a dash for the iron front gate. He was nearly out to the sidewalk when the huge hand clamped around his neck. After that, he could not cross the garden to use the privy without Longers ghosting his trail. He thought about sneaking off while the giant was sleeping, but odds were he'd be arrested or even shot if he was caught trying to slink into Christophe-Colomb in the dead of night. There was no way around it—either he was going to have it out with Longers or stay here and go out of his mind.

"I'm leavin' this time—and don't yuh try stop me!" he declared, confronting the astonished sailor with his fists at the ready.

"You're gonna fight in the Lord's own house? I thought you were a Christian—"

"I don't want to fight yuh, Longers, but I can't spend my whole life sittin' inside here—it's time me reach my friend, Thomas—"

"You done waited this long—" Longers contended, "a few more days can't hurt you. Anyway—what make you so sure he means to help you? You been waiting to see him nearly six whole months—your friend hasn't exactly broken his neck to see you."

"Mas' Tom told me to come—I have his letter!"

"Miss Estelle didn't have the heart to tell you, but it's better you should know—she thinks you're setting yourself up for a big disappointment. He's just another rich man's son that—"

"What the hell does she know?" Byron cut in angrily. "Thomas is not like those fancy-pants she caters to. Tom Judah is my friend—he mashed up his ribs to save my hide."

The fierceness of Byron's loyalty seemed to take the wind out of Longers' argument. The sailor sat down looking stumped. "What to do now?" he murmured with cheerless eyes. "This'll probably just end up a wild goose chase...but a promise is a promise and I gave Miss Estelle my word I'd look after you. I believe in loyalty and seeing as I'm learning what it means to be a Christian I suppose I shouldn't find it hard to take care of you as a brother."

"Me not askin' yuh to take care of me! I just want to move on—I feel like I'm your prisoner—"

"Nobody's making you a prisoner—it just don't make sense to be sailing from port when yuh not sure where yuh going or if the storm is even over."

"Look around!" Byron cried, pointing inside the empty church. "You see any ships inside here? Everybody done sailed! You can stay here wasting up your life—I'm not the one pining for a loose woman's favors!"

Longers stood with his own fist raised then held himself in check. "You sauce-boxes think you know it all—that's why you're such a nuisance to try and teach how to manage a ship. You can't just jump and do everything quick—it takes experience to handle your sails. Life is the same. You need to take time—take things easy and learn to be smooth."

"Patience is a virtue but too much will hurt you," Byron quoted impudently, suddenly no longer afraid to face Longers' fury.

"One day that attitude is gonna cost you—" Longers sighed, wagging his head. "All right, you win—but will you grant me one favor?...come pray with me before we go?"

"We—? How yuh mean, we—?"

"Since you're set on being stubborn I'm going with you—but if we don't find your friend up in Cristobal you're coming right back here and waiting for Miss Estelle."

"Why? I never ask you!"

"No more argument!" Longers snapped. "You heard me—I'm coming with you. Now kneel down here beside me and show me how to pray."

Byron gaped at Longers with his mouth hung-open. "You want me to teach you how you should pray?"

"That's right. I've lived a wandering bare-knuckle life. The minute I stepped inside this place I started to feel different—strange—as if I'd been led here for a purpose. I always went along with a nose for a nose and a tooth for a tooth, but now that I've been in here thinking, I wonder what it got me...I got no wife—much less a son to carry on when I'm gone. The vicar says that if you learn to love, God's light shines through you and can change a person's heart. He said I should pray for what I want—but how? I figure if I'm gonna speak to God in person before I go trouble him with all what's on my mind I should know some proper words to pray."

Longers moved in closer to Byron who drew back, on the lookout for a trick. "Don't fret—I'm not looking to trap you. I already gave you my word. You're being reckless, but I'm not gonna stop you."

The two men knelt down together and Longers turned to Byron with a whisper. "Go ahead and start and I'll try follow..."

Byron racked his brain, not knowing how to begin. He vaguely remembered a handful of verses he'd had to memorize for his Sundays of schooling but doubted he could still find them in the Bible or if those words were from actual prayers.

"Come on—start," Longers hissed.

"Mi not rememberin'—"

"You mean you used to go to church almost every Sunday and you never pray?"

"Sure, mi pray!"

"Then start!"

He wanted to recite 'the Lord is my shepherd' but feared he'd be lost once he strayed past the second verse. Finally he shut both eyes tight and ventured the single passage that had been drummed inside of his head. "O, my God...I be ashamed and blush to raise up my face to thee..." he paused to peek up at Longers who stayed kneeling with his tall frame perfectly erect and his eyes tightly closed.

"Go on—why you stop—?"

"—O, my God—for our iniquities are bigger over our head, and our t-trespass is risen to the heavens—I can't—"

"Keep going!"

"Since...since the days of our fathers have we trespassed...and after all that is come upon us for our wickedness...we cannot stand before thee—A-Amen!" Byron sputtered, bringing the ad hoc prayer to a hasty end.

"Amen! That was fine—just right!" Longers said approvingly, grabbing Byron by his shoulder. "Come—let's go and ask Father Chickering to bless our journey and be on our way."

At Longers' request, the vicar graced them with a parting prayer then warmly bade them God's speed. The friends were almost at the front gate when he came hurrying after them.

"Joseph! You forgot your weapon—" he said, holding out the old flintlock.

"Thanks, Rev," said Longers, tucking the gun in the back of his waist. "But I plan on burying it once I get the hang of what it takes to be a good Christian."

"Ours is not the easiest path but you'll find it is the road to the serenity you seek," Pastor Chickering said, his waxy face shining as he smiled his encouragement.

The two exiles thanked the reverend again and veered east for Christophe-Colomb. They were barely past sight of the church when a patrol of federal troops swooped in and surrounded them with bayonets pointed. The soldiers' eyes were on the long-limbed sailor as they circled the men like cautious spear-hunters rounding an eight-foot bear. Byron stood scarcely breathing, too scared to move or say a word. He was stunned that Longers seemed content to wait for a member of the platoon to speak first and take charge. When moments passed and no one had said a word or come forward, he inquired politely why they were being detained. The sailor's patois-flavored English seemed to raise their captors' hackles.

A copper-skinned soldier, his dark-billed cap askew above the blood-stained poultice on his forehead, swaggered out from the pack. His dull brown uniform appeared a size too large and his haggard face wore the leaden look of a man who had not slept in days. He gave his new captives a surly look then abruptly reversed his rifle and rammed the butt in the center of Longers' spine.

Bawling a command in Spanish, the platoon-leader had the troops form in line and with a wave of his bladed gun had them steer the two Jamaicans back past the Freight House and down to the railroad's terminal yard. They prodded them across the long snaking bands of iron tracks and into an open space where a detachment of United States Marines were loitering in back by a refitted flat car armored with skin of half-inch steel and mounted with two murderous-looking Gatling guns. The Marines all shared a contemptuous careless pose that conflicted with their smart blue jackets and shiny helmets. Their faces, burnt pink from the tropical sun, held a sheen of boredom that faded instantly seeing the platoon parading in their mismatched prisoners, one a giant, the other almost tiny.

Longers, who had been putting up a fuss the entire way, sent his voice booming across the main yard, antagonizing his Colombian guards who simply wanted him to shut up and wait. Longers was still loudly attempting to explain that he worked at the nearby shipyard when an officer with mutton-chop whiskers and a chestful of ribbons came ambling into the yard on a small red pony. The animal was straining piteously beneath his heft and one of the Marines yelled out to ask if he couldn't find a horse his own size to cripple.

The cheeky challenge drew gales of Yankee laughter which the officer haughtily ignored. His solid back poised, he slipped lightly out of his stirrups, which were close to scraping the ground. He continued to pretend not to hear the raucous *gringos* and after strolling past Longers with an icy glance, stopped a foot from Byron's nose and stared him up and down with intense fascination. He snapped out a question in Spanish and Byron froze in a deaf and dumb panic, his brain distracted by the whiff of stale beer and strong tobacco.

"*¿No habla español?*" the lieutenant mocked, winking back towards his men who bared several rows of crumbling teeth stained black from a diet of coffee and gnawed cigars.

"Hey, boy!" the cheeky Marine shouted over to Byron. "Tell the spick he needs to learn to speakee-de-English!"

There were more waves of Yankee laughter and the lieutenant stood rigidly still, preserving his majestic self-possession. Then all at once he wheeled back at Byron, who quailed to see that his grin was a mask of pure malice.

"*¡Mire, la manguerita negra se está retirando del fuego!* Look—his little black hose is helping put out the fire!" the lieutenant exclaimed, pointing to the dark patch spreading at Byron's crotch.

His captors doubled over, gasping with laughter. In his fright, Byron had experienced a strangely pleasurable release and now a second warm stream, this time of urine, was leaking down inside his thigh.

"A little late though, eh, *muchacho*? The nasty fires you *changos* started have all been extinguished!" the officer taunted in impeccable English. "Aha! And what have we here?" He exclaimed, pointing to Johnny's fiddle-case with sham surprise. "Look, *amigos! ¡Un instrumento!* So—you are a *violinista!*—or did you steal it?"

Before Byron could respond the officer snatched the fiddle from his hand. Longers jumped to intercede but was checked by the alert platoon-leader who stuck the point of his bayonet in the sailor's rib. Longers sagged, as if seriously wounded. When he stayed on his knees the soldiers lowered their rifles and bent towards him curiously. Longers was back on his feet in a flash and with a smooth swivel-hipped pivot, kicked the long gun from the platoon-leader's grip, sending it spinning through the air.

The Marines broke into full-throated cheers, applauding the fluency and power of the move. With the Colombians briefly stunned, Longers crouched close to the ground and, pulling the flintlock from his back, took dead aim at the haughty lieutenant.

The officer coolly held up his hand, disdaining the slightest show of fear. "What are you going to do—?" he sneered, halting his men when they rushed to take aim with their rifles, "shoot an officer of the Colombian federal guard in front of twenty witnesses?"

"I'm not out to shoot anybody," Longers answered truthfully. "I just want you people to stop and listen to—"

Before 'reason' was out of his mouth, the eight man platoon had him surrounded.

"Why are you assaulting us?" Longers cried as he easily brushed off his first few attackers. "We've done nothing wrong! You have no right!"

A sudden gunshot paused the scuffle and the sergeant quickly wrested away the old flintlock. The lieutenant stalked up to Longers and pressed the barrel of his smoking gun to the middle of his forehead. "I have no right?—have you forgotten this is my country? Be glad I must show our Yankee friends we are more civilized—we honor our laws...but please—" he warned in a whisper, "don't test me!—*¡Sargento!*" he thundered abruptly. "*¡Cuerda para atar sus manos!* Get some rope to tie his hands—then bind it around his black neck!"

"*Si, Teniente Rivueltas—¡si, señor!*" replied the troop-leader, scurrying off to one of the railcars nearby with a bright salute.

The rest of the platoon trained their rifles on Longers and the lieutenant tucked away his pistol then flipped open the black-cedar case. He lifted out the fiddle and admired it with a critical eye then ran two of his fingers gingerly across the catgut. "You need new strings," he said flatly. Reaching for the bow, he shoved it and the violin into Byron's chest. "Play us a tune. If you're any good, your *higueputa* goes free," he promised, tipping his head back over at the giant squatting on the ground inside a circle of bayonets.

"Spit in his eye!" Longers yelled, then gave a gasp as a soldier's boot slammed his ribs.

Byron stared at the magic fiddle and felt ill. He set the bow on a string and every muscle in his body locked tight. He stood there helplessly, too ashamed to glance back at Longers. His shoulders drooped and he let the fiddle slide down, slowly, from under his chin.

"Worthless apes—" Rivueltas hissed, grabbing the violin. "*¡Bueno! Sargento,*" he rasped, seeing the platoon-leader return, "*¡lleve los ladrones al centro y átelos con los otros!*—take these vermin and put them with the others!" He snapped his arm towards the Marines. "We shall show our *gringo* champions we don't need big noisy guns to deal with a few jack rabbits."

"*¡Si, comandante!*" said the sergeant, jumping to salute, though his blank look suggested the lieutenant's added words in English had not been comprehended.

Rivueltas slammed the fiddle back in its case and the Yanks responded with more hoots and whistles that grew into a taunting ovation when the struggling platoon finally restrained the powerful giant. Rivueltas turned his back to the cynical cheers and gave Byron a long malevolent glare. Then, gathering up every ounce of his dignified weight, he remounted the little sway-backed pony, dug his spurs into its tender flanks, and trotted off with Johnny's violin pinned high against his side.

The Marines retreated from the hot open yard, still chuckling as the sergeant mustered his troops back in line and ordered the prisoners marched back to the Front Street square. As he approached the fire-razed boardwalk, Byron could see the white bungalows of Christophe-Colomb tantalizingly within reach, a few hundred yards beyond the grassy divide. Seeing the pristine cottages peeking out from behind their slender palm-trees filled Byron with such anguish he started to purge fluid from every pore. Great flows of sweat poured out from his groin and armpits and at each step he felt his legs growing heavy as lead. "Longers—" he gasped in a quavering voice, "where yuh think we gonna end up?"

"Who can tell...maybe the nex' life—"

Without warning, the sergeant dashed up from the rear and poked Longers in the back with his bayonet so viciously the sailor hollered in pain. Longers cursed, roaring with anger as he squirmed to escape the binding rope, but the more he struggled the tighter it drew around his throat. Byron shuddered seeing his friend begin to choke as a dark spot of blood seeped out of the back of his jacket.

He nudged for Longers to keep still as he glimpsed the vengeance in the sergeant's shining eyes. He had seen eyes that cruel only once: they had belonged to men inflamed by a rumor that one of the plantation's young bucks had molested the cook's ten-year-old daughter. He remembered how breathlessly they had rushed to excite their posse, as if they were announcing a last-minute dance on Saturday night. What haunted him still was knowing these same men, who'd always been quick to complain about life's injustice, had managed to whip themselves into such a fury that none of them realized they had the wrong man until they had broken half the bones in his body.

The memory gave Byron the shakes. How absurd it would be for him to have survived Culebra's perilous faceless toil only to meet his death after being picked out falsely—it would certainly make a lie of Longer's notion that life obeyed some natural order. As he staggered along the street felt slippery, cushioned with powdery ash, and the air, with its sickly-sweet smell of roasted flesh, was making him dizzy. He shut his eyes, telling himself he was too young to be judged without mercy, but when he opened them again the world was tilting. He struggled to stay on his feet but his legs were failing and his head was spinning. He begged the sergeant to let him stop and catch his breath but the soldiers yanked him by his arms and hauled him back upright. He managed to stumble a dozen more steps before he collapsed, curling in pain as a vicious kick smashed one of his kidneys.

As he lay in the dust, he could hear the sergeant spewing obscenities. He bravely tried to stand, but again he slumped and two of the soldiers, one bracing him on either side, dragged him by his elbows while he heaved and spat blood.

At last they made it to the square, sitting like a field of dust in a realm of devastation. A long black stripe left by a burning locomotive covered the Front Street tracks like a marker between segments of hell. Mercifully his head was no longer spinning and Byron felt himself beginning to gather his bearings when he glimpsed his antagonist sitting on a low platform by the plaza's ruined clock tower. The lieutenant was engrossed in conversation with two other officers, their prominent chests even more splendid with medals and ribbons. A crowd had begun to gather at the fringe near where four black half-naked men stood roped together under guard. As they stood with their hands tied behind them the men were gulping in feverish breaths that made their dark, glistening abdomens swell and contract like bellows.

The platoon drove their two new captives showily across the square and as they came closer Byron saw that one of the roped prisoners was the Haitian, Reynal. Stripped of his sword and the grand tricolor sash the militant looked shrunk and broken. His eyes were fixed on his shoeless feet and he never looked up as Byron and Longers were put to stand by his gasping cohorts. Byron glanced over to try and catch his eyes and nearly toppled in a second faint seeing the scarlet skin hanging from the Haitian's back in papery shreds.

Byron told himself to pray but hopelessly failed. He tried to think of the magical words that might save him but his throat promptly clenched as one of the soldiers strode up to tie his wrists. He was close to tears when a stentorian voice rang out across the square and began a clipped recitation. The pronouncement alleged that with capital punishment now legally reinstated in the United States of Colombia, by order of President Nuñez' provisional government, all enemies of the homeland were henceforth subject to death. The amendment, which was read in Spanish, fell meaninglessly on Byron's ears. As it ended, the officers on the dais all stood, looking grave. The one whose chest displayed the most adornment solemnly raised his right hand. From somewhere in the square there was a hushed snare roll followed by the thuds of a deep bass drum. A dark cloth encircled Byron's face and the world went black. His eyes left useless in their blindfold, he felt his heart quickly shiver as the guards began leading him back to the edge of the square. He stumbled as his knees knocked together and he started to snivel.

"Hold up, boy!" Longers snarled, hearing his whimpers. "Don't let the spigotty bastards see you bawling!"

Byron truly wished he possessed the sailor's defiant bearing, but his only urge now was to plead for pity. He thought, what use does a dead man have now for his dignity? There could be no heroes where there was no honor and honor could not exist in a world where men had no qualms about killing the innocent.

The short march came to a halt and Byron's heart gave a shudder at the blast of a cannon. Through the big gun's dying echoes the slow bass drum beat on. The crowd, now sharply multiplied, was growing fevered. Without the aid of his sight, their babel thumped him like a crashing wave. His mouth was dry and tasted of ashes and he could feel his pulse racing madly ahead of the drum's slow pounding. Suddenly, there was a shout and then another and he felt his arms being gripped, then roughly tugged. "Longers!" he wailed, twisting back for his anchor. There was the rata-tat-tat of gun-shots joined by a savage human roar, then sinking silence.

By the day's grim end, twenty-one men, nineteen of whom were completely blameless, had been murdered without trial, but the man deemed Panama's most wanted terrorist was still at large and *Teniente* Alphonso Rivueltas was still angry and profoundly ambitious. He had rushed to inform his superiors that one of his captives bore some resemblance to Pedro Prestàn and had requested their consent to detain him. To his annoyance, his proposal had been met with chuckles and perfunctory dismissal. Then, just as the condemned men were about to be shot, the American warship's brigade commander showed up for the ad hoc tribunal. Noticing one of the prisoners shared the rebel leader's unusually small stature, he suggested that the tiny Jamaican be held for interrogation. The presiding general, not wanting to appear ignorant of the acclaim the Yanks had received for the extraordinary intelligence they were able to extract using their latest methods, had hurried to concur and ordered Byron removed from line.

Chapter 19

"Psst!—Judah!—yuh 'wake?"

Thomas had been in the midst of a delicious dream. Genevieve looked ravishing beside him, her plain habit exchanged for a white lace gown and pearls. Now, as he rose to the surface, the sweetness of sleep was displaced by the soreness in his tendons.

"Yuh 'wake?" Cuffie whispered more urgently.

"Jesus—!" Thomas complained, turning onto his side, "I never knew one man could have this much pain in so many different places—it's morning already?"

He strained up his neck with one groggy eye open and saw the barrack pitch black. Outside the Culebra night was still and moonless. "Damn, Cuffie!—it's the middle of the night..."

"Lissen! I heard sumpen—like somebody crawlin' up the verandah..."

"Man—you off your head! Go back to sleep—"

Thomas covered his head with his sheet, praying he could pick back up his sweet dream, but as he closed his eyes he heard what was definitely the sound of scraping feet. His immediate thought was that it must be the night watchmen. No doubt they were on extra alert since the previous night they'd had to run off several drunks caught sneaking through the camp. As he held his breath to listen for more footsteps he could hear Cuffie hunting for his secret tin of matches. He was about to murmur to his friend when he heard a startled gasp from somewhere in the dark and then a scratchy whisper.

"*¡Digo!* Give us your gold!"

"*¡Olvídese de él, corta gargantas de un tajo y toma su dinero!*"

A second menacing voice hissed out and Thomas sank back fearfully inside his covers. There was a rustling noise right near his bed and he could sense Cuffie groping frantically at the shelf for his candles. He was again tempted to mumble to his friend but was afraid to poke up his head. He could hear the sound of scuffling start up deeper inside the barracks, followed by more soft scraping feet and the whisper of men moving lightly through the darkness. He finally found the nerve to raise his head and promptly flinched as a droning groan, like air being squeezed from a bladder, sighed out close by him.

Knifing fear stabbed inside his chest as the tussling sounds increased and he heard a short stifled scream and then another. He hunkered back down in the bed, straining to lie still with his heartbeat in his mouth. He was trying to conjure some magic escape when a rough hand reached through the dark and rubbed his scalp.

"*Usted tiene pelo suave. ¿De donde es usted?*"

Thomas marveled at the bizarre demand "—why stop to tussle my hair and ask where I'm from?" he wondered. "*Soy de San Blas*," he lied on a sudden hunch.

"*Bueno, usted habla español*," the intruder commended in a grating whisper as he stroked Thomas lightly on the cheek with the edge of a razor-sharp knife. "*Dénos su oro y usted puede vivir para besar a su madre otra vez más*—give me your gold and you can live to kiss your mother."

Thomas was about to entreat that he had only been working in Culebra a few days and hadn't been paid when he remembered the coins still in his good trousers. "*Un momento*," he begged, springing up to search under his bunk and then bumping into his unseen assailant.

"*Nunca mente, compañero*—" the man grunted, abruptly out of patience as a loud fracas erupted.

The entire barracks had come alive and in the black confusion diggers were blindly pummeling each other. The robbers who had not already escaped finished ransacking the nearest pockets for dollars and gold before quietly slipping away inside the darkness.

"Somebody strike a goddamn light!" an injured digger bawled and Thomas raced to find the candles he had left thoughtlessly under his bed earlier that night. He grabbed the box up quickly and crouched on the floor by Cuffie's bunk. He clutched for the tin of matches then froze, feeling his arm touch warm flesh. After a few feverish tries he managed to light one of the long candles and was again stopped cold. Cuffie had fallen with his back to the wall and was lying with his naked legs sprawled out. A sticky puddle was expanding on his shorts from the blood trickling down from the slit across his throat.

Thomas felt his insides turning over as his brain flashed a mirroring image of Diego. He sensed his being tumbling back into a deep dark pit but his spirits rallied as he noticed Cuffie's powerful chest faintly rise and fall. He hurried to light a second candle to inspect the seeping wound then sank in horror as he glimpsed the rest of the barracks. Men lay dead in their red-smeared beds, their bodies oddly contorted, their eyes still wide in surprise.

He shoved the grisly scene from his mind to focus on Cuffie. Crawling back to his own bunk, he reached for the white cotton shirt he'd left folded by his pillow along with his trousers. He quickly ripped it into strips and hurried to wrap Cuffie's wounded neck. Out on the grounds he could hear the shouts of a spreading riot but he felt strangely detached and lucid, his mind free of panic, absorbed with saving Cuffie.

After he was through gently pressuring the skin around the gash, Thomas undid the blood-soaked bandage and replaced it with a fresh band of cloth to wrap Cuffie's neck more tightly. He had just gotten through fixing the new binding when the tramp of urgent strides shook the barrack's floor and a dozen diggers burst in, still stoked from the rush of combat. The sight of their comrades, lying with their throats slashed and bloody, brought the mob to a shuddering halt. Aghast, the avengers shifted their lanterns to better see Thomas who was on his knees quietly attending to his friend. They rushed to surround him, demanding to know which way the killers had fled. Thomas glanced up at the men standing around him breathing fire and suggested in a firm calm voice that they put down their sticks and shovels and find a doctor.

It was hours after sunrise before the Jamaicans were able to repel their attackers and restore a semblance of order. The French arrived from their neighboring village to learn that the night's fatalities included both watchmen and, at last count, sixty-four diggers. The assassins turned out to be a company of unpaid government troops. The dozen or so renegades the Jamaicans managed to capture had tried to protest that they had tracked the outlaw Prestàn into camp and been assaulted by the workers until a quick search of their pockets yielded a hoard of stolen gold.

Poor Cuffie had been fortunate in that, unlike the murdered men, he had been awake before the ambush and possessed a thickly-muscled neck. As a result, even though his attacker's merciless blade had sliced between two vertebrae and pierced a vessel in his spine, it had missed his jugular. Thomas earned the company doctors' praise for his alert application of a tourniquet and constant pressure. Without it, they said, his friend would not have survived.

When he was sure that Cuffie would pull through, Thomas packed away his friend's old dungarees and borrowed one of his coarse blue shirts to wear with his own dirt-stained trousers. Old Deggy insisted on handing him a full week's pay and joining him for his walk to the station.

"I confess you truly surprised me, Judah. You may be a little bit soft in the head," the foreman gently needled him, "but you're damn tough when it counts."

"I don't know—" Thomas answered glumly, as his mind's eye again showed him standing frozen while Diego screamed. "Culebra proved I'm not nearly as tough as I thought."

Old Deggy raised his hand and held it to his heart. "You're solid in here—that's what counts."

Thomas smiled back thinly but didn't reply. They continued on to the platform and as they stood waiting in silence he sensed the foreman had something on his chest that he felt hesitant to express. Finally the train to Colón appeared from beyond the ridge, tooting its shrill steam whistle and as it slowed and approached the station Old Deggy held back Thomas by his arm.

"Don't just forget about us now. We need fellows like you helping to deliver us from this bondage. A hard-working boy like Cuffie deserves a country where he can live and die like a man. You're a bright-skinned chap—think about it!"

Old Deggy's parting comment preyed on Thomas the entire ride back to Christophe-Colomb. He'd been through enough to have learned by now that he was nobody's Moses. But the foreman's challenge had struck a nerve because it reminded him that he had once been vain enough to think he was meant to be the small man's champion. It had been a vague presumption conceptualized no further than his returning home to antagonize his father's complacent circles by penning great paeans to his comrades' epic Panama labors. Instead, he would leave here knowing that men like Cuffie, if they were lucky enough to make it out alive, would be going home to be at best abused, and at worst discarded.

Although his own close brush with death had left him chastened and prepared to repent, he felt strangely indifferent about receiving Henri's forgiveness. His emotions were still too raw to feel all that charitable, but as he arrived back at his mentor's comfortable residence and saw the garden's fresh-cut grass and flaming crotons he could not restrain a surge of joy.

He came in quietly, praying that Henri was away or engrossed in his work so he'd have time to change clothes and come up with a story to explain his nine-day absence. He was still limping through the foyer when Duvay came charging out from his study. The Frenchman launched at him in full fury. Thomas heard himself declaimed as an overindulged ungrateful whelp who would end up a pitiful failure but his mind was too distracted trying to process the butchery he had witnessed to make sense of so much yelling. He was dying for a tall cold drink and a nice warm bath. He possessed neither the strength nor the desire for an all-out battle. He tried to explain, but Henri railed right on, dragging up every old error Thomas had committed, throwing fresh logs on his blazing temper until his whole body was trembling and his face was purple.

"This is totally unacceptable!" Duvay blared, hot with righteous anger. "Because of you my work is now a full week behind!—you slouch!—you faithless ingrate!"

"It's over, Henri," Thomas said wearily, when Duvay finally stopped for breath. "Whatever great cause burns in that fevered brain of yours is finished. *C'est fini*. Ended. Dead."

"*Mon Dieu!* I am to be ruined by shiftless shirkers! Look at you!" Duvay exclaimed, as he caught sight of the rumpled blue work shirt under Thomas' red vest and the filthy gray trousers, "sloppy as a vagrant! I suppose you think I should overlook your irresponsible behavior because you've been out ministering to layabouts with that precious nun of yours..."

"What on earth gave you that idea?" Thomas blustered, shocked to think someone he knew had seen him with Genevieve and then gone out of their way to mention it to Henri. It was some relief to know that whomever it was did not seem to suspect them of being in love. "Really, Henri—you have developed quite an active imagination—"

"Oh, have I...? When you were still gone the day I returned I had Monique inquire at the hospital, fearing some ill may have befallen you. The Mother Superior told her that you'd been there twice to inquire about her young nurse novitiate. She suggested to Monique that you may have gone to find Genevieve who is apparently off somewhere providing comfort to the sick and homeless. So tell me—how did that wholesome little nun get you to throw up your job? Did she promise you your own harp and cloud?" Duvay asked sarcastically.

"You've got it all wrong—I haven't seen Genevieve in over a month."

"So then, where in the devil have you been?"

"I would have told you by now—had you given me the chance—"

"I've given you nothing but chances!" Duvay snapped, then suddenly seemed to tire of his temper. "All right—come inside and let's hear it!" he said, leading the way into the open sitting room."—but don't expect you're going to charm me into taking you back!"

As Thomas described the midnight ambush in gory detail, Duvay's purpled coloring slowly turned white. "I must cable your father!" the Frenchman cried, charging up abruptly from the divan where they'd been sitting.

"My father—?" Thomas murmured, blinking in astonishment. "I tell you well over sixty men were just brutally murdered and all you can think to do is to rush and inform my father that I've been fired?"

"*Non, non, non! Ce n'est pas ça du tout!* This is not about your being derelict—we'll discuss that later. No—what little I'd been hearing of this matter has been rather garbled—first reports tend to be hysterical. From what you've said, the number of casualties is insignificant—but if those really were government troops on a rampage there will be political ramifications. Your father is an influential man—he will be able to help us counter the exaggerations that are bound to be printed in the papers." Duvay lingered, tensely rubbing his hands. "That should reassure our investors—"

"What are you saying—?" demanded Thomas, looking dumbfounded, "that my father is in business with the company?"

"He's one of our loyal investors—in fact, his firm was formerly engaged with providing us good laborers. I need to alert him to start recruiting replacements—" His normal color returned, Duvay surprised Thomas with a sudden warm pat on his shoulder. "I'm glad you're home, *mon fils*. Now I must go, quickly!"

Duvay rushed off to compose his telegram and Thomas sat in a stew of disgust and self-loathing. So! he thought, fuming—from the very beginning, while he was basking in the delusion that his great wit and charming character lay behind Henri's peculiar affection, the conniving bastard had been in cahoots with his father. He had been nothing but a pawn—a useful tool. How large a fool he had been to think that Henri Duvay could actually harbor some genuine feeling for a living being. People were valued only so far as they boosted his power or aided his great plans.

Thomas lugged himself slowly up the stairs and for the first time in his life felt beaten. His mind, like his body, felt whipped. He slumped inside his bedroom then wandered to the large French window and absently drew the gauze-white curtain. His jaded gaze finally settled on the far-off cove and he stood there bewitched, seeing the turquoise bay glittering with golden threads of reflecting sunlight and the white masts of gently sailing ships. After the bloody carnage at Culebra it was hard to believe a place on earth could be that serene.

He didn't bother answering as he heard Duvay call out to say he was off to send the cable. He was already lost in the blue-green water, imagining the luxury of a bath and the clean feel of soft white linens. He moved to the armoire to find his bedclothes and was surprised as he glimpsed a frightening stranger. It took him a few seconds to digest the fact that the image with the coarse swatch of black stubble and morbid eyes was his own reflection. Where he was used to seeing a dapper pose and a defiant violet gaze that seemed to smirk, he now saw the score of death and sorrow.

Duvay returned from the cable office much more upbeat. He hounded his sullen assistant until he'd dragged out the rest of the story then showered his protégé with praise for having cleverly kept his wits and foiled his attacker. Thomas' absence was abruptly forgiven and for days afterward Duvay's mood remained determinedly chipper. On his part, Thomas felt he had no other option than to resume his work and try and stay hopeful even as he worried more each day that his father had intercepted his mother's crucial letter.

Henri persisted in his stubborn good temper, but as Thomas had predicted, his countrymen had been shocked by the ambush and were quitting the canal works in droves. Duvay appeared to take the mass exodus in stride. He even listened thoughtfully when, in response to his questions, Thomas described the workers' resentment, feeling they'd been made scapegoats for Panama's internal troubles. But Henri seemed to go deaf when Thomas argued that beyond the fear that any night they could be butchered in their sleep these men were fed up with risking their lives for a cause with such diminishing rewards. Instead, Henri inured himself inside a cocoon of unyielding optimism. Even as the stream of departing workers swelled beyond a thousand he confidently insisted that once they were over the natural trauma that followed the slaughter, diggers would come flooding back to the isthmus.

His attempt to hide the canal's latest dire threat within a web of tendentious expectations fell apart a fortnight later as the deflating wire arrived:

MUCH REGRET. UNDER CURRENT CIRCUMSTANCES PROCURING NEW WORKERS IMPOSSIBLE. SAMUEL JUDAH.

The truce which had seemed to knit a tighter, more cordial bond between assistant and mentor began to unravel that very night. Henri Duvay reacted to Samuel Judah's rejection by plunging into more of his spitting tantrums. For days afterwards, he would conclude his every snapped instruction with an invective against merchants and bankers. He cursed the former as liars and the latter as thieves. When that earned him no satisfaction, he turned his venom onto his handy assistant. Duvay again castigated him for the sloppiness of his drafts, yet if Thomas labored to avoid the tiniest imperfection, he berated him for the slowness of his work.

Consumed by his inner doldrums, Thomas accepted the lash of Henri's sharp tongue without a murmur. Perversely, his new meekness only provoked Henri Duvay to show more anger. He began to think that the harried engineer was baiting him to respond so he could unload his own frustration. When Duvay would bluster and smack his ear in irritation, he simply steeled his spine and swallowed his spit. Finally, just when he knew he could restrain himself no longer, his mother's letter arrived. Alone in his room, he tore it open and held his breath. Seeing the generous draft inside, he yelled with joy and started packing.

His knock at the study door received a brusque '*entrez*' and Thomas stiffly stepped in. He paused to observe the man he had lived with for the past thirty months. Duvay stood with his back still turned, muttering to himself as he pored over a prodigious onion-skin chart that stretched clear across his desk before flowing down its side and curling onto the floor. Seeing him standing there hunched over, Thomas was reminded of a cartoon in one of the prospecting magazines he'd just purchased—Duvay could be that lampooned old miner squinting fiercely in his pan for the elusive nugget. For a moment, he was moved by his mentor's confounding dedication. Like his darling Genevieve, Henri was afflicted with an excess of belief in a world ruled by the devil's randomness.

"I'm leaving, Henri."

Duvay gazed up sharply, then bent promptly back to his work. "Oh, I see—it's been what...nearly a month? Must be time for another vacation," he murmured sardonically. "If you're testing me, Thomas, I'm flat out of patience. Go upstairs and finish those drafts or don't bother coming back!"

"You don't understand...I'm not testing you. I'm leaving Panama...for good..."

Duvay stood up to face him and all the fateful adventures they had shared seemed to flow between them. In that short glimmer Thomas saw that their bond had been much like Culebra—what once seemed solid had been exposed under steady assault and though their divergent makeups created a color of excitement, like the mountain's contrasting layers, under duress it had finally crumbled.

"So you're giving in like those other weaklings! Why am I not surprised?" Duvay spat out with distaste. "I should never have wasted my time."

"I don't wish us to quarrel, Henri. I promise to reimburse you for every wasted minute."

"Don't flatter yourself—real accomplishment is beyond your capacity! Pity, your father was right. You have talent, but it won't amount to much."

The comment sliced precisely at Thomas' tender spot but he controlled his urge to hit back. Instead he let an ironical smile play on his lips. How wrong you are, Henri, he thought dryly. "I hope you live that long, *monsieur*."

As he picked up his bags and walked down the hallway Thomas could feel the smoldering gaze burning his back. He had wanted them to part as friends. As difficult a man as Henri was to please, he had never discouraged him from dreaming big, unlike his own father, and as he stepped out to the landing he sensed the missing wag had been suddenly reborn. Only now he had his sights set on a greater world. Strolling for the docks to find his ship, not once did he stop for a backward glance to the dark shuttered walls of his master's residence.

Chapter 20

Estelle had missed having Longers along for protection but, with the *federales* on the hunt for insurgents, the giant's dark presence would have made the trip to Portobelo much too risky. Neither had she been able to bear letting innocent Byron fend on his own while Prestàn's men and the displaced thousands were out fighting each other for food. Panama had been created for traders, not farmers, and she'd be willing to wager that a king's ransom in slaves and gold had never fed a single rebel on the run—much less an entire city.

She had not been looking forward to facing Constancia, who was certain to see the Last Frontier's destruction as celestial punishment. Once she'd pried enough telling bits and pieces from little Isabella, Connie had been furious to realize that her sister's wealth was even more tainted than what Estelle claimed to earn from selling liquor and running a little boarding-house. Constancia had written to denounce her for promoting the basest of sins, but Estelle needed to believe that her own flesh and blood would not reject her.

She had left her damaged brothel with an anxious heart after picking out all the valuables she could carry. From there she had struggled to a Cristobal stable where, for a hefty deposit, she was able to procure a horse and buggy. Then, for a very steep bribe that would cost her two of her gold rings and her jeweled barrette, she had finally persuaded the captain of the occupying garrison to lend her one of his men as an escort. It had not disappointed her at all when Corporal Arias turned out to possess the kind of Spanish good looks that paid their way into a woman's bed or that he showed her unusual deference for a federal soldier. He sounded almost shy as he took the reins from her hand and suggested they would be safer veering inland.

"It will take us twice as long I'm afraid, *señora*—but the coast-road to Portobelo is likely being watched and you would be an easy target for the rebels."

"As you say, corporal—" Estelle replied with the hint of a come-hither smile, "if I'm to be a target I would not want to be easy."

So after leaving the garrison's bivouacked camp near Monkey Hill they had digressed from the main cobblestone road to one of the offbeat trails blazed by escaped Africans fleeing into the forest after sacking some opulent trader's convoy. Estelle was surprised by the skill with which the young corporal was able to steer them along such thin and twisting paths. When she asked how he came to acquire this ability, he explained that he had grown up near Buenaventura. "I'm quite certain Captain Becerra had that fact in mind when he selected me to accompany you," Arias said dryly.

"You have problems with the captain?"

"Let's just say it's not easy being from the so-called 'dark province'—especially now that half of our people seem to be supporting the rebellion. My officers all hate being here—but then, most of them would rather call themselves Spaniards than Colombians. They look at *Panamá* as nothing but a backwater full of ignorant negroes...if it wasn't for our canal and the money from the Yankee railroad they would be happy to see it sink into the sea."

"But you support President Nuñez?" she pressed him, her interest piqued.

"I support the federation."

"Even if Nuñez ignores our Constitution?"

Arias checked the gray mare with a firmer rein and stared sternly off into the distance. "The Church says we must support President Nuñez to save the federation—I put my faith in the Holy Church," he answered flatly and Estelle, sensing he resented being asked to say more, put off her questions.

Although the little buggy had proved sturdy and nimble enough to maneuver the inhospitable trail, the going was slow and Estelle constantly had to duck and hide her face for fear of losing an eye to some infringing brush or low-hanging bough. The rough path finally widened and became almost smooth as it snaked alongside a ravine before plunging into the leafy cool of a bamboo grove. They were picking up speed, traversing the flat sheltered vale when their way stood blocked by fallen branches and stalks of bamboo. Arias hopped quickly down from the carriage but no sooner had he started clearing the impediment than a pair of bandits skulked in and shoved him roughly to the ground.

Estelle snatched up the corporal's Remington rifle and with a cautionary shout took aim at the closest brigand. The young robber turned and, seeing the gun aimed right at his head, stepped back skittishly. As he stared with his knees beginning to shake, his partner drew out a revolver and held it to Arias' throat. Estelle coolly kept her gaze and aim on the shivering young bandit and addressed the one with the gun. She informed him that she was on an urgent mission of mercy and would gladly hand over her gold except she could not promise not to shoot his friend here in the head if he did not hurry and put down his weapon.

The young robber stared at the long rifle in the madam's steady hand and pleaded with his accomplice who scowled then said he would refrain from putting a bullet in the soldier's neck—but only if she included the Remington as part of the bargain. Arias blanched then wagged his head ferociously, but Estelle, who found men to be more troublesome than fearsome or logical, ignored his indignation and saved his life. She slowly lowered the rifle then flicked its barrel, smiling when the bandit obediently released the red-faced corporal and shoved the revolver back inside his belt. Estelle set the Remington on the floorboard by her feet and reach for her heavy suitcase. As she threw it open and exposed her crystal candlesticks and expensive silverware, the bandits' eyes grew wide and they both came tearing up to the carriage.

After the outlaws had stumbled merrily off into the forest with their new rifle and cumbersome plunder, Corporal Arias, still visibly seething, insisted on ditching the buggy.

"We hardly need it now since you let those criminals rob us blind," he grumbled, his red face livid. "You'll lose your deposit if they come back and steal it but we might get to Portobelo alive."

"Whatever you say, Corporal Arias—" she nodded, sounding contrite, "I am in your hands."

The ensuing hour spent perched on the mare's bare rump had put a lasting hurt in Estelle's own hindquarters. She began to regret letting Arias have his way when the trail descended to a steep-sloped gully and vanished under streaming water. The course was far too swift and rocky to venture across. Their only choice was to dismount and lead the mare back up on foot to find some other way around. They plodded on valiantly through the afternoon's blistering heat with Arias' prudent instincts their only compass. After struggling up more jagged terrain, they finally arrived at a stretch of open scrub-land, but as they remounted the foaming mare they were greeted by a swarm of green biting flies.

Estelle's ankles and neck were quickly covered in painful bites and the hot uphill slog had her weak from fatigue and dehydration. Her eyes began to tear as they neared a crossroad she recognized from the line of peddlers making their way home from the district market. The hampered women, hunched beneath their unsold bundles of cane-brooms and charcoal, looked like drifting husks. As they spotted Estelle straddling a horse's wide haunches with her loose skirt hiked up to her thighs the women shot her revolted looks that tore through the madam's normally tough hide like flinted arrows. Seeing the familiar frowns, Estelle squinted the tears from her eyes with a chuckle. 'Yes,' she rued to herself inside, 'you old crows would rather lose all your hair and be covered in boils than be a woman like me.' She tightened her plump arms boldly around young Arias and complimented him wryly for having found his way to the loving bosom of her old sweet home.

It was nearing nightfall when they arrived at her dead mother's farmhouse. As the mare straggled to the fence's front gate, little Isabella came rushing up from the porch with arms spread wide while Constancia stalked up behind looking grave and ashen. Arias hurried to dismount and help Estelle to the ground. While he went to tie the mare at her hitching post Constancia drew her sister aside. "What do you mean coming here—and with a soldier? Don't tell me he's one of your clients!"

Estelle shrugged. "They set fire to Colón. My business is ruined. I came because I need a place to stay. The town has gone crazy—I was lucky to get Corporal Arias to escort me."

"He can't stay here!" Constancia hissed angrily under her breath. "Tell him to go!"

"Don't you understand? They've got us caught up in this silly civil war! The man risked everything to get me here!" Estelle pleaded. "We were robbed on the way—then the dry-bed was flooded—we had to climb back through the hills. Please, Constancia! The poor man is weary!"

"No!"

"Why, no? At least let him stay for a meal—he could sleep out on the porch and be gone by morning."

"Look—" Constancia whispered, darting a harsh glance back to Arias who was politely occupying his time showing Isabella how to make a church and steeple with her fingers. "I know about the trouble in Colón...no listen to me, *hermana!*" she insisted when Estelle started to interrupt, "you'll understand me later. He has a horse, he can ride up the coast—the *federales* are still in charge in Puerta Pilón."

"Puerta Pilón?—that's over an hour away! Oh, all right!" Estelle snapped when her sister stood scowling with her frail arms firmly folded.

Estelle went and apologized to Arias for her rudeness. She blamed their poor manners on her sister's failing health. Crestfallen, the corporal stood speechless. Then, all at once, his eyes lit up and his face wore a stunned admiring smile as Estelle reached inside her bosom and handed him fifty of the hundred and thirty dollars she'd cunningly kept from the two young bandits.

"For the rifle and all your trouble," she said, rising onto her toes and kissing him on both cheeks. "Now fetch me your canteen—at least we can make sure you have enough water."

Before he left Arias promised to return the mare to her stable, adding that once the rebels were defeated he would see about retrieving her carriage. Isabella started running behind to wave him good-bye but Constancia jumped and hauled her back, barking for Estelle to hurry inside.

"Why do you insist on punishing yourself like this?" Estelle demanded, feeling the heat trapped in the dirt floor dwelling like an oven.

"This is what I get for wanting a quiet life..." Constancia muttered, fidgeting in her long Mother Hubbard dress as she bent to kindle a pair of glass lamps. "Hardship is the only prize for an honest woman."

"*Pero la virtud es su propia recompensa*—but virtue is its own reward."

At the unexpected male voice Estelle gaped at the shadow creeping up from deeper inside. She stood in a fog and from somewhere in her brain's anxious muddle she heard Constancia commanding Isabella to take a lamp and her book and read on the porch until supper.

"That little child is a gem. Perhaps by the time she is grown she will not suffer for her intelligence," the shadow's cultured voice continued.

Estelle marched up and struck Prestàn hard with the flat of her hand, first on his mouth and then harder across his cheek. "One for me and one for my sister! How do you dare come and hide in this house—!"

"Stop it! You don't live here any longer!" cried Constancia, jumping between them. "This is my home now!"

"So!—this is why Corporal Arias had to be turned away without so much as a crust of bread."

Prestàn implored Estelle to sit and let him speak. "*Por favor*—I can explain..." he entreated, rubbing the smart in his jaw.

Her strength used up, Estelle collapsed in the tattered armchair and wearily shut her eyes.

"I should never have trusted the *norteamericanos!* Had they not double-crossed us, today Panama would be free," Prestàn expounded bitterly. "They pretended they would back us against Nuñez and his traitors—I paid them to get us guns then when they arrived the swindlers refused to release them!"

"So you burned down the city—" Estelle broke in acidly.

"Who dares say so? Of course I gave no such order! The *gringos* may have turned it into a sewer, but Colón is still home to my wife and child. I would never risk their lives—never!"

"So, you leave them to run and hide in my sister's skirts?"

Prestán flinched at Estelle's stinging words but stayed calm. "I'm leaving for the mainland to join the resistance. Your sister has kindly offered her help if Maria is forced into hiding with little América."

"I should have had a gun instead of only my bare hand—" Estelle grumbled, sneering at the swelling starting to show on Prestàn's cheek, "you'd be lying dead at my feet! How dare you! How dare you put my family in such danger?"

"Pedro didn't need to ask!" Constancia broke in passionately, her brown face flushed. "You don't know anything, *hermana!* Pedro has been a godsend since Julio died. After I got sick, we would not have eaten had it not been for his help."

Estelle stared at her sister, speechless. "You take this man's money...and refuse mine?"

"As Mother said—*mejor ser pobre y limpio que rico y sucio*—better to be poor and clean than rich and dirty."

"*Necio*—idiot! You are ready to condemn your own child! Listen to him!" She mocked Prestàn's words with a high nasal whine. "Poor me—I trusted the *Americanos. ¡Estupido!* I don't know which of you is the bigger fool!"

"Enough, *hermana*, enough!" cried Constancia. "I'm going to make some supper. This is still my home—I expect you two to make peace and not upset Isabella."

"I'm sorry," Prestàn conceded with a tiny drop of sarcasm, "your sister is quite right. I should not have been so trusting—"

Estelle jumped up and stomped out to the porch. She sat trying to quell her rage while she listened to her niece's untroubled chatter. She was repulsed by Prestàn's smugness, his stiff unrepentant back in the face of so much pointless destruction. But what rubbed the very heart of her soul was knowing her family was in his debt and, unlike Prestàn, who was bound to be praised for his noble gestures, she would never be warmed by her sister's gratitude. All through supper she refused to respond when the rebel attempted to engage her in conversation and deafened her ears when he launched into his fantasies of Panama's future. When she was tired of nibbling at the red beans and rice she got up from the table and promptly dozed off sitting in the armchair. She woke surprised to see the sun and that someone had lifted her to lie on a quilt-covered mat on the floor. She jumped up quickly to check through the house, and sighed in relief when she saw that the rebel-leader had gone.

"How long has that rogue been keeping you?" she asked, finding her sister in the backyard over a fire frying up *huevos y plátanos*. Constancia looked frayed and thin as ever, dressed in the same unflattering Mother Hubbard gown she'd been in the day before.

"Honestly, Estella—you've become so crude! No one is keeping me. I know that must come as a shock to someone like you. If it's any of your business, I've only seen *Señor* Prestàn twice since mother died and that was when Isabella was still a baby. He's been sending us a hundred dollars every year—ever since Julio was killed."

"I was wondering how you could afford to be this stubborn! What will you do now? Your little hero is a fugitive. Even if he escapes being shot or put in prison he won't be practicing law here anytime soon..."

"We'll manage. I'm over my sickness and it's easier now that Isabella is older. Now all I need is to teach her how to cook *plátanos*," said Constancia, smiling wanly. She wiped the drips off her brow and began transferring the three sunny-side up eggs from the heavy skillet on the smoking wood stove to a platter.

Estelle felt a mix of frustration and pity seeing her sister's thin frail arms as Constancia stood shuffling the pan of green fried plantains. Though her sister was still in her twenties, and twelve years younger, the toll from a recurring illness and the rigors of country life with a child and no husband had marked her with the sagging lines of age. Add to those slender anemic looks a proud and sensitive nature and Estelle worried that Connie was as doomed as that brave butterfly trying to fly against storming winds.

It was curious how differently the two sisters had dealt with fate. When their mother passed away Estelle could not wait to flee the dull poverty of peasant life. Eleven-year-old Constancia, on the other hand, had been so unhappy after Estelle sold half of the family property to send her to school on the mainland that she had dropped out to become a teenage bride and then persuaded her city-raised husband to move home with her and become a farmer. No doubt the oppression of a place untouched by invention for close to three centuries was what impelled that noble man to fight for those who were dying to face forward instead of back. Constancia was eight months pregnant with Isabella when poor Julio was murdered for his trouble.

Portobelo was no longer a stronghold for Peruvian gold and Spanish plunder but its fortress mentality lived on. The ruling *encomenderos* still rued the theft of their inheritance by English buccaneers and African pirates and saw even the progress from a well-paved road as a threat to their shrunken dominion. In her grief, Constancia canonized her gentle Julio and placed him in a shrine inside her heart. Estelle had tried once again to cajole her sister to sell the old farm and move to a city but, as always, she was rejected. It would be disloyal to Julio, Constancia insisted, piously rounding her lips the way she did whenever she breathed his name as if he were Simon Bolivar or Christ himself. To her heartbreak, Estelle realized that tussling to uproot her sister's fantasies was as useful as plowing furrows in the ocean—the words might be heard but their sense was instantly lost beneath fresh waves of anguish. It was one more reason, though admittedly unjust, that Estelle no longer felt any gratitude towards Pedro Prestàn. For had he not saved her mother's farm from the grasping landlords, Constancia would have no land in which to plant her guilt and feed old sorrows.

It upset Estelle to think that her intelligent niece could end up like Constancia, and their poor mother before her, but as she adjusted to the quiet life of the country she forgot her sadness a little more each day. Somehow, Isabella's bright spirit remained undimmed by her mother's bouts of gloom. Constancia had bought two large hives, planning to sell the honey and augment the farm's meager income, and Isabella could not wait to terrify her aunt by showing her how she let the bees cover her legs and arms and even crawl across her cheeks.

"Don't worry, *Tia Estella*," said the child as her aunt nearly swooned into a faint, "the girl bees are friendly and the boy bees have no stingers."

If that's true, thought Estelle, as she watched her niece gently coax the fuzzy insects back into their hive, then God should have made men the way He made bees.

As much as she hated leaving her darling Isabella, Estelle knew she ought to start looking for a safe place for Longers and Byron to stay. According to her sister's young farmhand, the rebels were all in hiding, but she worried about venturing out too soon. She was trying to decide if she dared ask Constancia to let them stay with her for a while in Portobelo when a message arrived from Theresa saying that Longers had been shot and Byron was in prison.

Her hiatus shattered, Estelle pressed twenty dollars upon her sister and insisted that she buy some new clothes for herself and Isabella. Then, after hugging her long-faced niece good-bye, she tracked down the local water carrier and paid him to rush her to Colón in his wagon.

Byron had long lost track of the days. Just like the timeless year he'd spent chipping down Snake Mountain, his existence had a dismal sense of unreality. Only this was worse. The cell was damp and lacked a single window—walking in the dark was like roaming inside a roomy casket. He could barely move without stumbling against a wall and unless one of the guards came in with a lantern he had no notion if it was night or day. He might have stopped believing he was actually still alive were it not for the tireless insects.

Besides the ants and some unidentified crawlers, which thankfully did not sting but insisted on searching every crevice in his body, what plagued him more than anything was the silence. He took to howling at the top of his voice or imitating a lost cow's moans just to defy its unbearable authority until odd animal noises began sounding in his skull and he could not tell if they were coming from him or if his mind was simply toying with his ears. He would find himself unconsciously holding his breath, excited by the clicks of boot heels descending the jail's short steps, only to realize when no one arrived that it was only his muddled imagination.

With nothing to do but think, he kept returning to the same dark question: could he truly be a living being if no one cared if he was dead? It made him wonder how many men being eaten by worms not far beneath this very cell had never been missed, much less forgotten, and he had the sudden creepy notion that those rotting thousands were his kin. As the days blended and silently dragged on he found himself wishing he could slip inside their nameless graves and sleep forever in the restful company of their bones.

The alerting clicks drew Byron from his dark musings. A yellow shaft of light expanded along the opposite wall and he watched his jailers make their clicking descent down the wooden stairs. He was surprised when instead of setting down another gluey plate of mashed yams, the first guard directed him to stand back and his partner moved to unlock the bars to his cage.

Byron obediently stepped back and the first guard came in and tied his hands while the second one covered his head with a woven sack. Even inside the scratchy hood, Byron was able to discern the change in the air and light as they pushed him up to ground level. After a short walk out in the sunlight he felt himself being turned and then guided through a doorway. One of the jailers took his hands and shoved him down on a rickety chair. As he sat nervously and collected his senses, his nose picked up the smell of the lieutenant's cigar.

His jailers slammed closed the door and left without a word, and he guessed with a tiny shudder that he was back in the room where he'd first been questioned. The smoke from the strong cigar was making it hard to breathe inside of the hood and when it seemed he might choke from fear he bravely rallied his lungs, telling himself that they must have realized their mistake and were about to release him. The wish slipped painfully down his throat as he heard the officer's syrupy tone.

"How are you finding our accommodations—is the diet to your liking? I'd say you've gotten a bit fat by the looks of it—but then that is our greatest fault—we are a very hospitable people..."

He could sense the lieutenant mocking him but the words went without leaving an impression. When he did not respond Rivueltas grew more exasperated.

"No answer. Would you like me to take off that silly hood?"

Although he no longer really cared, Byron nodded out of instinct.

"I'd be happy to—" Rivueltas said more pleasantly, bending to Byron's ear and touching his shoulder, "but you need to reciprocate my goodwill. First you repay my country's generosity by siding with anarchists and now you refuse to tell us their plans or where to find them. Answer me this!—how does one little *chango* cause so much trouble?"

The cynical question carried Byron back to the days just after his mother died. Too young to take her place in the fields, he'd been sent to help the workhouse cook whose scowl could scare a rooster into laying fresh eggs. Big Rosie did not abide having little children romping in her kitchen, so Byron used his pent-up energy running his mouth. He assailed the poor cook with all the questions vexing his tender senses, until he found himself across her large knee, baffled and in tears for asking one too many times, 'Miss Rosie, where is heaven?'

"Don't just sit there like a dog! Answer me—*¿cuál es su nombre?* What is your name?"

Byron remained dumbly unaware. His mind was back reliving those early plantation years when he was looked upon as nothing but trouble.

Rivueltas again bent down and warned him in a menacing whisper. "We will catch that terrorist, Prestàn, whether you choose to help us or not. Don't worry—we will get him to tell us that the two of you share blood! And then I will track down your father and your brothers and all your cousins. Every man in your family will hang—along with your *chombo* friends."

"Mi gots no family for yuh to hang."

"Why do you keep on lying?" Rivueltas shouted, banging his fist against the back of Byron's chair. "That giant you were with has quite a violent reputation. I know he could not have been your father—so where is he? I don't care if you're a bastard—tell me his name!"

Inside his hood, Byron felt his face grow hot with shame, knowing he had no answer.

"*¿Su madre?*"

"Cooper," he mumbled, offering the same lie he had given the recruiter to get his traveling papers.

"Speak up, thief—I can't hear you!"

"Me not a criminal! Me's a honest British subject!" Byron protested then sagged, stunned by the sudden power of his own voice.

"Liar! We both know better!"

"Me's an innocent man. Yuh got nutting against me..."

"Oh, you think so?!" Rivueltas shook Pautrizelle's pamphlets, pointlessly in front of Byron's hood. "I have the evidence right here in my hand. They were hidden in the case with your stolen violin. You were seen talking with those radicals."

Byron kicked himself inside for keeping those stupid leaflets.

"Enough of your impudent silence—put out your hand!"

Before Byron could budge the lieutenant had clutched him by his wrist. He heard himself scream as the hot cigar seared the flesh on the back of his hand.

"If you did not steal it, then tell me where you got such a fine violin! Were you holding it for that rascal lawyer? I hear the little scum is somewhat cultured—"

Byron let loose a second yell as Rivueltas held down his hand and let the cigar slowly burn through more sensitive layers of skin.

"Why are you being stupid?" The lieutenant implored, sounding genuinely crushed as he let go of Byron's hand. "I am a civilized man! I am not a monster, but I will defend my country's honor and you are making us look like fools. Come. Tell me anything you like," he wheedled as Byron nursed his throbbing hand. "Just give me something that can satisfy the papers and I'll see to it the general spares your life."

"Me dun tell yuh everyt'ing. I took those pamphlets but me never join wid dem," Byron insisted, trying not to sniffle. "Dat instrument did belong to Johnny Fingers—the Fiddler...but the Fiddler done dead..." he moaned, dissolving into tears inside his hood.

"Idiot—" Rivueltas spat. "Guards!" he bellowed at the door. "Take this scoundrel for some warm reflection," he commanded as the jailers came rushing in. "A taste of the cat should help him perceive his position more clearly."

The warders hustled Byron back down inside his dark catacomb. Removing the burlap sack, they ordered him to remove all his clothes and stand outside the cell. Byron watched, naked and quailing, as the first guard returned carrying a cloth-covered wand with five long strands of leather cord kinked with knots spaced every few inches. As his companion came in with a bucket of water neither man seemed to be relishing his task. One of them shoved Byron lightly and had him spread his arms and legs out wide against the cell's iron bars. After they had strapped him to the metal by both his wrists, the guards appeared to grunt a quick agreement that they would each administer no more than five lashes.

Their reluctance strangely moved Byron's sympathy. He endured all ten whistling strokes from the cat-o-nine-tails, clamping his teeth inside his lip until it bled to keep from crying out and adding to their remorse. Byron could sense the guards' unspoken appreciation as they untied him and laid him gently face down on the cold earth floor. He cringed, just managing to muffle his scream, feeling them swab the healing salt water to his savaged backside which began to sting as if it had been slashed by a thousand hot knives.

After his jailers had gathered up their sponge and bucket and departed glum-faced, Byron lay wincing inside his skin. His body felt as if it had been wrapped in thorns then set on fire. At last the pain began to ease and he could feel himself slipping gratefully out of consciousness. Every so often he would wake to sip from the small urn of water on the floor of his cell before drifting back to dream of worms and buried bones. It took the smell of feces he had apparently expelled right after his beating to remind him he had not eaten in days. He was not sure how long it had been since his tongue felt this hard and a high hum was droning inside his head. He could sense his body's desperate cravings but as he lifted the urn to his lips he realized he had drained the last of his water.

Still no help came. Part of his brain seemed to be receding while the rest was now under the control of a loathsome stranger. The usurper's thirst was savage, unsatisfied by the few trickles of urine Byron strained to squeeze from his aching bladder. When that too ran dry the stranger turned manic. Now a desperate animal, it crouched on all fours, scratching and clawing to pull nobs of dirt from the floor to cram into its mouth.

Meanwhile the aloof half of his brain looked on in disgust, one ear cocked back towards the stairs, keen for the boot-clicks that would chase off the repulsive stranger and bring someone to whom he could confess. Whatever they wanted was true. He would admit to plotting to murder Mr. de Lesseps or the English queen if someone would just let him have water. Exhausted and out of hope, he finally curled up on the dank earth floor, lost in an infant's world of dim sensations. He saw himself tight inside the sling molded to his mother's stooped back as she weeded the fields. He smelled her familiar odor blend in with his as they lay touching on the wattle hut's hard husk mat. He felt her nestle him close and heard her velvet voice crooning the lullaby she sang him to sleep with each night: 'Moonshine baby don't you cry—mumma gonna bring somt'ing fi yuh by and by...' The dreamy song broke off and in his mind he could hear her calling.

"Byron? It's going to be all right. I'm here."

His weak eyes fluttered open then quickly shut against the sudden light. He heard the velvet voice start pleading for water and tried to shape his own parched lips to echo the remote request. Never mind, he thought, sensing the rush of his returning soul as he recognized the generous voice. Alive or dead, he mattered to someone, which meant he must matter to the Lord.

———

Rivueltas had struggled to conceal his fury as he finished reading the general's order. He tossed it lightly aside trying to guess how large a bribe the well-dressed woman waiting in his office had paid for his prisoner's release—and why.

"Your little thief must have remarkably hidden charms, *Señora* Morales," he responded finally, unable to disguise his disgust at the stench of corruption and the corrosion of his sway.

"Byron is no thief!" Estelle objected. "He is as honest as a priest and a fine young fiddler."

Rivueltas leaned back at his desk and gave a loud guffaw that jiggled the medals on his chest. "A fiddler?—that monkey couldn't play a note to save his friend's life! But fine. Take him if you like. He's not worth anything now that Prestàn has been captured."

"Prestàn has been captured?"

"Caught him hiding on the mainland near Barranquilla," the lieutenant replied with a smugly sinister smile as he stamped the order and handed it back. "They say he was betrayed by his own *mulatos*..."

Rivueltas' diabolical parting grin had haunted Estelle for days after she rescued Byron. She feared that if Prestàn had been captured alive, he might break under pressure and incriminate both her and Constancia. She could have saved herself all those sleepless nights. Pedro Prestàn faced the gallows as he had lived, starch-backed and unrepentant. His sole declaration, shouted to the largest crowd Colón had ever seen as people from all over the province came to witness his hanging, was—*¡Viva Libertad!—¡Viva Panamá!*

The rebel lawyer's execution foreshadowed a sudden end to the entire resistance. On the mainland a Yankee blockade had cut the insurgents off from their vital supplies, while back in Panama Commander Aizpuru was arrested and sent into exile. The speed with which the *norteamericanos* were now quelling the crisis had left Estelle beside herself with anger. She still could not fathom why they had waited this long, seeing that they paid the Bogotá government a ransom for the right to protect their interests. She did not buy Harcourt's excuse that the Yanks were reluctant to get involved in Panama's affairs. If it was true, it would have been the first time in thirty years they'd shown an ounce of respect for her country's sovereignty.

For the first time in her life Estelle was close to losing hope. She had no home, her establishments were ruined, her girls had all scattered, and Longers was dead. She thought of going back to stay with her sister until she saw that Byron was in far too much pain to make the journey. With the vice-consul's help she was able to rent a two-bedroom cottage at the edge of town where she subdued her grief while she coaxed the tortured youngster back to life.

Though Byron let her feed him broth and salve his carved up bottom with buttered honey, her attempts at mothering were met with a hollow stare and stony silence. When his ragged rump had healed to where it no longer resembled chucked meat she tried to lure him out of the bed but he blankly resisted. She took to scolding him gently, warning that if he lay like that his sore bottom would get even sorer. He simply gazed at her with the same wooden look, as if he was far beyond the reach of mere physical pain. Then one day, after she came in with her cheeks washed in tears and mumbled Longers' name, he surprised her and did not flinch when she sat down and rested her head on his shoulder. Encouraged, she put her arm around his waist and sensing him surrender, helped him from the bed and out to the wicker porch swing.

It became their ritual each day at the start of sunset. She would ease him onto the seat with a pillow already in place, then nestle herself beside him. They would sit like that for a length of time without speaking. Finally Estelle would sniffle and blow her nose and resume her misty-eyed recollection of her devoted sailor. Somewhere in her story she would always bring up the time one of the Bottle Alley pimps sent three of his stooges to smash up her *cantina*. More tears would fill her eyes as she again quietly admitted that had Longers not been there that night she would never have stayed in business and become a success. Then her eyes would begin to sparkle as she described the lopsided brawl.

"Longers picked up two of those hooligans by the scruff of their necks and cracked their heads like peanuts. Then he drew out this old round pistol and said if they ever came in my bar again he'd be waiting to shoot them! It was fate sent him my way—that dear man stayed here all these years just to protect me. I knew he worshiped me—" she said, the longing words fading inside a shrug heavy with guilt, "but by the time we met I was a used-up woman—I'd been robbed of my healthy desires. Curious ain't it?—this hash we make of life...I wanted my own brothel so I'd be free of deceitful men and I succeeded by deceiving poor Longers. I abused the one good man I should have trusted—and now he's gone..."

Estelle rattled on, eager to also share the more humorous offbeat moments she'd spent with the poker-faced sailor. Through it all Byron sat unmoved, wearing the same blank stare, his eyes fixed on the horizon's violet sky or the lurching sea. The only hint that he had heard a word came when she would try and mimic Longers' gruff voice to recite one of his quirky sayings and Byron's upper lip would show the slightest twitch of a grin. After a week went by like this, Estelle could no longer bear his stone-faced distance. She decided she would try and shock him from his trance by relating the horror that took place at Culebra while he was in prison. Before she finished describing the massacre, Byron erupted.

"Dat's it! Time dis *chango* get himself a gun! I'm gonna blast all them spiggotty soljas straight to hell!"

Startled to hear the gentle youth snarl with such venom, Estelle feared her attempt to shock him had been a grave mistake.

"That's not the answer, *negrito*." She started to caress his arm but Byron twisted away his shoulder.

"Let mi go! Mi gonna rip out them bowels and give it feed rat!"

"No, *caro*, the weak need to use cunning—not violence..."

"So what me must do? Nutting? S'pose Longers did do that? Yuh'd be sitting here now?" he shot back fiercely. "They treat us worse than dogs!"

"I understand, my love. Who wouldn't want to fight men like Rivueltas? But take it from a woman who's seen her share of spiteful men. It's better to keep the devils close and prey upon their weak spots."

"The only spot dis man need find is where to put a bullet!"

Estelle grew frightened seeing his wasted body trembling, worried that she had him dangerously inflamed. "Listen to me, Byron!" she said, holding him firmly by both his wrists,"—there are only two kinds of people in this world—those who sell and those who steal. Prestàn's problem was that he was too proud to do either. Don't end up like him. You'll only be wasting your precious life fighting lost battles."

"Precious life? What precious life you be talking 'bout? Strainin' my back on a shovel gettin' hammered by rain one day then wicked sun-hot the next? Is precious life gettin' blown up by dynamite or perishin' from swamp fever so them can plop you under some rubble without even troublin' to read a verse of scripture? Is that the precious life yuh talkin' 'bout?"

Estelle moved so their shoulders touched, but Byron reflexively wriggled away. Not to be put off, she kept her tight grip on his hand. "Let me tell you how you fight and survive," she counseled him while he continued to tremble. "You're right Longers easily whipped those thugs—but I knew that sooner or later he'd wind up with a bullet in his back and even if they didn't kill him I'd be spending most of my profit paying for protection. I hadn't yet figured why anybody wanted me out of business—I'd barely gotten started—then it dawned on me: here I come insisting that any girl who works in my place stays clean and my tavern is sitting less than a stone's throw from one of the nastiest chancres on the earth. Back then a man dropping his trousers in a Bottle Alley stall was paying for a crotch full of diseases and was more than likely to end up getting robbed.

"That's when I started planning the Last Frontier. I knew that if I wanted to make real money I needed a better location—but I had to survive long enough to afford it. So I dressed up like I'd stepped straight from a couturier in Paris and went to see the harbor master who was known to be smuggling in liquor for the underground market. I could see him start licking his lips the minute I stepped in—I was still quite a looker back then—I barely had to say two words before he agreed to sell me his bootleg wholesale in exchange for my services. That's when I casually brought up the problem I was having with the Bottle Alley thugs. He put his fat sweaty arm around my shoulders and said if the meat in the tamale is as fine as its wrapping my troubles were over. I was fairly sure a man in his line of business could handle the matter but I wasn't about to take chances. I took part of the money I started saving on booze and paid the whores to have their pimps stop harassing me. Everyone has something to sell—the trick is knowing what your enemy will buy."

"Sure. You can count on coming out fine—it's your people and you're a nice-looking woman. Me's nothing to them," Byron said, looking down miserably. "Naw, it's time this boy go on home. At least back-a-yard they respec' humanity. They're not gonna brand me like some cow!" Holding back more tears, Byron stared at the raised red circle where the cigar had scorched close to the bone.

Estelle bit her lip and let her finger trace the ring of darker skin where the two angry burns showed signs of healing. "What can you sell if you go home now? Another back to chop more cane? Longers was right, you know—you don't have to settle for what they're selling. You can learn to live on the intelligence God gave you. Isn't that what drew you here to Colón—the hope that you would find that helping friend? Why give up that hope when you're not even twenty?"

"The bastards done stole my little money. I could kill that wicked lieutenant—he stole poor Johnny's violin—" Byron caught himself too late and the pressure of holding all that guilt and grief finally overwhelmed him. He buried his face in Estelle's lap and confessed through a stream of heaving sobs.

"It's all right, *niño*," she said, stroking the soft black wool grown thick on his head. "I'd be lying if I said I wasn't disappointed to hear it—" She paused and stared sadly out to the sea, "but I'd be a bigger hypocrite to condemn you for pretending to be something you're not. Now, I have my own confession to make. Your friend with the violet eyes did come asking about you. I never told you because you were being such a help and I didn't want to lose you. Funny, before I met that hunk of a sailor I didn't believe any man could be loyal. But you've shown me that Longers was not so exceptional—or perhaps—" she bent and kissed Byron's tear-stained cheek, "I just know how to cheat the best Jamaican boys."

Byron looked up to regard her expression and his sad eyes grew luminous. He parted his lips to thank her but the words spilled out inaudibly. Telling him, 'hush,' Estelle opened her arms and held him to her breast, then set the wicker seat to swing and started singing.

Chapter 21

Bolivar City, Venezuela

Thomas had not expected to pay for his voyage playing poker. He had learned a good deal watching Henri fleece his victims and after being pressed into a game on board he had been pleasantly surprised by how quickly his five dollars had swelled into fifty simply by being patient and counting every card. He landed in Caracas having won well over a hundred dollars and he might have put off his plans and spent the year gambling had he not been sure of earning Genevieve's condemnation.

He had been unhappy leaving Panama without seeing her, but reasoned that the sooner he started panning the sooner he'd be ready to woo her. He had spent his five days in Caracas with her constantly on his mind, wondering how much gold it would take to start up a business and truly impress her. Thinking the distraction might ease his mental turmoil, he had passed his evenings gambling while he waited to start the overland leg of his journey. By the time his mule train was due to head south he had won so much gold and silver he had to stop and bank the lot, keeping just his wad of fresh dollar bills which seemed both sufficient and more convenient for his travels.

As he rightly anticipated, the trip had been arduous going across jagged terrain, but despite the distressingly slow pace he and his fellow travelers had made it to Bolivar City just as the river's weekly passenger-boat south was being loaded to depart. Had Simon Bolivar succeeded in uniting Latin America, Venezuela and Panama would have still been part of Gran Colombia. Thomas would then have known not to insult his partisan pilot by laughing in disbelief when the boatman refused his Yankee greenbacks. He had apologized profusely once someone explained why the republican had been offended but before he could find anyone willing to trade bolivars for some of his dollars the pilot had cast off and left him stranded.

Bolivar City lies on a graceful green slope at the point where the milky Orinoco narrows. As he wandered its riverside walk Thomas found it hard to believe this placid setting had been the battleground for a great revolution. He was annoyed by his turn in luck, but the soft breeze coming off the water made it an inviting spot to sit after a three day ride on the back of a burro. By the time he roused the energy to continue, the breeze had died and the sun was scalding. He asked a passing fisherman where he might hire some other transport and felt his temper steaming when the man said it was doubtful he'd find a pilot willing to take a single fare as far as the gold-fields. His mood did not improve when after searching for a place to stay and escape the afternoon heat he finally found an open hotel only to be told that the last room was taken. The receptionist, a suave young *mestizo* in a double-breasted waistcoat, was sympathetic.

"It's not the hour to be out and about," the dapper clerk advised, cooling his light brown brow with a palm-leaf fan. "Why don't you leave your gear with the valet and have a drink in the bar? Certainly—" he smiled when Thomas asked if he could exchange some money, "but don't worry—we are pleased to take your dollars. Why don't I sketch you a map with the addresses of some other lodgings while you enjoy your refreshment? Perhaps by the time you feel rested one will have reopened."

Encouraged by the clerk's advice, Thomas left his bags and after choosing one of the tavern's small marble-topped tables ordered tapas and a draft of beer. He was enchanted after days of drinking cheap whiskey and quinine to find that the beer was fresh and very cold and with enough flavor to make him want to linger and sip it slowly. When he got around to retrieving his luggage, the receptionist suggested he return to the hotel for a late dinner. "We have a first-rate chef and if you care to leave the night clerk a note with where you are staying I'll try and find you a new guide when I come in tomorrow."

Thomas thanked him with a comradely smile and a new dollar bill and left to search out the row-houses on the Colónnade facing the river. Following the clerk's instructions he knocked at the first dark blue door he saw but got no response. He cupped his hands to peer through the narrow French window's long frosted pane then quickly reared back, hearing a dog's low growl. He tried the second address five doors down and again received no answer. When none of the lodgings appeared eager for business he decided to try his luck on a shady avenue leading through a bower of trees bearing fruit which smelled amazingly like malted milk.

After he had walked a fair piece without encountering a single pedestrian he realized his prospects would only get slimmer the farther he strayed from the heart of the city. He was about to head back and await the end of siesta when he noticed a rustic planked-wood fence with a sign protruding from its low hinged gate that read Pension. As he drew closer, Thomas could see the cream-colored walls of a rambling hacienda deep inside a large dirt courtyard with an eroded cast-stone fountain. The sparse green from a dying hedge and a set of bending palms appeared to impinge on the property as if its former acreage had been sharply lopped off.

Glimpsing a human outline nodding in a rocking-chair on the hacienda's iron-barred verandah, Thomas rapped at the gate hoping to draw the person's attention. He had been banging for almost a minute when the figure snapped up and snarled out, *¡calla un momento!—¡no haga ruido!* Tall and ungainly, the man rose from the chair and hopped to grip the bars of the verandah. He beckoned to Thomas impatiently to come through the unlocked gate and cross the courtyard. Thomas was nearly at the steps to the shaded porch before he realized that the prune-faced *gringo* clutching the verandah bars was missing one of his legs.

He was about to climb the porch stairs when the old man barked for him to stop. Even half-concealed by the filigreed ironwork, the long whiskered face, its gray eyes sharp and steely, showed a character used to shaking men down to their boots. The old man balanced on his one good leg with a hand against the grating and peered belligerently down at Thomas who felt less and less heartened as he inquired about a room.

The old proprietor cut him off midstream, his Spanish betraying a startling Irish brogue. "You can have the one in back across from Mrs. Alvarez—you'll have to go and wake her for the key."

Thomas thanked him and turned to leave.

"Where do you think you're going?" the old man growled, summoning him back and sticking a hand through the grill. "I'll need two nights cash in advance!—and I'll not have you bring back any loose company or come here pestering me again!"

After he had paid the old grouch Thomas followed the path beneath the hacienda's dark sloping eaves and found the off-set garden cottage. He had to knock for several minutes with tactful persistence before a shrunken old woman came slouching out in her slippered feet, rubbing her eyes as if to knead them out from deep sleep. She looked up at him blankly as he politely asked if she was *Señora* Alvarez, then prodded the air with her wrinkled forefinger to cut him off. Shambling back inside, she returned a minute later with a jug of water and a long iron key. She handed Thomas the heavy clay jar leaving him to inch along behind struggling to juggle both it and his two heavy bags.

Arriving at the hacienda's even seedier-looking wing, she unlocked the door to a darkened room that treated Thomas' nostrils to a potpourri of smoked tobacco, mildew and dust. A few stubborn threads of light managed to shine through the coating grit on the only window, revealing a sagging four-poster bed, an old wardrobe with a broken mirror, and a muddle of nailed-on slats of lumber apparently meant to double as a towel rack and washstand. He was about to leave and ask the old geezer for his money back but as he set down the jar of water he realized he was too tired to hunt a step further. And with some better luck he could be gone by tomorrow.

"There are towels and soap in the dresser," said *Señora* Alvarez, scraping away on her sleepy feet to finish her siesta.

Thomas threw himself onto the bed and promptly fell asleep. He woke up with a start, hours later, expecting to find himself lying on a blanket on the ground across from his pack-mule. He fetched a towel from the battered wardrobe and after pouring half the water from the jug into a basin, rinsed the grime from his face and neck then put on a fresh shirt. When he had the bags with his gear safely stowed he decided that rather than stay in here swallowing rancid dust he would return to the pleasant hotel for an early supper.

The clerk's claim that his establishment was renowned for its fish did not disappoint. He ordered a second garlicked flank of the fried piranha and topped it off with another tall glass of cold beer. He dallied over a cloyingly sweet cup of black coffee then strayed to where a group of delta *rancheros* sounded as if they were enjoying an evening away from their cattle and beer-hating wives. A pudgy fellow whose boisterous cackle occasionally jarred the whole room spotted Thomas eyeing their table and invited him to join them for a round of *La Viuda*.

"Sorry, gents, that's not a game that I'm familiar with," Thomas replied, employing a bit of the cunning he'd picked up from his mentor.

"It's nothing! Come on!—we'll teach you," insisted the husky rancher winking to his *compadres*. "Bartender," he called to the man with the slick, pomaded black hair standing at the tavern counter, "set up our friend here. Tonight his drinks are on our table."

Thomas sat reluctantly in the pulled out chair and after a few jovial nudges while he followed the next hand he let himself appear to be persuaded, having realized that *La Viuda* was a simple variation of what the railway's Yankee leathernecks called Whiskey Poker. By his third deal in, he had dispensed with his wide-eyed ruse since it was clear his hosts saw the game merely as an excuse to spend the night drinking. A few swigs of dark rum or bourbon washed down with a flagon or two of beer and those men whose rugged faces seemed steeped with wisdom were far too soused to bluff. They would either curse and toss down their cards or a cat's grin would sneak to the edge of someone's lip, alerting Thomas it was a good time to fold.

When the game finally broke up in time for the men to be home by midnight, the plastered *rancheros* could barely stagger to their feet. As the five all stumbled out together, locking arms to keep from falling over, the husky rancher nicknamed Gordi warned Thomas that he'd better come back tomorrow and square things. Thomas found the threat quite surprising seeing that while Gordi and his *compañeros* were busy drinking he had been soberly doubling his money. But if he was going to be stuck in this town for one more night he was happy to oblige.

Thomas had chosen to travel by mule to skip the delay and expense of stopping at an inn each night but after his rough and tumble trip he was ready for a long night's sleep in bed. Even though his fusty mattress was old and lumpy he did not wake up until noon. He hurried back to the hotel where the helpful receptionist informed him that he'd found him a guide and the pilot was waiting for him down at the marina. Thomas dashed straight for the pier but by the time he made it to the landing, the pilot had lost patience and left.

Feeling stymied at every move, as he trudged back to his room to wait out another siesta he thought seriously about becoming a card-sharp. The impulse became even more compelling when his second night playing cards with the tipsy *rancheros* netted him another one-hundred percent return. Waking early the following morning, he spent the entire day until noon trying to hire a boat to the gold-fields to no avail. He told himself not to be discouraged, that the cards could be fickle and in the long run he'd be better off sticking to his plan. To keep up his spirits he found a store selling mesh and plywood and spent the afternoon constructing special panning equipment of his own. By evening he was over his frustration, feeling proud of his hand-fashioned tool and looking forward to doubling his bets for a third straight night. But as he came inside the hotel tavern he saw that the *rancheros* had come in early and were all slouching at their table with hard expressions. As they watched him with stony stares, fingering their five empty glasses, he could tell that his new friends were in a far less accommodating mood and dangerously sober.

"Why come back?" demanded Gordi, his chubby frame puffed up accusingly. "You've already picked us clean, you two-faced hustler—"

Thomas had heard of men getting plugged with a bullet for an innocent misdeal so he approached their beef with tentative care. "What are you saying, I'm a cheat?"

"Worse," the rancher grunted, spitting on the tavern floor, "you're a *tacano—¡un piojoso!*"

What Thomas had failed to apprehend was that his friendly *rancheros* were all related, either through marriage or as third and fourth cousins. In his outsider's ignorance, he had let two evenings pass without paying for their drinks from his winnings. As a consequence they had arrived to find that their credit was now as dry as their throats. Thomas appreciated that for the ranchers this was a crisis, but seeing he did not share their blood or a bed with one of their sisters, he failed to see why he was expected to stand the whole tab, especially since over the course of two nights he had sipped a total of four beers.

He did appreciate, however, that their parched anger presented a pressing risk to his own skin. He begged their pardon, pleading innocence for having violated their custom, then walked over to the barkeep and asked to see their tab. When he saw the amount of liquor five *rancheros* could guzzle in under eight hours his jaw nearly fell to the floor. Not about to part with more than his two-night's winnings, he gave the barkeep fifty dollars, a mere quarter of the total tab, and told him to serve his thirsty friends one more round while he dashed to get more money.

The promise was a complete pretense but it got him safely away. After sprinting a mile in the opposite direction from the rambling hacienda, he started cautiously rounding back, hoping the wide detour would throw the *rancheros* off in case they became tempted to trace where he was staying. He doubted his long dash had drawn undue attention as it was already past sunset and, as usual, the streets of Bolivar City were growing festive. The quiet promenades were now filled with troubadours tossing sly winks as they strolled by the chirpy young girls selling flowers and stacks of steaming *cachapas*. Drifts of laughter and contented murmurs seemed to rise at every corner as folks emerged from their long *siestas,* lured by the smell of cooked cheese and the seductive pulsations of lyrical drumming.

He blocked out the varied enticements competing for his senses and rushed past the malted-milk trees and on through the Pension's front gate. He hurried across the dark graveled courtyard towards the back and was suddenly rocked back on his feet, stopped by the red glow from a burning cigarette right at the entrance to his room. He swerved around, gasping with fear, and as he leapt headlong for the verandah step he crashed against the old proprietor, knocking him flat.

"*Fàn fada ort!*" the Irishman cursed in his native dialect, scowling up from his rump. "What the devil are you doo-in' tearing at me like a scalded cat? I tole ya you're not to come troublin' me agin!" Even as he swore in three different tongues, the old man accepted Thomas' quick hand to help him back up and then balanced on his one good leg. "Don't bother yappin' in my ear!" he snipped when Thomas tried to explain that he was a hunted man. "I've lived here long enough to know you half-breed mulattos have a tough time taking orders! Ain't nobody after you, you darn fool!—the Indian's been waitin' on you for an hour—I was about to tell him to skedaddle!" he said, jerking his gray head to the figure smoking back in the shadows. "Another harebrained fellow!—had to tell him to come on in and stop his hammerin'. Damned Indian ruined my supper. Anyhow, good riddance—he says you'll be gone tomorrow—"

Sure enough, just after dawn the next day, Thomas and his new pilot met at the quay to make the lengthy river trip to the minefields. As they latched the gear onto the bamboo raft Thomas was still riled over last night's encounter. "I was his only bloody guest and the old goat talks to me like I'm a criminal."

The guide, who went by Lagarto, clucked his tongue. "Don't mind the *Colónel*. I told you last night—he's not all that right in the head."

"How the devil does the old coot survive?" asked Thomas as he settled in the center of the raft and watched the loose-limbed Amerindian untie from the landing.

Lagarto laughed as he grabbed his long pole and slipped aboard light as a cat. "That old coot has *mucho dinero*. A lot of people around here think he's a hero. He inherited that place from his wife's family, they were wealthy *criollos* who'd backed *El Libertador*. Word is his wife was the most beautiful woman in the province but she died trying to birth the big Irishman's child. People tell me the reason *Colónel* Kerriman hates to be disturbed is because the two of them still dine together every night. *Señora* Alvarez is his wife's own mother but she has to stay out in the cottage so as not to scare her spirit..." Lagarto dipped his pole to shove off then paused for a thoughtful chuckle, "—maybe the old *gringo's* not so crazy."

They had been breezing down the somnolent pearl-gray river for eight or nine minutes when Thomas suddenly realized that in his hurry to bank his gold in Caracas he had forgotten to stop at the government house for his mining permit. He was about to ask his guide if he'd made a serious oversight when he glimpsed the magnificent tepuis. Sparkling as crystal in golden sunlight, the massive tables of sandstone and granite appeared like giant red-brass crowns.

Imaginings of the riches dripping inside the veins of those godlike *mesetas* supplanted all thoughts of the forgotten permit. Thomas was still fantasizing about returning to Panama with a monarch's share of gold when the raft made a jarring bounce and went plunging down a stretch of stony rapids. He clutched the edge of his seat sure that any moment the raft would shatter into pieces. As they shuddered downstream, glancing from boulder to rock, the gap between life and death seemed as slender as the pliancy of a six-inch bamboo log. When his guide seemed hardly troubled Thomas tried to mask his terror. He asked Lagarto with forced casualness how critical it was for a panner to carry his permit and felt his rising courage sink when the pilot replied that the gold-fields were patrolled by the army and poachers were discouraged by being shot.

By some miracle the pontoon survived its battering and Thomas' awestruck mood returned as they skimmed, rattled but intact, onto the Caroni's still blue waters. Thomas was relieved, seeing Lagarto hoist back up his long pole to steer the craft to land, that he had made it to the fields with hours of daylight remaining. He thanked his guide with a generous tip and left him to firm up his raft on the sand while he shouldered his voluminous gear and went hunting for a promising site.

At the river's lower reaches he was dismayed to see over a half-dozen miners crouched intently by the bank, their bodies so encrusted with shining mud they looked fashioned from metal. His misgivings increased seeing an even larger number of men spaced out in the shallows, all patiently swirling huge black saucers. Poised with their necks deeply bowed to their chests, they looked like a wading flock of migrant birds hunting food at low tide. Every so often a miner would siphon some of the silt in his disc into the bag at his waist then dump the balance back in the water, but from the lament on their dark perspiring faces, Thomas reckoned it had been a long hot day of slim pickings.

His guess appeared confirmed as he noticed the slit-eyed stare that tracked his way the moment one of the miners spotted him plodding up the bank with his cumbersome gear. He began to worry that those stories he'd read about men panning a fortune from these rivers had been fakes just to sell magazines. He thought back to Lagarto's warning and was again musing about life as a gambler when the obscuring woodlands suddenly parted and the mighty tepuis loomed back into view like lustrous megaliths. No, he thought, his belief restored seeing the gleaming gold mountain, a fortune was here, waiting to be found. He could almost taste it.

He took heart from what seemed to be less than common knowledge that while there was easier gold to be found where the river ran slowest it was also away from the true mother lode. From the numbers he saw mining the same choice area, more likely than not by now most of the good-sized nuggets had already been panned. So instead of spending hours sloshing about hoping for a few small grains he decided to search out a promising seam then use the river's own power to get at the deeper deposits of gold. On a hunch, he tracked a line of shrubs and brush tinted amber and an hour later was rewarded as he came to a secondary stream gurgling down from the distant *meseta*, its metal-rich water like ruby-red wine.

Thomas labored on, scrambling across a fair-sized boulder in his path then through some low-hanging foliage, nearly down on all fours to safeguard the precious burden still strapped on his back. When at last he could stand upright, he was unsettled to hear ripples of laughter coming out of the forest. He cautiously followed his ear and was even more amazed that the voices seemed to be conversing in English with a mellifluent patois that reminded him of home.

The sky was turning indigo as he arrived at a grassy clearing and saw five men hunched around a fire, their dark limbs mottled in the metallic lacquer of the riverbank miners. Four of them were enjoying some good-natured sparring while a spare young chap with barely enough flesh to cover his bones knelt by the crackling flames and started to carefully coat the bottom of a cast-iron frying pan with a thick silvery liquid.

Thomas approached the men guardedly and was charmed to see their faces beam with smiles and their hands start fanning him welcome when he called to them in a lilting West Indian salutation.

"He calls it tinning," a panner with a sparse wool beard explained when Thomas crept in to ask what the scrawny little cook was up to. "Just watch—! Sparky's about to do some magic with his mercury!"

As Thomas looked on in awe, young Sparky took a bundle from one of the men and dumped its ball of black mud into the gray-coated pan which was now smoking-hot. He jiggled the frying pan deftly from side to side and when a tiny lump slowly began to take shape he poured it into the hollow of a cored green mango. After pressing the hard fruit tight with a stick, he plopped it straight in the flames. He repeated the whole process five more times, removing the ones already blackened to a crisp and setting them to cool. When all six mangoes were done he split the first three open and proudly presented their owners with three shining lumps of gold.

While the miners finished collecting their new bounty and went to drop it with the other nuggets they each kept in a small marked bag, Thomas congratulated the skinny young cook on his impressive wizardry.

"Where me learn it—?" Sparky muttered, echoing the question with touchy surprise. "I picked it up from the smartest panner around—he could find a rock full of shit with his nose..." he boasted glumly.

"He's no longer around—your friend—?"

"Him dead. Robbers caught him panning alone last year and put a bullet in his head."

"Sorry," Thomas whispered, promptly regretting having pried.

"It's awright," Sparky said with a shrug, climbing up to his feet, "you cudden know."

The miner with the scant fuzzy beard came and pointed to the equipment Thomas had tied across his knapsack.

"What all dat you carryin'?"

"I'm like the tortoise, man," Thomas answered with a chuckle. "Got all I need right on my back."

"Yeah? What for—?" asked another miner, eyeing the long contraption skeptically.

"Oh, this?" said Thomas, seeing the men all come and surround him, their attentions riveted on the riffled sluice box he had copied from a mining magazine. "That's my ticket to El Dorado," he boasted then heard the miners all start wheezing with laughter.

"Young boy," drawled the oldest panner, a thick scar-faced fellow with a gap between his two front teeth, "don't you know? El Dorado is a phantom...a made up story."

The little alchemist fixed Thomas with an incredulous look. "You don't have a *batek?*"

"Sorry?"

"Your pan, man," the bearded miner said impatiently, as if tired of dealing with an idiot. "How you expect to find gold widout a *batek?*"

Thomas did not bother to explain that if he found a lode-bed in a fast-moving stream his lightweight mesh and plywood box would be filtering out more nuggets in two hours than their big pans could probably sift out in a day. He didn't like being laughed at and since they were eager to take him for a fool he decided he might as well turn their perceptions in his favor. "Golly—then I'm sure glad I ran into you chaps—" Thomas lifted his hat and scratched his head. "Whatcha all call it—a *batek?*—guess I should've got me one of those. I'm still pretty green about this prospecting business—but at least out here in the bush I can learn and not keep getting sidetracked."

"How you mean, sidetracked?" piped up a smooth-cheeked fellow with slivers of gold glinting between his teeth.

"You fellas know this game they call *La Viuda?* The Yanks I know call it stud poker—or some such thing. Cut a sad story short—these *rancheros* got me hooked into their game up in Bolivar City—near cleaned me out—"

His tiny speck of bait reeled them in. Practically in chorus, the miners insisted that Thomas should join them for supper. Thomas happily contributed a can of mashed pumpkin in exchange for a slice of smoked pork and a flour dumpling until he realized it had been boiled to such a dense solid he could have easier used it to kill a man than chew it. Afterwards, as everyone sat sipping some steaming bush-tea, the gap-toothed miner produced a pack of greasy cards from his back pocket and proposed they help the young fellow brush up on his game. Thomas kept up his phony resistance, not wanting to tip his hand until the panners were convinced he was a dumb goose, ready to be plucked.

"Well—maybe some practice would do me good...but just a round or two—if you like, we can use my new cards..." he offered innocently, pulling out a fresh deck of his own and clumsily trying to shuffle.

The minute he saw the gold-lust bright in their eyes as he fumbled to deal the six hands, Thomas knew that these men in their cheap rubber boots with their damp breeches rolled up past their knees were a bunch of diehard optimists. And sure enough, the more good fortune began to desert them the tighter they clutched to the flimsiest of hands, as the casual game changed and grew intense. Like the consanguineous ranchers, they accepted their bad luck philosophically, the one difference being they were losing their shirts to him completely sober.

Thomas found it even harder to enjoy his winnings when he learned over the course of the night that the five of them all hailed from the same Guyana plantation. He tried calling the game off twice, saying he did not deserve his run of luck, but the gap-toothed panner wouldn't hear of it. To his dismay, it seemed his gracious hosts were as proud as they were honorable.

"So, yuh been a little lucky—no pork-knocker worth a vein of shit gonna quit this easy. Play on!"

Hearing the declaration tossed out a fourth time, Thomas asked the maroon-skinned miner why they all stuck to panning in the river.

"You can spend a month knocking rock and never find a mother lode—gold's a sure bet in the river," said the bearded panner nicknamed Phinny.

"Don't listen to him! Doing one thing don't rule out another—but yuh gotta know where to look or you'll never trace that rock full of shit," the man with the fine gold slivers between his teeth stuck in with a grin.

"Lookie here," exclaimed the miner the others called Bounce, "can we stop the jawin' and deal—? A Jamaica monkey can't be lucky all the time!"

"That's right," nodded Phinny, "—even a black cat don't live forever! I feel the tide is ready to do some turnin'."

The cards disagreed and one by one the others all folded in disgust, leaving just Thomas and Big Daddy, the pork-knockers' elder statesman. Thomas felt good about his hand, but he was starting to feel almost ashamed about taking his money.

"Come on now! Don't go limp on me now because you think I might finally whip you!" Big Daddy complained when Thomas stood pat and declined to raise.

"Hey, if I can't meet you then the last pot is yours."

"Sure, with a few loose grains and a couple red pesos. Here, let's make things interesting." The dark-skinned panner dug out his little cloth bag and pulled out what looked like a dirty marble.

"Big Daddy, no!" gasped Sparky over his comrades' troubled murmurs.

The miner tossed the rough-edged pebble into the hat on the ground with the rest of the bets. "Looks like our Jamaican cousin has been playing us like a fiddle. Let's see what our young Judas is made of—"

"But yuh don't even know how much that stone you found is worth!" said Sparky. "It could fetch two—three hundred dollars...maybe more!"

Big Daddy squared his scarred face fiercely against his young opponent.

"That there's a diamond. You heard Sparky—it's worth at least two hundred. I'll stake it for that pile of winnings." The miner nudged his nose at the stash of cash and gold on the ground and for the first time all evening Thomas sensed a current of hostility. "It's mostly our money," Big Daddy muttered, "what d'ya really got to lose—?"

"How many?" Thomas asked coolly.

The big miner grinned as Sparky blew out his breath and looked away.

"Two—and make them pretty!"

With teasing slowness Thomas slid back his three last cards and checked them one by one. His demeanor stayed expressionless as he paused to calculate. If he proved a shabby judge of men, making the wrong choice could put him in even worse jeopardy. "You first—" he said quietly, delaying while he made up his mind.

"Bow to her Majesty three times!" crowed Big Daddy as he proudly laid out his three queens and his buddies jumped up hooting, dancing and hugging with smiles of delight.

When Thomas was slow to concede, the miner called Bounce reached for his wrist and impudently exposed his hand. The men all froze with bated breath, and Thomas wished he had folded sooner. The silence seemed to weigh a thousand pounds as Big Daddy sat gaping at the three winning kings. Thomas could feel the miners simmering and he felt strangely dispossessed, as if he had just traded away something precious. He wanted to tell them to take back their gold, but before he could the miners had walked off comforting Big Daddy and left him there alone. When he saw that they were preparing to bed down for the night, Thomas sought out young Sparky and offered him part of his take.

"Here—I did wrong. I shouldn't have taken your gold."

"Thanks all the same..." Sparky demurred, his chin tucked down firmly to his neck, "once coconut fall from tree him can't fasten back."

"Man, you're not a coconut, take the money! Or look—" Thomas picked up the deep-crowned hat with the greenbacks and gold and began to finger hastily through its loot, "you probably know which was yours...you can have it all back."

The skinny pork-knocker shook his head. "Can't do it. Out here you never know when bandits or some outlaw soldier might try and rob you. That's why the five of us all band together. We share and share alike—except what's in your pan—that stay yours. Same if you get lucky and hit a rock full of shit. Same way we like to gamble—winners, keepers—only to ward off hard feelings we always limit how much to raise each bet."

"Nobody said a word about any limit, tonight!"

Sparky lowered his eyes. Thomas couldn't tell if it was to hide shame or resentment.

"Big Daddy figured you'd be easy pickings. But you was bluffing us from the start."

Thomas did not know what to say. He'd come to like these happy-go-lucky pork-knockers. The idea of a game had only popped in his head because they'd laughed at his sluice-box. Did it make sense for him to feel bad about winning if all their good-natured ribbing, the jokes over dinner, had simply been an act to soften him up for the kill? Or was it fairer to say that these men were no different from him—once gold came into the picture, even a friendly game became serious business.

When Sparky refused to share in his winnings Thomas left to retire at a cautious distance. He did not think these men were the type to creep through the dark and slit his throat but harking back to Sparky's murdered friend he bedded down with a grip on his shiny new pistol. As he lay on his blanket halfway between the bush and the river the jungle noises grew frantic. The night choir of whooping frogs and screaming monkeys was not only more discordant than he recalled from Panama, their cacophony was sustained by the hum of a billion insects. He was hunting for a shirt to tie around his ears when he heard his name being shouted above the racket.

"Hey—yuh can't sleep down there!"

"Why not?—maybe coral snake is his cousin!"

"No man—widow spidah is his muddah and scorpion is his fahdah!"

Thomas rolled lazily onto his side and saw Sparky's wiry frame hanging above him in the dark. "What am I now—an outcast to be mocked and bullied?" he snapped, hearing the pork-knockers' rippling laughter back in the forest as they bandied about mordant jokes at his expense.

"Look around—" Sparky urged him.

Thomas rose partway up from the ground and strained his eyes through the spectral light of the wasting moon. He made out nothing beyond the contours of the river and the silhouettes of the vine-covered kapoks looming above the bush like long-haired creatures.

"Yuh see anybody else sleeping out along the riverbank?"

Thomas gave a shrug. He could barely recognize shapes ten feet away.

"Yuh can't lie here on the ground—yuh didn't pack a hammock?"

Thomas shook his head then glowered back at the woods, hearing one of the pork-knockers chortle that maybe that big cat is gonna fill his belly tonight.

"I hear those jaguars are partial to some tender brown-skin meat!" quipped another.

"They're just teasing me—right?" Thomas whispered to young Sparky.

"Maybe—but I wouldn't count on it. We been hearing talk that there's a big-ole tiger living somewhere back inside the bush. Big Daddy thinks he saw him out prowling one night further up along the river—"

"Jesus—now you tell me!" Thomas squeezed his hand around the gun and snatched up his bedding. It had not dawned on him until now that when he'd camped in the jungle with Duvay there had always been a scout on lookout all night.

"Relax, young Thomas!" Big Daddy's voice came blaring from the forest. "Sparky is just worried because an ole Indian told him the big cat can only hunt someone small..." The miner's wry humor sent the others howling one more time. "But he's right—that there ground is not the place a man in his right mind wants to be sleeping. Never mind," Big Daddy continued when the bellowing laughter subsided and Thomas stood lingering at the edge of the grove trying to decide if he should climb up and sleep in one of the trees. "You fleeced us good tonight but we're not cruel—we won't make you spend the night like a bat on a branch—you can have one of our hammocks."

Thomas thanked Big Daddy earnestly and insisted on buying his extra hammock for double its worth. After hovering restlessly half the night, unable to find a comfortable position or block out the buzzing insects and a noisy parrot, he decided to be on his way before the miners woke, perhaps more inclined to get even. His instincts said it was wrong of him to mistrust them, but he could not tell when one of these pork-knockers was being dead serious or when an offer made with complete sincerity would somehow sting their pride.

He was in the middle of redoing his pack to wrap his goods and machete inside the cloth hammock when Sparky came up and asked where he was headed.

"I'm gonna try my luck further up. Why not join me? If there really is a big cat out there I could use the extra eyes."

"More gold down there," said Sparky, jerking his thumb back towards the river.

"Maybe before, not now."

"Risky—pannin' on your own—that's how Papa went and got himself shot."

Thomas glanced sharply at the skinny pork-knocker. "That miner you said got killed—that was your father?"

Sparky stared off into the dawn's pink distance then nodded faintly.

"Sorry to hear—sounds like you two were pretty close."

"So I thought—" Sparky whispered, looking solemn. "You're a born-lucky gambler, Tom Judah, but I'd think twice about panning gold in these parts on my own."

"Thanks for the warning, old boy." Thomas grinned as he finished wrapping his shovel inside the folded hammock, "but like you said—looks like I was born to be a gambler."

Chapter 22

December, 1885

Before he met Estelle, Byron had looked forward to Christmas like an asthmatic looks forward to catching the Spanish flu. As a child, he was the one with no relatives to visit for a day of games and feasting after the five A.M. service. His first two holidays in Panama had left him no less despondent. While the rest of his crew were back home with their sweethearts and being pampered by their jealous mothers, he'd be sitting in his bunk trying to think up a cheap way to pass his vacation. His sense of friendlessness had been dispelled last season when Theresa alerted him that the 26th of December was the one day all year Estelle refused to do any business so she could lavish her attention on her devoted staff.

First had come a sumptuous one o'clock dinner prepared by Mattie, the brothel's widowed cook, which Estelle insisted on serving herself. When they were nearly bursting she ordered everyone out to the sitting room where they lounged on the big harem pillows while she passed each of her girls a little present and Byron a thank-you card filled with cash. After devouring the last of the fruitcake and coffee, they whiled away the lazy afternoon sipping pineapple punch, playing charades and solving riddles.

Byron had gone to sleep that night drunk with happiness, his cheeks still warm from Miss Theresa's tipsy kisses. But this year the thought of Christmas made him even more downcast and gloomy than ever. His back had almost healed but increasingly there were days when he feared he was losing the connection with his senses. He often ate his food without tasting and found himself unable to follow what Estelle was saying. When she was away he would sit alone in the wicker porch swing wishing he had died in that dismal prison.

As he lay bleeding all alone inside his cell, weak from thirst and starvation, what had pained him the most was knowing he was ready to confess even though he was innocent. Yet now that he was free from that physical torment the remorse stinging his conscience made him miss the strokes from that knotted leather lash as if they had been caresses. How could he wish Miss Estelle a Merry Christmas when they both knew Longers was dead because of him? How, he wondered, could she ever forgive him?

Each time he had tried to bury his guilt beneath an eruption of hate for the sadistic lieutenant, he pictured the bullets striking Longers' body then saw himself standing inside the firing squad like a fool, with Johnny's silent fiddle in his useless hands. When Christmas Eve arrived, he started to walk away from the cottage thinking he would drown himself in the sea. But as he stepped to the sand he heard Longers growl inside his head—'boy, show some courage!' Ashamed that he had lost his spine, he wandered back to the porch and sat down heavily. He wished back his brighter spirits but sensed they had flown far beyond the darkening sunset. When finally the last bit of light was gone, he got up and went to bed, too depressed to watch Estelle put on her brave cheerful face all through dinner.

———

"*Caro*—are you awake in there?"

For an instant, Byron imagined the whispering voice in his head had been part of a dream. And then he heard the loud knock at his door.

"Byron...don't tell me you're asleep—it's Christmas eve!"

"What's de time?...I been feeling a little bit tired..."

"Tired? You looked pretty spry this morning! Come on—I don't want to eat alone again tonight—it's Christmas. You can't stay in there sulking all your life, you'll have a relapse."

"Mi not good company tonight—I'll be better tomorrow...promise."

"Promise, hell—rouse yourself—I'm coming in!"

Before Byron could finish brightening the bedside lamp and find his trousers, Estelle had stepped inside and shut the door. As he rushed to drag on the pant-legs she stopped to pose in a purple Chinese robe cut from plush silk taffeta embroidered in floral bouquets and insects couched in floss and golden cord. With her black hair swept up high and pinned with a diamond-studded amethyst brooch she could have passed for an Eastern empress.

"*¡Feliz Navidad, querido!*"

Byron blinked at her with both hands frozen to the waist of his trousers. When he gaped at her dumbstruck, Estelle strode in and kissed the side of his mouth. "I bought myself a present for Christmas—what do you think?" She twirled around so he could see the back of her luxurious new robe and its large cinching bustle. "Exquisite, don't you think? Almost makes me look slender again—do you believe I'm about to turn forty?"

Byron could not recall when she had looked more ravishing. He had seen her dressed to the nines in the Last Frontier, but seeing her tonight, after these many weeks when she had either draped herself all in black or worn a plain blouse and dark skirt, the effect was astounding.

"Well—aren't you going to say anything?" Estelle fumed, spinning lightly around like an ingénue showing off before her first ball.

She turned to him with a frown and her perfume's heavy fragrance wafted into Byron's nostrils, leaving him even more lightheaded. He managed to rise out of his fog enough to gloomily stammer, "uh-huh, yes, miss...very pretty..."

"Oh, Byron, it's Christmas! Longers is in heaven and my dear little sister is sure I'm going to hell—please, for this one night, let us not grieve!" Estelle's dark eyes began to shine behind a brief film of tears. She came and kissed him deeply on his lips then stood there close, so close that her breasts firmly pressed his naked chest.

Byron budged back awkwardly, embarrassed by her kiss and the heavy smell of whiskey on her breath.

"You're right, miss. I shudden be draggin' yuh down like this—but from I was small people used to say I turn into a sourpuss come Christmas—" Byron strained to smile, though neither his heart nor soul was in it.

"It's not good for a child to grow up sour," Estelle responded in a moody whisper. "How old are you now?"

"Twenty, miss."

Estelle slid her hand up from his shoulder and cupped it to the nape of his neck. "Twenty..." she echoed with a dreamy smile. "I was probably a sour woman by then... Tell me, Byron, would you stay on in Panama if you had an honest girl as company?"

"I don't know what yuh mean, miss—"

"You're twenty, Byron—don't you think it's time you knew what I meant? You do like pretty women, don't you?"

"Sure, miss—but I came here to save up enough for a piece o' farmin' land back-a-home. I cudden go waste my money on fancy wimmens."

"I wasn't talking about having a good-time on Saturday night. I meant suppose you'd met a nice Panama girl who'd make a good partner?"

Byron recoiled at the notion. "No way, miss! Man must marry his own nation!"

"How quaint!" Estelle exclaimed as she snaked herself around him and perched at the edge of his bed. She turned him back to face her then crossed her legs seductively inside the front-split gown. "So you plan to leave me now—just as you're getting back your strength?"

Byron tried to step back but she reached out and held his wrists.

"You really want to go back and cut more cane?"

Estelle gazed at him deeply and Byron promptly shied his eyes. He knew that with things this uncertain he could not abandon her and live with his conscience—yet he could not bear the shame he felt in her sight.

"Why yuh want me to stay—don't yuh hate me for what happen'?"

Estelle shook her head. "I blame myself. I should have sent for the two of you sooner...I wronged that poor man. He—" she stopped and stared off sadly. "He loved me you know..."

"All of we did know. Miss Theresa—Miss Mattie—ev'rybody!" Byron's meager frame shrank in sudden distress. "Oh, God—how me gonna face them?" he blurted fearfully. "Don't mark me as ungrateful, miss, but sometime—when I think 'bout Longers—I wish yuh never did boddah come look for me an' bring me back to life..."

"I wouldn't call sitting here moping all day being alive." She placed the flat of her hand on Byron's bare abdomen. "I see you've finally been doing some exercise," she said, smiling when his muscles clenched at her touch. "If you stay I'll help you finish that trade—like Longers wanted." Estelle uncrossed her legs and pressed her cheek against his stomach. "I didn't know how much I'd miss him! Without a man—what will I do?"

Her fragrance was arousing and Byron felt his palms grow moist and his loins flush with blood. He closed his eyes to fight it.

"You want me try take Longers place?" he stammered, confused as he felt her hand slide to the wetness on his trousers. She massaged the moist dot gently, and her rub's excruciating pleasure made him fear, for an instant, that he might suddenly pass out.

"And where was his place?" Estelle asked. Her baiting words were slurred as she boldly unbuttoned his crotch.

"I don't really know, miss—" Byron mumbled, feeling more and more flustered.

Estelle grabbed his hand and shoved it high between her legs. "Right there—right there is where he belonged!"

Byron stood in shock. He had never seen her behave like this. He tried to draw back but Estelle shot her hand to the bulge at his crotch.

"What—are you saving this for some stupid little island girl?" She taunted as her nimble fingers found their target. "A good husband is like a carpenter—he knows how to use his tools."

"Preacher said we should try and stay pure before—MISS!"

The yell burst out before Byron could control it. He shut his eyes to absorb the surprise and felt a moist feathery sensation more pleasurable than one he'd ever imagined fluttering down his member like wings on a butterfly. He felt his twitching legs give in as Estelle lay back on the bed and pulled him on top of her. He tried not to tremble as she opened her robe and guided his frightened fingers until they found what he pictured in his mind as a miniature cave of custard. When she seemed satisfied that he followed her intricate motions she grasped the rod between his legs that had been blindly poking her stomach.

The hard shaft slipped into the wet warm cave and Byron's toes began to curl, feeling his heartbeat double its tempo. He was face down on a bumpy raft, riding across a string of cresting waves and then plunging to the breaking surf until a massive charge smashed ecstatically into his brain and he was floating limply back to shore.

Estelle let out a loud deep moan and Byron lurched up from his blissful stupor. Sure that he had caused her some terrible injury, he cried to her in panic and felt foolish when she gazed at him with a chuckle and patted his cheek.

"You need to learn what a woman wants before you run and get married."

"How yuh mean—I don't quite follow..."

"Men spend a lot of money to see my girls because they never think about their wives and so their wives don't bother to think about them."

"Most folks back-a-home say only whorish women trouble themself with things like that. They say a good woman only does it to please her man."

"Idiots! A woman has blood inside her flesh just like a man. She needs caresses a lot more than she needs some poor husband." Estelle's voice fell off and her sad eyes flashed with annoyance. "He could have had me...but that stubborn sailor wanted to marry me..."

"I knew it—"

"What do you know?" Estelle chuckled as she leaned up abruptly and grasped Byron by both ears. Teasing out his tongue, she spread her legs and showed him how to make a lonely woman his forever. He was beginning to enjoy the taste when she lifted his face and kissed him softly. "Merry Christmas, *corazon*," she murmured drowsily. "I have another surprise. Dear Mattie made us dinner...please—I need you to come..."

She left to set the table and Byron knew that he had just been granted a rare and special gift. It had called back his spirit and made him hungry for more. And yet he was perplexed and uneasy, afraid that what they had done was not wholesome or natural. He heard the preacher's voice in his head warning him of fire and brimstone and of bad boys going blind. Then it occurred to him that he had spent his life running away from superstition. Maybe in his hurry to escape he had been going about the whole thing backwards. Instead of holding fast to a single vision he should take full value from the present and let the future unfold as it would.

While he lay basking in the glow of his remade desires, two amorous whistling toads started peeping. Their quiet antiphonal calls grew into a chirping serenade. They had found the perfect key to make their own sweet song.

Chapter 23

Something in Sparky's expression as they shook hands good-bye had reminded Thomas of the way Byron had stood looking lost and downtrodden as he left for the hospital in that pig-farmer's foul-smelling dray. It was the look of someone who, despite having no reason to nurture great hopes, saw in Thomas Judah a reason to believe them. Now, as he dragged the loaded hammock along behind him, Thomas wished he had not let Estelle Morales deter him from seeking out his faithful little buddy. Had he thought of it in time he would have asked Byron to come and pan for gold with him. At least he'd be sleeping easier knowing he had someone else on the lookout.

He tracked the meandering tributary for an hour, unable to settle on the ideal spot. Finally he came to a small lagoon enclosed by steep banks on all three sides. After searching in vain for a path to the higher ground, he circled back and up a gentler slope through brush with spiny burrs that clung like ticks to his shins and ankles. He was nearly to the top when his pulse set to racing at the siren call of a second tributary gurgling in the distance. After what felt like an eternity, he came to a passage so bereft of nourishing light that even the thorn bush had not managed to stay and scratch out a living. As he set down his load and began to unpack he had an unsettling sense that he was infringing upon an inviolable preserve.

"*Hé! Que faites-vous?*"

Thomas turned in time to see a spider of a man scrambling up through the sunless murk, furiously shaking his finger. Thomas had just started piling rocks inside the river to speed the downhill flow through his sluice box.

"*C'est mon secteur! ¡No puede minar aquí!*"

The man accosted Thomas in a fiercely startling voice, mixing French with his bumbling Spanish, and accused him of encroaching on his territory.

How was it possible? Thomas thought in shock as he stood gripping his shovel. It seemed absurd that he could have come all this way to be confronted by a cock of a Frenchman.

"*¿Usted sordo? ¡No puede minar aquí!*—You deaf? I said you cannot mine here!" The spidery man bounded up closer still, waving his finger as he blustered in Spanish and French, pointing for Thomas to pack up his things and go back down river.

After lashing back with a stream of French vulgarities, Thomas vouched, without pausing for a breath, that he would pan wherever he pleased. Before he could finish, the man bent down with his hands on his knees, gasping with laughter.

"*Pardon*," the man wheezed, wiping tears from his eyes with a grimy brown sleeve. "*Je suis surmonté! J'ai pensé que j'ai eu un cadeau de* bluster...I thought I had the gift of bluster—haw, haw, haw!"

Thomas advanced on the slip of a Frenchman with his shovel half-raised. "Oh—so you think I'm bluffing? You want me to leave?—show me your markers! I haven't seen a single one!" In his frustration, Thomas had thoughtlessly reverted to English.

The man had shied back from the shovel but now suddenly regained his nerve and held his ground with a beaming grin. "*Mon Dieu!* You also speak English—*Quelle bonne chance!*" he exclaimed in a thick Gallic buzz. "You are wrong, of course, the river at this point is *à moi*—so to say—mine to mine," he said, pointing impishly to his chest. "My claim *à droit*—my first marker is by the lagoon—but you knew zis already, *non? Bien!*" he cried before Thomas could say no. "Now we shall be calm and consider...so! Here is what we can do—*oui?* You help me with my work and you can stay—I can pay you something too—much better, *si?*"

"Work for you?" Thomas's eyes ran disdainfully from the man's coarse shirt to the filthy felt hat stiff with resin. "Now who's pretending—or do you take me for a sap?"

"Ah, *touché, mon jeune homme!*" the man grinned, politely bending the brim of his hat. "Pierre Joubron," he continued, springing closer with one hand out, his belligerence slipping into oily familiarity. "Forgive me—I have been without civilized company for too long and it has affected my manners. Naturally you must be free to seek your fortune, but trust Pierre, he knows where to find more gold than you ever imagine!"

The mention of gold keened Thomas' interest until Joubron explained that, although he indeed had a permit to mine, he was a scriptural geologist by calling.

"No pretend," Joubron assured him when Thomas sniffed that he had never heard of such a profession. "Actually I consider myself to be an evangelical explorer." The Frenchman took off his hat and placed it to his heart. "Praise God for opening my eyes in time to see! Clearly, He guided you here so that I could finally finish my treatise—one's faith must be strong to appreciate His mysterious ways. I had an assistant but sadly he died. A terrible accident—we were climbing the great tepui when the rocks suddenly gave way. He was impaled on a shard of crystal—most unfortunate." Joubron shook his head at the dead-looking arm hanging oddly against his left side. "God spared me for the sake of our work but, as you see, one of my wings got badly damaged. I would only need you three or four days a week—the rest of the time you may mine my claim and keep..." the geologist stopped to rub the dark spikes of stubble on his chin, "shall we say—forty per cent?"

Thomas sharpened his violet eyes and leveled them on the Frenchman. "Make it eighty and you can forget the salary—so long as you add my name to that permit. I wouldn't want to find myself accused of taking what was not mine."

Joubron raced up and pinched him on the cheek. "You are perfect, you quick rascal, but I am no sap either...first you help me, then whatever gold there happens to be we split fifty-fifty—agreed?"

Thomas was not inclined to jump at the offer, yet as curious as the prospect sounded, this was a promising spot to test his sluice box. And if Joubron was on the level, it would solve his problem until he could secure his own license. Besides, if he was here to discover new gold he could do a lot worse than teaming up with a mineralogist, even a half-lame biblical one.

After agreeing to Thomas' terms with a binding handshake, Joubron insisted that his new partner come back with him to camp. Thomas began having regrets when on the way there the Frenchman never stopped talking. As if he'd stored up a year of dissertations waiting for an audience, Joubron proceeded to expound on his mission to counter Man's drift from God, employing a raft of bible quotations and his own misconstrued methods of science to prove the scriptures' unerring truth. "The written word is a mighty tool!" the geologist asserted when Thomas ventured to suggest that it seemed a lot to ask of a single book. "We Christians cannot cede its power to the Devil's publishers!"

Much to Thomas' relief, Joubron left off his fevered discourse as they came to a spring bubbling up from underground. They stopped to sip the crisp refreshing water then took a thin trail that ended at a palm-roofed hut raised on a wooden platform set on stilts. They were almost there when four native boys, naked except for their grass loincloths, rushed up to greet them. The oldest looked no more than ten and Thomas was intrigued to see the children's eager brown faces delicately flecked with tiny red and green dots. The boys all ran and encircled the Frenchman, excited as a brood of puppies as Joubron stooped to kiss them on the forehead.

"These are my students," he explained as the children tried to tug him to come along faster while the oldest boy kept turning to stare at Thomas. "They are so anxious because it's past time for our afternoon tea."

"They stay out here with you?"

"*Mais non!* Their people have a settlement a few miles inside the forest. The boys help me collect my samples and I am bringing them to God by teaching them to read the Good Book. All right, that's enough!" Joubron barked in a language Thomas did not grasp when the two largest boys innocently yanked his injured arm a bit too forcefully. "Here, put these inside," he said speaking more slowly as he reverted to English and handed them Thomas' knapsack of canned provisions. "Peter, you fix the tea like I showed you," he told the oldest-looking boy, his accent far less discernible now that he was calm. "There are dry leaves in the pit for the fire."

"You're teaching them to read English?" asked Thomas as the boys rushed on ahead, carelessly dragging the heavy pack along the ground.

"Of course—why do you ask? Because my speech is not so perfect?"

"It just strikes me as odd...I spoke English half the time when I was in Panama, but I've heard nothing but Spanish since I've been in this country and besides, you're obviously French—"

This seemed to insult Pierre Joubron and he launched into a long heated diatribe and excoriated all things French. Thomas felt he should protest the prejudiced assault but realized that any defense on behalf of science and humanitarianism would only bait the evangelist further. He sensed that his new partner was the sort who allowed nothing to penetrate his cranium that might disturb his confident views. He could not help a tiny snicker when Joubron roundly condemned Diderot and Voltaire for destroying the Catholic church then, in the very next breath, declared he'd been saved the spiritual bane of French pride thanks to his Protestant upbringing.

"Ah—you are wondering, why do I write all my books in English when my French brothers are the ones most in jeopardy?" Joubron noted somewhat apologetically, seeing Thomas' ironic smile. "It may be too late to save them, and the English are much more receptive. It might surprise you to know that the main sponsors of my work are North American."

As rickety as was its outward appearance, once they had scaled the rustic dwelling's three-foot, notched wood pole and stepped inside, it disclosed unexpected trappings of comfort. On the floor, side by side, were two wool-covered pallets next to a swaddle of black-spotted gold fur with tufts of white. The rug lay rolled up by two saddlebags beneath a wide red and green hammock half folded between two stalks of bamboo that were part of the hut's main frame. Near the back were three kerosene lanterns on an old rum barrel and in a corner by a large sack of flour sat a square homemade table with legs so low Joubron would either need to be kneeling or squatting on the floor to use it. At the table's edge, piled on two large tin plates, was a stack of little orange husks, while in the center an ink-stained notebook lay open next to a glass-faced barometer, a protractor and a brass transit compass. Higher up, raised on a log, was a small bookcase about two feet tall. It had two rather lengthy shallow shelves, the lower holding several reams of writing paper and two thick bound journals while the upper was jammed with a collection of small glass jars, one with red currants, raisins and dry figs, another with assorted nuts inside their shells and the last with little colorfully wrapped sweets beside a large brown tin labeled *sucre cristallise*. All of which, when taken together, suggested to Thomas that over the course of his alleged long solitude this enigmatic Robinson Crusoe had made more than a few trips back to civilization.

As they settled down onto the two covered pallets, Joubron suddenly realized that he had been so busy talking he had not yet asked Thomas for his name.

"Your father is a Judah?" he asked with a glare of horror. "Is that not odd for someone like yourself? Forgive me—but I must ask this now before we march onwards—have you been redeemed by our Savior, Jesus Christ?"

Thomas was not sure how to respond. Most people who were surprised by his name seemed more curious about his blood than his religion. He remembered his mother dragging him to church every week until the twins were born and she no longer seemed to have the energy. It had been one of the few early developments in his life for which he'd been grateful. Yet, as unconnected as those Sundays seemed to the person he'd become, he resented the Frenchman's question.

"That's a bit presumptuous—don't you think?" he answered tartly and then, happily for him, three of the boys came barreling in ahead of the boy named Peter who had managed to inch up the foot-holed pole carrying a pot of scalding-hot tea.

The boy set the boiling tea down on the floor then raced up to Joubron who smiled in approval and tousled his satiny crop of black hair.

"Thank you, Peter—you did very well!"

The boy grinned with pride then ran to join the other boys busy helping themselves from the pile of hollow squash shells. Joubron left to fetch the jar of sweets and the tin of granulated sugar. "One cup each then it's time to go home," he said firmly, as each boy expectantly waited his turn to stick out his bowl for a teaspoon of sugar and then his greedy free hand for a piece of hard candy.

The children left to huddle in a corner and enjoy their treats and Joubron slowly filled two more orange husks with the steaming black tea. Thomas reached for the large tin of sugar but the Frenchman quickly snatched it from his hand.

"The bark's salubrious effects are best when unsweetened," Joubron snapped and promptly returned the jar of sweets and the granulated sugar to the hut's long shelf.

"So—you came here from Panama," Joubron said in a friendlier tone as he sat back on the floor next to Thomas. "Then you are familiar with that mountebank de Lesseps and his fantastic canal."

The mention of Panama sent Thomas back dreaming of Genevieve standing beside him, looking tall and light golden brown in her white lace dress. "Sure am..." he murmured distractedly, "I was part of the project."

"*C'est formidable!* I was in England when *Monsieur* de Lesseps was there trying to raise money for his grand inspiration. Everywhere he went there was some scandal or excitement! So, how is the charlatan's magnificent project progressing?"

"Not well, I'm sorry to say. The canal seems cursed—"

"You see?" exclaimed Joubron, beginning to gloat. "The French have doomed themselves with all their cleverness. They imagine they are smarter than God."

Joubron again began to defame his countrymen, from Napoleon to poor misguided Rousseau. As Thomas listened with quiet amusement he was tempted to agree—Joubron was perfectly right—all Frenchmen were out of their heads. He was reflecting on the merit of that notion when he noticed the boys had finished their tea and were gazing towards Joubron with anxious stares, their slim bodies braced with expectancy. All at once, Joubron careened at them baring his teeth like a panther preparing to strike. He arched his spine and feigned to pounce, clawing at their backs and snarling when the boys ran screaming. As Joubron stamped behind, swatting at their bottoms and bellowing ferociously, Thomas was not sure if the boys were yelping with glee or real terror.

"Don't worry...they look forward to our little game," Joubron assured him, seeing Thomas' dumbstruck look as the slowest boy scooted down the notched-pole ladder and dashed after the others still shrieking as they vanished inside the forest. "They'll be back here tomorrow, bright as ever."

"How far is it to their village? They seem a bit young to be roaming through the wild."

Joubron leered at him with contempt. "Too young? Would you ask such a thing of a monkey or a bear cub? The forest is like the sea and they are fish," he said curtly, squatting down heavily then pouring them both some more of the bitter lukewarm tea.

"If you count them as animals why go to the bother of teaching them to read? I'd wager a monkey would make better use of a house with running water than the precepts in your impenetrable Bible."

"I'm here to spread God's Word not corrupt them with our decadent amenities," Joubron said ardently. "If I had brought back thirty iron pots and sixty machetes I could have convinced their whole tribe to pray to Jesus but I would have polluted their unblemished souls and they would still lack genuine understanding. That's why I train their young. Eventually these four boys will grasp His Truth and share it with their people."

"So, you're really here as a missionary. Does the government know you're out here turning their natives into Protestants?"

"I prefer referring to myself as an emissary scientist for Christ. The Papists had their chance but they earned themselves a bad reputation among the Pemon. I'm still learning their language—I find I'm far better off not speaking to them in Spanish." Joubron paused and took a long slow gulp of tea then turned back to Thomas with great seriousness. "Do you trust the Bible, Judah? Or are you one of those who believe men are nothing but monkeys put here by accident?"

"I believe the part about being born in sin," Thomas replied with a sardonic inward grin. "Other than that, I believe whatever can stand the test of science."

This threw Joubron into yet another long tirade. He warned that such apostasy would reap the whirlwind. "What is science but God's tool? Is there a need to interpret the use of a shovel?"

"I suppose not—but just because I use one to dig doesn't mean I'm digging up gold...it might turn out to be nothing but pyrite."

"His Holy Scriptures is your proof! The moment I laid eyes on those *mesetas* rising in the sky like red-brass tabernacles I said, Joubron! *c'est là*—there is your revelation! Here is the key that will unlock the riddle of life—of our existence! You doubt?" he cried, jumping to his feet with sudden agitation. "Wait—I will show you!"

Joubron charged to the saddle-bag across the floor and pulled out an odd-shaped rock about double the size of his fist. He hurried back, pointing to the faint outline of a wing embedded in the pink and yellow sandstone but Thomas' eyes were bulging on the rock's feathery crest of gold.

"This fossil is of a bird only found in northern Europe. Tell me, *Monsieur Savant!* How did a lapwing get buried in a South American tepui? I'll tell you how—Genesis 7, verse 19!—and the waters prevailed exceedingly upon the earth and all the high hills that were under the whole heaven were covered—verse 21!—and all flesh died that moved upon the earth, both of fowl...and all that creepeth—all across this whole earth!...now do you see? That was Noah's cleansing flood. This is our new world God sanctified and gave us to keep pure—cast down our sins and return us to being like children!" Droplets of spittle flashed onto Joubron's grubby whiskers as he pressed the rock into Thomas' hands for him to take a closer look.

What little Thomas divined from the scriptural geologist's theory made very little sense but he made no effort to dispute him. He was far more enthralled by the sample's fleecy tiara of sparkling gold. If Joubron was going to steer him to finds like this he was willing to overlook his suspicion that this new partner of his was more than a little bit mad.

Chapter 24

February 17, 1886

It had been less than a year since Colón's incineration but the city appeared shining and reborn. Even the weather seemed eager to confer its blessings, the port's usual morning clouds having evaporated into a clear blue sky. The rebuilt boardwalk sat freshly painted and lined with a staggering number of flags and every storefront stood draped with bunting in honor of *le Tricoleur's* red, white and blue. The city garrison, decked out in splendid new uniforms, had paraded admirably as a courageous local band squealed the *Triumphal March* from *Aida* with enough raw zest to make up for the scene's missing elephants. From his seat near the end of the plaza's front row, Henri Duvay was surprised to see a large portion of the country's elite mixed in with the darker masses, their faces all sharing the crowd's bright expectancy. No doubt they were counting on his company's knack for pomp and show to lift their spirits now that they realized Panama's coffers had been bled and the province's rich future was being hijacked by Bogotá's dictatorship.

Unlike the crowd, Duvay found Ferdinand de Lesseps' bombastic return both offensive and tiresome. He had braced himself for the inevitable week of banquets filled with flatulent speeches only to learn that he was also expected to be part of today's traveling circus. Surrounded by his star-studded entourage and a gaggle of newsmen, the Great Savior planned to make his appearance at every railway stop along the canal-line until his caravan arrived in Panama City for the gala evening ball followed by a grand display of fireworks. Duvay considered it an inane extravagance when the company had yet to find replacements for its three thousand departed workers and the American press was busy turning both de Lesseps and the canal into the world's greatest laughingstock.

Duvay's ill-humor soured further as he heard the hat-waving cheers announce the Great Canal-Builder's dramatic entrance. "If you could only be reasoned with—" he grumbled inside the thunderous ovation as de Lesseps leapt sprightly from the back of a mighty black stallion and vaulted into the box of honor, "the new locks might already have been in place and all this wild jubilation would have been warranted. Instead, you come back here thinking you can hoodwink your investors—as if your showing up dressed like an eastern potentate would induce some kind of mass amnesia that allowed us to believe you had mastered gravity and time itself." The old fool has lost his senses, Duvay thought dejectedly, watching de Lesseps stand and preen for the cheering crowd. No one in his right mind could ever imagine that the mere sight of a robust octogenarian sporting a tarboosh and gaudy silk robes would magically placate his critics and persuade the gods to let him replicate his past glories in Egypt.

The most bitter pill for Duvay to swallow was knowing that de Lesseps had praised his revisions in private, but no sooner had he launched into his speech than the Great Persuader was back carping on the absolute necessity of a sea-level passage. To amend that plan, he proclaimed to more blind cheers, would dishonor not only those who'd entrusted him with their fortunes but the thousands who had sacrificed their lives for this priceless endeavor. Of the sixty engineers de Lesseps had enlisted for his tour, not one had disputed Henri Duvay's meticulous documented evidence that only a lock canal could succeed in Panama. Yet still, despite all the evidence, not one of them had enough clout or courage to tell France's beloved living legend that his vision for an 'Ocean Bosporus' was a scientific impossibility.

As the Savior's caravan pulled into Culebra, Duvay quickly ducked from the halted train to inspect the Cut's progress without some sycophant truckling in his ear. He had not been back this way since mid-December, after a ferocious hurricane had obliterated months of hard digging. By the time it had finally stopped raining, the Chagres had surged more than thirty feet, flooding the canal-line, so that when he set out weeks later Duvay was able to cover the entire distance from Gatun in a *cayuco*. He remembered paddling down the bloated trench and seeing the carcasses of donkeys, dogs and men floating by just below the peeking treetops black with a million roaches and furry tarantulas.

Now here it was the middle of February and he stood on dry land, feeling just as shocked and discouraged. The belly of the trench was clogged with a silvery-brown gravy, the Yanks' corpulent new machines stuck like beasts in a tar-pit. Out of Culebra's once thousand-strong crew barely three hundred men remained, and though they appeared to be digging valiantly, the formidable mountain seemed to silently mock them.

"This morning was my first time seeing him! What a performance for a man his age—and he still has such perfect skin! Amazing, *n'est-ce pas?*"

Duvay wheeled back with annoyance, expecting some smarmy nitwit from de Lesseps' cortege, and was astonished to recognize Thomas' willowy young nurse from the hospital. Her healthy glow was gone, and in the unsparing sunshine her complexion seemed less tawny than a qualmish yellow. The signature wings sprouting from the sides of her head seemed to droop in the midday heat but she stood hugging her spare-boned frame as if fighting a chill. Before he could reply she pointed across to the opposite ridge just as a roar rang out from down in the Cut. De Lesseps had galloped the powerful black stallion clear to the mountain's crest and was waving triumphantly to the diggers' wild cheers.

"What an inspiring man!"

"He relishes his own fantasies," Duvay retorted with terse disgust, seeing de Lesseps soak up the diggers' stirring accolades.

"Oh, but how can one not admire such youthful vitality—he makes you believe anything is possible!"

"Indeed—even the impossible."

"Surely, *monsieur*, you still share his belief? Everyone has struggled so hard for this project—" the nurse's voice grew thin and her expression clouded over, "so many have died. It would be terrible if we stopped believing..."

"Tell that to the Americans!" the engineer snapped. "Haven't you read the papers? They're calling de Lesseps 'the Great Undertaker.'"

Sensing Duvay's dark mood, Genevieve changed the subject. "We haven't met by accident, *monsieur*. I saw you sneaking to escape and I followed, hoping you'd permit me a moment to speak with you—"

"You want to ask me about Thomas—well, I can't help you. He's no longer my assistant. I had assumed he left because of you but I see he has deserted you too."

"He spoke of us?" she asked, sounding more hopeful than surprised.

"We did live under the same roof for almost three years. Did you think me oblivious—or simply hard-hearted?" he asked her irascibly. "Thomas was more to me than some valet-secretary. I cared about his welfare—his chances. Thanks to you he has thrown it in my face and abandoned me."

Genevieve's gaunt face grew flushed. "If you think I encouraged him to leave you're quite mistaken! Thomas was going to throw up his job right after his friend Diego's funeral. It was I who convinced him to stay."

"Bah! It is not the day the fruit first rots that it drops from the tree!" Duvay's sharp green eyes flashed at Genevieve with anger as he recalled the sight of Thomas strolling off with her the day of the funeral. He had arranged for Valladares' expensive service thinking it would earn back Thomas' loyalty and perhaps even his affection. He had left the burial ground that day incensed that this sanctimonious nurse had spirited away Thomas' judgment. "You hide beneath that saintly attire but you pious types are worse than trollops...at least they're honest about what they want."

Genevieve's face drained back to its anemic pallor. She held a hand to her cheek as if her crime had been proved and she stood convicted. "So he told you," she mumbled weakly.

"No one had to tell me anything! Thomas used to be a tough young nut with a hard-nosed bent. He never would have mourned that Valladares fellow like a sap had you not filled him with your mawkish notions—"

"Pardon, *monsieur*! If you think Thomas is a sap then I doubt you know him at all."

"I know that when he came here Thomas was ready to balance his worth against the measure of his cause and not fret over every little death. Of course you're probably not rational enough to understand that. You believe in saving lives—no matter how pointless or redundant! Do you think the great pyramids or the castles of Europe were built at no cost to human life? Stick to saving souls and don't go damning mankind to the living hell of ignorance."

Genevieve started to giggle and quickly clapped a hand to her mouth. "Forgive my laughing, *monsieur*," she stuttered, halting Duvay in haste when he started to curtly bid her good-day. "I thought you were about to denounce my lack of virtue. You have to understand—when Thomas cried over Diego he was also crying for himself. I don't know if that makes him mawkish, but to me it seemed perfectly rational. I can assure you he did not leave because of cowardice..." Genevieve paused with her frail arms folded and looked bereft, "although it would be nice to think it was out of sorrow or sentimentality...No, *monsieur*, I think Thomas left because he decided you and I were both incurable failures."

Duvay appeared taken aback, as if some hidden secret that hurt and surprised him had suddenly been exposed. He turned his face away in time to see de Lesseps race his snorting black steed down from the slope to be engulfed by another adoring fold. Beet red as he dismounted after his gallop, the eighty-year-old looked ebullient as a crush of dark-eyed schoolgirls ran to smother him with nosegays and ruby-lipped kisses. Meanwhile, a second train had arrived and a dozen ladies in breeze-catching pastel frocks with parasols to match were being helped up to the treeless overlook by eight or nine businessmen in stylish sack-suits. As they reached the top and passed around a pair of field-glasses to peer at the Cut's scarred slopes, they might have been a group of languid birdwatchers waiting to be served a picnic lunch. "No doubt they're tickled," Duvay grumbled, seeing them point and stare with awe at the mountain's vivid flanks. "It makes no difference to them that this great cause may end in disaster—the butchers and bakers and candlestick-makers have all made out like thieves thanks to our squandering old hero."

"Take heart, *monsieur*. He may be pompous and stubborn but he has brought us joy and renewed our faith," Genevieve observed, looking over at the station where two inspired souls were affixing a huge pink banner that read, 'Hail to the Genius of Our Century!' across the dark green train. "Perhaps that is what we've both been lacking."

How dare she speak of faith, Duvay muttered after Genevieve had quietly nodded good-bye and left him alone with his thoughts. It was too much faith and not enough science that had hamstrung their labors in Panama from the start! Watching de Lesseps bask in all the ephemeral adoration, the engineer wondered if he and the proud old visionary were the only ones who had ever truly believed the canal would succeed. Or was the truth that, so long as the old man had a knack for raising money, most were pleased to simply spend it? It was clear from the latest editorials slandering the French and ridiculing their efforts that the Yanks would be quite happy to see them fail.

So, was this the end? The final virtuoso performance that dazzled briefly, but finished with its hero's disgrace? For despite all of de Lesseps' inspiring charm, it would be a miracle if his investors let him throw away more of their money. Ironically, it was the very mulishness that saw him conquer all foes in Egypt that was turning out to be the Great Man's defeat. If mere stubbornness allows that to happen, a grand possibility will be lost, and that, thought Duvay, would be the real tragedy.

After she had left Duvay to sulk, Genevieve abandoned the Great Savior's expanding retinue and took the train back to Colón. She felt strangely relieved and yet, at the same time, hurt and empty. She had wavered about approaching the prominent engineer lest he fly into one of his tempers and denounce her in public. Instead, she'd been blind-sided by the fact that he blamed her for Thomas rejecting him and quitting Panama—not because he suspected she had seduced him, but for teaching him empathy. She had always been puzzled by Duvay's unusual forbearance when it came to Thomas, who had boasted that he could get the Frenchman to forgive him almost anything. She saw Duvay's needy secret more plainly now: the satisfying role he had created and was able to play each day with his handsome and witty young assistant. So long as the two of them were together, pursuing *La Grande Cause*, the whole world was free to doubt him for there was Thomas, under his command, believing, supporting, or at least pretending. No wonder, Genevieve reflected as she settled inside her train, the poor man looked lost without him.

Close to a year had gone by since she'd last felt Thomas inside her, and though God, in His wisdom, had induced her body to reject his seed, his essence lingered. At first, during the nights when she had camped on the beach along with the homeless, she would lie back on the sand imagining the seductive habits of his hands and the softness that showed in his eyes when he was unguarded and in her power. Later she would pray that, just as the tissue of her sins had bled from her body, she could expunge her persisting desire and send it floating out to sea. Often too wound up to sleep, she would stare up at the stars and try to form an image of her mother's face looking down at her from heaven. She wondered whether to picture her wearing a smile or a frown for having birthed such a trollop. But once she finally drifted to sleep, Nana Binta's was the face in all her dreams.

Always in a white robe and bandanna, the old woman appeared years younger, her small slim frame even more vibrant with life than she remembered. In her left hand was a pure white rooster and in her right a basket of sweet sop, mangoes and peaches. She would beckon Genevieve to come closer and suddenly a cleaver flashed in her hand and the rooster's head fell to Nana Binta's bare brown feet. Plucking a feather from the dead bird's body, she would carefully daub the ground with its blood while chanting a threnody to the invisible spirits. Palming a stone, the Senegalese woman shut her eyes for a silent prayer that ended each time with her trembling, then crying out, 'beware thy loss! Death follows the precious stray!' and all at once, Genevieve was kneeling in her place, feeling drained of life as she swabbed the dark stain from her father's temple with the rooster's white feather.

The vision left her as plagued by grief and fear as the day she had found her father lying there, still in her bed, with a pistol by her pillow and the hole from a bullet gaping in his skull. Why—she asked for the thousandth time—why did she tell Nana Binta that daddy hurt her when she loved her father with all her heart? How was it that she'd always known, from the first night he climbed in bed beside her, murmuring her dead mother's name, that the comfort and joy she felt having him that close was sure to bring about some terrible end?

She had planned on returning to work in the hospital once the wing was restored and the homeless sick comfortably resettled, but as it came closer to Christmas all she could think of was Thomas. It left her feeling humiliated and physically unclean. Too ashamed to face her sisters, she had obtained permission to join a surgeon-priest on his way to aid some poor lepers who had been expelled from their village. The trip had been her first exposure to the jungle, and its lush secrets had acted as a needed tonic until they arrived at the outcast colony. For all the suffering she had seen, it took every fiber of her will not to break down in tears to think that God could permit such horror; men without hands and feet, their ribs like branches trying to poke through sheathes of pustulated skin; balding women with their joints and ankles swelled out like balloons made of elephant hide. But what tore at her heart was seeing the children with their tiny bodies so shrunk from malnutrition they looked like hundred-year-old midgets.

With the frenzy of a swimmer flailing in a riptide she put her resurgent guilt aside and threw her energy into making such unbearable misery bearable. Every day she would rise before dawn and walk miles to find fresh fish or a tin of sweet milk and some ripe star apples so the starving infants had more to eat than a few kernels of roasted corn or the broth from dried-out marrow and boiled intestines. After doing what she could for their mothers, ailing with dysentery or speckled with pox, she would command the older children to look after the toddlers while she scrubbed the camp's infected hovels until the stench of excrement and death no longer overwhelmed her. For a month she carried the lame, divided the sick, treated sores and administered enemas with a tirelessness driven by compulsion. Finally, seeing her eyes peering out from two deep black hollows and her habit hanging on her anemic body like a large loose shroud, Father Contreras insisted on taking her back to Colón so she could rest and regain her strength.

Genevieve was horrified when the sisters welcomed her back with much joy and fussing as if she had accomplished some great deed. She listened and held her tongue while they glibly condemned Prestàn and praised the Americans for having so generously rebuilt the town, and restrained herself from interjecting, 'yes, but isn't it sad that the ghetto looks as wretched as it did before the fire.' After a few days in bed, as she was starting to feel stronger, her sleeplessness returned, thrusting her back into deep depression. She felt she should unburden her sins to Mother Agnes, but each time the urge would seize her she would think of Thomas and relent. How could she ever earn forgiveness when she was struggling so mightily to deny that from the beginning she had wanted Thomas to touch and bring life to the dead spot inside her? How, when her love had started out so pure, like the tenderness one feels for a child, could she have strayed this far? It was because of him. Because of him she no longer felt like a tainted vessel that would always be unworthy. She was a flesh and blood woman who could both love and find a way to serve God.

Chapter 25

The Great Undertaker's junket through Panama had proven more infectious than the summer's scourge of swamp fever. De Lesseps' whirlwind visit had breathed life back into the dying canal and left every barkeep and swindler in Colón dreaming of a champagne sky raining francs once again. Even Estelle, who had cautiously banked her insurance claims while she judged the new climate, was stirred from her doubts and depression. Before de Lesseps was back in France, she had hired a master builder to repair her brothel and restore the Last Frontier.

For his part, Byron had stuck to his promise and put off agonizing about his future. Estelle's special Christmas gift had helped to mend his spirit, but after each new urge pulled them close to try and ease the same old hurt, he would think about Longers. Even dead, Longers remained a towering, almost mystical, presence whenever Byron presumed to take his place, looming like a judge, to demand that Byron do everything in his power to see his beloved Estelle back on her feet.

Once the damage to his body had healed Byron had thrown himself wholeheartedly into the madam's service. When the bordello stood ready to receive its new furnishings he persuaded her to have one of the carpenters help build him a small cabin in the back garden so he could stay there at night and keep watch. He spent his days dashing between the brothel and the unfinished saloon. He lugged her barrels, fetched her new lumber, varnished her floors and laid her Arbor Wreath wallpaper entirely himself, rarely stopping for a meal much before midnight. He drove himself so tirelessly for those two months Estelle began to worry about his health.

"I love you for what you've done, *negrito*, but I won't let you go on slaving like this unless you promise to start eating during the day. You'll get sick if you get any thinner—then what use will you be when it's time to open the New Frontier?" she chided.

"There'll be plenty time for me to rest and fill my belly once yuh open. Besides," he grinned, "so long as Miss Mattie keeps leaving me some of her good stew I'll be fine."

Estelle frowned at Byron's hollow cheeks. "At least let me pay you for all this work."

Byron kicked at a slat of wood coming loose from the saloon's parquet floor and looked sullen. "What sorta wutless man would take your money after all we been through?"

"If you're not going to let me pay you, how are you going to save up any money—or have you changed your mind about going home to buy that nice piece of farming land?"

"I never change me mind 'bout it!" he answered her, pouting. "Once I see yuh back on top I'll try reach my frien', Thomas, one last time. If it don't work out I can always go back and do more shovelin' while I figure things out."

Estelle hid her unease at the sudden intensity of his devotion but she still needed his help so she refrained from pressing him further. When the Fourth of July arrived and the New Frontier was finally set to reopen, she called Byron out from behind the bar where he'd been setting up the crystal champagne glasses in long neat rows.

"I have a surprise, *querido!*" she said, beaming as he joined her inside her private room in back. "I spoke with Mr. Bragg—he has agreed to train you."

Byron was ready to leap with joy but wanted to make sure his heart had not jumped to the wrong conclusion. "Train me, miss?"

"That's right, he's taking you on. You're going to be a carpenter—you're going to have that trade Longers always talked about!"

———

Those seven summer weeks starting in July saw Byron daring to believe that the sailor had been dead right; for a man with a good-paying trade the living came easy. Mr. Bragg's outfit had won a contract with the canal company to build three huge machine shops near Tiger Hill. As it happened, the site was a short train-ride from Estelle's refurbished bordello which meant that Byron could sleep until a quarter past six and still get there sharp at seven. Better yet, he could work his whole shift in the same light cotton shirt and be back in his garden cabin by sundown feeling nearly as fresh and dry as when the long day started. Best of all, he had made a good first impression on his crew-chief. His third day on the job the spry white-haired Jamaican, who rumor claimed was pushing eighty, came to join him as he sat on his haunches munching his lunch.

"Hey there, landsman—" the old carpenter flashed a perfectly even row of slightly-stained teeth and crouched down easily beside his newest apprentice. "Mr. Bragg tells me you're from back-a-home—I just wanted you to know you show real promise."

"Thanks, Mister Lau," Byron replied, hurrying to swallow the bite of sandwich.

"You done carpentry work before?"

"Not really, sah—I picked up some pointers watching while you-all was working for Miss Morales."

"Looks like you caught on right quick. I confess I wasn't too pleased when the boss told me he'd brought in a new apprentice. The last thing I need when I'm being rushed to meet a deadline is having to be wasting precious time teaching some knucklehead how to start a notch for his handsaw."

"I reckon that ain't much to know, sah—"

Lau shifted his sights to the bare crossbeams on the open-walled machine-shop's skeleton roof. "You'd be surprised the little our young folks know when they get here. Not that I blame them—who they got left back-a-home to bring them along? Look at me—I been here over thirty-odd years. There's not enough building going on in Jamaica anymore—not like after slavery when everybody was dying to leave the plantation so a man could live with his family in a nice new house." The old carpenter pulled a tin of tobacco from his shirt pocket and offered Byron a plug. When he politely declined Lau stared off with a misty-eyed look. "Don't mind me," he said in a whisper, sticking a chaw inside his cheek. "I've made my peace...I know I'll probably die here in foreign. But I miss my roast breadfruit and my ackee and saltfish...I miss my country."

Lau's words stayed with Byron the whole time he was working. He figured if a master carpenter could not make a decent living back home Miss Estelle was right—he needed to earn enough now to have some money left over after he bought that nice piece of farming land. At least, once he mastered his trade he could go home and build himself a house. He did not fancy spending thirty years in Panama, but the one thing he would never do was go back to living in some wattle and mud shack roofed with cane trash.

The three machine shops were nearly complete when the construction firm that had parceled him the contract informed Mr. Bragg that, despite having wrapped up the job in time for work on the locks to begin on schedule, he should not expect to be reimbursed any overages above his initial proffer. Furious, Bragg appealed to the canal company directly but failed to win what he considered fair compensation. The Barbadian builder, a man of principled Irish stock, paid his men for the extra time from his own pocket, then left the isthmus, swearing Jesus and Mary would have to come back to earth for him to ever trust another stingy, little two-faced Frog.

Bragg's abrupt departure knocked Byron's brave new outlook flat. For two whole days he stayed inside his cabin in the brothel's back garden. He stopped showing up at the kitchen for his evening dish of stew and refused to open the door when Mattie brought him his supper. When he failed to come out for a third straight night, Estelle demanded that he let her inside the cabin. She planted herself down beside him on the narrow single bed.

"Why are you doing this? I thought you were feeling better..."

"What's the use," Byron mumbled, sitting shirtless as he sulked, "God either curse me or me born unlucky."

"Don't talk like that—you'll bruise my feelings," scolded Estelle, nudging him lightly.

Byron shook his head. "Yuh don't understand—this is the second time me lose an apprenticeship. I loss my chance when me was twelve...just like me loss this one now..."

"You haven't lost anything. Mr. Bragg isn't the only builder in the world. And from what I hear you're going to make a damn fine carpenter. You'll get that trade—just like Longers wanted—"

"I wanted to be a blacksmith like Sir Reynolds..." he said, gazing glumly at his chipped chest of drawers reclaimed from the brothel's old furniture. "Sir Reynolds was the one man I knew when me was growing who got respect—and he made good money. The other boys were mad when Sir Reynolds chose me, the smallest runt on the whole plantation, to be his helper. He used to get me up in the dark before the cock even crow to go haul in his heavy irons he had soaking all night in the river." Byron stopped and held up his head with a tiny smile of pride. "I had to lift his big anvil so many times while I was cleaning the ashes out from his forge my skinny arms did bulge up pure muscle—that's what turn me into a fierce fast-bowler. After I bounce a few balls at their heads playin' cricket those nasty boys finally stop harassin' me."

He again started to sulk and Estelle curled a mother's patient arm around him. "So what happened—why you didn't finish your apprenticeship?"

Byron stared down at the cabin floor. "After I done clean out the forge I had to go fetch coal from the storehouse. Sir Reynolds was particular about the grade of coal he used so he kept it in a burlap bag and mark it as his with blue chalk. This one mornin' I done flame the kiln an' I'm there dodging sparks, working the bellows feeding air into the fire while Sir Reynolds start up hammering. Next thing mi know—crack!—the red hot iron split right in two.

"Sir Reynolds stare into the flames, then him stare at me—him stare back at the flame, then him bend to it an' took a sniff. Him ask where me get this coal from. I tell him I took it from the same bag as always. He looks at me real hard and says the coal have in too much sulfur an' that's why it not holding the heat for his fire. I didn't know what to answer—I was telling him the truth. Sir Reynolds quick grab me by the ear and haul me down to the storehouse. Him kneel to check the sack with his mark and there's the good coal right inside it. Up to now I can't swear how it happen but I believe somebody switched that sack and chalk up the wrong one just to confuse me." Byron's eyes glazed with brief tears. "No way I was gonna mix up Sir Reynolds' bag with that big blue mark for the one with the charcoal for the boiling house...not as much as I did covet that job."

Estelle tightened her arm around him. "You need to stop moping about what has passed down life's river. Think about this—" she said with one of her sly cheeky grins, "had you stayed on that plantation, you would never have gotten to taste a fully-ripe woman."

After losing his second apprenticeship Byron was finding it hard to respond to Estelle's affections. He felt strangely removed, despite her dominant caresses. He knew that, although she claimed that love was not a lasting transaction, she was still mourning Longers. But despite not feeling right about receiving so much of her attention, he recovered enough over time that by November he was able to work and even taste his food. With Estelle's businesses starting to rebound, he found his former strength had suddenly come back. He busied his days tending to her garden then spent time each night helping out at the New Frontier. He was there working in early December when Henri Duvay spotted him as he went about clearing the used tables.

"Come sit here, *garçon*," Duvay commanded, pulling him up a chair. "I'd like to ask you a few questions."

"Sure, sah...just one minute..." Byron replied, leaving to set the basin with empty bottles and glasses on the edge of bar.

"Aren't you the chap who's been searching for Thomas Judah?" Duvay asked as he returned. "Did you ever find him?"

Byron could not drag his eyes off the man's impressive black moustache. He was fascinated by the way it twitched like the tail on a kitten. "No, sah—we keep on missing each other. But I did get a letter from him last year, before the fire."

"Did he say where he was going?"

"Going, sah? No, sah—he didn't say nothing about going anyplace. He promised to help me. If yuh remembah, sah—when I first met yuh I was looking for a job."

The big moustache gave another odd twitch and Byron politely let his eyes roam to the saloon's new, stained-glass gaslight fixtures. As the Frenchman quietly studied him behind that jumpy moustache, everywhere he looked there was shining brass and gleaming pine.

"I remember that we met, but I don't recall your name."

"Byron, sah."

"As I recall, Estelle mentioned that you were an honest worker—does she pay well for washing dishes and clearing tables?"

Byron stared meekly at the varnished floor. "I don't rightly know, sah. I'm only here helping—paying her back some kind favors."

"I see—" Duvay touched a finger to the rim of his glass, half-filled with champagne, and pondered his answer. "Are you still interested in having that job?"

The offer touched Byron's ears as if it had come from a great distance. His brain seemed eager to grasp it, yet he felt joyless. "Sure, sah," he answered softly, wondering if the Frenchman was about to suggest again that he go back to Culebra and do more digging. "I been hoping to find more work in construction. I helped put up those new machine-shops near Tiger Hill in September."

Duvay tilted his head, seemingly intrigued. "Really! You were part of that team? I understand some of the finish work was left undone but otherwise the job was done expeditiously and thriftily."

Byron was tempted to point out why but thought better of it. "Thank you, sah—I like workin' as a carpenter—" he was about to add 'helper' then alertly bit his tongue. After all, he had learned a great deal since he first started working with Mr. Lau, and as satisfying as the experience had been, the apprenticeship had earned him but a pittance.

The impressive moustache made another tiny quiver. "Anything, so long as it doesn't entail lifting a shovel, *n'est-ce-pas?*" said Duvay with a shrewd half smile.

Byron gave a shrug and did not answer.

"Would you be interested in a job that pays full carpenters wages?"

"Yuh mean it, sah?"

"Of course. Do I strike you as a joking man?" Duvay retorted, touching a hand to his black cravat with annoyance. "Monday morning. Seven o'clock. The dredging platform outside Mindi. Meet me there and I'll give you the details. Now, be a good chap and tell *Señora* Morales I'd like to speak to her about stocking some better champagne."

Byron was impressed when he arrived very early Monday morning to see the Frenchman already there waiting to address his workers. When two dozen men had gathered on the floating platform Duvay proceeded to stress the importance of their pending endeavors. He even dared to suggest that the future of the world might hinge on how precisely they followed his instructions. By the end of the grand exhortation, Byron was both proud and convinced that if they succeeded here in Mindi they would be praised as the ones who finally solved the conundrum of Culebra. If things turned out as Duvay described, instead of more futile digging, the big dredgers would be sailed down on ships and the spoil from the Cut floated back out on barges. The engineer's hidden goal, unknown to the great de Lesseps himself, was to dig a series of pools that would be flooded by waters diverted from the Chagres and finally linked by the giant iron locks.

Byron's excitement vanished almost as soon as his training had begun. Had he not been determined to impress Henri Duvay, he would not have found himself here, weeks later, trapped in an oilskin suit, breathing air through a long rubber tube with a brass and copper helmet around his head. He had hoped he'd seen his last days hoisting a shovel, yet here he was wielding a twenty-foot round-head spade, digging underwater like a mud-eating fish.

Today, the mighty City of New York had stalled against a submerged boulder so Byron and the five other drillers were back below in their diving helmets, boring the rock with holes so it could be packed with more dynamite. To Byron, the giant American dredge, steadied by a pair of spud-anchors over sixty-feet high, bore less resemblance to a teeming city than to some mythical snout-nosed mammoth. The first time he saw the monstrous dredge lumbering up the channel on its diamond-toed digging feet, spraying mud through its two hundred-foot-long nostrils, he had found it hard to imagine something stout enough to stand in its way. As it turned out, Panama's volcanic bedrock was proving to be more than its match. Fortunately, the dredge's black-diamond cutters had stripped enough of the boulder's surface so that after laboring several hours with the long-handled shovel Byron had managed to dig another twenty-foot hole.

He was anxious to see the longest stage of his task be over and done with. The compressed air being pumped inside his helmet was making him lightheaded and he worried that by the time it came to handle the dynamite cartridges he was bound to get nauseous. For the sake of safety as well as efficiency, the procedure for each dive was for them to drill in three two-man teams, so when he tackled his final hole and found his long shovel's sharp metal blade making no headway, Byron signaled for his partner's assistance.

It had taken no longer than the end of their first day of training for Byron to regret being paired with Tomby. He would have said the instant dislike had been mutual, except that his forty-year-old partner seemed to have a grudge against the world. When it took over a minute for him to draw the Jamaican's attention it wasn't because Tomby was deliberately ignoring him. His comrade was just one of those odd characters who insisted on doing everything in his own sweet time. Seeing that Tomby was also a man who had to labor for his daily bread, it was a trait Byron had a hard time trying to fathom.

Finally Tomby ambled over in his bulky diver's suit and Byron pointed brusquely for him to help set up the brace for the auger spoon drill. The two of them clamped the drill's long rod with its added torque from a tightly twined rope, and after straining with all of their might, they were able to turn and twist the metal bit through the granite. The exertion left Byron feeling faint and he quickly tugged his safety line to have them hauled up to the surface. As they lounged on the platform taking their short breather, Tomby slipped off the heavy metal weights clipped to the cuffs of his diving suit and held them near Byron's face.

"It's a sad thing, *bolow*. My daddy fought to get out from under slavery and here his son gotta work in shackles."

Byron shoved the weighted clips away from his nose. "Big difference—your daddy never got paid."

"Ain't it true—" Tomby murmured with a chuckle, "and I done used up all my inheritance."

Byron didn't get the joke so he shifted further aside and said nothing.

"Yuh out here busting your tail for that big-talking Frenchie but yuh wasting yuh strength if yuh think yuh gonna impress him. Heck—he got machines that can drill these holes three time quicker—they just don't trust us dumb monkeys to use them."

"Yuh lie..." Byron scoffed, although inside he felt uncertain.

"All right—maybe that was me exaggerating when I said they wouldn't want us using them," his partner conceded, "but I've seen them have drills they can power using that same pumped air we been breathing. Then again—machine cost money and chaps like us come awful cheap."

"Maybe you—not me—"

"No, no," the older man sneered, "they all know yuh's one of a kind."

"Damn right."

Tomby leaned back on his elbows and studied Byron with a languid grin. "So, tell me something, *bolow*—if a toad was to race a donkey, which one would win?" he mused, a twinkle glinting in his light brown eyes.

Byron started to get to his feet. "I don't have time for foolishness—"

"See what I mean? Yuh nearly pass out down there under that water and still don't want to go slow and take time. Siddown, rest your spirits! The Frenchies can wait one more minute."

Byron plopped back down on the platform knowing the stubborn man would hound him until he replied.

"So which one would win—the toad or the donkey?" Tomby persisted.

"I don't know—the donkey...?"

"Wrong! Yuh forget to ask how long was the race!" Tomby teased him. "If it was a straight out sprint I'd go with the jackass—but if it's gonna mean a lotta hopping around I'm putting my money on Mr. Toad."

Byron shot his partner a disgusted look and again said nothing. He was tired of Tomby's constant little jabs and the fact that of all the other divers his partner always seemed to take the longest to finish his drilling.

"Yes sir, that Mr. Toad—" Tomby went on wryly, "he takes his time. Changes his color when he needs to—now once Mr. Donkey done wear out you can't budge him—"

"Enough with the country parables and this beating around the bush—you got a problem with me, just say it!" Byron was fed up with Tomby hectoring him.

"How old are you, boy?"

"Four and twenty," Byron lied, adding three years to boost his dignity.

The older man cast a cynical eye to the faint line of fuzz starting to show above Byron's upper lip. "Yuh ain't foolin' Jon-Crow! Yuh favor eighteen—nineteen, at most. Listen to a man who done labor thirty years of his life and bury all three of his brothers to Panama fever—take your time on this job—otherwise the only man you're gonna end up pleasin' is the goddamn undertaker."

"Yuh needn't fret over me—I'm not looking to make this job last forever. I'm just biding my time before I go back to doing construction." It was a wish, but it was a wish that Byron was determined to nurture. He figured that if he went ahead and gave this job his all, Mr. Duvay might yet be persuaded to help him find work in his chosen trade.

The junior engineer shouted above the City of New York's grating engines rumbling downstream and the divers obediently donned their helmets to return underwater. When they were back in place on the bottom, each pair tugged its line for the men on the platform to lower the first set of the twenty-pound waterproof cartridges. Byron waited to grasp his own after Tomby then set about pressing the dynamite inside the hole using the spoon on a long wooden pole. Next came the primer, a stick and a half of dynamite capped with nitroglycerine gel kept inside the pouch tied to his waist. This was the part that made him sweat. Even though an underwater hole did not need tamping with gravel, unlike setting charges on land, it was critical that the cap and primer stay dry in their casing and that he place them deep inside the slot with the utmost care.

The last stage was just as tricky. Once the explosives were all in place, the drillers had to lay in the gunpowder fuses wrapped in fabric and clay then splice them to the cord leading to the electro-magnetic exploder back on the platform. As he worked through the panic throbbing in his ears, Byron tried not to think of the one-eyed man missing his arm and half of his cheek that he'd met while searching for Johnny. The delicate operation now complete, he closed his eyes once again and prayed to be out of the water and safely away before the boulder accidentally blew to pieces.

Chapter 26

Before Thomas Judah showed up in the forest, Pierre Joubron had begun to question God's purpose. He had worried when his arm healed poorly that he was not meant to see his grand thesis, *The Great Flood: How Our Lord Remade His Pure Earth*, established in print. Now that God had delivered him a strong young back he believed more fervently than ever he would find the evidence to see his theory withstand all scientific doubts. This early morning, as he had done each day for a fortnight, Joubron roused his new partner from sleep an hour before sunrise. After sharing a quick meal of an orange with bitter palm and walnuts, the two of them set out for the great tepui by the light of a lantern. The morning air had an icy nip and their progress was slow as Joubron constantly shifted their direction to avoid the nasty corners likely to harbor nests of drowsy scorpions and poisonous spiders.

The red start of daybreak made weaving through the tannin-rich brush seem as if they were wading in a marshy lake of blood. As always, Thomas was burdened with the heavier gear so that by the time they had reached the foot of the *meseta* his joints were stiff and aching. Only the burning memory of that rock-sample's feathery crown of gold kept him coming back to the mile-high mountain. Thomas prayed that today would at last be the day he dug up a fortune.

After a short rest and some more nibbled nuts, he set to digging. The base of the tepui was extremely slick and, conscious of his mishaps back at Culebra, he was careful to mind his footing and not try to work too quickly. He had been wielding the Frenchman's pick for nearly two hours and was about to take a break when a crack in the rock revealed a layer of gold-flecked crystals. He hacked at the shiny quartz with savage energy but despite his zeal the vein yielded a mere sprinkling of gold and no fossilized treasures.

"These segments are all worthless," said Joubron, looking dejected as he picked up each of the twenty-odd striated rock-chips and turned them over in his hand for one last time. "Take a rest—then we must try higher up."

"Are you crazy? I'm staying right here!" Thomas protested, gasping as he caught his breath. "This seam has got to be crammed with gold!"

"That is fine and well but it is not showing me what I'm looking for!" Joubron snapped. "Have you forgotten? My work comes first. We can concern ourselves with finding more gold after I've found my fossils."

"We agreed this would take up only part of my time. I've been straining my back on your account for two weeks and we haven't found a single one of your priceless specimens. I am going to keep on right here. If you don't bloody well like it you can pick up that other shovel and go and dig for yourself!"

"All right, all right! Let's be calm—we can both have our cake, as they say. You can stay here and labor all day with that pick if you like—and end up with a few dollars worth of dust. I know of a place that will surpass your young dreams but if Joubron is going to trust you to be his partner you must swear to obey!" the geologist commanded, riveting Thomas with two fiendish dark eyes. "And be warned—the father punishes those who would dare obstruct his exalted designs!"

"Show me this place," Thomas said bluntly, "then I'll see if it's worth it."

Joubron stopped and eyed him coldly, trying to decide if he should take the gamble. "Fine—" he snapped abruptly, "we can go there tomorrow."

Early the next morning after a bark tea and cornmeal breakfast, they set off inland through the northern forest. After a while they came to a scorched black trail that led across a stony expanse to a dense growth of trees of a type different from the ones they had passed in the jungle. Pressing through the sunless woodland they came to low hidden knoll. Thomas climbed the slippery knob behind the sure-footed Frenchman into what he took to be a limestone grotto carved out by some extinct underground river. Joubron led them down beneath a rocky overhang and through a passage covered in pebbles. The Frenchman stopped to light his lamp and announced that they were in part of an old abandoned quarry.

"Did you notice the remains of the brick foundations back in the clearing? A few centuries ago those woods were home to a papist monastery," Joubron explained as he held up the kerosene lantern. "See how that foot-trail winds back up to the other side of the hill?" he asked, pointing towards a slit of light shining in from the distant outlet. "That's where they went and hid their ore.

Those rascal priests did a good job concealing what they were up to," the Frenchman chuckled.

They squeezed through a fifteen-inch-wide crevice then crawled on their hands and knees through a waist-high tunnel, the entrance to which had been obscured by huge stones. From there the underpass opened into a fair-sized mine shaft breached by several patches of revealing sunlight. Thomas held up and stopped his breath, hearing his footsteps begin to crunch on the desiccated ground. After a moment he realized that what he first took for pebbles and unlikely scattered bird eggs being crushed underfoot were, in fact, tiny nuggets of gold.

"Leave them!" Joubron snapped, seeing Thomas drop to one knee and start to stuff the precious lumps into his pocket. "I understand the temptation but remember our agreement." The Frenchman came within an inch of Thomas' face and leered at him threateningly. "You will need me if you want to take out the whole lode...And I wouldn't want to see you shot for stealing before you can enjoy your reward."

Joubron made his point with a smile of malicious glee. Thomas was ready to snap and assign him to hell then remembered Lagarto's caution. Even with a day's head start, Thomas doubted he could find a boat to take him upriver before the Frenchman could seek out a government patrol and have him nabbed as a thief. He glared at Joubron's maniacal grin with a rebel's scowl then slowly opened his fist and let the nuggets fall back to the ground.

It did not take long for Thomas to realize he had been tricked into a Faustian bargain. With the greater part of his days spent hunting Joubron's elusive fossils he was left little time to apply his sluice-box. And while his heart was with Genevieve, his brain had not stopped burning at the thought of coming back with a fortune. He knew he would never free himself from this crazy Frenchman until he was sure he was not walking away from a gold mine. Yet there was no way to guess how long it would take for Joubron to be satisfied he had found the ultimate proof he was sure would condemn the modern world and redeem humanity.

Thomas saw only one way out of his fix. He had to get Joubron to add his name to that license. So far the Frenchman had stuck to his tactic, using the promise of gold to put him off. Until their partnership was official Thomas was afraid to risk even a quick trip to Panama, but he also knew that all the gold in the world would do him no good if Genie had vowed her life to God before he found her. He decided to try and win Joubron's trust by being cheerful and compliant. A stroke of luck aided his cause when on their next journey to the mountain a chunk flew from his pick and caught the sunlight like a marble of fire. The chip turned out to be a good-sized diamond which Joubron conjectured would fetch them each around five hundred dollars. Seizing his chance to soften the Frenchman, Thomas insisted that Joubron be the one to hold the valuable stone. "I trust you as a man of God to do me right."

They excavated at the mountain twenty more times over four arduous weeks, but after hauling back dozens of samples, Joubron had still failed to obtain his proving fossil *nonpareil*. Discouraged, the geologist announced that he was putting off searching for now to spend time with his slighted students. "I must be patient and wait for Revelation," he conceded piously, but his new tone was bitter.

The unexpected pause gave Thomas a chance to do more panning. Inspired by the thought of being able to provide Genevieve a lifetime of security and comfort, he tirelessly plied his sluice-box at countless spots along the river. But a week of sifting through sand ten hours every day had netted a grand total of three measly nuggets. He was through being patient. The time had come to confront Joubron and put his cards on the table.

He was on his way up the notched-post ladder to the hut when he heard what sounded like a large cat purring. It was past the time Joubron usually sent the boys home to their village after their daily treat, so he paused stunned to hear a buzz of urging whispers. He doubted those suggestive moans came from any reading of the Bible. Hoisting up inside he saw Joubron lying on his back in the hammock naked, a snuggling boy curled under each armpit. A third lad had his head at the Frenchman's groin, his slight frame draped in the spotted gold fur Thomas had first seen balled in a roll by Joubron's saddlebags. The boy named Peter sat cross-legged on one of the pallets on the floor, a grim fist tucked under his pouting chin.

Joubron gave a salacious sigh then motioned his misshapen arm to Peter who scrambled up eagerly to take the third boy's place, his little face brightening like a light. The perverse tenderness of the unsavory scene collided with Thomas' immediate drive to do violence.

"What was the lesson for today, you degenerate?—the rankness of sin...or naked I drink to thee?" Thomas rounded furiously on the reclining Frenchman who glanced up with an inebriated grin.

"We must be like zee children to enter God's kingdom..." Joubron smiled back impishly as his tongue wove lazily around his words.

"You dastard!—you're high as a kite!"

The boy Pierre Joubron had shamelessly named Peter reared up scowling while the others sat up with their black startled eyes on Thomas' fists. Joubron swayed forward to lift himself up in the hammock then flopped back like a fading fish.

"Time to go, *mes enfants*—father needs a little nap," Joubron garbled.

Thomas restrained himself from pounding out whatever was left of the drunkard's senses and started pulling the boys roughly out of the hammock. He had nearly herded the four of them outside when Peter ducked out nimbly from under his arm. The boy raced back to Joubron who had started to groan, his deformed hand rubbing his naked white stomach.

"It's all right, Peter," Joubron warbled, lifting his hand and resting it weakly on the anxious child's shoulder. "Father will finish the lesson tomorrow..."

"Why must go?" Peter demanded, crossing his arms when Thomas reached for his hand to drag him back from the hammock.

"Teacher is not well," Thomas explained as Joubron stopped moaning and passed out cold.

"Father sick?"

"Yes, very, very sick!—so you must go home and not come back until he says. Teacher does not want you getting sick..." Thomas pointed to the boys and shook his head then rubbed his own stomach, mimicking Joubron's weak groans.

"Great Spirit no get sick!" Peter declared.

Thomas stared at the child, aghast. Was Joubron so abhorrent he had not only used these boys as his playthings but induced them to confuse him with God?

"You're right, Peter—the Great Spirit does not get sick. But Joubron is not the Great Spirit, he is only a man like your real father, or me. Look—see?" Thomas nodded back to Joubron who had started to snore in his inebriated stupor. "The Great Spirit does not moan from bellyaches then fall asleep."

Peter hesitated, his little body tense. He seemed to reflect on this for a moment then he returned to his three companions cupping his fingers for them to come huddle around him. The boys whispered softly back and forth then

Peter abruptly shunted the others aside before darting a shifty-eyed glance back to Thomas.

"We go village—get father medicine—"

"No!" Thomas shouted but Peter turned and made a quick dash behind the other boys already scooting down the ladder and scampering into the forest.

With the children gone, and he hoped not soon to return, Thomas bent and gave Joubron a heavy shake on his shoulder. The Frenchman peered up with his eyes half-open then turned drunkenly onto his side, smacking his lips as he sank back into a sensuous dreaming sleep. Thomas backed up in disgust and his glance strayed to a near-empty bottle lying on its side beneath the hammock. He picked it up to take a sniff then flinched from the pinkish liquid that smelled like bourbon mixed with raw corn liquor and a bizarre sweet hint of yams.

He dropped the reeking bottle back on the floor and heard Joubron's breaths deepen again with drunken snores. Thomas crossed to the low stump-legged table and scanned inside the stack of notebooks with the geologist's scribbles. He flipped the pages of the books behind him on the shelf. When that desperate hunt came up empty he pried open the large metal box of rock samples and was surprised to see a pack of bullets tucked in a corner. After a search of Joubron's two saddlebags still produced no sign of the license Thomas smiled suddenly, hit by a devious hunch.

Reaching for the high shelf in back of the table, he retrieved the large tin of sugar and snapped the lid. He chucked some of the tiny brown crystals onto the floor to peer down inside and saw that the tin was lined with a doubled sheet of thick yellow paper. Holding his breath, he pulled it out and unfolded it slowly, trying not to feel giddy. At the document's bottom right corner was a small red seal granting the permit's signatory the right to all minerals found generally within the boundaries described.

Chapter 27

Samuel Judah was incensed that both his good name and part of his fortune were now in jeopardy. While he admitted in his more sanguine moments that he was largely to blame, he could not put aside his inner conviction that, directly or not, his unmanageable son was again the source of his troubles. He had agreed to assist the canal company chiefly to repay Henri Duvay for taking on Thomas. And though the arrangement did yield financial value, once it became known that his firm was enticing men to work in Panama he had drawn the ire of his country's planters, furious to see their once overflowing pool of dirt-cheap labor about to run dry.

So when news arrived that sixty-four Jamaicans had been brutally murdered, the growers seized upon the tragedy to inflame the public. Overlooking the fact that canal accidents and Panama's rampant diseases had killed three hundred times that many, they used the presses they controlled to print lurid daily columns under the recurring headline: CULEBRA MASSACRE. When one of the papers slanderously accused the Colombian government of encouraging the slaughter, the Jamaican people had been primed and began calling for blood.

Swift indictments against the renegade soldiers failed to silence the sugar-growers' cunningly planted cry—'repatriation for the insult to our nation!' Alarmed by a surge of heated editorials predicting unrest should more innocent Jamaicans be murdered in their beds, the island's English governor felt forced to take action. Samuel Judah was among those summoned to Colonial Headquarters where he was asked why, as an agent for the French, he could not insist that they evacuate his fellow citizens—particularly since he was the one who had placed so many of them in harm's way.

Samuel had humbly explained that he had no influence on the canal company's policies and at the moment its overriding concern was ensuring that the project survived. Pressed to elaborate, he confided that he had knowledge that Ferdinand de Lesseps was preparing to sell new bonds with numbered tickets to be drawn in a lottery. The hope was that, for the chance at several large cash prizes, the French public would be inclined to purchase more bonds and provide the cash the canal desperately needed. Until that happened, he told the anxious governor, the company was simply in no position to repatriate thousands of workers.

With the public's anger continuing to rise, the governor appealed to the Crown's London office for emergency aid and was tersely rebuffed. Left no alternative, he declared that the cost of return would have to be borne by Jamaica's own impoverished government. The growers, who made up the bulk of the island's legislature, saw that their cunning little plan was about to backfire. They had already taxed the poor to the bone so any new levies would have to come from their own pockets. Unless of course, they could find some other source of revenue. The likely temptation was not lost on Samuel Judah. Even though many of the planters remained his close friends and allies, he knew it would not take long before their eyes turned hungrily on him.

He wrote Duvay a long involved letter sharing the dangers he was facing because of the massacre. He said he appreciated the project was in financial difficulty but, if he was to be of service to him in the future, Duvay would be advised to persuade the canal company to ship home their wounded men as a goodwill gesture. Duvay's response had been shocking. He termed Samuel's suggestion presumptuous and niggardly, and ended by saying he found it unfortunate that a family as esteemed as the Judahs had been reduced to breeding ingrates like his thankless son.

Samuel was infuriated by the letter's sheer gall but under the circumstances he dared not respond in anger. Fortunately, the contracts themselves were on his side. The canal company's agreements clearly stipulated that any worker incapacitated during his indenture was to receive severance and a free trip home. His best hope was to use Duvay's extravagant French pride against him by making an issue of the fact that his company was dishonoring its promises. Yet the longer he reflected upon Duvay's outrageous affront, the more he was convinced that the Frenchman's harsh tone had far less to do with him than with Thomas.

"It appears your son is no longer earning glowing reports from his benefactor." Samuel dryly handed Josephine the letter. "I had been encouraged to think he was learning how to make his way in society—now it seems he has tainted my good name—"

As her eyes raced through Duvay's crass screed, Josephine's beige cheeks slowly burned crimson.

"All right, Josey. You're much too forthright to be good at bluffing. What do you know that you aren't telling me? We both know how that boy runs through money. I hope to God he hasn't stooped to stealing..."

"Samuel! What a horrid thing to say—and totally unfair! Our son has too much of that Judah pride to do something so disgraceful. I've been wanting to discuss Thomas with you for months, but whenever I've seen you you've been awfully short and distracted. I finally gave up waiting—" Josephine stopped and looked at him pleadingly. "Thomas isn't in Panama. He's gone to Venezuela."

"Venezuela! What in the world is he doing in Venezuela?"

"I'm not sure, exactly. He mentioned something about a stake in some mining venture, but I was just as happy to know he'd be leaving that hideous country. What kind of a government sends its soldiers to rob and slaughter poor innocent workers—?" said Josephine, squeezing her small hands nervously. "I suppose one should have expected it. I read in the papers that once the war started the Colombian military had so many defections it filled its ranks with cut-throats and desperadoes...I was worried sick—"

Again! Samuel mused in annoyance, ignoring his beloved's high-strung prattle. Again that impulsive hotspur had impaired his affairs! He slumped on the mahogany settee and tried to decide on the best tack to pursue. If Thomas' departure was behind Duvay's refusal, it couldn't hurt to try and smooth things out in person. Yes, he said to himself after thinking it over—a courteous little trip down to Panama might just rescue his good name and save his fortune.

———

The Caribbean's salt-tipped spray felt bracing as Thomas lounged out on the hot forecastle deck trying to picture Genevieve's face when he told her he was going to be rich. Would it show a flash of happiness or cloud in rejection? He was ready with any number of philanthropic proposals to try and overwhelm her but he had no confidence as to how she would respond. The uncertainty was driving him mad, as it had for those interminable weeks he'd been compelled to stay on in Caracas until his rights to the mine were ruled legal. After his miraculous good luck, if she turned him down now, all that pent-up hope and joy would be crushed.

It fit so perfectly together—everything that had guided him this far. He was even starting to believe there was some omnipotent hand tipping the scales to balance the score. After Joubron's abominable end, he could not stop thinking about that last night up in the tower when Genevieve finally disclosed her dark secret. The fierceness with which she had defended her father had shocked him. No man, no matter how sorely he missed his beautiful dead wife, can be excused for raping his ten-year-old daughter. Yet rather than place the blame on him, where it rightly belonged, Genevieve had been blaming herself ever since. Thomas had argued against her all night, unable to shake her wrenching conviction that had she not betrayed him to her Nana Binta, her father would have recovered in time to repent and still be alive.

He believed that, like Joubron, Genie's father had lacked the courage to live with his own shame. It struck him that each of those monsters must have possessed two tragically differing minds: one trained to do good, the other so evil he could see a child's simple wish to please as consent to his depravity. Perhaps it was that profound offense to nature that moved some benevolent invisible hand to steer each man to grab his gun and put a bullet in his sick tortured brain. He remembered racing for the hut after the gunshot and finding Joubron lying sprawled with a hole in the side of his head, his chest striped with blood and specks of brown sugar. Each time he recalled the morbid image, he thought at least those four innocent little boys had been spared the shock of discovering the body, unlike his poor Genie.

He began to sweat and grow tense in the reclining chaise lounge then reminded himself that Joubron was dead and his claim had been approved. And while he was dying to know her answer, he could afford to give Genie as much time to decide as she needed. After all, they were both still young. What need was there to rush once he found her? In fact, an extended courtship would fit nicely with his plans. For apart from a few nuggets of gold and the twenty eight hundred dollars he'd received for those two precious diamonds, his newfound wealth was still somewhere underground and its actual extent yet unknown.

As he sipped his drink out on deck all alone, Thomas wondered what had happened to the luxury-hating rebel who had left Jamaica. If someone had told him he would choose to travel first-class just like his father, he would have spit in their eye. Yet here he was, bathing in the sun on the S.S. Archimedes, trying to decide whether to dine on pheasant in wine sauce or sirloin tips braised with saffron and ginger. He hated to think his sympathies for the honest working man had been subverted by his first taste of real money, but he had to admit that after laboring months in the jungle it had been bliss to trade those dirty dungarees for a smart English tweed.

Those last weeks walking in Caracas, he had often felt he was being trailed by admiring looks. In retrospect, those long glances may have simply been drawn to the slightly wicked smile that lingered on his lips weeks after Joubron's suicide. He had not wished the Frenchman a morbid end when he forced him to initial the permit beneath Thomas' name while threatening to kill him if he caught him abusing those boys again. But it was hard to feel sad knowing that an insane molester was out of the way and that he now possessed the sole rights to a gold mine. If the God of Good Fortune was weighing in on the side of Justice, who was he to turn luck down?

"Excuse me, sir..."

It was the steward, whose ruddy squeezed-in features, elongated neck and set of near-invisible eyebrows created the impression of a talking eel. "I recall marking the sirloin," Thomas interjected, assuming he was being asked to confirm his selected main course.

The steward stiffened and flushed. "I'm terribly sorry, but there's been a bit of awkwardness with some of the other passengers. If you don't mind—er, I've been instructed to ask that you take dinner in your cabin."

Thomas sat for a moment, tongue-tied. He noticed that although the dining-room's long table showed settings for seven, the only one seated, apart from himself, was an elderly woman whose frumpy traveling dress with its lack of frills and puffy shoulders suggested she was English. "Sorry—I don't understand—whose request?" To Thomas' annoyance his voice came out sounding high and pinched. Further up, from across the table, the gray-haired Englishwoman peered at him above a silver-rimmed pinch-nez.

"A request was made...er—and the captain has complied," the steward explained, fighting his embarrassment. "He offers his sincere apologies but thinks it best for everyone's contentment."

The picture began to crystallize in Thomas' mind. He recognized that sudden stiltedness in the steward's tone, having heard it often back in his high school days. It seemed that when it came time to share a meal, the slightest brown hue interfered with certain northern digestions. "Well, I don't find it to my contentment. I paid my full fare the same as everyone else. Exactly whose comfort is it that I am upsetting?" Thomas recovered his voice and kept his even tone cool. He knew the thin Irishman was not at fault, besides, the chap had been more than decent, returning to refresh his drink all afternoon without his asking.

The steward bent and spoke confidentially in Thomas' ear. "It's those Parkers...they're American—you know the sort..."

Thomas had actually already guessed who the steward meant. He had glimpsed the lumpish Parkers and their lumpish daughters start to come on deck while he was sunning. He was about to say hello when the mother's round pudgy face seized in horror. She had gathered her ugly daughters and hurried them aft as if there had been a ghastly accident and she feared the gore would upset them. That was the last he'd seen of them. He smiled at the thought that his presence had scared the four of them so silly they'd spent the rest of the afternoon skulking indoors. "Then might I suggest you tell our American friends they are free to eat in their cabin—or would that be too harsh—limiting them to their own company?"

"Sir, it's only a double berth and there's one o' you and four o' them—once you count the two young ladies..." In his distress the steward's well-oiled voice had risen sharply but he caught himself quickly and tried an appeal to Thomas' hidden comradeship. "I can have the cook serve you up nice extra portions—"

"See here, steward—I could not help overhearing! Is that really your place?"

Hearing the Englishwoman's abrupt interjection the Irishman bristled. "Beg pardon, madam." The eel-faced steward stood back crisply from the table and his injured gray eyes shot a cutting glance at Thomas who blithely stayed seated.

"Tell Captain Riley the young man had already committed to dine with Lady Higginson and should that prove unsatisfactory he can take the matter up with me!"

His discomfort now bordering on panic, the Irishman rubbed his palms with tight agitation. "But madam—I—the captain—" he started to plead then wilted under the frost of an arch English glare. "Of course, Lady Higginson..." The steward straightened himself with a nod and yanked down on his waiter's vest to restore his composure and steel his spine for more unpleasantness.

"How terribly uncouth!" the lady fumed when he'd left. "Never you mind—they're nothing but blowhards and bullies. I fear what England's inattention has unleashed on the world!" She sniffed almost mournfully. Her eyes seemed to gape at Thomas through her adjusted lenses like small blue planets. "I must compliment you," she went on, smiling at him kindly, "for such a young man you certainly handle yourself adroitly. The right touch of force yet with charm, Master—?"

"Judah, Thomas Judah," he replied, his violet eyes warming to her compliments.

"Pleased to meet you, Master Judah. As you've already gathered, I'm Lady Higginson. Why don't you change positions and sit up here with me? That way I can shield you in case we are burdened by those horrid Parkers," she said with the tiniest of grins.

Disarmed, Thomas returned the grin and complied. With Lady Higginson as an ally, the episode had gone from being an insult he felt forced to parry to a diverting lark. Who would win the struggle for pride of place, he wondered impishly as they awaited the captain's arrival, the bumptious Yanks or the imperial British?

Thomas had no sooner settled in his new place when an urbane gentleman in a white dinner jacket joined them at the table. "*Buenas noches*...Vollmer," he introduced himself with a gracious nod, then sat where Thomas had just been sitting. The look on the man's huge pink face was strained and gloomy.

"*Buenas noches, Señor* Vollmer, would you be offended if we conversed in English? My Spanish is not up to par, I'm afraid—"

Vollmer's ice-blue eyes blinked at her vacantly.

"*¿Todo correcto si la señora y yo hablamos inglés?*" Thomas intervened gallantly when he realized the man had grasped almost nothing that Lady Higginson had said.

"*Sí, por supuesto. No me ofende, pero gracias por preguntar.*"

"What did he say? I think I got his gist but I'd like it confirmed," Lady Higginson whispered anxiously.

"He doesn't mind, but he thanks you for asking," Thomas explained as Vollmer looked on, smiling thinly.

The steward returned bearing the look of man who had just been sternly chastened. He announced that the captain extended his apologies but would be unable to join them for dinner.

"What a pity—is he not well?"

"I couldn't say, my lady," the steward answered woodenly.

"And the Parkers—are they taken ill as well?"

"They have chosen to dine in cabin, madam."

"Splendid. Perhaps by tomorrow they shall have recovered sufficiently for decent company," Lady Higginson snipped.

"I highly doubt it, my lady—it appears their discomfort is expected to last—" he paused and tilted his head towards Thomas ever so slightly, "until we dock in Colón the day after tomorrow."

The steward went about serving them in stone-faced silence while Lady Higginson turned her attentions upon Thomas. She joked that it had been ordained that in her later years she would travel the world as an ornithologist since her late husband had been the rarest of English birds—an enlightened member of Parliament. "Had Sir Edward been here he would have put those Parkers in their place. He had no patience for these coarse *poseurs*," she said with a superior little sniff. "They aspire to nothing more than being retail accountants and the best among them seem to believe that good breeding can be acquired by the pound."

Even though he had developed a taste for fine food and a good Bordeaux, Thomas had not yet shed his distaste for snobs. His contempt for the presumptions of class confused how he felt about this charming old Englishwoman. Years of being snubbed by half of his classmates had led him to believe that people like Lady Higginson possessed genetic intolerance. Yet, unlike his father's family who faintly criticized prejudice and then only in private, she spoke her mind with unflinching candor. There were hints of humor and self-deprecation to her smiling pomposity and he was enchanted by the fact that when she moved her dress gave off the same soft scent of lavender he recalled from his childhood sitting in church beside his mother.

Nevertheless, as their conversation wandered past the light consommé, he found himself on guard to be tested, sure that as the meal grew more meaty Lady Higginson would mutate into one of his dissatisfied schoolmarms and oppress him with quotes from Milton and Lord Tennyson after failing to pry out his unformed thoughts on Locke or John Bunyan. Instead, as their main course arrived (and as he'd hoped, the steak was first-rate) she was more eager to listen, responding to his action-packed tales with parted lips poised to softly gasp—oh, my word!—as he described another life and death episode. When it finally came time to bid good-night and stumble to his cabin, steeped in a fuzzy glow from the wine and his dizzying confabulations, Thomas realized that apart from his nights with Genevieve, he had not enjoyed a more satisfying evening.

———

Lady Higginson remained on his mind as he retraced the path he'd taken the day he first arrived and came to Colón's red granite monument, still standing in all its massive ugliness. He wondered how a person of her fine sensibilities would respond to that hideous tribute to the city's railroad founders. Would she see it as a Colombian architect's crafty revenge against the powerful *gringos*, or simply another product of modern man's vulgar taste and indifference? The monument inspired nothing except a nagging horror that its presence, like the shore's depressing ghetto, would be here forever.

He turned his dark thoughts to the brighter hope that Genevieve was back from wherever she'd gone. He considered going straight to the hospital then decided that he should wait until he'd taken a bath and was looking his best before trying to impress her. He went instead to the central post office to see if they were holding his mail and felt a rush of joy when the window clerk came back with two letters. He tore the first one open and saw it had been written in a flourishing hand on behalf of his neglected buddy, Byron, who was apparently in touch with Henri Duvay and was still hoping to find him. The second letter was from his mother scolding him for not having shared his expected address when he cabled her after arriving in Caracas.

Vaguely discouraged, he stopped to buy a copy of the daily *Star and Herald* and put off finding a hotel room to look up Henri on the off chance Genevieve had tried to contact him in Christophe-Colomb. He left the post office and walked back to Fifth Street, struggling to manage both his bags with the folded newspaper under one arm. The day had turned hot and muggy and the last thing he wanted was to arrive at Henri's looking sweaty and rumpled. He was about to signal to one of the little carmiettas sitting idle outside the train station when he felt a hand clamp the back of his shoulder. He spun back irritably and found a smelly *desgraciado* grinning right in his face. The man's large teeth were stunningly white and his slightly psychotic gaze and woolly growth of facial hair bore the look of a wounded wild animal.

"Move! I have no coins!" Thomas snapped, shrugging off the filthy arm about to boldly hook in his elbow. It was not unknown for a traveler arriving in Colón to be robbed in bright daylight, so after clasping his bags tighter, Thomas pondered whether it would have been better to let one drop and reach for his gun.

The vagrant drew back looking deeply offended. As he lifted his head to buffer his pride a grisly line appeared like a slash across his dark throat. Thomas froze, seeing the band of shiny scar tissue. "Jesus..." he gasped, "—Cuffie?"

The derelict partly repaired his brilliant white grin.

Thomas had to stiffen his knees to keep from falling over. Never in a thousand years would he have believed this dirty stooped fellow in that slovenly night-shirt was his strapping friend. "Jesus...Cuffie?" he breathed out again. "What the devil happened?"

Cuffie tightened his heavy shoulders and started to croak a reply then shrugged feebly.

"You lost your voice!" Thomas cried, feeling a sick twinge surround the ball in his gut. "Never mind—it's good to see you alive! Sorry it took me awhile, but you look like puss after it done fight mongoose!" he said, trying to make light of his shameful confusion. "You hungry?" When Cuffie's bright grin widened eagerly, Thomas passed him his bags and sent him to wait in the park nearby while he found one of the roadside vendors. After ordering the peddler's best two water coconuts, Thomas approached a heavy-set woman with one blind gray eye seated on a box behind a tray piled with homemade savories. Buying a large slab of her fried cassava along with three hard-boiled eggs, he hurried them over to Cuffie who licked his lips as he arrived.

By the time the first vendor showed up with his coconuts, Cuffie had gobbled down the snack without bothering to unwrap the little brown packet of salt and pepper. He quickly drained the green husks of their sweet cooling liquid then used one of the slivers cut from the top of each coconut to dig out the hidden white jelly. Thomas started to ask how he had been managing to survive when Cuffie gave a sudden belch and hastily covered up his mouth, looking surprised and sheepish.

"I see you can't talk—but you can't work either?"

Cuffie put two fingers to each of his eyes then shook his head to show he'd been having a hard time sleeping. After some weak hand movements punctuated by a few weary shakes of his head, Cuffie managed to convey that he had lost the strength to do a full day's heavy labor.

Thomas patted him on the arm and was about to promise to do what he could when a sudden thought made him pause. "You know—come to think of it—the company should have paid you compensation! Where have you been living since they let you go from hospital...out here on the street?"

Cuffie's spread his arms and looked down.

Thomas reached inside his jacket and counted out ten dollars from his billfold. "You need a bath and nice clean shave—and for God's sake, get yourself some trousers! If you don't look like you're out to frighten little children maybe when I get back I can talk one of the merchants into having you wash his windows and sweep out his shop."

Cuffie managed to look pleased even as his eyes remained woeful. He stroked the offered bills as if touching a lover's cheek and a gargling sound rumbled out from his throat that seemed to say, "honor to you, my friend."

Thomas nodded with a frail glum smile then left to hire one of the standing cabs. He was anxious to be out of the sun and, though it shamed him to admit, to be away from poor Cuffie. He simply could not square the chap he knew with that smelly lice-ridden wretch who'd struck him as just one more homeless beggar that he, like everyone else in this worthless town, claimed to pity but scorned getting near to.

He directed his driver to Henri's address then rested back in his cane-bottomed seat and opened his paper. He read the lead and shook his head with a shudder. A canal diver had been killed when a dynamite charge exploded near Mindi—'the accident comes the day after three more Jamaican diggers perished when a steam-shovel boiler exploded leaving dozens burned and injured.' So much for there being a god inclined to justice and mercy, Thomas muttered as he read the column's grisly estimate that twenty-thousand canal-men had been killed or died of swamp fever since the project first started. Why was it that the ones who had least to gain were always the ones forced to risk the most, he grumbled, slapping closed the paper. And how many more, like Cuffie, had been left uncounted and set adrift among the walking dead.

———

Samuel Judah was not accustomed to be the one playing the weaker hand, and he knew that in life, as was the general nature of business, sometimes a man must be prepared to accept his losses. He had prolonged this fractious relationship so that Josephine could not accuse him of discarding his own son, but even if Thomas was no longer a factor, he could not risk any more damage to his reputation. That was why he felt obliged to visit Panama for a second time this year and his canny host knew it.

"I assure, you, *monsieur*, I've been employing the meager influence I have left with the governor. I realize your company interprets his new bond as some kind of indirect extortion, but I can assure you that is not its purpose. The planters are using the public's rage about the massacre to institute a ban on export-workers to Panama altogether. The governor perceives an exit tax as the only way out."

"Ridiculous! He wants to tax poor men for wanting to leave and find jobs? Instead of trying to sneak that tax onto the company, he should be paying us for taking them off his hands."

"Had you taken my advice and agreed to repatriate those disgruntled men right after the slaughter we might have cooled some of the heated passions."

Duvay glared at the elder Judah from behind the expanse of his chart-covered desk. "Are you wanting me to believe that an English governor felt intimidated by a few black pick and shovelers?"

"Naturally not. No—what I need you to appreciate, *monsieur*, is that each time another injured worker's letter appears in the papers complaining of ill-treatment, the closer the masses in my country come to a violent rebellion. My providing you with replacements in such an atmosphere is simply out of the question."

"Out of the question—" snapped Duvay, sitting up aggressively, "what is out of the question is expecting gratitude from someone named Judah—or being foolish enough to consider one a friend."

Samuel took a long soothing drag on his host's excellent cigar before he replied. There was a dolor hanging inside the engineer's dark shuttered room that was making him claustrophobic. It felt as though he was being strangled by some nebulous paranoia twined with resentment and despair.

"I am sorry you view my encumbrance as a sign of ingratitude. I assure you I appreciate every kindness rendered me. Nevertheless, our governor is well aware that Mr. de Lesseps' lottery subscription has failed, which means your project is facing bankruptcy. Rather than attempt to obtain workers you will not be able to afford, my advice is to seek out a buyer. That way, if it appears the canal can still be salvaged, the company could pay part of its debts and have the rest restructured—"

"Aha! So that's the sinister scheme behind all this!" Duvay erupted, slapping the desk with his palm and nearly spilling his espresso. "These rumors I've been hearing are true—you vultures want to buy the company and sell the scraps! Who have you been plotting with—a cabal of New York bankers?"

"I have not the slightest notion what you are referring to," Samuel Judah responded icily. "I am not involved in any plot and resent your implying it! I am as anxious as anyone to see the canal open new markets. I am prepared to be of whatever service to you that I can, but someone like myself is forced to see things plainly. If you are determined to acquire new labor just to try and keep things going, then I'm afraid you need to look elsewhere. Perhaps in Malaysia—or Bombay—"

Duvay resettled the demitasse he had bumped from its saucer then glowered at his guest through the haze from their cigars. "Very well—let me speak plainly. I hired your son and paid him lavishly, despite his modest qualifications, and in return you agreed to act as our agent. I understand ours was a gentleman's agreement. However, if you intend to blatantly abrogate your word, I imagine I can make a fair case in court for breach of trust." He paused for pointed effect. "I'm sure the papers would be intrigued by the less than savory details."

"Now see here!" Samuel exclaimed, his uncomfortable neck warming inside its collar. "The arrangement was that I would help you to recruit some more workers—it was not open-ended. I came here hoping you and I could hammer out our differences in a cordial manner—but I will not stand for being blackmailed."

His indignation appeared to bounce off the Frenchman as if he were stone. Duvay's face never changed expression but now his tone was pure acid.

"And here I had assumed I was dealing with a gentleman. It was silly of me to forget that men of your persuasion care not for blood nor bone if it lies against your interest."

Samuel Judah found the bluntness of the insult staggering. Usually when good Christian men sensed their advantage slipping, they resorted to stealthier ways to try and browbeat him. "I'm familiar with such fiction and I reject its characterization. I came to see you as a courtesy and expect no less respect. As for my gratitude—as I said before—I appreciate what you've done for Thomas and I shall be happy to repay you in any sensible manner. But I cannot squeeze blood from a stone. Nor will I allow you to drag my name through mud so you can have someone else to blame when this damned project fails and is left a laughingstock."

Arguing voices came in from the hall and Duvay shot up bursting with rage. As more sharp words drifted in through the door, the Frenchman wobbled on his feet as if he had suffered a stroke.

"No! I will not wait any longer—!"

Thomas came barging into the study followed by the frantic Monique.

"Father!"

"*Monsieur!*" The alarmed maid raced to steady Duvay who stood ashen-faced, his arms braced heavily against the cluttered desk.

Samuel Judah leapt up, speechless.

"Shall I go for a doctor?" Thomas asked, seeing Duvay's gray face drain white.

"No, no—just give me a moment..." Duvay demurred, hiding the fact that, unlike the elder Judah, he had gotten a jolt the instant he placed the voice in the hall.

"You!" Samuel wheeled to confront his son as Monique hurried out to bring water. "What the devil are you doing back in Panama?"

"Lovely—the inconstant father chides the prodigal son," Duvay muttered bitingly.

As Monique returned carrying a tray with three glasses of water, the two seething older men faced off across the sea of charts and sketches spread between them.

"Were the two of you battling over me—or how to save mankind?" Thomas asked mischievously.

Samuel glowered at his son while Monique made a quick escape and shut the door. "What do you know about this?" he demanded, struggling to sift through the layers of suspicion. "Is this another of your stunts—did the two of you cook this up to try and embarrass me?"

"Naturally not!—how dare you suggest it!" snapped Duvay. "I'm no less curious to hear how he found the gall to show his face here now!"

Thomas unveiled a happy grin. That he had happened upon the two men he most wanted to humble surely meant that Fate was firmly behind him. "I came back, *monsieur*, because when I left you claimed I would amount to nothing—" he paused for his crowning moment, "and since good fortune has arranged to have my father here as well, I hereby offer to repay you both for the great kindness you've so generously shown me." Thomas turned to his mentor with a sarcastic smirk. "Is, say, a thousand dollars in gold about right for all your trouble—?"

"Impudent as ever," Samuel muttered, shaking his head. "I apologize, *monsieur*—he's been in the Venezuelan jungle—it must be some hallucinatory fever..."

Duvay made a dismissive twitter. "*Quelle blague!*—the twig does not fall far from its branch..." He leaned towards Thomas, his expression filled with hurt. "I offered you my friendship. Do you think money can ever make up for betrayal—for lack of loyalty?"

"Loyalty?" Thomas almost shouted, forgetting the promise he had made to himself to keep cool and collected. "Betrayal! Loyalty! How about developing a conscience? How many widows were we going to send to the poorhouse before you accepted reality?"

"Who do you think you are fooling? If you cared a whit about the poor, you would have stayed to help your darling nun care for the homeless. Oh yes—she sought me out!" the Frenchman cried, seeing Thomas flinch. "The poor thing wanted to know where you had gone..." Duvay dropped back into his chair and hid his face in his hands. "You speak of conscience. You have no conscience...Get out—please—the both of you," he said in a choking voice. "All of a sudden I'm extremely tired."

Samuel tugged his son's arm for him to follow but Thomas resisted.

"No—you go along. There's something I must ask Henri in private."

"As you like!" Samuel snapped before addressing Duvay. "I'm at the Washington Hotel until tomorrow, *monsieur*. I should like a chance to clear the air."

Duvay nodded back faintly, and the elder Judah stomped through the study door without a glance towards his son.

"I don't know where she is..."

"*Monsieur...?*"

"We both know why you're here," Duvay said wearily. "I could see that she loves you—with all her hopeless religious zeal. Strange—until you chose to insult me along with your father I'd been hoping you'd come back to see me."

The suffering in Duvay's meek whisper gave Thomas pause. He had never heard him sound this earnest or so downhearted.

"I thought my leaving as I did ruled out staying friends."

Duvay reached for one of the desk's glass paperweights and gazed at the colorful little figures jumbled tightly inside. "I'm a scientist. I trust our chaotic impulses will ultimately be put in order by our intelligence."

"Does that mean you're ready to accept that this great dream of yours has been a tragic failure?"

"You still don't understand," Duvay said sadly, putting down the kaleidoscopic little globe to face his former protégé. "Whether this was a crazy dream or not does not mean we could have abandoned things sooner. Even had we never tried, somewhere men would have died, there would still be a failure. We need this canal. Without it there will never be light across the whole sorry world and the poor that you pretend to care for so deeply will perish in darkness. What we have started is not the end. This canal shall be. You will live to see it."

Chapter 28

Byron opened his eyes as a noisy mosquito made a dive through the dark and buzzed inside his ear. He brushed away the staggered insect and suddenly stopped breathing, thinking he was back in the Monkey Hill prison. He was straining to make sense of his dark surroundings when his heart gave a shiver at what sounded like rattling chains and pitiful groans. As his anguished brain pictured men being tortured, he feared he had died and descended into hell until his cheek touched the pillow. He gasped in relief, feeling safe to judge that the damned were not rewarded with comfortable beds, but then if he wasn't in hell—where in the devil's name was he?

He started to sit up and instantly winced, feeling a grinding pain near his groin. He raced a hand down inside his sheet and felt a frightening bulge, as if a cricket ball had gotten stuck on its way through his intestines. The pesky mosquito flew back for his ear and its ardent whine made him think of the Fiddler's last plea. "Sure, *bolow*—plenty men go into their hospital—but how many yuh ever see come back out..." Now it seemed that was exactly where he was—injured and alone among the dying.

That hard bulge scared him, but he'd risk letting it heal on its own rather than leave this place inside of a casket. He hauled himself up, ignoring the pain as he slid from the bed, then shuddered in surprise when his bare toes touched water. He squinted down and saw what appeared to be a saucer beneath his bed-leg. It seemed an odd place to put a dish of water but he'd heard that hospitals were known to try all sorts of weird experiments. Another good reason for him to hurry and find his way home.

He was out of the bed, creeping despite the eye-watering pain, when he realized he was about to leave the ward dressed in his undershirt and drawers. He searched beneath the sheet for the rest of his clothes then gave up with a grunt of frustration. As he stopped to scratch the swelling from a new mosquito bite and heard the constant moaning, he decided he could not bear to stay here until the morning. Since it seemed a fair bet that his clothes must be somewhere nearby, he tiptoed out through the aisle of beds groaning with tormented bodies.

Out in the hall there was just enough light for him to recognize the outline of a cupboard further on his right against the wall. Sensing victory, he hurried to try its panel door but discovered it was locked and missing its key.

"Stop right there, young man! Who gave you permission to leave the ward?"

Byron's hands were still on the cupboard door as the wide form rose from the shadows and was on top of him with fierce flapping wings.

"What are you after—more morphine? Or is it that flask of licorice brandy no one thinks I know about?"

Unluckily for Byron, the burdened mother superior had been unable to sleep and had come on duty a few hours early. He stared at her, quaking and blank-faced. In her high dudgeon Mother Agnes was a terrible presence.

"Speak up! If you cannot explain yourself you'd best get back to bed before I decide you're a thief and deserve a good hiding!"

"Me not no thief!" he almost shouted, Rivueltas' sadistic malevolence burning in his ears. "I just want my clothes so I can go home—I don't need to be in any hospital!"

"What's your name? I don't recognize you—" Mother Agnes quizzed him sharply.

"Byron, sister," he mumbled, growing meek as he realized he was standing there in his underwear, rebuking a middle-aged white nun.

"Well, Byron, since you have submitted to our care what you may or may not need is up to your doctor and he'll decide that when he sees you tomorrow. Now get back in that bed!"

Byron wanted to tell her that he never agreed to any such thing, but since he could not explain how he had ended up here in the first place, he realized it would make her even more certain he was ill and off his head.

"All right, miss," he conceded, putting up no resistance when she started to lead him back to the ward by his elbow, "but tomorrow I want to go home."

It seemed as if he had only just crawled back in the bed and fallen asleep when Mother Agnes was sweeping up the window shades with a booming 'good morning!' Byron opened his eyes to a splitting headache and noticed there was a second nun stooping alongside him refilling the saucers beneath his bed.

"Good morning, Byron!" Mother Agnes chirped brightly, coming over as the younger nurse left with her large clay pitcher. "Feeling better?—how's that tummy?"

"Not too bad—" he lied, trying to smile his way through the murderous headache. He was not about to volunteer more reasons for them to keep him. "Sorry about last night..."

"Apology accepted! I realized once I checked your records that you were still in shock from the accident. Never mind—you have much to be thankful for!"

Yes, very thankful, Byron thought sullenly behind the pounding in his skull. He wondered what on earth she was talking about.

"God has chosen to spare your life—you should take the time to fully recover. You've come through quite an ordeal."

"I'm all right. Can I speak with the doctor now and get him to release me?"

Mother Agnes moved the small stand near the foot of his bed and sat to face him. "There are many new injuries the doctor still needs to attend to—and we're already shorthanded. Try to be patient—you've had a serious trauma." She reached for his hand and cradled it in hers. "You may need to have surgery..." she whispered, her blue eyes piercing him gently.

"Surg'ry?" Byron gasped. "Doctor wants to cut me open?"

Mother Agnes aimed a grave gaze towards the bottom of his stomach. "We can't let that bulge down there get any bigger."

"No-no-no! No surg'ry! No, sister—that's not for me!"

"You don't understand," the nun told him gently. "If that knot below your navel is bleeding you could die—"

The notion struck Byron as fantastical. He had had far greater pain than the one in his groin and even now his head felt a whole lot worse. The thought of being cut open had the old cooper's famous joke scaring his mind—'so how did the operation turn out?' the patient's wife asks the surgeon. 'Well—' the good doctor replies, 'the surgery was a great success—but unfortunately your husband has died.'

"Thanks all the same, sister—but I think I'll trust God and take my chances."

Mother Agnes' smile grew warmer. "It's good that you trust in God! Remember, he saw fit to bring you here. I understand that you're fearful, but you really must wait and speak with the doctor. If you promise not to fret, I'll make sure he sees you today. You can trust us, Byron—" she said as she stood to go, "we want what's best for you."

After she left Byron rested on his pillow and thought about his choices. The nun seemed kind but he'd heard about these new doctors. They liked to cut live people open to look and see what folks are made of. For all he knew this one just wanted to practice on him!

The sunlight seemed to have quieted the more agonizing whimpers and Byron was thankful to feel his headache begin to recede. He turned to say hello to the patient in the bed closest by, but the man lay still as a rock with his sheet drawn up past his head. Byron shrank, afraid the man was dead, and waited tensely until he saw the man's chest rise for a tiny breath. Relieved to know he had not spent half the night beside a corpse, he scanned the rest of the ward and was shocked by what he had passed blindly by in the dark. Men lay curled in their beds, shivering despite the room's stagnant heat. Others were sprawling uncovered, barely visible in their bulky white bandages. The few whose features he was able to distinguish had patches of pink skin showing where the brown had been burnt from their faces.

The misery radiating from these men shook Byron to his toes. He avoided meeting their eyes, fearing his next depression might have no bottom and he'd be left in that barren abyss. Feeling his hands turn cold and clammy, he forced his mind to dwell on happier things. He remembered how he'd been uplifted by Estelle's caresses and tried to think of the ideal gift he should buy her this Christmas. He was mulling the idea of finding her a country fiddler's portrait when a short round nun with a downy pink face came in pushing a laden trolley and started passing around trays of breakfast. The nun who had gone about earlier refilling the bed's clay saucers returned with more water and set about helping her young sister feed the sorriest invalids their toast and porridge. When most of the room had been fed, the plump nun came over to Byron carrying a half-filled glass of water and a bottle of quinine.

Watching as she topped off the glass with quinine, Byron realized the dull new burn in his stomach was actually hunger. "I don't get no breakfast?" he asked her peevishly.

"Sorry—Mother Agnes says you're not to have any solid food just yet," the plump nun replied, setting the bottle with the remainder of the quinine on the night-stand by his bed.

"Why not?"

"Shh—" she hushed him sternly, "just until the doctor has a chance to examine you. Now I need you to drink this whole glass, then I want you right back down on that pillow."

Byron sulked but drained the bitter glass. There was an air about these nuns with their big flapping wings he was unable to defy. "Why you doing that?" he demanded anxiously, when she helped him lie back in the bed before lifting his undershirt and starting to prod around the worrying lump above his groin.

"Don't worry—I just need to check. Does that hurt?" she asked with a tiny frown when she pressed her experienced fingers a bit more firmly and saw him wince.

"Not really," he fibbed.

"How about here?" she asked, probing an inch higher.

"No, no, I'm fine," Byron insisted, denying the odd tingling pain he suddenly felt in his shoulder.

"Good boy," she said with a reproachful smile that said she knew he was lying.

"Could I have just a little something to eat?" Byron entreated, when she moved to open the bottle. "My stomach—it's burning with hunger...sister—?"

"I'm Sister Nathalie," the young nun replied with a sweet caring smile. "If you promise to be patient until you speak with the doctor I'll see if there's any soup left in the kitchen."

All at once Byron felt immensely tired and had nearly drifted off to sleep when the nun reappeared carrying a bowl of warm bouillon. After she helped him sit up and started plumping his pillow, he asked if she knew if there was a patient here named Tomby.

"Tomby? No, I don't think so—but we have so many new patients."

When the nun had departed after assuring him the doctor would be in to see him soon, the man who'd been lying lifelessly beside him rose up with a disturbed glassy stare.

"Don't drink it!" he hissed, seeing Byron lift his spoon for an eager sip. "S-Satan d-done roused God's f-finger!" The man's lower lip twitched in spasms as he bent close to whisper in a broad Jamaican accent, "—it have in poison!"

"Relax, old boy," said Byron, making a face at the thin salt-free soup. "If Satan was out to poison me he'd disguise it with a bit more flavor—"

The man's protruding eyes looked as if at any moment a yolky yellow would come spilling out of their sockets. "Don't t-try figuring with Satan! He c-can wear wings j-just like an angel! He c-connived us down to Egypt and now G-God's finger done smite dis land with in-insects!"

Byron nodded back with a smile of mild condescension but then set the thin bouillon aside and closed his eyes while the man went on rambling. He realized that either the poor fellow would outlive his feverish visions or he'd be dead within a week, but that did not mean he found it entirely insane to think he was here among the cursed.

Sinking back under his covers, Byron tried to fill the blanks in his memory. The last he remembered was being underwater wrapping a fuse to the primer then helping Tomby set in the cartridge. Then, all at once, the ground seemed to rise above his head and everything went black. He guessed it was an explosion that had knocked him unconscious. They must have fished him out of the water and brought him here to the hospital. That still didn't tell him how he had ended up with a lump below his belly as big as his fist. It scared him what the nun said about it bleeding, but there was no way on God's green earth he was going to let them cut him open.

His fears were fighting off a mighty urge to sleep when he noticed Sister Nathalie rushing out from the ward with a balled fist jammed to her mouth. An instant later, she came hurrying back followed by a long-haired man in a rumpled white smock who Byron guessed was the doctor. Behind him two black orderlies came carrying a lacquered-wood screen which they used to shield two of the beds across the room then left as Sister Nathalie and the doctor vanished behind it.

The commotion sent men's tongues gabbling until a tremulous voice wailed, "damn—and he was talking to me so strong! All morning, sister!...all morning!..."

Immediately, the ward became silent as a tomb. Byron heard Sister Nathalie whisper, 'shush!' as the frantic voice began to mewl, its squeezed pitch a plaintive whistle.

The doctor staggered from the ward looking gray and when the orderlies returned bearing a stretcher Byron could smell the room's sweaty panic.

"Please, Lord, don't let me perish in here," he muttered as the orderlies came inching out with the white-draped body. As they shuffled back through the ward he could sense every man going rigid in his bed. He tried to plot how he might lay his hands on some trousers and find his way out but the drowsiness was pressing on his eyelids, and despite a determined struggle, his eyes could not stay open. He had been asleep for hours when he woke to feel a gentle hand shaking his shoulder.

He opened his eyes to see Sister Nathalie smiling down at him.

"You have a visitor," she told him cheerfully, "but for just a few minutes!" she announced as she left.

"So you wouldn't rest until you could copy me, eh, Sir Eggshell?"

Byron sat up with his mouth hanging open and started rubbing his eyes.

"Don't tell me your vision has gotten so weak you don't recognize Wolmers' best batsman!"

"Thomas—? I don't believe it!" Byron gasped, seeing the friend he remembered looking more like a prosperous businessman and several pounds heavier. "Is it you...for true?"

"Well, it's not the bloody Queen of England! What the devil are you doing in here flat on your backside? I thought I told you not to follow me to the hospital!" Thomas teased him.

"How yuh know to find me in here—? I been trying to reach yuh this whole year!"

"Pure luck, *bolow* boy—I came here hoping to see one of the sisters and I ran into Estelle Morales. She's out in the hall waiting for you—it's past regular visiting hours but I managed to sweet-talk Sister Nathalie into sneaking me in to see you for a quick minute—"

"Can yuh find me some clothes so I can get outta here—? They just haul out a dead man this morning!"

"Don't be too hasty. They say you were damn lucky—one of the other divers ended up dead. You look pretty gray—is the pain real bad?"

"Not bad, not bad! Nothing to speak of at-all. Thomas—" Byron whispered, darting a quick glance around the ward to make sure none of the nuns were in earshot, "they're threatening me with surg'ry—I want no part of that!"

Thomas sat at the edge of the bed and spoke more seriously. "Look, old boy—you'd be better off getting it done. You think they'd go to all that trouble just for the helluvit?"

"You think these people care a wink about my life? All they care about is testing out their new science."

Byron's neighbor, who had been mumbling to himself on and off, suddenly bawled out towards the ceiling, "magicians! Dust to insects! Beware God's finger!"

Thomas cast the bulge-eyed man a revolted look. "Poor fool—"

"That's just how me gonna end up if me stay inside here..." Byron grumbled with a shiver. "Yuh don't know how lucky yuh was to walk out of this place."

"Sir Egg—what you just said isn't as cockeyed as it sounds. But I was lucky. I found an angel to save me. Funny—" Thomas added thoughtfully, "I came to find her and she's brought you and me back together."

"That's what yuh been doin' all this time? Searching for her?" Byron queried with a trace of resentment. "She must be pretty—"

Thomas gave a doleful smile, thinking 'Genie's a lot more than pretty!' "I've been doing a lot more than searching, *bolow* boy—after I get back I'm gonna hand you a surprise that'll blow your socks off!" he said with a big fat grin as he jumped up to go.

"Yuh leaving a'ready?" Byron asked dejectedly. "Could you do me a favor? Would you stop and ask Miss Estelle to have them bring me my clothes so I can get out of here?"

"You sure you ready to walk? I wouldn't want you hurting yourself."

"Sure, I can walk. Me not no invalid!"

"I tell you what—" Thomas hedged, looking far from convinced. "I'll ask Sister Nathalie if you can get a smock and you go and talk to that panderer yourself. That way if you die because you refused the doctor's advice I won't feel bad about missing your funeral."

"I wudden want yuh to go takin' any extra trouble," Byron retorted, recalling all his messages over the years Thomas let go unanswered. "I just don't share your faith in their precious science."

"It's not a matter of faith—it's a question of knowledge. Sorry to see you've gone back to hiding behind our people's childish superstitions."

"What—yuh think every word the Frenchies say is true? So then tell me how come their canal been having so many problems? Obviously they don't know everyt'ing."

Thomas smiled and shook his head. "For a chap who knows so little, your logic is worthy of Aristotle." He said it flatly, suggesting it was meant neither as an insult nor cynical praise. "Just promise me you'll be alive and well when I get back," he commanded. "Since I can't stand funerals I'm gonna give you something to live for."

"Thomas—?" Byron called his friend back as he started to leave, "yuh said one of the divers got killed—yuh know who it was?"

"The paper didn't say but I heard somebody mention the poor chap's name. Now what was it—?" Thomas paused to wonder. "I remember it sounded a little bit like mine..."

"Tomby..." Byron whispered.

"Yes, that's it—Tomby. You were lucky, old buddy. That could've been you."

Chapter 29

THOMAS DID NOT PASS Estelle Morales in the hall on his way from the ward and he was not about to spend time looking for that pushy madam. She had cornered him coming in, hoping to pry out what he knew about Henri's thoughts on the canal's survival. She had heard that the bond offering had failed and was afraid that if new buyers could not be found all would be lost. After he had explained that he was no longer the engineer's assistant and refused to divulge his opinion that Henri would never accept the defeat of his life's great obsession, she had asked if he had come to see poor Byron. That she appeared to care deeply about his trusting young buddy had surprised him and made him wary. From the few times he'd observed her in action, Estelle Morales did not strike him as the caring kind.

He was no more eager to run into Mother Agnes for a second time. Whether she'd been annoyed to see him with Estelle Morales or because she wished to discourage him from pursuing Genevieve, Mother Agnes had greeted him with unusual coolness. Apart from his relief at finding Byron alert and in one piece, the entire visit had oppressed him. He'd been stunned when he arrived and saw the hospital grounds in their parlous state, the small green lawn taken over by weeds, the priory's sheltering hedge growing wild and untrimmed. Inside, the signs of an overwhelmed staff had been even greater. The once spotless floors were thick with grime and no longer were the omnipresent sisters seen flapping briskly through the ward and down the hall.

When Mother Agnes seemed resolved to be unhelpful, Thomas decided he would wait out in the garden for Sister Nathalie to come off duty.

"Steady on!" he said, lending his arm as the plump nun was about to stumble.

"Saints preserve me! Is that you, Thomas?" the sister exclaimed when he stepped out from behind the hedge of wild hibiscus to intercept her.

"Hello, Sister Nathalie—sorry if I gave you a start—"

The nun's soft features hardened. "Why were you lurking out here like a fiend? You nearly stopped my weak heart!"

"Not you, sister—you're as fit and rose-cheeked as ever!" said Thomas, letting his violet eyes rest on her fleshy sweet face admiringly.

"Oh, go on with you!" smiled Sister Nathalie, flushing a deeper pink but clearly enjoying the compliment. "I remember that silvery tongue."

Thomas turned and glanced around the untended hospital grounds. He knew better than to jump straight into asking about Genie. "What happened to the lovely sage and sanchezia that used to color this garden? I confess it was a shock when I came back and saw how badly this place has fallen off! The colored ward appears woefully understaffed—"

Sister Nathalie's plump shoulders squared defensively. "We're doing the best we can! We count ourselves lucky to still have a doctor. The ones who aren't dead have mostly all sailed for home."

"I'm surprised. No one I met here ever struck me as faint-hearted."

"I can't blame them!—it's been a strain, what with the fire. Once the company started sending our French patients to the hospital in Panama City it could no longer spare us a piaster..."

Thomas immediately regretted his thoughtless comment. A wave of anger rushed through him to think that these brave women who had sacrificed, not for glory but to bring comfort, could be treated so abominably. "Forgive what I just said—I had no idea. Under the circumstances, I would say you are all coping magnificently."

Sister Nathalie smiled up at him gratefully. "We do what we can...most of these poor men cannot even afford the dollar a day we have to charge them."

"It's a disgrace! I'd suggest they sue the company for breach of contract except it's nearly broke."

"The Lord provides—" the nun replied with no emotion. "We still have use of the orchard in back of the cloister. We've been able to grow flowers and fruit that we can sell. It keeps us going, but there's little left over to try and buy medicines...we can't go on this way very much longer..." she said as her frayed voice trailed off. "I know it's wrong of me, but frankly," she shrugged, "sometimes I find myself praying for the whole thing to end."

"It will have to end if there's no money," Thomas stated grimly. "I see now why Mother Agnes looked so unhappy. She was so distracted when I saw her I forgot to ask about Nurse Genevieve. Do you know how she's doing? I was hoping to see her—" He tried to sound offhand but a lover's passion had inflamed his countenance.

"So, it is true the serpent of desire bit the two of you!" The nun's dark eyebrows rose to indignant peaks on her wide pink forehead. "It's the tropic heat! It puts unnatural pressure on the brain!" she declared authoritatively. "Genie had clearly been out in the sun for much too long the last time we saw her—why, she was as brown as you!...but so thin—even worse than before when she'd gotten so pale. You could tell the poor girl was ill."

"Genie was ill?! Dear God, not the fever?"

"No, no—nothing that serious, thank the Lord!" said the sister, crossing herself quickly. "It was sheer exhaustion. We weren't happy to see her leave so soon again, but she insisted God had called her to work with those poor lepers alone in the wilderness."

"Lepers?—in the wilderness?" Thomas echoed, suddenly feeling chilled. "Where is she? I must find her! Please, Sister Nathalie!"

"Suppose she doesn't want you to find her? You handsome charmers are a good woman's torment. Now I see why she—" the nun stopped herself midstream and turned a dark shade of plum.

"Why she what?" Thomas demanded, willing to speak more openly since Sister Nathalie clearly knew more than she was admitting. "I know what is causing Genie's torment! Believe me—her demons are not because of me."

Sister Nathalie frowned then glanced away, veiling her quiet deliberations inside her winged wimple. "Genie has never been at ease in her mortal skin," she said, her air growing diffident. "I don't suppose it's easy—trying to stay pure when you are blessed with that kind of beauty. But this last time when I saw her she truly seemed content." The plain nun paused and shook her head, "no, not quite content—but more at peace."

"Where is she, Sister Nathalie?" Thomas pressed her more forcefully. "Genevieve is tormented because her heart was broken. All I'm asking for is the chance to try and mend it!"

The nun sighed in surrender. "I don't suppose anything I say will stop you from hounding her. Perhaps it's best you both air things out. I don't know exactly where in the jungle she is, but it's somewhere not far from Gorgona. When you get there just ask for Padre Contreras."

Thomas bent and kissed her quickly on both cheeks. "You're an angel, Sister Nathalie! Now I remember why you were always my secret favorite!"

"You are a charming liar, Thomas Judah!" she replied, smacking him lightly on the hand. "Just you promise not to go on pestering Genie if you don't like her answer."

He set off with cold anticipation, distressed to think that while he'd been picturing their life in a golden castle Genevieve had been trying her best to forget him. He had clung to her image as his bride as if it were some magic talisman. So long as he worshiped its promise and stayed faithful, past wounds would heal and he and the woman he loved would share a future filled with good deeds secured by the blessings of wealth and happiness.

Debarking as his train arrived at Gorgona, he went directly to rent a mule from the local hostler. He was hoping, though his instincts knew better, that Genevieve would be so swept up by his story she would want to ride back with him and be betrothed straightaway. His whimsies got a boost when the moment he mentioned Padre Contreras the old chestnut-skinned hostler grew warm and solicitous, just as Sister Nathalie had suggested. The hostler hunted up paper to draw him a map: Thomas was to take the byway east until it forked by the first culvert on the river. From there he was to take the trail on his left side and keep his sights on a cluster of kapoks and giant black palms. "Trust me, *amigo*," the stableman assured him, "you'll be there before you make it past those trees."

As he approached the forgotten village, Thomas thought he had come to the outcast colony itself. The humble settlement appeared to be no more than a dozen-odd large thimbles thrown up haphazardly. Each little rickety hut with its grass-topped roof hung in the air above the ground and could only be accessed by clambering up a woven ladder. He tried to imagine Genevieve's long body struggling up to safety ahead of some ferocious night predator then trying to sleep on a hardwood pallet designed for humans twice as limber and three quarters her size.

A handful of men were engrossed in conversation by a small wood shack on the ground in the middle of the settlement. As Thomas dismounted and walked the mule towards it, he saw that the hut appeared to serve as both a popular meeting place and a small items store. He approached the proprietor, a brown broad-chested *mestizo*, standing by the open doorway with his soiled shirt tucked inside a pair of white pantaloons. When he asked for Father Contreras the man glanced up quizzically then replied in a guarded tone that the padre was away and advised him to come back on Sunday. Thomas asked if he could tell him where he might find the colony of lepers and the men who had crowded in to listen jerked back with a start as if they feared he might infect them with disease.

When he kept up his appeal the shop-keep spat on the ground and showed Thomas his back. The men promptly moved off and picked up their discussion as though Thomas was suddenly invisible. After briefly thinking it over, Thomas tied up the mule and headed inside the store. He reasoned that if he made a purchase the shop-keep might be nudged into being more forthcoming.

Inside, the shack revealed three half-bare shelves with packets of blue soap, some tins of oil and colored bottles of aerated water. A pair of lanterns hung from spikes behind a waist-high table holding a large box of nails, a ball of zinc wire and wide glass jar half-filled with powdered tobacco. Half hidden by the box of nails was a three-inch folding knife with a beige pearl handle. Thomas was about to bend for a closer look when the shop-keep came in and stood at his elbow.

"Go ahead and pick it up. It's a beauty—got it off a Lebanese trader for some hobnail boots. Double blades—pure steel—never been used."

Thomas picked up the knife and pulled out the two small well-finished blades. The pin action was tight but smooth as velvet.

"How much?"

The stocky *mestizo* hesitated, stroking his sparsely haired jaw. "Make me an offer."

Thomas decided it wouldn't hurt to overdo it and butter him up. He proposed a hugely inflated price and the ploy worked like magic.

The proprietor could not conceal his grin as he tucked the six gold dollars deep inside his calf-length trousers. He slipped the knife inside its cloth bag and handed it to Thomas apologetically, saying that while everyone in the village loved Father Contreras they wanted nothing to do with the *leprosos*.

"Padre is a good and holy man but he does not understand that some are cursed."

When Thomas assured him he had not come to help with the lepers, the shop-keep relented and offered to guide him.

"But take care out there, *amigo*—few are blessed to be the *padre*."

Thomas climbed back aboard the mule and the proprietor led him to the start of a meandering trail through the grove of tall palms. Leaving him there, he told Thomas that so long as he stuck to this path, beyond the giant ferns and *zapateros* he was sure to find his way to Father Contreras and his *malditos*.

Thomas had barely pierced the gloom when the mule dug in its heels, spooked by the shadowing trees, their black roots twisting up from the earth, clutching for air and water like a dying man's baleful arms. He slipped from the animal's back to drag it beyond the malignant branches but the mule proved stronger. Realizing he was not going to coax it a single step further, Thomas cursed the timid beast and rode back to the isolated village. He paid the happy proprietor another dollar to water the useless mule then set off on foot.

A half an hour later he was still slogging through the jungle's deep underbrush, wishing he'd thought to bring a machete, when a scorching pain seared his thigh and he sank to the ground as if struck by a bullet. Cursing both the hostler and his worthless mule, he yanked off his trousers and hunted for the pocket knife he thanked his stars for steering him to purchase. He drew out the smaller blade and carefully sliced around the welt spreading an angry red circle across his thigh. Trying not to tear out too much of his healthy flesh, he clenched his teeth and after an agonizing operation pried out a blood-covered ant the size of his thumb.

He crushed the insect bitterly beneath his heel, then tied his handkerchief around his bleeding thigh and with laborious effort managed to drag on his trousers. He started up to his feet and almost fell when his left leg sagged and nearly gave way. He drew a deep breath and blundered on, shifting his weight from the aching leg and fixing his thoughts on Genevieve to avoid the pain. He started rehearsing what he would say when he finally saw her, wondering how hard he should push if her first impulse was to refuse him.

That uncertainty was so heavy on his mind, he scarcely noticed how badly he was hobbling. The poison from the ant's sharp pinchers had turned his whole leg stiff and the left side of his body felt as if it was pressing up against a wall of fire. By the time he sighted the ramshackle huts swaddled in gray mist he could barely lift his leg. He shambled towards a group of naked children sitting out on the ground in a cross-legged circle, half-heartedly at play, flicking twigs and rolling tiny pebbles. He limped towards them smiling and held out a shiny gold coin, saying it belonged to the first one who would take him to see the pretty nun with the golden eyes.

The children glared up from their listless play, their little mouths all set in the same quick grimace, as if they'd been slapped for no reason. A cocoa-skinned girl with black springy hair in untidied plaits shot him a scowling look that seemed unholy from one so young. He shuffled towards her, holding his smile, but as he extended the tempting coin, she suddenly leapt up and ran ahead of her playmates who all scampered in chase. Mystified, Thomas stuck the shiny coin back in his pocket and staggered in behind.

As he came to the first crude hut he saw two bareheaded men who appeared to be not much older than him, resting outside on the ground. Shiny lesions oozing with mucous mottled their bony brown arms and legs. One was missing both feet. They waved to him, smiling welcome and Thomas tipped his hat and rushed to limp by, ashamed that they had glimpsed his jaw drop in horror. He avoided the three swollen-legged women sitting with their backs turned and their heads bowed low as they silently husked corn and went to join the youngsters now clustered at the entrance to the settlement's largest shelter. Seeing him approach, the children policed him with dark suspicious eyes, their little chins sullenly pressing their chests as they parted grudgingly and let him hobble inside. A burly *mestizo* in his middle thirties rose from his table to greet him.

"The children said I had a new patient!" the surgeon-priest laughed, before turning aside to hack a rattling cough into his fist. "Pardon—I haven't been able to shake this confounded cold—" Father Contreras pulled a grubby handkerchief from the sleeve of his black cassock and wiped his lips. After Thomas introduced himself, the priest gently urged the frowning youngsters to go back out and play. The children lingered there a moment like deaf and mute zombies then the little cocoa-skinned girl aimed Thomas another blistering stare before bolting off ahead of her tiny followers.

The main shed proved to be a tent made of rawhide walls hanging from a roof of braided palms stretched across four stout iron poles. From what Thomas could see, the space appeared to function both as an office and an infirmary. There was a pair of standing cabinets with papers stacked in files and a six-foot table covered in a stained white cloth upon which lay a set of forceps, a hand drill, a hypodermic syringe and a sinister-looking hack saw that drew a shiver as he recalled the footless leper. The air inside was like steam and reeked of chloroform and harsh antiseptics.

Father Contreras gestured for Thomas to sit and face him in the other ponderous hardwood chair, an ornate church relic that seemed hugely out of place in its rustic setting. The priest sat back heavily at the unclothed table and pushed aside an untouched plate of black beans and green banana. He wore the look of a man whose courageous resistance had eroded.

"Hatred?" the weary priest mused, hearing Thomas describe the little girl's reaction when he asked to see Genevieve. "No, what you saw wasn't hatred...far from it—Sister Genevieve was their angel."

"Was? You mean Genie is not here?"

Father Contreras touched the tips of his thick rough fingers together and gazed towards the shed's palm roof. "God willing, she will return to us someday. In the meantime I pray to receive her strength—and that we will not dishonor such a priceless gift."

"A priceless gift?" Thomas echoed, still somewhat baffled.

The priest reached down to his right and pulled up two wide tumblers and a quart of whiskey two-thirds empty. Without asking, he poured two fingers of liquor into each smutty glass and eased one across the table to Thomas. "Your Spanish is quite good. How long have you been in *Panamá*?" he asked in English, overdoing the proper stress on the province's last syllable.

Thomas caught the attempted diversion and bypassed it smoothly. "I suppose you're wondering what brings me here—"

"No—although your showing up now did surprise me."

"I appreciate, *padre*, that for you Genevieve is simply a good novice with great zeal for her calling—" he paused to find the right tone, "no one can question Genie's strong faith, but you see, her past is very complicated...Genie and I—well...we have shared a great deal. It's no one's fault. I hope you understand!—"

"Please—drink—" Father Contreras urged, then covered his mouth to rasp more heavy coughs into his handkerchief. "No need to hurry. Time waits for all in this forgotten country...*¡salud!*" he exclaimed, raising his glass and gulping most of his whiskey.

Thomas saw he had no way out if he was to avoid being rude. He returned the toast and ventured a sip, surprised to find the whiskey pleasantly aged and exceptionally smooth and enjoyed a longer swallow. He opened his mouth to return to his quest but Father Contreras was alert and broke in first.

"You see these poor souls—?" Contreras swept a vague arm towards the rest of the colony. "They have more vision and understanding than you or I will ever possess. They're your true brothers." He stopped and gave a wan smile while Thomas cringed, remembering the amusement on the lepers' faces as he hurried to limp by. "Your fathers could read the heavens—how could they stay sane bowing down to the ground? They were happy to die out in our jungle but we holy men had to save them," he muttered with a chuckle. "The stupid ones pleased us the most. If they were lucky, after they'd been enlightened and we'd given them shoes, they got to know the pleasures of bottled beer and a juicy scandal sheet before they were hanged or doomed to strong drink." Father Contreras finished off his glass and started to laugh before being seized by another fit of coughing.

With his leg still sore and aching, Thomas was in no mood to sit and listen to a priest's acid rambling. "You might consider curtailing your sermons, Father—we dark rabbits have short attention spans." He got clumsily out of his chair, straining to contain his anger. "If you will not tell me where you've sent Genevieve, I shall thank you for the excellent whiskey and be on my way!"

"Please—please—" the priest urged, motioning for him to sit. "I meant you no slight. You shall have your answer—but be kind enough to hear me out."

Despite his worn-out posture, Contreras' voice carried a cleric's irresistible sway. Thomas loosened his clenching fists then sat back down impatiently.

"Sufferance, young Judah," the priest continued. "It costs you nothing and you'd be better served managing that temper. I appreciate your anger, but we are damned to be hypocrites. We blame it on Eve, but gold more than lust has been our undoing. We've even impressed it on the humble cross and now it gleams like Jeroboam's false virtues. We seized your fathers—chained them and my mothers to the bowels of the earth for a golden throne and a place in heaven." Contreras sputtered a liquid cough then slumped back for a restoring deep breath. He clamped his mouth with the handkerchief to suppress another sharp spasm and grabbed the bottle to pour himself more whiskey. "We all are cursed, my young friend—cursed by our fathers' great vanity. That is why the leper can grin—he has looked into the pit..."

Father Contreras threw back his head and drained his glass while Thomas looked on uneasily, thinking all religious men were surely mad when he heard the priest start mumbling rapidly in Latin.

"Angele Dei, qui custos es mei, me tibi commissum pietate superna; illumina, custodi, rege, et guberna..." He ended the supplication, signing his chest with the cross then set a boiling gaze on Thomas. "So, you are in love with Genie as well!" the priest's haggard voice was suddenly aflame and intense.

Thomas stalled, unsure how much to admit. "I care about Genie, deeply...her pain is my pain—if that means love, then so be it...yes—I love her!"

"You do, huh? Then I despise you—and I sneer at your suffering!" Contreras' sage features had become jealously deformed. He sat immobile, like some glowering graven image, then abruptly hid his face behind his thick hands and softly wept. "Forgive me," he said finally in a constricted voice, pulling the gray handkerchief from his cassock's black sleeve and wiping his face. "I was daring again to believe in goodness—but it has perished." He slumped and shook his head. "Such goodness is too precious—too precious for base desires. She was too tender to bear life. She gave us her all. Now she's free..."

"She's free? You mean Genevieve—my Genie, she's...?

Father Contreras wiped his moist red eyes and nodded weakly. "Yesterday morning. She'd taken to having dizzy spells. She swore it was nothing, but I should have known it was serious when she gave in and stayed in bed. Last week, she was back to caring for the children—we all thought she was getting better..."

Thomas was numb, unable to speak. The end he had feared from the moment he saw the padre's face was actually here.

Father Contreras reached a comforting hand across the table. "She knew you were coming. She wanted you to know that she's at peace. Resist your grief. Her true love belonged to God and Genevieve saw God in everyone—especially these children. She told me you convinced her that every joy, no matter how brief, serves its purpose. She said that so long as we are like children there is no sin—joy is heaven and heaven is our joy." The priest withdrew his hand with a heavy breath then picked up his empty glass and stared down through its filmy bottom. "Only a soul that precious could trust her faith so honestly."

Thomas barely heard the priest's last words. His spirit was limping through the graveyard of his dreams searching for the tombstone labeled Joy. He sat staring at all those empty years ahead, wondering if he would ever again trust the sound of his laughter. He thought he had finally found his purpose, the light for his soul, his healing angel. He knew now that he could never trust in her God and expect to find happiness. Not when that God was such a cruel and remorseless judge.

Chapter 30

"I don't understand you. They told me you up and jumped out one day without having the surgery! Can't you get it through that thick head of yours that you still could die?"

The two brash wanderers were back together, sipping drinks in the New Frontier, dueling stories.

"Do I look like a dying man to you?"

It had been over three weeks since Genevieve's death, but it had taken Thomas all that time to summon up the will to leave his hotel and search out his faithful buddy. He had not been surprised to learn that Byron had checked himself out of the hospital but he had experienced a moment of shame and disgust when Mother Agnes whispered distastefully that his friend had left with Estelle Morales and was said to be living in the back of her brothel.

"What about that nasty lump next to your stomach?"

"It's gone, Thomas! I woke up one morning and it was gone—no more lump—no pain—nothing! The doctor says it's a miracle. I guess all that book learning you got in school didn't teach yuh everything."

"I guess I'm not the man to argue that," Thomas grumbled, grieving for his beautiful innocent lover lying senseless in her early grave. "I'm just not sure luck is enough to carry you if you don't have good sense."

Byron grimaced as if his face had been splashed with ice-cold water. "Well, that's a fine howdy do! Yuh sound like yuh sorry the lump never killed me."

"Don't be stupid! Of course, I'm glad that you're better. I just don't think it's all that smart to trust in fate." Thomas scowled at the mug of cold beer he had barely touched. "Hell—never mind! I don't even know what I'm saying—"

"If you're happy I'm better, for truth yuh sure don't look it," Byron answered, looking confused though a little less hurt. "Something else vexin' yuh?"

Thomas had avoided bringing up Genevieve, afraid of losing face if he let slip any tears. He did not know why he continued to feel this bitter, but after these tragic last four years he recognized the clanking bell in the dark recesses of his mind was the tolling of guilt. First with Diego and then his beloved Genie—each time he had meant to intercede but had been too late.

"I'm sorry, Egg—I guess being back in this rotten town has me down. Enough crying about all the trouble we've both been through," said Thomas, sitting up eagerly. "It's time I tell you my proposition—you're not going to believe it!"

"Oh, here it comes! More big talk from Massa Thomas!" Byron grinned. "Four long years I been here hungry, waitin' for some meat on your big fat promises."

Thomas reached into his vest and slung the nugget onto their table. "Pick it up and have a feel," he boasted, seeing Byron's face light up at the shiny gold lump. "That's more than two months worth of shoveling down in Culebra. Go on—pick it up. It's not gonna poison you."

Byron reached for the big nugget gingerly then promptly dropped it on the floor, surprised by its heft. He bent to retrieve it and began to examine the uneven lump trying to decide if it was real. Satisfied it was genuine gold, he started to push it back across the table but Thomas quickly shoved back his hand.

"That's yours, old boy. Call it a little taste to draw your saliva. Here's the best part—there's a heap more where that golden beauty came from, just waiting on you and me to go and bring it back!"

Byron squirmed around in his chair, looking none too eager.

"What's the matter—duppy woke your mother? You look like you're frightened!"

Byron put a finger to his lips and glanced furtively around the saloon. He rolled his eyes towards the bar's long counter where two of Colón's well known sharpsters stood with their backs half-turned, watching him and Thomas through the edges of their eyes. "Yuh can't come inside here showin' off that way!" he hissed to Thomas, leaning low across the table. "Don't think because your skin is lighter than mine these culprits won't be looking to cut your throat and steal that gold once you leave here."

"Well, I didn't tell you to go and drop it on the floor now, did I? But I don't doubt a word you said." Thomas gave a cagey smile then slyly lifted the lapel on his Brighton jacket and exposed the holstered revolver. "That's why my business partner is always close and loaded. You know how to shoot one of these babies?"

Byron flinched from the gun and shook his head.

"That's all right—I can teach you once we get to Venezuela. Take it from me, you'll be a whole different man after that."

"Me—? No, sah! I'm not about to kill anybody!"

"Who said anything about killing somebody? It's just some insurance. I think about how many of our comrades might have survived that Culebra ambush if they'd all had pistols under their pillows."

"I still can't believe you were there when it happened. Why would you want to leave off working for Mister Duvay to go slave with a shovel?"

"I had my reasons," Thomas snapped. "Anyway, all that is water under the bridge. The point is you're going to have to learn how to defend yourself."

"I can defend myself all right—by not go-lookin' trouble. I learned the best thing I can do is be patient and keep myself quiet."

Thomas looked askance. "What are you saying—you won't go back with me? Don't you understand—? You're going to be rich!"

"Sorry, Thomas. I want to trust yuh—truly!—I just can't see it. That gold is sitting in foreign people's country. How you know them not gonna wait 'til we dig it all up, then say we steal it? I could end up there in prison."

"You're talking rot! Try and follow me—" Thomas spat impatiently, "I'll make it simple. I came across an old mine—so old nobody knew it was still sitting there flush with gold. I went to court. I won the claim. I paid the taxes. No one is going to throw you in prison."

"So why yuh telling me I need a gun?"

"Like I told you—it's just for insurance. I'm not saying anything bad is bound to happen—but if there's two of us we can watch each other's back."

"I don't trust these people's government." Byron gave a jumpy look as Lieutenant Rivueltas' leering visage flashed in his memory. "They take their spiteful men and make them soldiers."

"Don't worry about the Venezuela government—all it wants is its five percent. I figure we'll come out of there with—at the least—fifty thousand buckaroos."

Byron sat fiddling with the nugget, battling both sides of his contrary urges. Thomas' proposal completely overwhelmed him. He could not grasp a number as high as fifty thousand, much less in dollars. But as the saying went—if something sounded too rich, it probably was too rich to be true. He cupped the gold lightly inside his palm and saw that the small pale circle from the singeing cigar had begun to fade. 'Here I came hoping to make a mark and instead I've been branded,' he silently brooded. Maybe men like him were not born to take chances. Thomas could afford to talk big—nothing he did seemed to try God's patience.

"Can you give me a little bit more time to think it over?" Byron said finally.

Thomas was dumbfounded. "I don't believe this! You want time to think it over? Did you not hear what I've been telling you? I'm going to make you a wealthy man! You should be hugging me and jumping with joy!"

"Yuh never let me finish tellin' yuh all what me been through," Byron rushed to explain. "It's not just on account of the accident—although being in hospital did alter my perspective. You and me is not the same—I'm not dying for anymore danger and big excitement—"

"You're afraid—is that what you're tellin' me?"

Byron let the nugget roll down his fingers and onto the table then started to fidget with his glass of watered whisky. He looked down as if wishing he could curl up and hide. "Maybe I am. Maybe I'm tired of risking my life."

"Risking your life? You're afraid of risking your life?" Thomas jeered, shaking his head in disbelief. "You? The man who nearly got killed planting dynamite underwater? What happened—did the explosion rip out your spine?"

"No, it never knock out my spine," Byron retorted, his own resentment brewing, "but it did knock a little more o' that sense yuh was talkin' 'bout in my head." He composed himself and tried to speak more deliberately. "Everything will come in its own sweet time. I know what I want from life—that don't mean I got to get it tomorrow. Like I was startin' to tell you—you and me is not the same—I didn't come here because I was restless. I came because unless I wanted to feel like a monkey all my life, I had no choice. I can't be like you, Thomas—I can't afford to be the rolling stone that gather no moss..."

"You're being a chump. What you got to show for all the slaving you been doing since you've been in Panama? An old man's back and hands rougher than the skin on a cowboy pineapple. You think you'll ever amount to anything working a shovel? Or do you plan on getting rich washing a floozy's dirty dishes?"

Byron winced at the insult directed sharply at Estelle. "What I'm doing here now is only temporary. Like I told you—I gots me a trade. I'm aiming to be a master builder and have my own crew one day."

"Sure, sure," scoffed Thomas, "but where? Damn sure not here! Once the canal goes belly up this place is cooked."

"What yuh talkin' 'bout?" Byron retorted, fighting not to lose his new confidence. "Yes, the canal done hit some hard times with all these accidents but your boss told Miss Estelle they will ride over them."

"Sorry to break it to you, *bolow*—the great de Lesseps is broke. The banks won't lend him a nickel. Heck, he may even end up in jail—seems the old codger's been cooking the books."

Byron drooped with vacant amazement. He had heard the same rumors and up to now he had looked for every excuse not to believe them. No one he spoke to wanted to go back home to work on a plantation, but more of his comrades were leaving every day. The diehards like him still held on because they hated to lose that good feeling the canal had inspired: the pride of being part of something great, being able to show the world what a humble quashie like him could accomplish given a morsel of respect and an ounce of praise.

"I don't believe you. Nobody is big enough to put Mr. de Lesseps in prison."

"You may be right," Thomas replied, shrugging with indifference, "but it doesn't change things. The canal is dead...finished."

"Why should I believe you over Mister Duvay?" Byron stubbornly insisted. "You don't know it all! He told Miss Estelle the company may try to get the Americans to take things over."

"Miss Estelle, Miss Estelle—you can't say two words without bringing up her name! Man! She sure has got you wrapped up in her apron. I bet she likes having her little handyman right on spot." Thomas gave a lecherous chuckle then picked up his beer and took a deep swallow.

"Say what yuh want—Miss Estelle been good to me. I owe her—"

Thomas slammed the mug down on the marble topped table. "You owe her? You owe a woman who makes her money selling white men booze and tender brown flesh? What the hell happened to your ambition?"

"Just 'cause I don't want to follow yuh, Thomas, don't mean I los' my ambition! Look—I appreciate yuh want to help me..." Byron picked up the gold nugget then dropped it as if it had suddenly become too hot for him to hold. "It's just—" he gazed down at his hand and a bashful smile stole proudly across his lips, "it's just that Miss Estelle and me...we been through it all...we come like family."

Thomas shifted his body and let his angry eyes skim the near-empty saloon while he mastered his fury. As his gaze roamed from the expensive teak counter to the Murano glass chandelier hanging above the deserted roulette table with its plush green felt, he hoped with all the bitterness in his heart that the canal failed quickly and the grasping madam would discover she had badly overplayed her hand.

"Family?" he scoffed, glaring abruptly back at his friend. "She's just tempting you with her honey so there's no need to pay you. You're nothing to Estelle Morales but her ready coolie-boy."

Byron lunged across the table and latched an iron grip on Thomas' throat. "Take that back! Take it back, Thomas!" The shrill threat caused Theresa to stop buffing the polished bar and glare towards them. The two customers closest by who'd glanced at the sudden commotion quickly shied aside seeing Byron's balled-up fist. "Me not nobody's coolie-boy!" he hissed, ready to smash the next insult back down Thomas' throat. "Don't you ever call me that!" he cried as his voice cracked and fell to a whisper.

"Sorry, sorry," said Thomas, gasping a lung-full of air when Byron's fingers relaxed on his windpipe. "You're right, old boy—I was wrong to say it," he admitted, checking the bruise on his sore neck. "I just don't want you making a mistake I promise you'll regret for the rest of your life."

The saloon seemed to breathe a sigh as the early patrons eased back in their seats and returned to their drinking. Chagrined after his violent eruption, Byron lapsed into absent brooding. In the meantime, Theresa had sidled across to their table and now stood over them from her imposing height.

"Byron—is there something going on I should know about?" Theresa kept her eyes on Thomas as he sat quietly rubbing his neck. "I'll toss him myself if your friend is out for a fight."

Thomas glared at the stately hostess then, glimpsing the bright twinkle in her eye, grinned winningly at her trenchant humor.

"No, no—everyt'ing's all right," Byron said quickly. "It's me to blame. I just lost my head for a minute—"

Theresa's doe eyes flickered with a hungry look. "He looks like he's a lot to handle," she said, holding Thomas with her droll half-smile as she spoke to Byron. "You make sure to call for me if you need me—I know what to do if he makes any trouble."

She left them with the pretense of a chastening look and Byron anxiously returned to his apology. "I'm sorry, Mas' Tom—I don't know what came into my head, but you're wrong about Miss Estelle. If she was just out to use me she wudden-a-did trouble herself to help me start in my trade. I just can't see deserting her now just so—"

"I never took you for one of our backward country-people," Thomas stuck in churlishly, "—always quick to complain about how hard life is when they're the ones keeping themselves in slavery."

"What you know 'bout slav'ry?" Byron snapped, his jaw set fiercely. "Yuh know what it is to spend your twelve light hours cutting cane, trying to keep your mind as sharp as your blade so yuh don't chop off a toe by mistake because yuh doin' the same thing over and over? Yuh ever try keep pace on a blasted Jamaica Train when inside that mill is hotter than damnation—knowing that if yuh slip yuh gonna drown in a vat of boiling molasses? Then when the whole day done and yuh lie down tired yuh still can't find a sixpence in your pocket much less who the bastard was that brought yuh into this mess of a world. So tell me, Tom Judah—what the devil you know 'bout slav'ry any-at-all?"

"I know how to avoid it," Thomas quipped, safely under his breath. "Look—I'll grant you your life here may be better, but you need to learn to think big. I knew it was a risk going to Venezuela. But I knew if I was ever going to feel like a respectable man I had to start making some respectable money—" he stopped and felt a pang, remembering the joy that had lightened his labors back when he was imagining his wedding day. "I'm giving you the chance to be a free man. Forget trying to figure the risk. Take it from me—this is a safer bet than banking on love—or even kindness."

Byron sat still while his temper cooled, feeling ashamed and more confused. He wanted to trust Thomas' wonderful words, but his instincts kept saying be careful. He had not forgotten that Thomas had risked his own skin to save him, but perhaps if his friend had made an effort to see him for all these years, he'd be in a position to judge how far he could trust him. And there was one last thing that gave him pause: for a man who came bragging about his newfound riches Thomas seemed awfully bitter.

"I'm waiting, old buddy," said Thomas when Byron still sat, not saying a word while he fiddled with the golden nugget. "Are we going to be partners or would you rather stay and be bribed with a harlot's nasty favors."

"I'll thank you not to call Miss Estelle by that word. As you can see she runs a very high-class establishment."

"I agree this place is a far cry from her tawdry little Bottle Alley tavern," Thomas replied, glancing across to the large fresco on the adjacent wall depicting a local country version of a Roman bacchanalia. "I guess the business she's in doesn't have a dry season. I have to hand it to her—she's got real initiative. Not too many whores end up owning a saloon with fine paintings and antique chandeliers."

Byron bristled then shoved the nugget back to Thomas across the table. "Take your gold! I can't go with yuh."

"I said it's yours—so keep it!" Thomas bellowed, pushing it back. "Last chance—I'll give you forty percent of the lot—but I'm warning you—if I leave without an answer, I won't be asking again. So, are you coming?"

The ultimatum appeared to puncture Byron's brave new shell. He slumped in his chair and a dark cloud came over him. For a long strained moment he sat toying with the shiny nugget, trying to measure the worth of its weight. Finally he cast down his eyes and shook his head.

"Fine," snarled Thomas, bolting up onto his feet. "Use it and buy yourself a coffin. I wash my hands of you."

Byron looked up imploringly, but his plea fell dead beneath two hard violet eyes now cold and ruthless as a gunfighter's bullets. He parted his lips to speak and Thomas drew a gold dollar from inside his pocket and flung it down so roughly it went skittering off the edge of the table.

"Better stick to white rum and beer," Thomas jeered as he jammed on his black fedora and made a show of patting for his gun. "You'll go broke trying to get sweet on Yankee whiskey."

While his stunned friend struggled to find something to say, Thomas turned his back without a parting word and left his buddy to pick the coin up from the floor.

Before Byron could urge out his voice and beg him to stay, Thomas swaggered up to the card-sharps still slouching at the bar waiting to spy a promising mark. He grinned at the slit-eyed sharks then threw Theresa a big wink and a kiss before he strolled on by.

Back at the table, Byron stared at the lifeless chunk burning his hand, wondering as he heard the New Frontier doors still swinging, what had gone sour with his first true friend.

Acknowledgments

I WOULD LIKE TO thank the staff at the Institute of Jamaica and the Main Library at the University of the West Indies for their general assistance. Without their patient expert guidance as I explored their remarkable collections, Panama Fever could not have been written.

I must also thank my dear friend Laura Simpson, who braved impairing her eyesight poring through countless spools of microfilm unearthing priceless nuggets for my story. My gratitude goes out to Julie York for affording me her fine artistic talent and drawing my map. Lastly, I must pay tribute to Abigail, my multi-talented wife, whose roles in seeing this book successfully to print are too numerous to reckon.

About the Author

W. B. GARVEY is a relative of the celebrated Pan-Africanist and Jamaican National hero, Marcus Garvey. A classically-trained violinist, W.B. Garvey has appeared as a recitalist, orchestra member, and soloist in major concert halls in

Chicago, New York, and Los Angeles. He has also played for studio recordings with artists such as Frank Sinatra, Aretha Franklin, Tony Bennett, and Wynton Marsalis and for more than a hundred film scores, including Martin Scorsese's *Age of Innocence* and Spike Lee's *Malcolm X*. W. B. Garvey was born in Los Angeles and is a graduate of the University of Southern California. He has lived in Kingston, Jamaica, and London, England, and currently resides in New York City.